DOLL PARTS

First Edition: September 2025

Cover design by Melissa Grace / Cover wrap by Allison Salvino

ISBN:

Print: 979-8-9905828-3-5 / Ebook: 979-8-9905828-2-8

DOLL PARTS

A NOVEL

JEN DAVIS

To all the cycle-breakers out there, this one's for you.

ALSO BY JEN DAVIS

For Eva

AUTHOR'S NOTE

Dear Reader,

Thank you so much for choosing to read *Doll Parts*. I feel unbelievably grateful and honored to have the opportunity to share it with you.

I want to let you know that this story contains the topics of drug abuse and drug addiction, which some readers may find triggering. Your mental health is of the utmost importance, so if now is not the time for you to read this book, I encourage you to put it down and come back to it when you're ready.

All my love, always,
Jen

1

OCTOBER 2009

There was a slight tickle on my shoulder—soft, mostly, with a hint of roughness—followed by a hand gliding across the satin fabric of my camisole. It moved over my ribs, then up to my breast.

My brows turned inward as I stretched my legs along the smooth percale sheets. The hand trailed down my stomach, slipping under the waistband of my shorts, and I immediately pulled my knees back up.

"Marcos, *nooo*. I'm asleep."

"You're not asleep," he said, his breath warm on my cheek. "You're talking to me."

I groaned and opened one eye to check the alarm clock on the nightstand. "It's four thirty in the morning," I grumbled, curling into a tight ball.

"Come on. I'll be quick. Unless you don't want me to be." He swept my hair off my neck, placing kisses from below my ear down to my collarbone.

"I'm literally drooling on the pillow," I said, wiping the corner of my mouth. "And I haven't shaved my legs in, like, two weeks. Go in the bathroom or something."

He snickered. "I don't think I'm fucking your legs."

"Well, then, I haven't *waxed* in two months." I kicked his shin. "Go back to sleep."

He pulled me close to him so I could feel his dick pressing against me. "*Por favor, amor. Eres hermosa, y te necesito.*"

"That's not gonna work," I said, attempting to keep my voice flat as I fought a tiny smile. He *was* sexy when he spoke Spanish, but that didn't mean I felt like having my body invaded before the break of dawn.

"It'll work." He chuckled. "It always works."

"Oh my God, *fine*." I huffed, unfurling myself from my cocoon and flipping onto my back.

I worked my satin shorts off my legs, and Marcos removed his boxer briefs before sliding his hand between my thighs.

"I'm good," I said, guiding it away.

"Really?"

"Yeah, just...hurry up."

"What about this?" he asked, tugging at my camisole.

I grabbed the material and forced it back down. "It's too cold."

"*Pero, nena, tus tetas son perfectas,*" he murmured, lifting his body over mine and nuzzling his face against my chest.

I didn't always understand everything when he spoke Spanish, but I knew what *tetas* and *perfectas* meant. "Well, you're not fucking my tits," I said, turning his words back on him.

He lifted his head up, and I could see him grinning in the soft glow of the clock. "I would if you'd let me."

I rolled my eyes and stifled a laugh. "Exactly how much porn have you been watching?"

He winked, and I couldn't help but smile as he rested his forehead on the pillow. The stubble on his jaw bristled against my cheek, and I threaded my arms under his, gripping his shoulder blades. I winced, wishing I hadn't been so quick to push his hand away, then let out an exhale, allowing my body to relax as he moved slowly inside me.

Maybe this wasn't such a bad idea after all.

"God, I love fucking you," he whispered against my ear.

"*Mmm,*" I moaned. "That feels so—"

"Mom, Marisol's sick and throwing—Oh my God! Oh my God! Oh my freaking God!"

Suddenly, the pale light from the hallway bathed the entire room. Marcos immediately rolled over, grabbing the sheets to cover himself while inadvertently pulling them off me. I screeched and scrambled for the duvet, yanking it from the end of the bed.

Our fifteen-year-old, Lola, stood at the door covering her eyes. "My stupid sister is puking her guts out, and you guys are just as disgusting! I hate this family!" she screamed before turning and slamming the door behind her.

"Jesus Christ," I muttered, frantically patting the mattress to find my shorts. "This wouldn't have happened if you'd let me fucking sleep."

Marcos turned to me. "Babe. Come on."

"I'm sorry. I just..." I dropped my head into my hands, pushing my tangled hair out of my face, hot with embarrassment. "How did we go all these years without any of the kids walking in on us, and *now* it happens when they're old enough to know what's going on?"

He sighed, pushed himself off the bed, and pulled on a pair of pajama bottoms. "I'll go check on Mari. And don't worry about Lola. She'll get over it."

"Sure, it's fine for *you* because she worships the ground you walk on. This is just another reason for her to hate *me*." I sighed dramatically and flopped against my pillow, still pantsless.

He stopped on his way to the door, chuckling as he extended his hand to me. "No, I distinctly remember her saying

'*You guys* are disgusting' and 'I hate this *family*.' That's both of us."

"I guess." I squeezed his hand, then let mine fall to the bed.

"Try to go back to sleep. I'm sure Marisol's fine. Probably just some twenty-four hour bug."

"No, it's okay," I said. "I'm awake now. I'll be there as soon as I find my shorts."

Marcos left the room, and I pressed the heels of my palms into my forehead.

He was perfect. The perfect husband, the perfect father. The perfect man. The kind who told you your tits were amazing, still thought fucking you after eighteen years of marriage was the best thing in the world, and insisted you go back to sleep while he took care of your sick kid.

The kind I didn't deserve.

And never had.

———

"No, Marta. No, she's fine."

Marcos walked into the kitchen, and I pointed to the cordless phone propped on my shoulder, mouthing "Your mother" and rolling my eyes.

He grimaced, poured a cup of coffee, and leaned against the counter to observe the exchange as I flitted around the kitchen in my robe, dark hair piled into a hasty bun, searching for anything our twelve-year-old, Marisol, might be able to stomach later.

Lola had already notified me that she wouldn't be eating breakfast because she was too disgusted by what she'd witnessed when walking in on us earlier that morning. It was shortly after she'd stomped back upstairs and slammed her bedroom door that the phone call came from my mother-in-law asking why Lola wanted to move in with her.

"What? No. Absolutely not. She does not need to move to Miami."

Marcos sputtered and slapped his hand over his mouth, trying not to spit out the sip of coffee he'd just taken.

"Because," I continued, "her mother and father and siblings live in Los Angeles. In a home where she is fed and cared for and clothed—quite nicely, I might add."

Marcos motioned for me to give him the phone, but I waved him off. We had a big meeting downtown that day, and he'd volunteered to go it alone so I could stay home with Marisol. I knew he could handle anything that came our way, but he didn't need his mother getting him worked up over something so ridiculous beforehand. Plus, they'd speak Spanish too quickly for me to understand everything they were saying.

"I don't know what happened to set her off," I lied as I rummaged through the pantry. "Lola's fifteen, hormonal, and generally dissatisfied with life. That's how you're supposed to be when you're her age."

And it is *pretty disgusting to see your parents banging*, I wanted to add.

I sighed and met Marcos's gaze as she rambled on. A smile spread across his face, and I could tell he was trying not to laugh.

"Well, that's because you had all boys." I closed my eyes and pinched the bridge of my nose while she insisted that her three sons had never been like this when they were teenagers.

Of course, they hadn't because they were perfect. She'd informed me of this the very first time I'd met her, along with every other time I'd seen her since over the past eighteen years.

"I know. I understand that as her grandmother, you're concerned. But I assure you, she is one hundred percent fine. And I'm sorry she called and worried you." I paused to let her speak as our son, Lucas, entered the kitchen. "Yes, Marta. I know it's stressful for you."

Marcos placed his coffee cup on the counter, his body shaking with silent laughter.

"Okay, well, I have to make sure she's ready for school. I don't want her to miss weekly mass," I said, knowing that was the only way I'd get my devoutly Catholic mother-in-law off the phone. "Yes, I do know how important that is. Even though I'm a Protestant. All right, I'm gonna go, but...Okay, we'll talk to you soon."

I placed the cordless receiver on the marble countertop beside me, then massaged my temples.

"What's so funny?" Lucas asked, grabbing a package of Pop-Tarts from the pantry and sitting down at the island.

Marcos chuckled as he filled another mug with coffee, loading it with cream and sugar. "There is no better form of entertainment than *your* mother talking to *my* mother."

"Uh-oh, Mom, what'd you do this time?" Lucas smiled, the dimple in his right cheek reminding me that even though he was eighteen, he was forever the little boy who used to clutch my leg and look up at me with his big gray eyes.

I walked over to him and ruffled his mop of dark, unruly curls, thanking Marcos as he handed me my coffee, made exactly how I liked it.

He's too good for me, I thought, staring into the mug. *And he always has been.*

"Mom? What happened with *Abuelita*?"

"Huh? Oh." I blinked and shook my head. "Apparently, your sister called your grandmother and told her she wanted to come live with her in Miami."

"Lemme guess. We're not talking about Mari, right?" He stuffed half of a Pop-Tart in his mouth. "Lola's insane, Mom. I find it best to just ignore her."

"I know. But can you ignore her in your car when you take her to school this morning?"

He groaned and threw his head back. "What? Why? I'm

covering part of the breakfast shift for someone and have to be at the restaurant at eight thirty. It's, like, totally out of my way. You're gonna make me late."

"Because Marisol's sick. I can't leave her alone, and your dad has to get to a meeting." I wrapped my arms around him. "I gave birth to you, Lucas. I also bought you that car. So you can either drive it ten minutes out of your way, or I can take it back. And we can revisit this whole I-don't-need-college-to-be-a-musician thing we agreed to let you try."

He wriggled out of my grasp and grumbled "Whatever."

"Hey," Marcos began, crossing the room to retrieve his wallet and keys. "Don't give your mom a hard time. Dealing with *Abuela* this early is enough stress for one day."

"Fine," Lucas said, rolling his eyes.

"Okay, then," I announced. "I'm going to get Lola. If I don't come back, she's obviously strangled me in a fit of rage and I'm dead, so just know that I love you both very much."

Marcos tucked his wallet in the back pocket of his navy suit as he stopped in front of me for a quick kiss. "I love you, too. Lucas, call me if Lola kills your mother," he said over his shoulder as he headed for the door.

"*Sí, mi viejo.*"

———

I placed the bag of saltines, chicken broth, and ginger ale on the backseat of my SUV, a yawn escaping as I hoisted myself behind the wheel. I hadn't gone back to sleep after the four thirty wake-up call and was running on empty by the time I turned into the parking lot of the coffee shop down the street from our house.

"Hey, there," the redhead working the espresso machine said as the bell on the door clanged behind me. "You're here late today."

"Didn't go into the office. Sick kid," I explained, tossing my purse on the counter and retrieving my wallet. "Which is why I'm gonna need that chai extra dirty."

"No problem," she said, moving to the register to swipe my card.

"And add a skinny vanilla to that, would you, Kat? I should get my neighbor something for watching my daughter."

"Absolutely, give me just a minute."

I shoved my wallet back in my purse and slung it over my shoulder. "Thanks, love. You're the best."

I stepped back from the counter and surveyed the room as I chewed on the tip of my thumbnail. A couple of hip-looking twentysomethings with laptops open. Several blond women in yoga pants sipping what were surely sugar-free lattes. A guy wearing sunglasses with his face buried in a book.

Typical coffeehouse scene.

I sighed and pulled out my phone to see if Marcos had called about the meeting or if our neighbor, Liz, had tried to reach me about Marisol, but there were just a few emails from work. After tapping out quick replies, I dropped it back into the black hole of my purse and gazed out the window.

"Order up, Denise!"

I turned and headed toward the counter, picking up my drinks, balanced in a cardboard cup holder. "Thanks again, Kat. Hopefully I'll see you tomorrow, normal time."

"Healing vibes to the kiddo."

She waved, and I smiled before turning to the door. I was about to press my shoulder against it when I heard a man's voice from behind.

"Let me get that for you." His hand landed on the glass and pushed it open.

"Oh, thanks," I said, turning my head just slightly to see it was the guy who'd been reading in the corner.

I stepped into the parking lot, and he followed behind me.

"Thanks again," I said, raising my drinks to say *cheers* as I started toward my car.

"Denise?"

I pivoted. "Hmm?"

It was an involuntary response, and before my brain had a chance to process that a man *I* didn't know somehow knew *me*, he spoke again.

"I can't believe it's you."

"Do I—" I grasped the drink holder with one hand, then swept my sunglasses off my head and over my eyes, imagining that would afford me privacy as I studied his face and tried to place him.

He was tall with shoulder-length wavy brown hair, and a mustache lining his upper lip, along with a goatee on his chin. Jeans and a T-shirt that looked deceptively inexpensive but probably cost a fortune hung on his slender frame.

Was he a dad from one of the kids' schools? *Possibly.* A film-maker we'd secured financing for once upon a time? *Maybe.* A homicidal maniac who wanted to strangle me in broad daylight in the middle of Bel Air? *Unlikely.*

"Sorry," I said, managing an uncertain smile while my brain scanned him for facial recognition. *No fucking clue.* "I, um...How are you?"

"I'm good." He paused and scuffed a Converse-clad foot against the asphalt. "It's, uh...it's been a long time."

He had to be some film guy I'd worked with in the past, but since I'd been in the business for over twenty years, I had no idea when.

"Oh? I...I'm sorry. Haven't had enough caffeine yet this morning." I gave him a nervous laugh. "I can't quite remember when we last—"

"It's me, Denise." He removed his dark glasses, dangling them at his side. "It's me."

I squinted.

Fuck.

My eyes widened and my breath quickened as I realized he was none of the people I'd imagined. He wasn't from school. He didn't work in film. And he wasn't a murderer.

He was *worse* than a murderer. Ten thousand fucking times worse.

He took a step closer, and I backed up.

"What are you doing here, Christian?"

"I need to talk to you, Denise. I haven't been able to stop thinking about you since I got sober. Hell, even before that." He ran a hand through his hair. "I just have so many things to say. So many things I'm sorry for."

My brain, my heart, and the rest of my body immediately became entangled in a dangerous wrestling match.

What exactly does this motherfucker have to say?

Remember how many times you've thought about him. How many times you've wondered.

Get the fuck away from him. Now.

It wasn't until I was unlocking my car that I realized my body had won. Hands trembling, I opened the passenger door and placed the cupholder on the seat, then hurried around the back of the SUV. He stood in the same spot across the parking lot from me, arms out to his sides.

Vulnerable.

Repentant.

I was all too familiar with that pose.

And it was always an act. A fucking *lie*.

"Denise, wait," he called. "I just want to talk to you. Things are different now. So much has changed."

I choked out a bitter laugh as I reached the driver's side and slid behind the wheel. "Good. Great. Happy for you, Christian. Have a nice rest of your life."

"Can you please just—"

I slammed the door, started the engine, and pulled out of

the parking lot. My grip on the wheel loosened slightly when I stopped at a red light.

Deep inhale, slow exhale. I'm okay now. I'm safe.

The signal turned green, and with one final exhale, I made a left turn, steering my car toward everything I'd known for the last eighteen years and away from the one man who could completely set it on fire.

2

APRIL 1990

I jotted down a reminder to call a client first thing in the morning, then glanced at my watch before retrieving my purse from the bottom drawer of my desk. *Six thirty.* By the time I drove across town, the Whisky would be open, and I could recover the credit card I'd left there the night before.

My friend Siobhan had dragged me to see a Led Zeppelin cover band, and though I'd sworn I was having only one cocktail, one had quickly turned into six plus several rounds of shots. Before I knew it, I was waving a lighter in the air and belting out the lyrics to a mediocre version of "Stairway to Heaven."

Siobhan ended up going home with fake Robert Plant, and I ended up face down in the back seat of a cab, somehow managing to make it into the office on time and finish out the day by chugging Diet Coke and popping Tylenol.

I flipped off the desk lamp and stepped out of my office, waving at my father, who was encased in glass across the hall, phone to his ear and feet propped on his mahogany desk. He raised his hand in a brief gesture of acknowledgment, and I started for the elevator, passing the empty offices of people who'd gone home to sit around dinner tables with their families while eating pork chops and mashed potatoes and talking about their days. I wondered if that was nice or boring. It was hard to say with no frame of reference.

"Denise," a voice called from behind me.

Dammit.

After the night I'd had, all I wanted was a greasy cheeseburger and my bed. No talking about deals or clients or any shit that could wait until tomorrow.

I turned around, managing a weak smile. "Hey, Marcos. What's up?"

He approached me, short brown hair slightly mussed, sleeves of his white button-down rolled up past his forearms.

"I got those documents together for *Night Comes Too Soon*," he said, raising the manilla folder in his hand. "We should be able to wrap that up in the next couple days. Can you double-check them for me?"

"Yeah." I nodded, a dull ache squeezing my skull. "Just toss them on my desk. I'm sure they're fine, but I'll look at them tomorrow. I actually have to run, so..." I signaled toward the elevator with my thumb.

"Dinner?" he asked.

"Huh?"

"I mean, are you going to dinner?"

I shook my head. *Ouch.* "No, I'm...Why do you ask?"

"Because if you weren't going to dinner, I was going to ask if you *wanted* to go to dinner."

I cocked my head, and a wide grin spread across his face as he added, "With me."

"Marcos, I told you I'm not—"

"It can just be as colleagues. Or friends." He raised his brows, and his hazel eyes lit up. "Unless you want it to be a date. Then it can definitely be a date."

I massaged my forehead and sighed. "I don't want it to be a date."

"Why not?"

I tapped my toe against the carpet, crossing my arms over my chest and shifting my eyes to avoid looking at his handsome face. "Because I've told you. We work together. It's weird. And I think it's against policy."

He chuckled. "Do we have a policy? Do we even have a human resources department?"

"Um..." I paused to avoid admitting that we technically did not. My father had founded Abbott Film Finance twenty years before, kept a relatively small number of employees, and pretty much always ran the show. "I mean, there's Deb in Payroll."

"I don't think she'd mind."

I raked my hands down my face, scrubbing away any thoughts about accepting his offer. He'd been trying to get me to go out with him for practically two years. Not obsessively, and never in a way that felt creepy. In fact, I was secretly flattered. He was gorgeous and successful, but not like the guys who sent expensive champagne over to the table when I had drinks with my girlfriends. The ones who bragged about how much money they made and the cars they drove. And he certainly wasn't like the musicians I met on the Strip who just wanted to fuck in the bathroom.

Marcos Navarro was one of the good ones.

And if he really knew me, he'd know I wasn't.

"How about we grab lunch tomorrow?" I offered.

"All right, all right." He blew out a breath and shoved the folder under his arm. "I'll take what I can get."

I smiled and winked before turning for the elevators. "Have a good night."

"One of these days, Denise..."

I waved at him over my shoulder. "It's not you, Marcos. It's me."

My chest twinged, and he laughed, neither one of us truly understanding how much weight those words held.

———

I teetered into the darkness of the Whisky on my four-inch heels, muscles aching and feet throbbing. The random guitar tunings and mic checks emanating from the stage attacked my already aching brain.

"Hey, doll, what can I get you?" the guy behind the bar asked.

"I think I left my credit card here last night." I plopped my weary body onto a barstool. "Do you mind seeing if you have it?"

The bartender nodded, his choppy black hair falling into his face. "Yeah, sure, lemme go check real quick. What's your name?"

"Denise Abbott. Thanks."

I placed my elbows on the bartop and nestled my cheeks between my palms as he disappeared into a back room. Within seconds, my arms slid down against the glossy wood, and my head landed on top of them.

"A little early to be passed out, don't ya think?"

"Huh?" I raised up to see a tall guy leaning against the bar, long wavy brown hair falling over his leather jacket.

"Seven o'clock, and you're down for the count," he said, his striking gray eyes sparkling along with his smile.

Jesus help me.

"I, uh—"

"Denise," the bartender called, stepping back behind the counter. "You're in luck."

"Ah, thank you." I retrieved my wallet from my purse and tucked the card back in its designated slot. "Appreciate it."

The guy in the leather jacket took a sip of the beer he was holding. "Rough day at work?"

On a normal night, I would've stayed and stared at him for hours before pretending I had to leave and casually inviting him to come with me. But the hangover was too intense and I was starving, so I slid off the stool. "I actually just left my credit card here last night, so I've gotta—"

"What exactly do you do? I mean, power suit...heels. You seem a little stuffy to hang out at a place like this."

I snorted, the smolder in his smoky eyes practically begging me to flirt with him. "Why? Because I have a *real* job?"

"Ouch." One side of his mouth turned up, and he arched a brow. "Since you're so mean, I'm guessing you're a...lawyer?"

Aaand he's flirting back. But no. No, I'm too exhausted to do this shit. Maybe I'll see him another night.

"Sure, fine, I'm a lawyer." I slung my purse over my shoulder and rolled my eyes.

He tipped his beer bottle at me. "So then, you're actually *not* a lawyer?"

I sighed and shook my head, my tender brain rattling in my skull. "Yes. I mean, no, I'm not a—you know what, never mind. I need a fucking In-N-Out drive-through, my bed, and ten hours of sleep. So," I added, saluting him with a sarcastic smile before pivoting for the door, "have a great night."

"Denise. Wait." He reached out and touched my arm. "It's Denise, right?"

My eyes fell to his hand, and my skin pebbled beneath my blazer. The reaction caught me off guard, and I turned as his fingers trailed down the fabric. "It's, um..." I brought my gaze to his and cleared my throat. "Yeah, it's Denise."

"Does it *have* to be In-N-Out? Because we can be at the Rainbow in two minutes and you can be eating a cheeseburger in fifteen."

No. Don't bite. Leave now, get your food, and go to bed. Don't do it, don't do it, don't—Fuck, why does he have to be so goddamn gorgeous?

I pursed my lips and planted my hand on my hip. "Huh. I'm surprised you want to go to dinner with someone as mean as me."

"I just wanted you to talk to me." He grinned and placed his beer on the bar. "I didn't really *mean* that you're mean."

"That's a lot of *means*. And you're very mature. Should I tell the teacher you're picking on me because you like me?"

He chuckled. "Well, that *would* make you mean. And a tattletale."

I held back a smile. "So odd how you're trying to convince me to go to dinner, yet you keep calling me names."

"I've got one more name, actually," he said, reaching for his beer and taking a long swig.

I watched as the liquid made its way down his throat, wondering why I found it so incredibly sexy.

"Oh yeah?" I asked, tugging my blazer over my chest. "What's that?"

He brought the bottle down to his side and locked his eyes on mine. "Most beautiful woman I've ever fucking seen."

I opened my mouth, ready to issue a retort, but closed it as his words registered.

"Is that better?" He tilted his head, waiting for my response, and his body shifted, a hint of nervousness peeking through the confident exterior.

"It is," I said, twisting my lips into a seductive grin. "In fact, I've decided not to tell on you."

His body relaxed. "Good. Now, how about dinner?"

I sucked in a breath as the scales in my mind tipped back and forth. He was hot. *Beyond* hot. And the way my skin tingled when he touched me...

No. I need to go. I need to be sharp tomorrow. I can't do another day hungover.

"Thanks for the offer," I said. "And the compliment. But I should get home."

His face fell slightly, and he ran his hand over his mouth in an attempt to hide his disappointment. He clearly wasn't used to women turning him down. "All right, then. How about you give me your number, and I call you in a couple days to see if you're ready for another cheeseburger?"

I blew my breath upward, sending strands of long bangs flying, as I pondered what to do. This would never be serious for me. Nothing ever was, really. But he was sexy as hell and the heat that traveled through my body as indecent images of us flashed in my mind made my decision for me.

"Fine," I conceded, my voice purposefully flat.

I grabbed a pen from my purse and a napkin from the bar, then scribbled my number down and placed it in his hand. He ran his thumb along my palm, causing my pulse to quicken when we locked eyes once again. I gasped, realizing I had been staring at him much too long, and quickly retracted my hand as he folded the napkin and shoved it in the pocket of his jeans.

"All right, gotta go," I said, readjusting my purse on my shoulder. "I'll talk to you...maybe."

He shook his head. "No maybe about it."

I turned before he could see my bashful smile and was about to push through the door when he called out to me.

"My name's Christian, by the way."

I twisted my head, forcing my girlish grin into a confident one. I hadn't purposely not asked for his name. In fact, I'd probably forgotten because all the blood in my brain had rushed to the lower half of my body. But I liked how nonchalant it made me seem about the whole thing. It was important to keep it that way.

"Right," I said. "See you around."

———

I catapulted through the door of my apartment, immediately kicked off my heels, and flung myself onto the couch with the grease-stained In-N-Out bag clutched in my hand. The fries were gone, devoured in my car on the way home, but I dove in for my cheeseburger and attacked it like I hadn't eaten in a week.

The blinking light from the answering machine on the end table caught my eye, and I hit the Play button as I took another bite of my burger.

"Hey, it's me!" My best friend Eva's voice burst through the speaker. "I'm calling because I miss the shit out of you, even though I can't afford the long-distance charges. I'm guessing you're still at work, so call me back. Love you, babe."

I smiled, wiping sauce from my chin. I missed her, too. It had been over six months since she'd moved back to Chicago, and I wished every day that she was still in LA. I'd call her after I crawled into bed to see how she was doing.

The machine beeped, signaling the next message.

"Denise. It's Christian. Just calling to check on you and your cheeseburger."

I choked, somehow managing to press the button to stop the recording before grabbing my soda and washing down the lodged food.

Had he really fucking called me already? I cleared my throat and played the rest of the message.

"Also, I meant what I said. About you being beautiful. Not mean. Although, I will think you're mean if you don't call me back." He snickered, recited his phone number, and the machine beeped again.

I balled up the paper from my burger and tossed it in the bag, a tiny giggle escaping as I thought about our encounter.

"Denise." I dropped my head and groaned at the voice coming from the speaker. "It's Sharon. Your mother. Bill and I are going to Hawaii soon and have a layover in Los Angeles. I want to find a nice, new restaurant for brunch before we fly out of LAX that Sunday. And you could join us, I suppose. I'll call you later with more details."

The fake, high society accent she used to disguise the fact she was the daughter of a mechanic from Fresno made me want to throw up everything I'd just eaten. She didn't want to see me. She wanted me to be her fucking concierge service. And since I was going to all that trouble to scout out places to eat, well, *maybe* she'd invite me to sit at their table.

After all, I *was* the human she'd pushed out of her body twenty-six years ago, no matter how hard she tried to forget.

The ache that had subsided crept back into my head as I leapt up from the couch and threw my trash in the bin. I stomped down the hall and into my bedroom, slamming the door behind me before flopping on the mattress and picking up the phone on my nightstand to call Eva.

3

NOVEMBER 1979

"Your father and I are getting divorced. I'm moving to Chicago."

My mother said this like she was telling me she'd fired the gardener or gone to a new hairdresser. Like it should have no impact on my life.

I peered at her over my glass of juice, then slowly set it on the counter. "Oh."

"I don't want to make a big production of it," she added, taking a sip of coffee from the delicate white cup in her manicured hand. "I think it's best if you stay here. Minimal disruption with school and such."

"Why Chicago?" I focused on her orange lipstick smudging the porcelain to keep my tears from spilling over my lids. I wasn't sure why I was upset. It wasn't like we had a functional mother-daughter relationship. Maybe it was because the hope of having one in the future was now crumbling in front of me.

"Bill wants to move his company there."

Who is Bill?

The sleeve of her floral kaftan billowed as she fluffed her chestnut hair. "I'm marrying Bill."

I swallowed the news along with the rest of my juice.

"I'm not thrilled about spending winters there, but at least I'll be able to use my furs," she continued.

"Does Dad know?" I asked.

My mother plucked a stray dark hair off my crisp white button-down. "Don't be ridiculous, of course he does. No need to worry yourself with it. You're fifteen, practically an adult. You'll be fine."

"But when are you leaving?"

She placed her hand on her forehead and closed her eyes, a telltale sign that she was done with my questions. "After the holidays. I've already planned the Christmas party, and I'm not letting all that effort go to waste. Johnny and Joanna Carson are coming, for Christ's sake. Now go on to school."

I nodded, picked up my purse and textbooks from the kitchen table, and headed to the porch of our whitewashed colonial. I leaned my head against the thick, ridged column by the top step, staring out at the lush green lawn mower stripes beyond the circular driveway. The lines blurred through the tears I still hadn't allowed to fall.

Doesn't the mother always get the kid in a divorce? Doesn't the mother always want *the kid?*

I pressed my fist into my heart as I envisioned the tiny flame of hope that lived there being blown out by my mother's tangerine lips. A silly girl's dream that things would be different one day. But now that dream was dead. She would never be there to ask me how my day was when I got home from school. She would never drive me to my friends' houses on the weekends while talking about school and boys and life. She would never help me pick out a dress for prom.

I'd started to fend for myself once I became too old for a nanny but always hoped my mother would wake up one day and realize that she had never actually been a mother at all. She'd throw her arms around me, tell me she was sorry, and we'd eat pizza on the couch while watching *The Love Boat* and *Fantasy Island*. I'd fall asleep with my head in her lap.

Guess I can forget about that now, I thought, although I supposed I could see if our housekeeper liked pepperoni and Saturday night television.

My father certainly wasn't an option. I wondered for a moment how *he* felt about my mother leaving, then realized he never felt anything at all. He worked twenty-four seven and had no use for emotional nonsense.

"There's no time for feeling, Denise. Only thinking. Because once you stop thinking, that's when they go in for the kill" he'd always remind me.

My eyes darted from the lawn to the driveway at the rev of an engine and a streak of cherry red. I sniffed and blinked back the tears as my friend Suzette's Camaro came to a screeching halt in front of the house. After pulling in a shaky breath, I hurried down the steps and opened the passenger door.

"What's happenin', hot stuff?" Suzette tapped her cigarette against the ashtray as I settled into my seat.

I reached for her smoke and took a drag, staring straight through the windshield. "I think my parents are getting a divorce."

She pulled away from the house, taking the curve of the driveway at a speed reserved for racetracks. "What? What do you mean 'you think'?"

I passed her cigarette back. "My mom just told me she's marrying some man named Bill and moving to Chicago."

"Well, good fucking riddance," she said, sucking in one last hit of nicotine before tossing the cigarette out the window. "It's not like you like her anyway."

"I—" I paused, holding back my words. I wasn't sure if that was true. I just knew *she* didn't like *me*.

I *wanted* her to like me. I wanted her to *love* me. But I was too ashamed to say that out loud. It was easier to pretend I didn't care. It hurt less, and she was leaving, so what did it matter?

"Yeah," I said, smoothing out the school-issued plaid skirt that fell just above my knees. "Anyway, I'm pale. I need sun. We should go to the beach."

"Oh, girl," Suzette crooned before turning up the radio. "I have major plans for us after school. Better than the beach."

I cocked my head. "What are we doing?"

"I met this super-hot new band the other night. They're staying over off Highland. But we can't go dressed in these stupid uniforms, so we'll have to go shopping."

I nodded, slightly nervous because Suzette was a senior and I was only a sophomore. She took me places all the time where people would offer me bottles of things I was too young to drink and drugs I was too young to take. But I was always worried I would act like a fifteen-year-old. That I would say something immature. Do something dumb. Giggle like the teenage girl I was.

She reached over and fluffed my hair. "We're gonna make you look like a fucking superstar, and every guy in that room will lose his mind over you."

I smiled, faintly at first, but the idea of someone losing his mind over me tugged my mouth into a full-on grin as Cheap Trick reverberated throughout the car. I dug my compact and strawberry gloss from my purse, rolling the ball over my lips while Robin Zander sang about wanting to be wanted. I studied my reflection in the mirror, then snapped it shut, wondering somewhere in the back of my mind if those lyrics had been written just for me.

———

I teetered into the hotel in an electric blue spandex minidress, a pair of Candies heels, and a white faux fur jacket. My lids were slathered with matching cobalt eyeshadow, pink streaks lined my cheekbones, and thick gloss caked my lips.

"Jailbait chic," Suzette had declared as we'd giggled and posed in the dressing room mirror of a flashy little boutique on Melrose.

Hanging out in the suite were five guys I assumed were in the band and a few girls with whom Suzette exchanged hugs. She introduced me to the girls, all with names that sounded made up and much cooler than mine.

"And boys," she announced, "this is my best friend in the *entire* world, so we need to show her a good time, okay?"

They all laughed, and I blushed, hoping the pink powder on my cheeks hid my nervousness. Two of the guys eyed me from the corner of the room, and I looked away, digging in my purse for cigarettes, before sneaking a sideways glance. One of them gave the other a quick bump on the shoulder with his fist and walked my way.

"Hey," he said, hovering over me. "So, you're friends with Suzette?"

I placed a smoke between my lips and was about to flick my lighter when he held a flame to the tip.

"Oh." I was thrown off by the chivalrous gesture and warmth rippled through my body. "I mean, uh, yeah."

"What's your name?"

"Denise."

He smirked as his eyes traveled up and down my body. "You like bassists, Denise?"

I scoffed, outwardly cool, as my insides fizzed like the Alka-Seltzer tablets my father plunked into his whiskey when he came home from work. "Only if they're good."

"Well, I guess you're in luck, then."

What would the girls with the hip names say?

I took a drag off my cigarette and cocked my head, blowing

smoke from the corner of my mouth. "Awfully sure of yourself, aren't you?"

He laughed, his shaggy dirty-blond hair falling into his face. "You gotta be in this business, baby girl. Now, we need to get you a drink."

He poured me a vodka and orange juice, told me his name was JD, and led me to the couch where we sat, his body shifted toward mine.

"You know, everybody always flips their fucking lids over blonds, but I really dig brunettes. And big brown eyes." He smiled and fingered the ends of my dark feathered hair.

I took a long pull of my drink and bit my bottom lip, thinking that's what a sexy woman would do. "Well, I guess you're in luck, then."

JD chuckled and let his hand fall from my hair to my thigh, sending a shiver through me. "I see what you did there. Clever *and* gorgeous."

I tipped my cup up and finished off the screwdriver in one swallow, dropping my cigarette inside. "*And* out of a drink."

"Whoa, mama. I'm impressed. I could use another, too, actually," he said, swirling his beer bottle before heading for refills.

"Denise," Suzette hissed, sliding onto the couch. "JD is a total fucking fox, and he wants you so bad. I've been spying."

I smiled at the idea, shifting my eyes to where he was pouring my drink and talking to one of his bandmates. "You think?"

"*Yes*, girl." She leaned closer, a mischievous grin painted on her face. "So are you gonna do it? Is tonight finally the night?"

All the nerves in my body fired at once, and my hand landed over Suzette's mouth. "Oh my God, *shut up*."

I knew I was a virgin. *She* knew I was a virgin. But no one else needed to know. Especially not JD.

She peeled my hand away and giggled. "This is it. This is the guy. I feel it."

My cheeks warmed. "He's been so nice to me. He lit my cigarette and is getting me drinks. He said I was smart and gorgeous."

Suzette squealed, and I raised my brows, warning her to keep her voice down. "You *have* to do this, Dee. Just remember, it kinda hurts at first but then—"

I cleared my throat as JD approached us.

"What kinda hurts?" he asked, narrowing his eyes.

"Oh, hey," Suzette said, popping up from the couch. "We were just talking about—"

"Nothing," I interrupted, taking the fresh drink from his hand as she giggled and sashayed away. I took a sip from the cup, trying to think of something cool to say. "So, uh, do you guys have any shows coming up?"

He told me they were recording their album, then lying low for a while. Maybe doing a couple random gigs. Music and voices echoed in the background as we talked about how he joined the band, and I made up stories about my life that had nothing to do with attending the tenth grade at a private all-girls school and living with my parents in Holmby Hills. I said I was studying to be an actress and roomed with a couple other girls in an apartment in Burbank. He told me I was beautiful and he wanted me backstage at the next show they played. We kissed, and I tasted my strawberry gloss as it rubbed off on his lips.

"You should get rid of this," he said, gently grasping my faux fur coat.

I smiled and handed him my drink while I slid my arms out of the jacket and tossed it on the floor. "Better?"

"Much." JD's calloused fingers brushed my shoulder, then trailed downward. "Did I mention how sexy you are?"

I gave him a playful shove and laughed.

"Like, I can't stop thinking about what's under that dress."

My scalp tingled. My skin tingled. *Everything* tingled.

Oh my God, this could really happen.

"So, you gonna let me find out?" he asked.

I chugged the rest of my vodka and orange juice, staring at the ceiling, knowing this was going to be a dividing line in my life. Something I'd never forget. I'd recount the story to my friends the next day. To my college roommates in several years. To my female coworkers when I left the office early for cocktails one day in the future.

If I even went to college. If I even worked. Maybe JD would ask me to go on the road with him, and I'd be one of those women who wore big sunglasses and backstage passes and traveled the world on private jets.

"Sure," I murmured, the two strong drinks making me feel fluid and as sexy as he said I was.

He stood and extended his hand to me, and I floated toward the bedroom connected to the lounge area of the suite, but the door was closed.

"Guess that's occupied." He grinned, steering me into the bathroom, flipping the light on, and shutting the door behind us.

I wanted to ask if we could wait until the bedroom was free but didn't want to seem like a child. Even though I was one.

I placed my purse on the back of the toilet and turned to kiss him. But instead of kissing me back, he moved his hands up my thighs, hiking my dress to my waist and positioning me over the sink so that my back was to him.

Oh my God, my underwear is in my purse. I'd taken it off at the store on Melrose because Suzette had insisted panty lines were tacky. *He's seeing me naked. He's seeing* everything *naked.* My cheeks pinked as I gripped the sides of the sink, and my pulse raced at the sound of his zipper, the feel of his bare penis pressing against me.

What's going on? Is it supposed to happen this fast? Is he just going to put it in? Thoughts crashed like waves in my mind as I looked at my reflection in the mirror to see him staring back at me. I wanted him to say something. To say I was special.

But all he said was, "You ever done this before, baby girl?"

Don't say anything stupid. Act like you're grown.

"What do you think?" I asked, like this was just another night, but my voice cracked ever so slightly, and I worried I'd given myself away.

My answer elicited a sly smile from JD, and I dropped my head as he pushed into me. I braced myself against the cold porcelain, staring at my white knuckles, afraid to look up and see his face contorted in pleasure—or mine contorted in pain.

He gripped my hips, his hands rough against my skin, and grunted with each thrust.

Holy shit, was every dick this big?

My only experience with them before that pivotal moment had been a blow-slash-hand job in the backseat of Johnny Morello's car the previous summer, but he was only sixteen, so I had to wonder if maybe it wasn't fully grown. Even though I'd been to parties with Suzette before, I'd somehow always managed to put off the guys who hit on me with excuses.

I can't tonight.

I want to, but I've gotta get home.

My boyfriend's waiting up for me.

I wondered if maybe I should've said those things this time.

No. He told me I was beautiful and smart. He picked me out of all the girls in the room. He wanted me.

He sped up, panting "fuck, fuck, fuck" over and over again until he pushed into me so hard I was sure my head would hit the mirror. My crotch was throbbing, but I sighed softly and faked the smile of a satisfied woman.

He slipped out of me and liquid trickled onto my inner thigh, so I quickly pressed my legs together, pulled down my dress, and stepped away from the sink, waiting for him to touch my hair and kiss me and tell me he'd meet me outside.

"Thanks, doll," he said, zipping his jeans and checking his appearance in the mirror before leaving the bathroom. "You really are sexy. Maybe I'll see you around."

Shame smacked me in the face, and I immediately locked the door and sat on the toilet, wincing as pee stung my no-longer-virgin skin. Hot tears rolled down my cheeks, his words echoing in my head.

"Maybe I'll see you around."

Was I not pretty enough?

Was I not cool enough?

Had I not done it right?

After I got up, I forced myself to stand in front of the mirror, grab my compact, and cover the black smudges under my eyes. I wasn't going to walk back into that party looking like an ugly, stupid girl who cried over boys.

I heard my father's voice as I swept powder over my face and reapplied my lip gloss. All I had to do was stop feeling. Stop feeling and start thinking.

We'd had sex. What was the big deal? People had sex all the time. And now *my* first time was done. I was glad it was over, even if other girls had made it sound like having their cherries popped was *so* romantic. Maybe they were lying. Or maybe I just wasn't that kind of girl.

I took a deep breath and stepped out into the lounge, scanning the room. Red heat spread across my chest and climbed up my neck as I saw JD taking a hit off a joint with some other girl.

Stop feeling.

I forced my eyes away to find Suzette straddling a dark-haired guy seated in the corner of the room. After grabbing my coat from the floor by the couch, I approached them on shaky legs and gently tapped her shoulder. "Hey, Suzy. I'm gonna call a cab and head home."

She rolled her head full of blond curls toward me, a faraway look in her eyes, like she'd washed down a quaalude with a shot of vodka.

Good. She won't ask too many questions.

"Hey, babe. What'd you say?" she slurred with a vacant smile.

"I gotta go. Not feeling the vibe here," I said, doing my best to sound bored. "But have fun, and I'll see you tomorrow." I leaned down and kissed her cheek, while she kissed the air and told me vibes were important.

The lights on Sunset blurred as I stared outside the window of the taxi, wondering if I would look different when I walked into the house. If my father would notice I was dressed like I should be standing on a corner in Hollywood. Or if my mother would look up from her martini glass long enough to glean that there was something unfamiliar about me that she couldn't quite put her finger on.

Neither of those things happened, so I headed straight to my bedroom, put on a record, and wrote HAD SEX in bubble letters in my diary.

That's all there was to say. He'd served his purpose. And it felt good to be wanted, even if it wasn't exactly how I had imagined. At least that's what I told myself as the ink on the lined pink paper blurred from the one tear I allowed to fall.

I closed my diary and looked to the corner of my room where the dolls I used to play with as a little girl were arranged in various poses, untouched for several years. *It would be easier to be one of them*, I thought. *Pretty face and pretty hair on the outside. No heart and no feelings to hurt on the inside.*

4

OCTOBER 2009

I pulled my SUV into the garage and cut the engine. Air streamed from my lips, and my body deflated like a balloon, sinking into the soft tan leather on the seat. I tilted my head back and closed my eyes, trying to regain my composure before I went into the house.

I couldn't tell Liz about Christian. She was just a neighbor who occasionally came over to drink wine, complain about her husband, and ask me how in the world I ever found a man as good as Marcos. I would always just shrug and say it was luck, I supposed. Which wasn't exactly untrue. Marrying him really *had* been a fluke. A series of missteps, accidents, and tangled-up emotions that by some twist of fate had given me the family I thought I'd never have.

I sighed and ran my hands through my hair, the image of Christian standing on the sidewalk engraved on my brain.

Fuck.

Would he be at the coffee shop the next time I went? Did he know where I lived? How had he found me after all this time? Did he remember...

I sucked in a breath and shook my head, not allowing

myself to think about that. Not allowing my mind to think about *him*, period.

I grabbed the drinks and grocery bag and hurried into the kitchen, placing them on the counter before plucking the vanilla latte out of the cupholder and following the sounds of the television in the family room. Liz flipped through a magazine in one of the chairs, and Marisol was curled up on the couch under a wool throw, eyes fixed on *Twilight*.

"Well, hey there, my little sickie." I kissed her forehead, which felt cooler against my lips than it had earlier that morning. "And here," I said, handing Liz the latte. "For being a gem."

"Mmm. *You're* the gem." Her eyes widened as she took a sip.

I perched on the edge of the couch beside Marisol and stroked her long dark hair. "You seem like you're feeling better."

She nodded. "Yeah. And I'm so glad they made a movie of this so I don't have to read the book."

I chuckled and turned to Liz. "Books aren't her thing. But please tell me you've read them all so I know I'm not the only middle-aged woman completely obsessed with teenage vampires and werewolves."

She shut the copy of *LA Weekly* and tossed it on the end table. "Every single one."

We laughed, and she pushed herself out of the chair. "Okay, I'll let you two enjoy the movie. Glad you're feeling better, kiddo. And thanks for the latte, Denise. Best neighbor ever."

Marisol raised her head off the throw pillow on the couch. "Thanks for coming over, Mrs. Hollis."

Liz smiled and blew Marisol an air kiss as she headed out of the room. "Anytime."

"Want some ginger ale?" I asked, rubbing Marisol's arm through the throw. "Or feel like eating anything?"

"Just ginger ale is good," she answered, snuggling farther into the couch. "Thanks, Mom."

"Love you, sweet girl."

I squeezed her shoulder before padding into the kitchen, where a notification dinged on my laptop. I grabbed my chai, then walked over to the island, sliding two fingers over the touch pad to bring the screen to life. My muscles immediately tensed, and I held my breath as the cursor hovered over the email.

No. No, no, no. Why is he doing this? Why now?

I closed my eyes for a split second, quickly clicked on the message, then opened them.

From: Christian O'Connor
To: Denise Abbott
Subject: I'm Sorry

Denise,

I'm sorry I surprised you this morning. I shouldn't have done that. I'm in town for work, and the coffee shop is near where I'm staying. I've seen you there but couldn't figure out how to talk to you, and I just had to take my chance today. I realize this sounds insane, like I'm a crazy stalker, but I don't want anything other than a chance to tell you how truly sorry I am for all the hurt I caused you. I'm in recovery now, and things are so different. I need to see you. Make amends. Can you give me a chance to do that? That's all I'm asking. Please.

Christian

He'd typed his phone number beneath his name.

I stared at the screen until it became a sea of fuzzy waves glaring back at me. It had been nineteen years. Nineteen goddamned years since I'd scrambled out of that ransacked house and driven away from him.

For months after, I'd worried what he might do. Show up at

my apartment? At work? All the times I'd thought we were over before, he'd reappear and beg for forgiveness. But that time was different. He'd finally chosen between me and heroin, and heroin had won. I tried not to pay attention as he rose to fame afterward, but once the band's first album came out, they were everywhere. And he was the front man. The voice with the looks that made all the grunge girls sweat through their flannels. The super-fucking-nova exploding in the sky.

When the band split up, I was relieved I didn't have to see his face anymore. I assumed he'd retreated into a life of solitude with a suitcase full of needles. But I thought about him. More than I wanted to. More than I should have.

And now this. Waiting for me in a coffee shop. Emailing me. How does he remember where I work? How does he know anything about my life?

My thoughts ran wild with images of him showing up at the office, causing a scene in front of my employees, *in front of Marcos*. Of him in the corner of the coffee shop every morning for eternity, peering at me over his dark glasses. Of him ringing the doorbell at our house and Lucas answering it and seeing...

I gasped and punched the Delete button before retreating to the kitchen table, out of reach from my laptop. I settled into the banquette and placed my elbows on the table, resting my head in my hands. I couldn't let my imagination run wild. Surely, he wouldn't do any of those things. If he was in recovery now, he'd call his sponsor, who'd tell him to respect my privacy, and he'd move on.

Unless.

The thought sent my stomach to the floor.

Unless he remembers what I told him at his house that day.

No. It wasn't possible. He'd been out of his mind. There was no way he'd remember I'd told him I was pregnant.

Absolutely no way.

5

MARCH 1982

I pulled one leg up on the tan wicker chair, shoveling a spoonful of boxed mac and cheese into my mouth while scanning the latest issue of *Cosmo* spread open on the kitchen table. The article's headline promised to teach me how to find the joy in sex. I frowned, sad that there were girls walking around out there who hadn't found it. I'd actually made it my personal mission after the asshole from that second-rate band had used me in the hotel bathroom.

I startled at the sound of footsteps against the tile floor and quickly closed the magazine.

Shit.

My father, dressed in a charcoal suit and maroon tie, set his tumbler of whiskey on the counter. "Where's Maria?"

"She's off for the next couple days," I garbled through a mouthful of food. "Visiting her family in San Jose. But she left dinner in the oven for you."

He glanced around the room, a blank expression on his face, and ran a hand through his short gray hair. "Okay. Well. How do I turn that thing on?"

I popped up from the chair and hurried over to the oven,

setting it to 350 and winding the timer. "She just fixed it a little while ago, so the oven's still warm. It shouldn't be long."

He nodded and loosened his tie while I returned to my seat. I was about to put my Walkman on so that Van Halen would drown out any awkward silence that was sure to follow, but he spoke first.

"How's school?"

Why is he talking to me? Does he not have any work to do? It's six o'clock, why is he even home?

"It's, uh…fine?" I answered, slowly placing the padded earphones back on the table.

"Good. And have you decided which college I'll be writing a check to for the next four years?"

I stared down at my bowl of noodles, stirring them with my spoon. I didn't know if my answer was the right one. If I should…if I *could* explain it to him when I didn't know how to explain it to myself.

"I, um…I was thinking—"

"USC?"

I shook my head. "No, I…"

"UCLA?"

Spit it out.

"I was actually thinking about DePaul."

My father rolled his lips inward and inhaled through his nose. I studied him, waiting for a flicker, a twitch, any sort of indication of how my words had landed with him. He remained stoic, but when he spoke, slowly and deliberately, I knew.

"As in, DePaul University in Chicago?"

I tried to nod but managed just one bob of my head, afraid to commit to a yes.

"So you've decided, then?" he asked

"It's a good school" was all I managed to eke out.

He took a long pull off his whiskey, then swirled the amber liquid in the glass. "It is a good school. But I'm not sure why you'd want to go there when USC and UCLA are in the same damn town where film deals get done. Do you not want to work at the company anymore?"

My face flamed. His trust in my ability to succeed in business—in *his* business—was the only connection we had, and now I was disappointing him. The one thing I'd been able to get right in our relationship was going wrong.

"Because I thought that's what we'd agreed on," my father continued. "Keeping the business in the family. I show you the ropes, you take over when I retire."

"No, I do want to," I assured him. "I want to work for you. For the company. But I also want to see if maybe Mom and I can..." I trailed off as he stared past me, his jaw tightening.

I cleared my throat. "I just want to see if I can spend some time with Mom before I come back here and start work."

He tipped his drink back, finishing it off before setting the empty glass down. "You're a very smart girl, Denise," he said, finally shifting his eyes to me. "If you weren't, I'd tell you to marry rich and hope for the best. But you've got my business sense, and you could be a very powerful person one day." He pressed his hands onto the countertop. "You've got just one problem."

My mouth went dry, and I rubbed my lips together. "What... what's that?"

"You have too much goddamn faith in people."

My nose stung, and a tide of tears swelled in my eyes. I wanted to tell him he was wrong. That his words were proof that he knew nothing about me besides the fact that I made good grades and shared his last name. If he'd known me even just a little bit, he would have understood that I didn't have faith in much of anything.

I didn't have faith in him to care about me if I got into a horrible car accident, lost all that "business sense," and couldn't run the company. I didn't have faith in the guys I slept with, except their ability to give me an orgasm or two once I told them what to do. I didn't have faith in half of my friends from school, as they would no doubt turn around and stab me in the back if it suited their needs. And I actually didn't have faith in my mother to love me like I needed her to. But the little girl who secretly played with her makeup and teetered around on her heels trying to look as beautiful as she did had to give it one last try.

"I—" My words got caught in my throat, and I coughed. "I called her. I told her I wanted to go to college in Chicago. She said that was fine, she would have me over to the apartment for dinner sometimes. Apparently, it's a penthouse right on the lake and—"

"I don't need the details of her life."

"Oh, I'm sorry, I didn't mean to...Sorry."

The timer dinged, and my father turned his head. "Anyway. How do I get the plate out of there? Where are those...things?" He held his hands out, palms up.

I walked across the kitchen, laser-focused on the oven, afraid I would cry if I looked in his eyes. They were the same warm brown as mine, reminding me I really was his daughter, and all I wanted to do was make him proud. But now I'd fucked that up.

I grabbed a mitt out of the drawer, pulled the plate from the oven, and set it on the stove. I placed a fork and knife on it before retreating back to the table and picking at my own dinner.

He blew out a long breath. "I'll write the check to DePaul, Denise. But don't say I didn't warn you about her."

I nodded, the cracks in my heart expanding. Maybe I *was* stupid for hoping my mother cared about me. I'd wanted so badly to crush my feelings for her like the beer cans that drunk boys stomped on at house parties. To turn all my feelings off like I did when I went upstairs to those same boys' bedrooms after they were done showing off. But I couldn't do that with her, no matter how hard I tried. I'd been so shocked by her leaving that I hadn't told her how I'd felt. I didn't have the words at the time. But I was going to try to find them. Move to her city. Show her how badly I needed to be the daughter she wanted.

"I do want to be a part of the company. And I'll come back," I told my father, my voice soft and apologetic, as if I was asking him to forgive me for trying to have a relationship with my mother.

"Oh, you will," he said, heading out of the room to his office, mitt and plate in hand. "I know you will."

6

OCTOBER 1984

"Well, you look amazing." My roommate and best friend, Eva, stepped inside our apartment and dropped her backpack on the floor with a loud thud. "Is that a new outfit?"

I twirled in my short red skirt, off-the-shoulder black sweater, and high-heeled slouch boots. "I skipped my afternoon classes and went shopping. The sweater's not too *Flashdance*, is it? I feel like that's so overdone."

"No way. You look fantastic," she assured me, flopping onto the sofa. "Did you actually say yes to a date or something?"

"Ha ha," I deadpanned, sitting beside her and crossing my legs. "I'm actually going to dinner with my mom. Her favorite spot downtown. And I say yes to dates, by the way."

"Denise. It's been two years since I met you in the freshman dorm, and you've been on *maybe* four dates, despite being asked on at least two hundred."

I shrugged and smoothed my skirt. "I prefer less formal engagements."

Eva twisted her lips. "Code for getting fucked and going home."

"And what's so wrong with that? Who needs all that small talk over a plate of mediocre fettuccine Alfredo beforehand?"

We locked eyes and burst into laughter.

"Okay, so, dinner with Sharon tonight, then," Eva said, tightening her long blond ponytail. "I'm glad things are still going well with her."

My shoulders tensed. When I'd first seen my mother after arriving in Chicago two years earlier, she'd gushed over me like I was a precious Cartier necklace she'd accidentally left in California. We ventured around the city, meeting for lunches and dinners and embarking on all-day shopping excursions. We went to upscale salons and lounged on heated blankets while one person painted our nails and another massaged our faces with silky lotions. It was everything I'd imagined mothers and daughters would do—the adult version of the attention I'd craved as a child. But despite the interest she'd taken in me, something about it still felt delicate, like a fluffy white dandelion whose seeds could be scattered by the gentlest of breezes. So I held it close, protecting it from any possible disturbances. Always agreeing with her opinions, always letting her make plans according to what she wanted to do. Never bringing up how alone I'd felt growing up as her daughter.

"Yeah," I said, my voice tinged with uncertainty. "She even invited me to come to some big gala with her in December. You know I usually go home for Christmas, but maybe she'll ask me to stay in Chicago this year." I paused and shook my head. "That's probably dumb, I just—"

"It's not dumb, Denise." Eva leaned over and squeezed my knee.

My mouth immediately turned down, thinking about the fact that she'd lost her own mother in a car accident when she was seventeen. "I'm sorry. Is it weird, me talking about my mom?"

She smiled, and her eyes softened. "Not at all, babe. I'm

happy for you. You deserve all the love in the world, and I'm glad Sharon has finally realized that."

Her words pricked at my heart, and I placed my hand over hers. I didn't deserve anything, but I hoped she never realized that.

"All right." I nodded and blew out a breath before standing and grabbing my purse from the coffee table. "I'm gonna head out. What are you up to tonight? Do *you* have a date?"

"I wish." She stretched out on the couch and sighed. "I just don't understand why I can't find the right guy."

"*Hmmm*. Do you think it could be that you're still hung up on your high school boyfriend? Is that possible?" I asked, smirking, as I slipped the gold chain of my handbag over my shoulder.

"No. Maybe. Yes." Her face crinkled, and she grabbed a throw pillow, hugging it to her chest. "I just wanna be in love, Denise. Like, stomach-hurting, heart-racing, can't-stop-thinking-about-him love. Is that so wrong?"

"*That* sounds like a disease I never want to catch," I said, scrunching my nose.

Eva chuckled and tossed the pillow at me. "Well, then, get the hell out of here before I cough on you."

I blew her a kiss and winked as I opened the door. "I think I'm immune."

———

"*Darling*," my mother exclaimed, kissing the air beside both of my cheeks before sitting at the white-clothed table. "So sorry I'm late. I couldn't find my silver Chanel clutch anywhere, and I refused to leave the house without a coordinating evening bag."

She looked elegant as her red nails fingered the diamond pendant resting just above the neckline of her ivory wrap dress. Her loose brown curls fell just over her shoulders and framed her perfectly painted face. I shifted in my seat and tugged at my sweater, so awkward I might as well have been wearing braces and acne cream.

"That sweater is cute," she said, placing her napkin in her lap. "Very...Oh, what's that movie called?"

I swallowed the lump in my throat and muttered, "*Flashdance?*"

"Yes, right. *Flashdance.*"

Goddammit.

"Oh! We need some champagne because I have exciting news to share," she chirped, signaling a waiter and ordering "that bottle" she liked so much the last time she was in.

"Of course, Mrs. Montgomery," the server said, glancing at me before hurrying off.

"Bill's London and Madrid offices are up and running now," she continued, "so he's finally going to stop traveling to Europe for months on end. Isn't that fantastic?"

A warm wave of uncertainty swelled above me as I reached for my water with an unsteady hand. I took a sip before dropping my eyes to the table. "Oh. Yeah. That's great."

"I swear, it's like I've been living alone the past two years. Good thing you were here, otherwise, I would've been bored out of my mind. It's practically impossible to make new friends in your forties," she lamented before clearing her throat and adding, "early forties."

"Anyway," she continued, "Bill will be able to go to that benefit gala in December, so you won't have to worry about it. You can go do...whatever you college girls do."

The wave crashed, and my face scorched as the words on the menu became blurry.

How could I be so stupid? How could I be so fucking stupid?

I blinked back tears and forced myself to look up as the waiter returned, displaying the champagne and placing two flutes on the table before filling them with liquid gold. His gaze burned into me as he turned his head so my mother couldn't see him. We locked eyes while she blathered on about Christmas in Aspen with Bill and his adult sons and how she hoped neither of them would have their *own* children soon because she was far too young to be a grandmother. He mouthed "Your mother?" and smiled sympathetically when I gave him a quick nod.

He had sleepy eyes covered by thick-framed black glasses and a perfectly straight nose. His dark hair was styled in a low-key pompadour, and his fitted white button-down, thin black tie, and black pants accentuated his tall, slim frame. He looked like an artist. No—a poet.

"Denise? Did you hear me?"

I shook my head and shifted my attention back to my mother. "Huh?"

The waiter cleared his throat and folded his hands in front of him. "I'll leave you ladies to look over your menus, unless I can get you anything else right now?"

"We'll be ready to order soon. Thank you...Oh dear, I'm sorry, remind me of your name again."

"It's Ben, ma'am."

Ben.

She flashed a quick smile as he made his way to another table. "Anyway, I was talking about Christmas. I'm assuming you'll be in LA, so could you stop by that little boutique on Rodeo and get me that face cream I like? They just don't have *anything* like it here in Chicago."

"Right," I said, her words pouring salt into my wounded heart. "Of course, I'll be in LA."

"Wonderful," she said, picking up the leather-bound menu. "I can't believe I haven't brought you here before. So quaint and *quite* exclusive."

I took a sip of my champagne and pretended to listen as she offered commentary on each of the dishes. I didn't care that the fucking salmon had been flown in from Alaska. I didn't give a shit if it had its own goddamn seat on the plane, just like she didn't give a shit about me. I'd been nothing more than someone to occupy her time while her husband was out of town. Like the friends I had in high school who'd disappeared whenever they had a boyfriend. But they were teenagers. My mother was forty-four years old and still the selfish bitch she'd always been. The lunches and dinners and shopping trips had everything to do with easing her boredom and nothing to do with her wanting to spend time with me. Why had I let myself believe it was anything other than that? I'd been so fucking naive. So fucking *blind*.

I grabbed my glass, polished off my drink, then immediately poured another one.

"Denise. That's what waiters are for." My mother's tone was hushed and disapproving.

I downed half of the refill, imagining it was concrete hardening my heart so she could never hurt me again. "Sorry, super thirsty."

"Well, next time, *wait*," she said, her jaw clenching before a false smile spread across her face. "Now, what are you having? I think we can start with the pâté and then I might do the—"

"Actually, I'm not that hungry. I think I'll just get a salad." I turned in my seat, scanning the restaurant, before grabbing my purse. "I need to use the restroom, so you can order for me if you want."

"But what salad..."

Her voice trailed off as I headed to the back of the room. I slid into the hallway that led to the restrooms near where Ben was serving an older couple their meals. When I saw him nod and back away from the table, I coughed. He whipped his head in my direction, and I delicately waved my fingers.

One corner of his mouth turned up as he approached me. "Hi."

I leaned closer. "Do you maybe wanna meet me in the ladies' room?"

"I, uh..." He sucked in a breath. "Are you serious?"

I nodded, my hand discretely brushing his arm as I held his gaze.

He glanced over his shoulder. "Okay. Give me two minutes."

I scurried to the bathroom, turning the brass knob on the dark wood and breathing a sigh of relief when I saw it was designed for only one person. *So much easier than a stall.*

My boots clicked against the tile as I walked to the counter, set my purse down, and checked my appearance in the mirror. I plucked at my bangs, fluffed the rest of my hair, and reapplied my red lipstick. There was a soft knock, and Ben's head appeared around the door.

"My friend's covering for me," he said. "I can't really stay long, but are we...Do you want to..."

I laughed as I leaned against the counter. "You think I invited you in here for some casual conversation?"

He stepped closer. "I wasn't sure what you wanted because you're, you know, Mrs. Montgomery's daughter and, like, seriously smokin' hot."

So maybe not *a poet.*

I placed a finger over his lips. "No talk of Mrs. Montgomery."

"Right. Sorry," he said, removing his glasses and placing them on the counter.

I slid my hands up his chest and gripped his face, pulling it toward mine. He pressed into me, kissing me hard, and I could feel him straining against his pants. I wedged my hand between us, stroking him through the black fabric as he groaned and moved against my hand.

His mouth traveled to my ear. "I kept looking at you and thinking about what it would be like to—"

"What are you waiting for, then?" I whispered back.

Ben's finger hooked on the black lace underneath my skirt, working it down my legs as we continued to kiss. I managed to step out of my underwear and kick it aside before unfastening his belt and freeing him from his pants.

"How are we doing this?" he panted.

I bit my bottom lip. "When you were at the table, did you think about bending me over it?"

He let out a long, slow breath. "Fuck, I can't believe you're real."

My lips twisted into a seductive grin as he turned me to face the mirror and lifted my skirt. The doorknob jiggled, and he gasped.

"They can wait," I said, staring at him behind me in the mirror. "Now fuck me."

He moaned as he pushed into me, and I leaned forward, positioning myself so that he'd hit all the right spots. Even though we didn't have much time, he moved purposefully, like he wasn't just in it for him. I would've tried to make it last, but we were on a tight schedule, so I decided faking it was my only option. I didn't really care if I came. I could deal with that later by myself or a simple phone call to someone I knew could make it happen. All I needed was to know how much this adorably unassuming waiter wanted me.

"Is this good?" he asked.

"Keep going...yes...yes," I said, pressing my hands onto the counter. "Oh God, I think I'm gonna..." I closed my eyes and sighed loudly.

With one final thrust and groan, Ben hunched forward. "Holy...shit," he managed.

When he slipped out of me, my skirt fell back into place, and I turned around, crossing one leg over the other.

"Wow. That was...unexpected." His chest pumped up and down as he zipped his pants, then looked in the mirror, wiping at the red smudges around his mouth. He positioned his glasses on the bridge of his perfect nose and took my hand. "I feel like a total dick saying I have to get back to work, so can I at least get your number or something? I don't even know your name."

I smiled. "It's Denise. And no need for numbers. Maybe I'll stop in for...*dinner* sometime, though."

He smiled back. "Make sure you request one of my tables."

I winked, and Ben gave me a soft kiss before returning to politely taking orders and pouring wine. I locked the door behind him, then cleaned up and tossed my underwear into my purse before staring in the mirror at my mussed hair and smeared lipstick. I started to retrieve my compact, but stopped, tilting my head and smiling at my flushed reflection. I laughed, tossed my bag over my shoulder, and headed out the door, ignoring the looks of several women waiting outside.

"Sorry that took so long," I said, sliding into the seat across from my mother.

Her eyes widened as she stared at me. "For God's sake, Denise. What happened to you?"

I ignored her question and picked up the menu, browsing the ridiculously priced meals. "I actually think I *am* hungry, after all. You said the salmon was good...right?"

OCTOBER 2009

"So, what's going on at school today?" I asked, taking a left onto Bellagio and glancing over at Lola.

"Nothing," she said, frantically tapping the keys on her cell phone.

I raised my brows above the frames of my sunglasses and turned my attention back to the road. "Nothing? Nothing at all?"

She sighed and dropped her phone in her lap. "Just the same old boring stuff, Mother."

"*Mother*?"

"Are you not my mother?" Her sardonic tone told me she was rolling her eyes as she flipped down the visor and appraised her reflection, smoothing her long toffee-colored hair. It was the exact color of Marcos's, minus the gray that had crept into his.

"I *am* your mother, which makes me wonder why you think you can speak to me like that."

"Whatever, fine, sorry," she mumbled, pulling a tube of gloss from her backpack and swiping the wand across her full lips.

A grainy image of me sitting in the passenger seat of Suzette's car when I was fifteen flashed behind my eyes. *Oh God, is she having sex with twentysomething musicians in hotel rooms?*

We'd had *the talk* when she was younger, and it was probably time for a refresher—but not on the way to Catholic school. She was a beautiful girl with a penchant for pissing me off, and I knew all too well what that could involve. I made a mental note to bring it up the next time I was driving her to the mall so she'd be trapped in the car with no means of escape.

I flipped on my blinker at a stoplight, the rhythmic sound lulling me into a trance as I stifled a yawn. We'd been so rushed trying to get out of the house that morning, neither Marcos nor I had time to make coffee, and I needed the comfort of a warm cup of caffeine. I couldn't go to my normal spot, though. Not if it meant there was a possibility of seeing Christian again.

I'd lain in bed the night before with Marcos snoring softly beside me and wondered if Christian was keeping a vigil at the coffee shop. It seemed he knew that was my regular place, which was unsettling. Had he been watching me? Following me? And the email...How many more would there be? The uncertainty made my stomach heavy, like I'd swallowed a cement block. I'd considered waking Marcos and telling him what had happened, but there was something inside me that didn't want him to know. Something warning me that if I confessed Christian had contacted me, I'd also have to confess my own thoughts. All the what-ifs that occupied more space in my brain than they should have.

I blew the thoughts out with my breath as I pulled in the front of the school and shifted the car into park. Lola did one last check in the mirror before grabbing her backpack and opening the door.

"Have a good day," I said, trying to sound upbeat, like I wasn't irritated that my daughter was a bitchy teenager, and my ex-boyfriend was potentially stalking me.

Lola grumbled "Okay" and shut the door. As she walked toward the entrance, tossing her arm around one of her girlfriends and throwing her head back with laughter, I thought about how funny it was that I had longed for a relationship with my mother when I was her age, but Lola seemed to want nothing to do with me. I hoped it was because she knew I loved her, and that no matter what she did, she'd never have to worry about that love being taken away.

The clamor of voices and smell of burnt coffee overwhelmed my senses as I stepped into the Starbucks, silently cursing Christian for forcing me to abandon my quiet little coffee shop a few miles away. Surely it wouldn't be long before I could go back. Maybe a couple of days, or a week at most, to be safe.

My heels clicked against the floor as I took my place behind two giggling girls in pleated skirts and polo shirts who appeared to be ditching mass for Frappuccinos. I chuckled to myself, silently pardoning them for their sins.

"What can I get started for you this morning?" the guy in the green apron behind the counter chirped.

"Venti Dirty Chai, please."

"All righty, one Venti Dirty Chai for…"

"Denise," I said, handing him my card.

He told me they'd have that up "in a jiff," and I stepped to the side with all the other people waiting to grab their drinks and get the hell out of there.

I fucking hate you—

"Christian!" a barista called, placing a cup on the counter.

An invisible syringe of adrenaline plunged into my heart. My pulse pounded and my ears buzzed as the liquid spread to my legs, preparing them for a quick escape from the person waiting to pounce like a tiger from the crowd.

There are thousands of Christians in Los Angeles. It might not even be him. Breathe, breathe, bre—Jesus fucking Christ.

His gray eyes met mine, and I immediately dropped my gaze to the floor. My chest heaved as my lungs tried to capture the little air that seemed to be left in the room.

Did he follow me? Did he fucking follow me?

I dug my nails into my palms and raised my head, ready to tell Christian to get the fuck out of my life forever. But he wasn't there. My eyes darted around the open space, landing on wavy hair and a black leather jacket walking out the door.

What the hell? Is he doing this just to fuck with me? Will he show up in the lobby of my office building tomorrow, casually sitting in a chair and reading a magazine like he's waiting for an appointment with one of the other occupants?

No. No way. I'm putting an end to this shit now.

I stomped to the door and shoved it open, planting my feet firmly on the sidewalk. "Hey!"

Christian stopped but didn't turn around.

"What the fuck do you think you're doing?" I asked as I approached him.

A passerby side-eyed me, and I shot her a look. *Like you wouldn't do this if your ex was stalking you.*

Christian turned slowly, coffee cup in hand, and shook his head. "I didn't know you were going to be here, Denise. I swear, I didn't know."

I barked out a laugh. "You expect me to believe that?"

He combed his hand through his hair and sighed. "I'm not following you or whatever it is you think I'm doing. I came here today because I thought you'd be at the other coffee shop, and I didn't want to freak you out."

I lifted my chin, considering his explanation. It *did* make sense. He couldn't have been following me if he'd already ordered his drink when I got there. But still, I suspected he was up to something. "Then why'd you email me yesterday? You didn't think *that* would freak me out?"

His leather jacket creaked as he shrugged. "I know I probably shouldn't have done that, but I…I just want to talk to you. I owe you an apology. *Apologies.* A lot of them."

I narrowed my eyes and clenched my jaw, considering my options. Hearing him out offered at least some level of comfort that he wouldn't contact me again. And the risks seemed fairly minimal, at least on the surface. He'd said he was in recovery, which was probably true because if he hadn't gotten clean, there was no way he'd be alive. If we talked in public, somewhere safe, maybe it would be okay. And I'd say nothing about my personal life. *Nothing.* Especially not about…

"All right, then. I need to know exactly what's going on, how you found me, and that you'll stop doing whatever this is once I listen to what you have to say."

His eyes widened, and he stumbled over his words. "I… Okay, yeah. Can we talk now? I've got time if—"

"No." I shook my head. "Meet me tomorrow at noon in…" I tried to think of somewhere big, crowded, and far enough away from the office that I wouldn't run into anyone at lunch. "Venice Beach. In front of The Sidewalk Cafe."

"I'll be there." He slid his free hand into the pocket of his jeans. "Thank you, Denise. This means a lot."

"One hour. That's it. Then *no more*," I insisted.

He nodded and offered a faint smile which I didn't return. My heels scraped against the concrete as I hurried back inside to retrieve my drink, unable to shake the fear of walking into the same tangled web we'd woven all those years ago.

8

APRIL 1990

T he room was lit by dim pendants hanging above the bar, the soft glow of red bulbs strung from the ceiling, and a few flickering neon signs advertising cheap beer. The smell of stale tobacco clung to the black walls, while a haze of fresh smoke lingered in the air like smog over the city. I wasn't familiar with the place when Christian gave me the name and address but agreed to meet him there anyway. A change of scenery was good. And I didn't want to run into any *acquaintances* at my usual haunts.

I stepped across the threshold of the entrance in my snakeskin pumps, careful not to trip over any obstacles hidden by the low lighting. There were a few people seated at tables scattered throughout the room, chattering over "L.A. Woman" by The Doors playing on the jukebox. I clicked across the concrete floor to the bar where Christian sat, the long dark waves that fell down his back unmistakably beautiful.

I couldn't wait for my fingers to be tangled in them, his breath warm against my neck as I wrapped my legs tightly around him.

But first things first.

I squeezed between his stool and the one next to him, planting my elbow on the scuffed wood of the bartop. He smelled like soap, or laundry detergent...something clean and fresh, neutralizing the staleness of the bar.

"You take all your women to places where no one will ever be able to find them?" I asked.

He turned his head, the corners of his mouth curling up as he took me in. I was positive that Christian was some sort of struggling musician, and we wouldn't be patronizing a high-end establishment, so I'd made sure to dress casually in the sexiest way possible. Faded jeans, black leather jacket, and a low-cut, tight white T-shirt complemented by a pendant necklace that dipped into my cleavage.

"Only the ones who look like they wanna get lost with me."

I brushed my bangs to the side and situated myself on the stool, hanging my purse over the back. "Guess you had me pegged all wrong."

He cocked his head. "You sure about that?"

I smirked as the disinterested-looking bartender approached me. "Miller Lite, please."

Christian shifted in his seat to face me. "You're a cheap date."

"Oh, I'm sorry. Do they have an award-winning chardonnay here that I simply must try? If so, we should get a menu. I'm sure it would pair well with the cheese plate,'" I said, rolling my eyes.

"Hey, Mick," he called to the bartender who'd retreated to the corner with his cigarette after sliding my beer in front of me. "Did you get that shipment of chardonnay in from Burgundy?" He paused and winked at me. "That's in France."

"Fuck off, Christian," Mick said, blowing a stream of smoke to the ceiling.

Christian raised his brows at me and stifled a laugh.

My mouth fell open. "How the *fuck* do you know about Chardonnay?"

"My mother considers herself a wine connoisseur. Everyone else considers her a drunk." He shrugged, lifting his beer to his lips and taking a sip. "But you know...potato, *potahto*."

I laughed sharply. "Well, I'm not sure what my mother considers *herself*. But *I* consider her a bitch."

He smiled. "So is there an apple-tree thing going on there, then?"

I took a long swallow of my beer and plunked it on the bar. "I'm only a bitch when it's called for. Which it might be right now."

He placed his hand on my knee and focused his smoky eyes on mine. "All right, no more name-calling. That was just to get your attention the other day. Which I seem to have now."

I held his gaze, hoping to convey everything I wanted to do to him and everything I wanted him to do to me. "I'd say you do."

"Glad that's settled." Christian's hand trailed from my leg, and he reached for his drink. "Now you get to tell me all about yourself."

I groaned. Had his brain not received the message my eyes tried to send? "Is that necessary? Can we actually rewind to the name-calling?"

He grinned and leaned closer to me. "Oh, come on. Who *is* Denise? What does Denise *do*? What is Denise's *last name*?"

"Okay, but this is like a genie thing where you get three wishes. Except you only get to ask three questions."

He sighed. "Fine."

I took a long swig of my Miller Lite. "Denise is twenty-six years old. Denise is from LA. Denise works in finance. Denise's last name is Abbott."

"That's all you're gonna tell me?"

"Yep."

He gave me a coy smile. "And what do *you* wanna know about *me*?"

I shrugged, trying to hide my own smile. "Same three things, I guess."

He ran his hand through his hair and rolled his eyes. "*Christian* is twenty-five years old and from Seattle. Christian is..." He paused, and I could see his cheeks flush in the light dangling above us. "A musician...a singer...a songwriter. Whatever you wanna call it."

I chuckled to myself at my ability to spot these guys a mile away but quickly cleared my throat. The way his voice quieted and he stumbled over his words wasn't something I was used to. His humility sent a tingle through my chest, and I fingered the pendant on my necklace.

"Christian's last name is O'Connor." He blew out a breath and scrubbed his hands down his face. "Are we going to refer to ourselves in third person all night?"

"No." I grinned and sipped my beer. "When's your birthday?"

"I thought it was only three questions."

"I changed the rules."

He drained his own drink, releasing a satisfied *aah* before placing the empty bottle on the bar. "February twenty-seventh. When's yours?"

"Oh, wait, I just changed the rules back."

"Nope," he insisted, shaking his head. "I match you, question for question."

"January thirtieth." I twisted a strand of hair around my finger. "Which, if you're only twenty-five, means I'm a whole year older. Makes me feel like I might be taking advantage of you, actually."

His lips quirked, and he arched an eyebrow. "Really? Because I don't currently feel taken advantage of."

I ran my tongue over my teeth. "Would you like to?"

"What's the tab, Mick?" Christian sputtered, turning his head to the bartender.

"Gimme ten, and we'll call it good."

I reached for my purse, assuming he could barely pay for his own drink, much less mine, but he threw two twenties on the bar before I could retrieve my wallet.

My eyes widened, and Christian smiled. "Mick's a good dude."

———

"Nice place." Christian's eyes swept around the apartment as I tossed my purse on the chair in my living room. "You got a roommate?"

I chuckled and leaned against the wall "No. Why? Don't want any potential witnesses when you murder me?"

"Nah. I just thought a threesome might be fun," he said, his mouth twitching as he winked.

I narrowed my eyes and let out a breathy sigh. "Ooh, that would be fun. Do *you* have a roommate?"

He laughed and gripped my waist, pulling me closer so I could feel what was hidden behind the front of his jeans. "I've got an entire band. But I'm not sharing you with any of them."

"Darn," I managed just before Christian snaked a hand around my neck and his lips met mine. I threaded my fingers through his hair as he kissed me deeply and slowly, setting my insides on fire.

His mouth roamed to my neck, and I moaned as he brushed my hair back, bringing his lips to my ear. "I asked if you have a roommate because I want to know if we have to be quiet while I fuck the shit out of you."

Mary, Mother of God, I'm gonna come right now.

My hands grasped his jacket, sliding it off his shoulders and down his arms, before tugging the bottom of his T-shirt up. He lifted his arms, allowing me to guide it over his head, and I ran my palms along his smooth, firm chest down to the faint trail of dark hair above his jeans.

"Hey," Christian said, hooking his finger under my chin, tilting my head up. "Shirt for shirt."

I kept my eyes locked on his as he stepped back so I could discard my own jacket and top, revealing a carefully selected lacy white push-up bra with satin trim. "Better?" I asked, twisting my lips.

He smiled and pressed into me, gliding his hands up my ribs. My nipples hardened as his thumbs brushed over the soft lace that covered them, and I sucked in a breath.

"Fuck, yes."

I bobbed my head to the left. "Bedroom's down the hall."

"I could fuck you right here," he growled, burying his face in my neck and massaging my breast.

I threw my head back and laughed, pushing him off me. "Let's save the wall fucking for another time."

He raised his eyebrows. "So there's gonna be another time?"

I grabbed his hand and pulled him toward the hallway. "Depends on how good this one is."

———

I exhaled and ran my hand over my forehead, brushing away my bangs as I made a mental note to never lose Christian's number. The way he worked his fingers, his mouth, his *everything*—it was like he'd gotten a goddamn degree in how to make a woman come. I rolled my head to the side to see his forearm slung over his eyes and long dark hair splayed across the pillow. His chest pumped frantically before settling into a steady rhythm, and a faint smile danced on his lips as he peeked at me from under his arm.

"So." I poked my finger into his shoulder, my mouth

curving into a satisfied smile. "Where'd you learn to fuck like that?"

He let his arm fall to his side and turned to face me. "Hard to say. I guess it helps to get a good, solid warm-up in before game time, so I really should be asking you."

I raised my chin. "Asking me what?"

"Where you learned to suck dick like that."

Our faces contorted and our shoulders shook until we were like twin volcanoes erupting with laughter.

"Natural talent, I suppose," I choked out as the laughter faded, and I swung my legs over the side of the bed. "Anyway, I guess you probably need to go, so—"

"Wait." Christian reached for my arm. "I don't need to go."

I looked down at his hand and slowly turned my head. *What the fuck is he doing?* "I mean, there's no need for—"

I gasped as he pulled me across the bed and into his arms. My limbs stiffened, and I held my breath. He cupped my face and gently brushed his lips across mine until I found myself returning his soft kisses and curling into the warmth of his body. My hand slid around to his back, lightly stroking the damp skin under his hair as my thoughts became soft and hazy.

I wasn't sure how long I'd been in the trance when the flares in my brain started signaling. *Abort, Denise. Abort.*

I cleared my throat, extracted myself from his cocoon, and rolled out of the bed.

"Where are you going?" he asked. "I thought girls liked that."

I chuckled as I hurried over to my dresser and grabbed a pair of underwear and a T-shirt, pulling them on as quickly as possible. "Well, Christian, *I* am no ordinary girl."

He pushed up on his elbows. "I mean, I thought we...I thought that was good...no?"

I twisted my hair up, securing it with a clip. "I have an early morning and need to get some sleep."

"Tomorrow's Saturday," he said, his brows turning down.

"I work a lot. Weekends and stuff." I picked up his boxers and jeans from the floor and placed them on the bed. "But we should do this again."

He looked at his clothes before bringing his eyes up to mine. "Are you kicking me out?"

"That sounds so harsh."

"But you are."

"Yeah, I am," I said, gritting my teeth, as if that somehow made me look like I was sorry for doing it.

He blew out a long breath before planting his feet on the floor and walking into the bathroom to discard the condom. "Well, Denise," he began, returning to the bed and grabbing his boxers. "What if I say I'm not going?"

"Ha!" I crossed my arms over my chest. "You can't just stay in my apartment if I tell you to leave."

"Oh, I think I can," he said, pulling on the boxers before stepping into his jeans.

"And *I* can call the cops."

He shook his head. "No, you can't."

"Oh, I totally can."

"I mean, you *can* but you won't."

I narrowed my eyes and propped my hands on my hips, opening my mouth several times. But nothing came out.

"Great," he said, strolling over and placing a quick kiss on my forehead before walking past me and starting down the hall. "What should we order for dinner?"

I curled my toes into the carpet, taking a deep breath through my flared nostrils before stomping behind him into the kitchen, where he was opening drawers like he owned the place. "What the hell are you doing?"

"Looking for take-out menus. It's, like, nine o'clock. Aren't you hungry?"

"No."

He cocked his head. *"Really?"*

I'm fucking starving, you lunatic, but this is not how it's supposed to go.

"My treat," he added with a grin.

I glared at him as I tapped a bare foot on the tile.

He needs to leave. He has to. Simple as that.

Shit. Why is he so goddamn gorgeous standing there shirtless with those eyes and those lips?

No. No. He needs to go.

But that sex was insane. Maybe we can do it again.

Fuck. Fuck. Fuuuck.

"Fine," I conceded, rationalizing that no harm could come from eating a few slices of pizza or a carton of lo mein before one more roll in the hay. "They're in the drawer to your right."

He flashed a victorious smile and pulled out a thick stack of menus, waving them in the air. "I take it you're not a cook."

"I told you, I work a lot," I snapped, scurrying over and snatching the papers from his hands.

"This is like the perfect Friday night, right?" He sidled up to me, his arm circling my waist. "And my God, you're short without those crazy heels on. How tall are you?"

"Five one," I said, glowering up at him.

"That makes you even cuter. Anyway, we should probably order before places stop delivering. And then we can put on a movie."

"Oh, Christ on a stick, Christian," I said, slapping the menus against the countertop and elbowing him. "What do you not understand about me wanting you to leave?"

He laughed and backed away, raising his hands in surrender. "All right, too far with the movie thing, I get it. But seriously, Denise. You want me here. You can say you're not that kind of girl, but you *totally* cuddled with me."

"I did not *cuddle* with you."

"You did."

"For like, five seconds."

"More like five *minutes*."

I rolled my eyes and picked up a trifold menu. "Can we do Chinese?"

He clutched his hand over his chest. "How did you know that's my favorite?"

"I really have no idea how you're still here," I said, my voice flat.

The statement was directed at him, but I was also asking myself why I was picking up the phone to call Number One Chinese rather than 911. What was going on with me? *The sex.* The sex had been too good. It had clouded my thinking, and I wasn't in my right mind. That had to be it.

After I ordered our food, I sat with my back against the arm of the couch, a copy of *People* magazine splayed across my bent knees. Christian, still shirtless, settled into the other end of the sofa, peppering me with questions about my life.

"Did you go to college?"

"Yes."

"Where'd you go to college?"

"Not here."

"Where do you work?"

"At a company."

"What company?"

"No."

When he finally decided I was, for all intents and purposes, ignoring him, he gave up trying to make conversation and flipped through the television channels.

But I wasn't ignoring him at all. I was well aware there was a ridiculously hot shirtless man with whom I'd just had maybe the best sex of my life sitting a foot away from me. One whom I couldn't stop stealing glances at as I pretended to read celebrity gossip. One who needed to get the hell out of my house before I started to get comfortable with the idea of him staying.

The doorbell rang, and Christian hopped up, digging his wallet from his back pocket as he headed for the door. I almost told him I would pay for dinner but remembered how much he'd tipped the bartender earlier that night and figured he had it covered...somehow.

I continued to flip through the pages of my magazine as he thanked the delivery driver and began to rummage through the bag.

"Holy shit, this looks awesome," he said, heading to the kitchen. "I don't think the orange chicken *and* the shrimp lo mein *and* the two egg rolls are enough for me. I should've ordered more."

"Do not fucking touch my orange chicken," I warned, tossing the *People* aside and hurrying after him. "Or my eggroll."

I picked up the plastic container, balancing the eggroll on top and retrieving a fork before starting back to the living room. He grabbed my waist, and I yelped as he yanked me back.

"Let go of me, *Christian*."

"Put your food down and turn around, *Denise*."

My jaw clenched, and my chest heaved as I slid my dinner onto the counter and pivoted to face him. "What?"

He grabbed my ass, barely covered by the T-shirt I'd thrown on, and pulled my body into his. My jaw relaxed as I met his gaze, and before I knew it, our mouths collided and my mind went blank. When he stroked his thumb over my cheek and gently pulled away, I stood motionless, lids closed, my breath the only sound I could hear.

A voice in my head finally instructed me to open my eyes,

which I did. "You can have some of my orange chicken if you want."

Christian chuckled. "What?"

Jesus Christ, what the fuck is wrong with me?

I cleared my throat and shook my head. "Uh, I mean, it's probably too much food for me."

"Fine. So, can we eat and talk like normal humans now?"

I swallowed hard and nodded, accepting that my brain was short-circuiting, and there was nothing I could do to fix it at the moment. I'd have to work on it later. I probably just needed to eat. Surely, I'd be back to normal after I had some food in my system, and then Christian would go on his way.

I picked up my container and turned to head toward the living room. "There's some beer in the fridge. Can you grab two?"

Even though I couldn't see it, I felt the warmth of his smile like the sun on my back.

"Abso-fucking-lutely."

9

OCTOBER 2009

The midday sun was warm on my bare arms, but it did little to ease the chill that traveled down my spine and pebbled my skin when I saw him standing in front of The Sidewalk Cafe. His shoulder-length waves danced in the breeze like the fronds on the palms in the grassy area separating concrete from sand. He was watching one of the artists on the boardwalk decorate a canvas with dramatic strokes.

I hung back, turning toward the ocean and clasping my hair as a few stray strands whipped around my face.

I can leave right now. I can leave, I can block his email address, I can find another coffee shop nowhere near the others.

But I didn't want to go.

I told myself it was curiosity. And that *was* part of it. What did he want to say? Why was he really here? The other part... Well, I was old enough to know better. To know that it was stupid to wonder if things could've been different. To wonder if I wanted them to be different. Because my life was good.

Too good for someone like me.

With that thought, I took one final inhale of salt air and

walked toward him, my brain telling me to turn back while my broken heart propelled me forward.

"Hi," I said, crossing my arms over the smooth silk of my sleeveless blouse.

He startled and rotated his head from the street artist to me. "Shit. Hi." His voice cracked, and he cleared his throat. "I, uh...I didn't think you'd actually come."

My chest tightened. Looking at him was like looking at Lucas, with his hooded gray eyes and strong, straight nose. Even the goddamn dimple on his right cheek was the same.

"Well, I did." I rubbed my arms, diverting my gaze and trying not to think about the fact that I was face-to-face for the third time in three days with the father of my son. A father my son had never known. A father he'd rarely asked about after we told him at eight years old that there had once been another man, but that man couldn't take care of him. And then Marcos came along and loved us both so much that *he* wanted to be his dad.

"Thank you. For doing this," Christian said. "Are you, uh... Should we get something to eat?"

I sniffed and shook my head, grateful for the sunglasses that covered my glassy eyes. "I'm not hungry. Let's just sit."

He nodded, and we walked in silence until we found an empty bench. Christian hesitated, waving his hand for me to sit first. My body hugged the arm at one end, and he kept his distance by sitting against the other, spreading his long denim-covered legs and placing his elbows on them. He dropped his head, hands threading through his hair, and let out a breath.

I looked at my watch and huffed. "Just say it, Christian. Say whatever it is you want to say so I can go on with my life and not worry if you're lurking around every goddamn corner."

"I...I don't know where to fucking start, Denise," he confessed, frustration fueling his voice. "It's, like, I know the feelings, but I don't know the words to explain them. I thought I did. All the therapy, all the meetings, all the conversations with my sponsor. I thought I knew what to say. But it was a lot easier when I was writing it down or saying it to myself." He paused and lifted his head. "But seeing you is making me relive all the shit I put you through. And I can't fucking believe I was that person."

I chewed my lip and stared straight ahead, the passersby blurring as memories of that last day with Christian pierced my brain. "Why are you here?"

"I...I wanted to tell you I was—"

"No, I mean, why are you *here*?" I jerked my head toward him. "I thought you moved back to Seattle. At least, that's what the magazines said."

"Did you...read about me?"

I snorted and rolled my eyes. *Yes.*

He sighed. "I'm here for work."

Right. He'd said that in his email.

"I'm working on some songs," he continued. "Not for me. Just helping out an industry guy I know."

"And you decided you might as well stalk me while you're in town?"

Christian pressed his fingers against his forehead. "Denise, I'm not...*Fuck.* All right, look, I'm staying at my friend's guesthouse in Bel Air near the coffee shop. I was there one morning, and I saw you. I mean, I wasn't sure if it was you, but then the barista called your name. So I went back the next day, and you were there again. And then I just...I kept going back, trying to work up the nerve to talk to you." He paused and leaned against the back of the bench, gazing up at the cloudless sky. "But if I'm being totally honest, I knew you were still in LA. I looked you up more times than I want to admit and saw you still worked at your dad's company. Or I guess it's your company now. And I thought about calling you or emailing you. But I didn't know you'd be at that coffee shop, I swear."

I studied his face, wondering if he had draped a veil of innocence over it while I wasn't looking or if he was being truthful. He'd lied to me so many times before. Back then, I'd believed him because it was easier. Easier to imagine I hadn't been so stupid as to offer up my entire self to someone who cared more about getting high than he cared about me. But now, I didn't have to decide whether he was being honest. I could let him say he was sorry, I could thank him for the apology, and I could go back to the office. The place where the husband who loved me—despite the fact that I wasn't quite sure I'd ever done anything worth loving—was working to support our family.

The tug I felt to stay didn't make sense. But it only grew stronger as Christian glanced over at me, the slightly weathered skin on his face and the creases of age on his forehead spurring my curiosity about what had become of the man I'd met nearly twenty years ago. Back when I believed it was me against the world. When I slammed the door shut on people before they could slam it on me.

But not him.

There had been something different about *him*.

I'd thought we were the same. That I was half a person, he was half a person, and with the right amount of thread, we could figure out how to sew one whole human. I didn't know how he'd made me believe that.

"I'm so sorry, Denise."

His voice startled me, and I blinked away my thoughts.

He scooted forward on the bench, clasping his hands and turning his head to me. "I was messed up. And I messed *us* up. And I know you probably have a whole different life now, and it doesn't matter to you, but I just need to say that I regret what I did. How I was. And I can't apologize enough for the hurt I caused you."

I swallowed, not quite able to dislodge the lump in my

throat, and managed a slight nod. I didn't know whether I forgave him, and I reminded myself that it really didn't matter either way. I just knew that even though I should have wished him well and headed to my car, I stayed there, tethered to the bench.

"How long have you been sober?" I asked, unintentionally flipping my sunglasses onto my head. I immediately felt exposed and crossed my arms over my chest.

His face softened as he fixed his eyes on mine. "Seven years."

"That's..." I pressed my lips together and nodded. "Congratulations."

"Seems to be sticking this time." He laughed, crossing his fingers on both hands, but a sadness coated his voice, causing my mouth to settle into a frown. He noticed and changed the subject. "What about you? Are things okay with you?"

I took a shallow breath before allowing a restrained "Mm-hmm" to vibrate through my tightly sealed lips.

"I'm glad," he said, wringing his hands. "You deserve a good life. I wish I could've given that to you. I wish I hadn't fucked it all up."

I shifted my gaze to the palms over his shoulder. "You don't know what would've happened, Christian. Even without all the...stuff. We were just kids."

"Maybe." His voice cracked, and he cleared his throat. "Did you, uh...did you end up...I mean, do you have a family?"

My eyes darted from the trees to the expectant look on his face. *Does he want the answer to be no? Does he think, after all these years, we're going to smile at one another, lock hands, and walk down the fucking boardwalk together like he didn't wreck my whole world?*

Or worse...does he remember what I told him that last day?

I steeled myself, not wanting him to see me sweat. "You *do* understand you don't have the right to know that? That you don't have the right to know anything about me other than whatever you looked up on the fucking internet?"

"Yeah. Yeah, I understand," he said quietly. "I'm sorry, I just...I hope you have, you know...good things in your life."

I stared at the pavement. *Goddammit. God-fucking-dammit. Why do I feel bad for him? Why do I feel one ounce of pity for this man?*

"I do," I said, lifting my eyes. "Have good things. A good family." I paused, unsuccessfully trying to stop the next three words from tumbling out of my mouth. "What about you?"

I wasn't sure why I asked. *No.* That was a lie. But I hated myself for wanting to know. I hated myself for caring and for secretly meeting a man whom I never should've agreed to meet in the first place.

He leaned back against the bench, resting an ankle on his opposite leg. "About twelve years ago, I got married. She was gone by our first anniversary." He sighed and turned his head to me, his faint smile tainted with melancholy. "I can't say I blame her."

I wondered what the nameless woman had endured as images of our relationship clicked in my brain like pictures in an antique slide projector. Things had probably been good at first. He was sober...then not. She cried, begging him to get clean, and he swore he would. And then one day, whether she came to a quiet decision on her own or he scared the living hell out of her, she ran away and never came back.

A bolt of reality struck my brain like lightning. *What the fuck am I doing here?*

I flipped my sunglasses over my eyes and sprang up. "I have to get back to the office. But I...I hope things work out for you."

"Oh. Yeah. Okay." He looked at me like there was something else he wanted to ask, but I wasn't going to give him the chance. "But, um...thank you. For meeting me. I'm glad you're...I'm glad you're happy."

I nodded curtly, refusing to look at him. "Goodbye, Christian."

I glanced over my shoulder several times on the way back to my car to see if he was following me, then rolled my neck, trying to relax as I settled in behind the wheel. I called Marcos, letting him know I wasn't feeling well and was going to head home for the afternoon. Once there, I swallowed a small blue tablet with a sip of water from the sink, then burrowed under a blanket on my bed, determined to wake up believing the past several days had been nothing but a dream.

10

____

APRIL 1990

"So you lied to me." I took a swig of my beer, then pointed it at Christian. "Which makes you a liar."

"*Aaand* we're back to name-calling."

I smirked. "Is it name-calling if it's true?"

He swirled his empty bottle at me. "Can I get another?"

"No." I pushed myself off the sofa and headed for the kitchen, the alcohol and conversation making me forget how badly I'd wanted him out of my apartment an hour and a half ago. "I'll get us both one while you sit there and think about what you've done."

"Do you have any idea how sexy it is when you punish me like this?" he called after me.

I giggled, grabbing two beers and padding back to the living room. "Don't change the subject," I said, handing him one of the bottles before settling back into the couch. "We're talking about the fact that you're not *actually* from Seattle."

He sighed. "You do realize this is a technicality, Denise. It's, like, fifteen minutes away."

I turned to face him, twisting my legs into a pretzel. "Christian, you are from *Mercer Island.* One of the richest cities in this

74

entire country. You can't live there unless you make a bazillion dollars. And yes, that's a real amount."

He shrugged. "Fine. You got me. I make a bazillion dollars."

"You do not. But—"

"My dad does. Or family. I guess it's my mom's money, really. He just married into it and took over her father's business." He sipped his beer. "We should talk about you now."

"No, no, no," I protested, pulling a throw pillow onto my lap. "I'm not done. I have questions."

"Get rid of that pillow, and I'll answer 'em."

My brows turned inward. "What? Why?"

"'Cause now I can't see your underwear." He flashed a salacious grin. "How do you know Mercer Island anyway?"

"I had to go there to meet with a bazillionaire who wanted to invest in a film."

"So, *that's* what you do for work, huh?"

"Yes." *Shit.* "I mean, no."

"I think you're busted on this one."

"Whatever." I rolled my eyes. "Oh my God, do you think it was Mr. Christian?"

His shoulders fell. "Have you seriously already forgotten my last name?"

"No. I was just being cute."

"It's O'Connor."

"Fine, do you think it was Mr. O'Connor?"

"Mr. O'Connor has watched maybe three films in his life. And they all have *The Godfather* in the title." He chuckled. "So, no, don't think so."

"All right, enough about him. Back to you. You came to LA for music?"

He shifted in his seat, and I narrowed my eyes, studying his face. There was something he didn't want to tell me, something that made him uncomfortable, but I wasn't sure I needed to know what it was. I wasn't sure I *wanted* to know. This was the longest we'd ever hang out. A total one-off. Going forward, all this would be was sex. *Just sex.*

"Actually, I kinda...I had trouble with things...back home. I needed to get away."

"Oh." I swallowed, attempting to digest the unexpected serious turn our conversation had taken. "Well, you don't have to—"

"It's fine," he said. "My parents have a house down here they never use. So, a couple years ago, I packed up my shit, got in the car, and moved in. I didn't expect my band to follow me. Our sound is more what's happening in Seattle than LA, but..." He looked at me with an expression that landed somewhere between surprised and grateful. "They did."

"So, your parents suck, then? That's why you took off?"

"I, um..." A flash of discomfort flickered on his face. "Yeah, that's pretty much it."

I raised my bottle to him. "You're in good company."

"Yours, too?"

"Mostly my mom. But my dad is only slightly less of an asshole. My friend, Siobhan, who's studying to be a shrink, calls him 'emotionally unavailable.'" I laughed before lifting my drink to my lips. "She calls me that, too, though."

The right corner of Christian's mouth turned up, high-lighting the dimple in his cheek. "Sounds like she's gonna make a great shrink."

I blew a breath upward. "I'm not emotionally unavailable, Christian. I'm just...*pragmatic.*"

"Pragmatic?"

"Pragmatic means—"

"I know what it means, *Denise*," he said, shooting me a look. "And you're way beyond pragmatic. I think you should consider the possibility that you're scared as hell."

I huffed. "Coming from someone who's known me for less than twenty-four hours."

"Well, you're definitely...guarded. I'd barely pulled out before you were telling me to hit the road."

"I just don't see the need for—"

"What?" Christian leaned toward me. "Having a conversation with me?"

I instinctually met his gaze, holding it a bit too long before looking away. "I don't want to get involved in anything, Christian. So, if that's what you're looking for, I'm not your girl."

"Tonight hasn't been good?"

I picked at the fabric on the pillow still in my lap. "It's been good. But I'm...not that person."

He downed his beer and set it on the coffee table before turning to face me. "Look. I could come over here once a week, fuck *you*, and fuck *off*, if that's what you really want. But I actually dig hanging out with you. Is that so hard for you to believe?"

I scoffed and ran my palm along my face as my cheeks flamed from his words.

You think *you like me, Christian. But you don't. You have no idea who I am, and once you find out, you'll...*

I took a deep breath, snuffing out the fire on my skin, and let my hand fall to the pillow. "I've just decided I'm better off by myself."

Christian began to move closer to me but stopped as my eyes widened like a cornered animal. "Is it because of your parents?"

"What?"

"Your parents. Because they're assholes."

I laughed sharply. "You know, I really should introduce you to Siobhan. You could talk about all the how-our-parents-screwed-us-up bullshit, and how we have to heal from it, and blah, blah, blah. You guys would totally hit it off."

"I don't need her to tell me my parents fucking sucked. That they *still* suck. To this day, I can't figure out why they had kids.

My father has never given a shit about anything but work and money, and my mother has never given a shit about anything but *herself* and money." He took a breath, his gaze still focused squarely on me. "So, yeah. Parents *do* fuck us up. And I spend a lot of time fighting the feeling that I'm fucking worthless because of them."

My lips parted, and I drew in a tiny gasp of air.

"But they don't get to say who we are, Denise."

I looked into his eyes and saw my reflection—not just me at that moment, but the young girl whose mother sent her nanny to watch her school play, a teenager who was left to her own devices, and a college student who spent Christmases in a quiet house with no shimmering tree. The images grew watery from the sea that swelled behind my eyes.

Had Christian and I lived the same life?

I wasn't sure what to do with the feelings that were knotting my stomach and clouding my head, so I did the only thing that made sense to me. "We should, um..." I managed, voice straining through the tightness in my throat. "We should go to the bedroom."

"You were staring at the wall when you said that."

"Fine." I slowly shifted my eyes until they settled on him. "You should fuck me."

He looked at me earnestly. "If I do, I'm not leaving afterward."

I pressed my lips together and nodded, then stood and headed toward the bedroom. When I reached the door, I paused, and Christian wrapped his arms around me.

Until that moment, I'd thought I was using him to shut myself off from all the things I didn't want to feel. To numb myself the way I always had, the only way I knew how. But that wasn't it at all. Because just for the night, just with him, I knew I wanted to feel everything. Absolutely fucking everything.

11

———————

OCTOBER 2009

Christian's hips press against mine as his long dark hair falls around my face, covering me like a blanket. His skin feels different this time. I'm absorbing every piece of him—every bead of sweat, every ounce of emotion. I slide my hands down his back, pushing him deeper into me, desperate to be closer to him. The muscles in my core tighten, and I press the back of my head into the pillow, waves traveling through my body, vibrating through my lips. I...I...Fuuuuu—

"Denise?"

"Huh?"

I forced my lids open and my eyes circled the room, finally landing on Marcos sitting beside me on the bed. My face was smashed against the pillow, thighs squeezed together, and the ache that pulsed between them sent a rush of warmth from my chest to my face. I gasped and pushed myself up, my pulse pounding in my neck.

"What? What time is it?"

"Just after six. You must've been out for a while," Marcos said, running his hand along my cheek. "You were, like, moaning. And you're all flushed."

Jesus.

I shook my head and blew out a breath. "I think I just got hot. I mean, warm. I'm fine."

Marcos's brows turned down. "You sure?"

I managed a smile as I wiped my hair from my face. "Yeah, I'm good. Really."

He narrowed his eyes and tilted his chin up.

"Marcos, I'm feeling better. I promise. I was just worn out and needed to rest," I assured him as I patted the bed for my phone. "Shit, I must've left my cell in my purse. Are the girls where they're supposed to be?"

I needed to change the subject. Erase all thoughts of Christian from my brain and focus on my family. My beautiful family, whom I loved more than anything.

"Yep. Marisol is at Violet's for the night, and Lola is doing whatever she does with Jasmine and those girls. I reminded her not to get in a car with anyone else and to be home by eleven, no excuses. Just like you said." He grinned, a proud husband who'd remembered his wife's instructions after she'd called him earlier and told him she felt sick.

A wife who'd lied.

A wife who went home and dreamed about fucking her old boyfriend.

How horrible of a human am I? Let me count the ways...

I sighed and fell back against the bed, my arm landing over my forehead. "How does she have friends who can drive? She was, like, four years old yesterday."

"We're old, Dee," he said, sliding his hand from my waist to my breast as he leaned in, his lips hovering over mine. "But you're still hot as fuck."

I smiled and raised my head to kiss him, wrapping my arms around his neck and tugging him on top of me. "Thank you. You're hot, too. And I'm not the only one who thinks so." I winked and placed my hands on his cheeks.

He gave me a cocky smile. "Oh yeah? Who thinks I'm hot?"

I giggled. "I heard Jasmine tell Lola the other day you're a DILF."

"Am I supposed to know what that means?"

"Per the internet, it's a Dad I'd Like to Fuck."

Marcos scrunched his face and rolled off me. "Fucking Christ. She's sixteen."

I turned on my side, still chuckling, and smoothed my hand over his chest. "If it makes you feel any better, Lola told her if she ever said that again, she'd tell Jasmine's boyfriend about the time Jasmine made out with some kid named Tyler while said boyfriend was in Tahoe."

Marcos rotated his head to me. "That actually does *not* make me feel better. Is *our* daughter making out with kids named Tyler?"

"She might be. I don't know. I looked over at her in the car yesterday morning, and I swear I saw myself when I was fifteen." I grimaced. "Maybe I should make her an appointment with my doctor. I can't be a grandmother at forty-five."

Marcos's eyes looked as if they would pop out of his head on two springs. "You think she's..."

I propped myself up on my elbow and shook my head. "No, no, I'm not saying that. I just need to talk to her because, you know...we all do things without thinking sometimes."

He covered his face. "I can't deal with this."

I pried his hands away, placing a kiss on his lips. "Don't give it another thought, babe. I'll handle it. Lola never tells me anything unless I make her. She could want to be a fucking nun, for all I know."

He smiled softly and ran his fingers through my hair. "She loves you, Denise. You don't see it, but I do."

I sighed, hoping what he said was true, even though I hadn't felt that way since she was in elementary school. "Maybe one day she'll tell me that. But until then, you can be her hero." My lips twisted into a saucy smile. "And her friends' DILF."

"Say that again and I swear I will pick you up, take you outside, and throw you into the fucking pool." He yanked me toward him, nuzzling his stubbled cheek into my neck, something he knew never failed to send me into an unhinged tickle fit.

My stomach muscles ached from laughter by the time I was able to wriggle out of his grip. "Okay, okay, I won't say it again." I paused to catch my breath and smooth my hair before scooting off the bed and heading toward the bathroom. "I'm getting in the shower. We need to leave soon for Lucas's show if we wanna get something to eat beforehand. Actually, shit. I don't think I can eat. I'm all of a sudden nervous."

"It's gonna be great." He crossed one leg over the other and grabbed the remote from the nightstand, aiming it at the television. "Now go shower while I lie here and try not to think about my daughter doing things I don't wanna think about her doing."

"Get over it, Marcos," I called as I lifted my blouse over my head and let it fall to the cool tile floor. "You didn't flip your shit when I found *actual* condom wrappers in Lucas's bedroom."

"He's my son, not my baby girl."

"You're being sexist."

"I'm being a protective Cuban father."

"You were born in Florida."

"Take your shower, *mi vida*."

I chuckled, slipped out of my black slacks, and turned the shower lever. But as I stared at the water glistening in the last of the sunlight peeking through the window, the smile dissolved, and my reality set in.

There's nothing I've ever done to deserve someone like him.
Absolutely nothing.

———

"Does this place have valet?" Marcos asked, his eyes scanning the scene as we headed into West Hollywood.

I turned in my seat and stared at him. "Marcos. Were you somehow under the impression we were going for a five-course tasting at Spago?"

"You mean I have to park my own car?"

I nodded. "And *then* you have to *walk* to the club. Just like one of those"—I paused and lowered my voice to a whisper—"*commoners.*"

He chuckled as I told him to make a right so we could try the lot behind the club. Miraculously, there was one space left that he agreed to squeeze his new Audi into after I told him the only other option was a garage ten blocks away. I wasn't sure if that was exactly accurate, but I didn't want to walk more than twenty steps in the thin-heeled boots I'd foolishly decided to wear.

Once inside, we found a space where we could see the stage but remain unobtrusive. I adored Lucas's girlfriend, Mia, and this was her big night: an artist showcase where the record label she'd recently signed with would introduce her and some of their other new acts to heavyweights in the industry. She and Lucas had sung and played guitar together since they started dating their sophomore year of high school. Never one for the spotlight himself, Lucas had encouraged her to start signing up for singer-songwriter events at local coffee shops and restaurants, where he'd sit behind her and play the more intricate parts to the melodies she'd created. Her manager had taken her on as a solo artist, and because labels often had their own plans, it was uncertain if Lucas would become a permanent member of her backing band. Guilt washed over me every time I found myself praying it wouldn't happen.

What kind of mother doesn't want her son to find happiness doing what he loves?

The kind who'd found his father passed out with a shoelace tied around his arm in a club just like the one they were in tonight.

"What do you want to drink?" Marcos's cheek pressed against mine while I tapped out a text to Lucas, telling him we had arrived.

"Just a vodka something." My hands trembled as I placed my cell back in my purse and thought about the fact that in thirty minutes, my baby was going to be onstage, playing to a house full of movers and shakers in the music industry. "Soda, tonic...whatever. Just tell them to make it strong."

He headed toward the bar while I stayed behind, chewing my lip and picking at the polish on my thumb as I scanned the room. Some of the crowd were in jeans and T-shirts with tattoos decorating their arms, while some wore professional attire, just to remind everyone that at the end of the day, the music business was just that—a business. I wondered who the bad guys were and who the good guys were. Who would take care of Mia. And Lucas, if he ended up being a permanent part of that world.

"Mami!"

I twisted my head to the right, where Lucas and Mia were standing, easy smiles on both their faces.

"Hey, kiddo," I said as his limp arms wrapped around me.

Is he not nervous?

I pulled back, narrowing my eyes. "You seem...relaxed."

He cleared his throat and lifted his shoulders in an attempt to stand a little straighter. "I, uh...What? Do I?"

Mia giggled, twirling her blond beachy waves around her finger, and Lucas placed a hand over his mouth.

I looked at her, then my son. "Oh my God, Lucas, are you *high*?" I pronounced the word exactly as my mother would've said it to me if she'd ever given a shit.

His eyebrows pinched together, and he waved me off. "What? No. What?"

I pressed my finger into his chest. "Lucas, how many times have I told you—"

"Come on, Mom." He rolled his head and sighed. "It's just a little weed to help us chill. It's not like I'm backstage plunging needles into my arm."

I took a shaky breath, and my fingers circled my wrist, trying to ease the ache from the memory his words unearthed.

"I'm sorry, Mrs. Navarro. I mean, Mrs. Abbott. I never know which one to call you 'cause it's, like, Lucas's name is Navarro, but you're still Abbott." She giggled again, then gazed up at Lucas. "I don't think I wanna change my last name, either."

I love her, but dear God.

"Anyway," she continued. "What I was going to say is that my brother, he grows his own stuff. It's totally organic, so it's, like, healthy."

I ran my hand through my hair and mumbled something about it being fine just to end the discussion. For as long as I could remember, I'd been terrified that there was some sort of genetic predisposition to drug addiction. That I'd walk into Lucas's room and find syringes instead of condom wrappers. And when he'd told me he wanted to put off college to see what would happen with his music, I'd considered getting into the car and driving myself to the hospital to make sure I wasn't having a heart attack.

Calm down, Denise. Like everybody in the entire state of California hasn't had a medical marijuana card since 1996. It's just pot.

"There they are!" Marcos appeared on my left and handed me my drink, which I promptly swallowed half of. He pulled both Lucas and Mia into a hug, then stood back, sipping his beer and appraising them. "Are you guys high?"

"So how many songs do you get to play?" I asked quickly,

hoping to steer the conversation away from organic weed. "Any new ones?"

"We're playing four total." Mia beamed up at Lucas. "Two new ones. I'm super psyched to see how they go over."

Lucas nodded. "Yeah, her manager brought this guy in and—"

"Hey, man, just wanted to say good luck. You guys are gonna sound great."

What.

"Dude, I was just talking about you. You have to meet my parents."

The.

"Mom, Dad, this is Christian."

Fuck.

Christian and I locked eyes like we were engaged in a staring contest and the punishment for losing was the goddamn guillotine. But I wasn't actually trying to win. At that moment, I would've gladly stuck my neck out for the blade to slice through it. Unfortunately, my blood had turned to ice, freezing me inside and out. I was paralyzed. And by the looks of it, so was he.

Words floated around me, but they were muffled, as though someone had stuffed cotton in my ears. Christian finally broke our stare, and the voices became clear.

"And this is my wife Denise."

I gasped and whipped my head to Marcos.

"What?"

His brows turned in, and he gestured to Christian. "This is Christian. He's been helping them write some of the songs for the album."

I opened my mouth, and a tiny squeak worked its way out.

Marcos cocked his head and placed his hand on my arm. "You okay, babe?"

Get it together. Get it the fuck together.

I took a discreet breath and turned to Christian as a curtain fell over my face. The same curtain I'd relied on for years to hide everything happening behind the scenes while I repeated carefully rehearsed lines and displayed acceptable emotions for whatever audience I was hoping to impress.

"Yes. Hi. So sorry about that," I said, extending my hand and a smile so wide my cheeks ached. "I think I drank my cocktail a little too quickly." A laugh launched like a missile from my throat. "Nice to meet you...Christian, is it?"

Had he not blinked, I would've sworn I'd grown snakes for hair, and my stare had turned him to stone. He slowly raised his hand to mine, clasping it while looking at me just long enough to read the message I was sending with my eyes: *You don't know me.*

"Nice to meet you." He looked at Lucas, then back at me. "Your, uh....son is very talented."

"Thanks." Marcos beamed at Lucas. "We think so, too."

Christian flicked his gaze to Marcos, as if he was surprised by his comment.

"My parents have somehow managed to get themselves lost in here." Mia groaned, rolling her eyes and sliding her cell phone into her pocket. "I've gotta go find them."

"I'll come with you," Lucas said, clasping her hand as they began to weave through the crowd. He called over his shoulder that he'd see us after the show.

Christian turned his head and watched for a little too long as he disappeared.

My eyes bounced back and forth. *Christian. Marcos. Christian. Marcos.*

I've got to get the fuck away from here.

"Well, I need a drink," I announced, finishing off the remnants of the clear plastic cup in my hand. "Marcos, will you come with me? It was nice meeting you, Christian."

I gripped Marcos's arm and headed for the bar.

He chuckled, gently tugging me back. "Denise is clearly nervous about the show. Can we get you anything, man?"

I turned to Christian and tightened my jaw. *He knows better. He fucking knows better…doesn't he?*

His lips pulled into an uncomfortable smile. "No, thanks, I'm good. I'm gonna head backstage for a bit. It was nice to meet you, though." He lifted his hand in a wave, giving me one last pointed glance. "Lucas is a great kid."

My stomach dropped so hard I looked down to see if it had fallen out of me. It might as well have. I felt like I'd been cut open, and nobody knew but me. Nobody *could* know but me. So all I could do was gather up the pieces and parts of me that lay on the floor and pretend that everything was okay. Which really wasn't so different from what I'd always done.

———

I stared at the cursor on my laptop, blinking like a beacon, warning me that if I didn't slam the gates shut now and tell him to stay the hell away from my son, my entire village was going to go up in flames.

My hand shook as I fumbled for the coffee mug sitting on the kitchen counter. It had turned lukewarm during the twenty minutes I'd been perched at the island, trying to figure out what to say to Christian. I hadn't allowed myself to believe he remembered much from that day so many years ago, but the way he'd looked at me and Lucas at the club scared the hell out of me. So that morning after the show, I opened my laptop and recovered his deleted email.

I never knew what happened after I told him I was pregnant. He'd made it very clear he'd heard the words in the moment. But where they lived inside him *after*—whether they'd buried themselves in the recesses of his mind only to be resurrected upon seeing his reflection nineteen years later, or they'd been haunting his thoughts all that time—I had no idea.

Either way, I wasn't going to ask. I wasn't going to give anything away. And I sure as hell wasn't going to let him into Lucas's life. So, I sucked in a deep breath and began to type.

From: Denise Abbot
To: Christian O'Connor
Subject: Re: I'm Sorry

Christian,

I'm sure you'll understand that I'm not comfortable with you working with my son. I don't know if you somehow planned this as part of an attempt to find me, or if it was just some unfortunate coincidence, but based on our history, I think it's best that you tell your "industry friend" that you can no longer be a part of the project.

Thank you for respecting my wishes.

Denise

I wasn't sure how long the cursor hovered over the Send button on the screen. I told myself I was hesitating because I didn't want to do anything to harm Mia and Lucas's chance at a music career, which was true. The new songs they played the night before—the ones I assumed Christian had helped write —were beautiful. But there was also a splinter of emotion lodged inside me that needled at my heart for being so cold to the first man I'd ever allowed myself to love. Even though I wasn't enough for him to love back.

But that was par for the course.

"Morning, beautiful."

I clicked Send and snapped my laptop shut, my heart hammering in my chest as Marcos padded into the kitchen wearing gray pajama pants and a T-shirt.

"Hey, hi," I said, clearing my throat.

He bobbed his head at my laptop before pouring a cup of coffee. "You working on a Saturday?"

I shoved the computer to the side. "Just catching up since I skipped out early yesterday afternoon." I picked up my mug but immediately set it back down once I realized it had gone as cold as my email. "Glad you slept in. You needed it."

"Midnight might as well be 3 a.m. these days." He leaned against the counter, taking a sip of caffeine.

"Oh, come on, Marcos," I said, twisting my lips into a smile. "Forty-seven is the new twenty-seven. Haven't you heard?"

"Says the forty-five-year-old. You just wait—next year, it's all gonna go downhill. The minute you cross that line, you pull muscles in your back you didn't know you had, your knees go out, and you start wanting to eat dinner at 4 p.m."

I tilted my head and narrowed my eyes. "You want to eat dinner at 4 p.m.?"

"God, yes." He strolled to the island, his smile highlighting the gold in his hazel eyes. "I've been harboring that secret for over a year now. Feels good to finally get it out."

I placed my elbow on the counter and rested my chin in my palm, crinkling my nose and mouth. "Well, what's a relationship if it's not based on honesty?"

My throat instantly closed, trapping a gasp before it could escape. It was supposed to be a joke. A joke about Marcos wanting to catch the early bird special. But the words fed my guilty conscience, and I couldn't cut the electricity that sparked inside me.

Was I lying to Marcos by not telling him about Christian?

He'd said he didn't want to know who the father was. That night when we were working late, and the facade I'd hidden behind finally crumbled because I no longer had the strength to hold it up. Christian had drained me of every last ounce. I'd told Marcos he was just a guy I'd known who was out of the picture, and that was it. No name, no details. Besides, Christian wasn't *Christian* at that point. No one knew then how famous the band would become.

So after we'd made our way to the bar the night before and Marcos asked me how I didn't remember "the guy from Soulever," I pretended I'd had a sudden lapse in memory. *"Oh my God, of course! I feel so dumb. Hi, yeah, can I get a double vodka soda, and what do you want, babe?"*

"You're, like, extra cute when you do that." Marcos set his mug on the counter and walked around the island.

I turned toward him as he approached the barstool. "When I do what?"

"Scrunch your face up like that." He smiled, smoothing the hair that had escaped my loose bun.

"This?" I tilted my chin up and crumpled my face so that my eyes were practically slits. "*This* is what makes you wanna pick me up and bend me over the kitchen table?"

"Oh my God, that is so hot," he choked out before pressing his smile against my lips and leaning into me as our bodies shook with laughter.

"Seriously, you guys are so gross. I'm, like, literally talking to Jasmine's dad's lawyer girlfriend about how I can be legally emancipated."

I looked at Marcos, my eyes rolling before landing on Lola, whose shorts peeked out from beneath her oversized sweatshirt as she stared blankly into the pantry. "So you decided not to move to Miami?" I paused, wrinkling my brow. "And wait, when did Jasmine's parents get divorced?"

"Only a million years ago." She sighed and shut the door, dissatisfied with her breakfast options. "Remember her mom went to that yoga retreat in New Mexico?"

I shifted my eyes to Marcos, who shrugged. "I thought she was doing an intensive certification or something. And wasn't that just in September?"

"Yeah, like, forever ago." Lola gathered her long locks into the scrunchie she'd removed from her wrist. "Anyway, I guess they're not technically divorced yet, but she's staying there. She said LA is a soulless void. She's living in a yurt."

"What's a yurt?" Lucas shuffled into the kitchen, yawning and pulling the orange juice from the fridge.

Lola leaned against the counter and sighed. "Duh, Lucas, it's a thing you live in. Maybe if you went to college instead of being glued to your girlfriend, you'd learn that."

Lucas took a sip directly from the container and snickered. "Like you know what it is."

"Whatever, I totally do."

"Then what is it? Also, where's the sister I actually like?"

I shot him a look. "Your *other* sister, whom you *also* love very much, is at a sleepover, Lucas. And let's not start the morning off by arguing about tents, okay?"

"Aren't yurts more like huts?" Marcos asked.

I sucked in a breath and forced a tight grin. "You know what? I want waffles. Who wants waffles? We should make waffles."

Lola and Lucas narrowed their eyes at me before Lola spoke. "You mean, like...*los congelados*?"

I gave her a blank look as laughter sputtered from Lucas. "What?"

"Geez, Mom," she said, shaking her head. "You should really brush up on your Spanish. Your husband is Cuban, you know."

"Lola, do not...I just don't know that word." I huffed and turned to Marcos. "What the hell did she just say?"

"She said"—he pursed his lips, trying not to join them in their laughter—"'frozen ones?'."

I scoffed at their lack of faith in my cooking skills. "Excuse me, but I can make them from scratch." I hopped off my stool and walked purposefully to the pantry. "Flour doesn't expire, does it?"

"Do we have bacon?" Lucas asked, once again opening the refrigerator.

"I think there's bacon," Marcos said. "And grab the eggs. This is good. Family breakfast. Sibling bonding time. Lola, ask your brother about his show last night."

She grimaced. "Okay, but, um, what if I don't actually care?"

"Lola," Marcos said sharply as he rifled through a drawer for utensils, and I peeked into the bag of flour I'd plucked from obscurity to make sure nothing had taken up residence in it.

"Fine. How was your stupid show last night, Lucas?"

Lucas snorted. "Stupid?"

"I'm sorry, I actually meant boring." Lola hoisted herself on the island and smirked.

"You know, one day you're going to regret how mean you were to one another," I insisted, repeating the words I'd said at least a million times but never really knew to be true.

"It's all right, Mom. I'm actually okay with Lola thinking our music is boring. You know, since her definition of exciting is bubblegum pop sung by chicks with pinwheels spinning on their tits."

"Lucas!" Marcos's eyes widened, and he slapped Lucas's arm with the spatula he'd located.

Lola's face contorted. "Oh my God, Lucas, you are *so* deranged. Do you know how sick and twisted it is to say *tits* in front of your *sister*?"

"Lola!" I cried.

Marcos shoved his hand in his hair. "*Ay dios mío,* can we please stop talking about tits?"

"Dad!"

"Marcos!"

The open bag of flour slipped from my hands, sending a burst of powder up from the floor, coating the front of my Dodger blue T-shirt in white. A tiny giggle escaped through the hand Lola had slapped over her mouth. I coughed, waving away the remnants of flour dust as Lucas snickered and a smile cracked across Marcos's face.

With Lucas and Lola both in their teens, it felt like we'd rarely had a moment together without him telling me to chill out or her stomping out of the room screaming. One where we'd just had fun and appreciated what we had as a family. My heart swelled, and I wished I could take both of them into my arms and hold them like they were babies again.

My phone rattled, signaling an incoming message, and my eyes immediately darted to the counter where it sat. Lola reached for it, and my skin tingled at the reminder I'd hit Send on an email to Christian only minutes before.

No. There was no way I was going to let Christian break the magic spell that had inexplicably been cast over the kitchen. No way I was going to let him ruin anything for me ever again.

"I'll get it later," I said, snapping out of my thoughts and into a pursed-lip smile. "Now, everybody calm your tits, and let's make some waffles."

12

APRIL 1990

Christian's thumb circled my nipple. "You know, you have amazing..."

I turned on my side and propped myself up on an elbow, pinning him with my eyes and a wry smile. "Is tits the word you're looking for?"

He laughed. "Right. Tits. Because breasts sounds too clinical, and boobs sounds too twelve-year-old boy."

"Well, thanks," I said, winking. "I'd return the compliment, but I don't know the male equivalent."

He grinned and lowered his gaze. "I mean, you could talk about my thick, hard—"

"You know, I really only like to *feel* thick and hard...*things*. Not talk about them at"—I glanced over my shoulder at the green digits on my nightstand—"10:18 in the morning. Which, wow, it's late. I need to get to the gym."

Christian reached for my hand, but my fingers slipped through his as I hopped out of the bed. "You can feel it again, you know. Just give me, like, seven minutes."

I coughed out a laugh and pulled on the pair of black biker shorts and a hot pink bandeau I'd plucked from my dresser.

"You have this down to a science, huh? Seven minutes between fucks?"

He pushed himself up, his back resting against the headboard as he grinned. "More like twelve because we've been talking for five. And you didn't say anything about the gym last night."

"Well, given the fact that you're still here, I was clearly out of my mind last night," I called from the bathroom as I gave my hair and teeth a quick brush.

"Why are you so mean, Denise?"

I watched in the mirror as the corners of my mouth flicked down. I knew he was joking—at least I thought he was—but there was something about him that...*mattered*. I didn't quite know why, but I didn't have time to think about it. I didn't *want* to think about it. So, I ran my hands down my face and exhaled, rolling my shoulders before stepping back into the bedroom.

"We'll hang out again, Christian," I said, shimmying into a black suspender leotard. I snapped the straps against my shoulders, hoping he'd take that as his cue to leave—even though I wasn't sure I wanted him to. But I'd sweat out whatever weirdness that was during class.

His wide eyes scanned my body. "*That's* what you wear to work out?"

I brushed my hands along the nylon fabric before planting them on my hips. "Oh, I'm sorry, do you think an evening gown would be more appropriate attire for step aerobics?"

"Are there guys in your class?"

"My neighbor, Beau, sometimes comes with me."

"And does he stare at your tits the whole time?"

"Only when trying to figure out how to get the fake ones he wears during his nightly drag show to look better."

Christian's face brightened. "I love Beau. You should go to the gym with him all the time."

I pressed my lips together in a feeble attempt to hide my smile. "My class starts in thirty minutes."

"All right, message received." He sighed and swept the sheet to the side, then made a quick stop in the bathroom before retrieving his clothes from the floor.

I sat at the end of the bed, pulling on socks and fumbling with the laces on my tennis shoes as I watched him out of the corner of my eye. Slightly faded denim buttoned just below his toned abs and white cotton draped like a curtain over his tan chest.

Jesus fucking Chr—

"You need some help there?"

Shit.

I cleared my throat and immediately turned my focus to my shoes. "What? No."

He snickered, and I sprang up from the bed, refusing to make eye contact with him.

"Come over tonight," he said.

I scoffed and headed down the hallway.

"Is that a no?"

"No."

"No, meaning that's *not* a no, or no, meaning you're not coming?" Christian appeared in front of me, unlaced boots now on his feet.

"That's a"—I squeezed my eyes shut—"whatever means I'm not coming."

"I'll make dinner," he continued as if I'd accepted his invitation. "Do you like Italian? If you don't, that's obviously fucked up, but I can make something else."

I rolled my eyes and shoved his leather jacket at him. "Christian, I'm not coming. Like I said, we'll...hang out...sometime. I have your number."

I chose my words carefully. I may have let him stay over the night before, but that wasn't going to become a *thing*. And we weren't going to go on *dates*. I needed to set some boundaries. And not just for him.

"Okay, I'll call you later to see if you've changed your mind and wanna stare at me shirtless again." He bobbed his head toward the hallway. "You know, like you did two minutes ago."

A small laugh escaped my throat as my cheeks pinked. "Goodbye, Christian."

"See ya soon, Denise," he said, flashing me a sly smile before disappearing out the door.

At the sound of metal clicking, I melted into the sofa and threw my head back, blowing out a long breath.

What is this guy doing to me? Why did I let him stay? So he understands what it's like to grow up with shitty parents. Don't most people have shitty parents? Don't—

I sat up, gasping at the knock on the door and turn of the knob.

"Well, hello, gorgeous!" Beau's southern drawl dripped of honeysuckle as he sashayed into my apartment wearing a tiny pair of shorts and a fitted tank.

I opened my mouth to greet him, but he spoke before I could get a word out.

"And I'm not talking about *you*, I'm talking about that man who was practically sizzling as he walked out your door." He leapt into the chair diagonal from me, crossing his lithe legs in one perfectly choreographed movement before leaning forward with his chin on his fist and a grin on his face. "Does he like boys, too?"

"Nice sweatbands," I deadpanned, pointing to the neon green fabric around his wrists.

"You're such a jealous bitch. Now tell me about your lover."

"He's not my lover. He's just a...good time."

Beau leaned back in the chair and folded his arms over his chest. "Oh, honey, I would not let that one go. I know how you are about relationships and blah, blah, blah, but he's hotter than noon on the Fourth of July."

"What is that land you come from again?"

"Alabama."

I chuckled and pushed myself up from the sofa. "Right. Anyway, let me grab a hair tie, and I'll be ready to go."

I walked down the hall into the bedroom, first scanning the top of my dresser, then the bathroom vanity, with no luck. The nightstand was the only possibility left, and I breathed a sigh of relief when I located a rogue elastic band in one of the drawers. As I secured my ponytail, a square brown leather object by the lamp caught my eye.

Are you fucking kidding me?

I huffed and picked up the wallet, then flipped it open to see Christian's Washington state driver's license.

Goddammit.

It was much too strategically placed to have been left by accident, and it certainly didn't fall out of his jeans and land on top of my nightstand.

"*Denise!* Hurry up. We need to get a good spot so we can see how fabulous we look in the mirror."

"Coming!" I tossed the worn wallet on my bed, deciding I'd teach him a lesson by not answering the phone when he called to let me know he'd *forgotten* it. He would get it back when I saw him next—on my terms.

I just had to figure out what I wanted those terms to be.

———

I skipped up the steps of the converted quadruplex and fit my key into the lock on my apartment door.

"Bye, sweetie," I called over my shoulder to Beau.

"Bye, sugar. And don't forget to fill me in after you have

dinner with your new boyfriend tonight." He wriggled his fingers and blew me a kiss.

"Not happening," I muttered more to myself than Beau, who had already disappeared into his own apartment.

I stepped into my living room, sorting through the mail I'd grabbed from the metal box outside, and kicked my foot behind me to close the door.

"Whoa, there."

I yelped and whipped around to a strange man taking a step back as if to signal he meant no harm.

"Sorry to frighten you, miss. Just delivering these."

I stood like a statue, my eyes wide and lips parted, staring at the clear vase he held in his hands.

A vase teeming with what had to be two dozen roses.

Hot pink and black roses.

"Should I...put them somewhere?" he asked.

"Oh," I said, blinking. "Are you, um...are you sure they're for me?

"The name on the card is Denise Abbott."

Card. Good, there's a card.

I nodded. "Okay, um, yes. Sorry." A nervous laugh sputtered from my lips as I tossed my mail on the console table beside me and took the arrangement, my arms shaking from its weight.

"You have a good day, miss." A look of confusion or concern or maybe both settled on his face as he stepped outside and shut the door.

I mumbled a dazed and delayed "Thanks" as I placed the vase on the coffee table. After plucking the small card from the plastic wand, I ripped open the envelope and held the note between my thumb and forefinger.

They're pink and black because I haven't been able to stop thinking about your tits. I mean your workout clothes. I actually mean you.

— Christian

As the card fluttered to the table, I closed my eyes and massaged my temples, weighing my options. I could call him and tell him to leave me alone. Ignore him and hope he'd go away. Leave a note on my door for when he came knocking, letting him know I'd taken his wallet to the police station. But as I thought about him standing at the door, pulling a piece of paper off it and laughing, I had to press my lips together to fight my smile.

No. Stop it. Stop it right fucking—

I sucked in a quick breath as the phone sounded from one of the end tables flanking the sofa. I stared at it, wondering if I should pick it up. What if it was Christian? And what if I said something I didn't mean to say? Or I said something I meant to say but shouldn't—or didn't want to—say?

I shook the ridiculousness out of my head and grabbed the receiver, shoving it against my ear. "Hello?"

"Jesus. I know I'm in a bad mood because it's April and forty-nine degrees, but why are *you* so pissed off?"

I sighed and flopped on the couch. "Sorry, babe. I thought you were someone else."

I could practically hear the thoughts swirling in my best friend Eva's head all the way in Chicago. "*Ooh*, who did you think I was? Who are you mad at?"

"I'm not *mad* at anyone," I said. "Just...annoyed. I think. I mean, I am. I am annoyed. I'm pretty sure." I bit my bottom lip, concerned at how ruffled my voice made me sound. At how ruffled I truly was. "Anyway," I managed, clearing my throat. "How are—"

"Did you meet a *boy* you like, Denise?"

Dammit.

I scoffed. "What? No! All I said was, I'm annoyed. Why is that...What would even make you think that?"

"It was really just wishful thinking. But now I'm guessing I might be right because you're totally flustered."

"I am not!"

"Well, then, I guess it's your mother who has you all worked up, so we'll just have to talk about her. What's Sharon been—"

"All right, all right, all right." I huffed and tucked my hand under the opposite arm. "I slept with this guy last night. Like, whatever, no big deal. But he just sent me"—I paused and rolled my eyes—"flowers."

"Flowers? Isn't *no flowers* number two in the *Rules for Engaging in Sexual Relations with Denise* contract? Right after *no sleepovers*, of course."

I winced, thankful she couldn't see my face, and after a few seconds of silence, she inhaled so sharply, I yanked the phone away from my ear.

Great. Apparently, she'd placed spy cameras in my apartment before she'd moved out last year.

"Oh my God, he totally slept over, didn't he? And now he's in love with you, and you're probably in love with him, even though you won't admit it, and you're gonna get married. Which, speaking of, when's the wedding? I swear, if you go to Vegas without me, we're done." Eva applied the brakes on her runaway train of thoughts with a dramatic sigh. "I can't believe this. I always thought I would be first."

She snorted, and I imagined her tipping over on her couch, hand covering her mouth.

"Ha, ha, ha. You're hilarious, Eva."

"I love this so much," she choked out.

"You're wasting long-distance money," I reminded her, a smile creeping across my face.

At that moment, I wished I was sitting beside her, and we could spend a lazy Saturday, like we did in college, nursing our hangovers with junk food and MTV before getting ready to go out and do it all over again—Eva always hoping she'd meet Mr.

Right, and me just hoping I'd meet the one guy at the bar who knew the right way to use his tongue.

Sometimes I wanted to tell her that dream men didn't exist, but I also wanted to believe they did for girls like her. Girls who were easy to love. Girls who had so much love to give. Girls who weren't me. Eva deserved someone who checked all the boxes and treated her like a fucking queen. So, I kept my mouth shut and prayed that she'd run smack-dab into him rounding the corner of Rush and Division one night as they each headed home alone after the bars closed. They'd slowly raise their heads, see the stars in each other's eyes, and live happily ever after.

"And then she was like 'Well, you'd think you'd want to spend Easter with your family, but if you already have plans, I guess that's fine.' *So* passive-aggressive, Denise. I wanted to say 'Actually, no, I do not want to spend Easter with the thirty-two-year-old woman who's married to my fifty-five-year-old father, but sure, I'll drive an hour to eat fucking ham with you if it really means that much.'"

I blinked, the thoughts in my head evaporating like a cloud. "Huh?"

"Fucking Kimberly wants me to come to their...Have you even been listening?"

Shit, shit, shit.

"Yeah, totally," I lied. "That woman's an absolute bitch."

It was always a safe response to Eva's complaints about her stepmother.

She gasped. "Oh crap, I gotta run. I didn't realize what time it is, and I'm supposed to meet Danielle for a movie. Call me later this week and tell me when I should start looking for my bridesmaid's dress."

"At half past fucking never, Eva," I said, rolling my eyes. "Now go have fun and tell Danielle I said hi. Even though she borrowed my signed Duran Duran Rio Tour T-shirt in 1984 and never gave it back. Do you have any idea what I had to do to get backstage at that show?"

"Smile and ask very nicely?"

"Sure. We'll go with that."

Eva chuckled. "Love you, babe."

"Love you, too."

I clicked the Off button on the cordless receiver and tossed it on the cushion beside me, the small card on the coffee table catching my eye. My cheeks warmed and a girlish giggle escaped from somewhere inside me—perhaps a part that wanted to believe something different for once.

Or maybe the part that just wanted to fuck him again.

Whatever the case, I picked up the phone and walked to my purse before allowing myself time to think about it. I flipped through my address book, then punched the numbers on the keypad, chewing my thumbnail while the phone trilled.

"Hello?"

My stomach tingled.

"So, um...what time tonight?" I asked.

A soft laugh tickled my ear. "Who is this?"

"The girl whose tits you can't stop thinking about."

"Yeah, that actually doesn't help me narrow things down."

"Never mind, then," I said in a tone that I hoped made him think I was going to hang up—even though I wasn't.

"Denise, wait."

I twirled a lock of hair around my finger. "You sure this is Denise?"

He laughed, and a snapshot of the dimple in his right cheek flashed behind my eyes. "Seven is good. Just bring yourself... and my wallet."

13

APRIL 1990

I swirled my wine in its globe, turning the dark burgundy liquid translucent in the moonlight. "How did you even find black roses, by the way?"

Christian turned his head against the back of the sofa, which I assumed had been strategically positioned by his mother's decorator to offer its occupants an unobstructed view of the Pacific. "There are a lot of spooky people in this city."

The corner of his mouth twitched, slowly curling into a smirk so sexy I felt it in my core. A corkscrew gradually tightening my insides until—

Stop staring. Stop fucking staring.

I cleared my throat and forced my spine to straighten so I wouldn't melt into the couch—or him.

"Touché," I said as I placed my glass on the wrought iron coffee table in front of us. "And that was very clever. The color choice, I mean."

"Well, it got you over here, so"—he tipped his beer bottle at me and winked—"I guess it was."

"Funny how you actually didn't have to leave your wallet after all."

"I told you that was an accident."

I turned toward him, bending one leg and resting it on the cushion. "You really think I'm gonna believe your wallet fell on top of a nightstand you were nowhere near the entire time you were at my apartment?"

Christian nodded and took a sip of beer, staring out at the light sparkling on the ink-colored ocean. "Yeah, that's right."

I glanced at the white glow of the waves breaking on the shore. "You're so full of shit. I don't even know how you bought the flowers and groceries for dinner without the stupid thing."

"Oh, I made sure to grab some cash before it fell on top of the nightstand." He looked at me out of the corner of his eye, then tightened his lips in a feigned attempt to stifle his smile. "Oops."

I slowly shook my head. "Wow. Has everything tonight been a lie? Did you really have an Italian nanny who taught you how to make lasagna? Did *you* even make that lasagna?"

Christian laughed, brushing wisps of hair from his face, only to have the breeze blow them back again. "Yes to both. I swear."

He reached over and squeezed my knee, the light from the moon turning his gray eyes to a shimmery silver as they locked with mine. *Liquid warmth everywhere.*

"Though I did leave out the part where she slept with my dad and was promptly put on a plane back to Palermo."

I took a shallow breath, attempting to inconspicuously regain the composure I'd lost from his touch. "Oh. Right. I don't recall you mentioning that."

"Yeah, it sucked," he said, sighing. "I loved her more than I loved my mother. Hell, she loved *me* more than my mother did. I didn't really understand why she had to leave, but my brother is six years older than me, and I guess he heard our parents arguing about it. He told me it was because she had sex with our dad and that was something only husbands and wives were supposed to do. So, naturally, I asked him if Natalia could be Dad's wife and our mom could go to Italy instead."

I reached for my drink and swallowed the last of it, hoping to wash down my own past. Even though I knew better than to ever hope for anything.

"I had a nanny, too," I began, the words refusing to drown in the wine.

Shut up. Shut up now before you spill your whole life story to this guy.

"Was she a hot *signorina*?"

"No." I placed my empty glass on the table and scooted closer to him, realizing a quick change of subject was in order. "Anyway, I have to go soon, so we should—"

He caught my hand as it slid up his thigh. "Tell me about her."

My shoulders fell and I sighed, freeing myself from his grasp. "I didn't come here for hand-holding and deep conversation, Christian."

His mouth fell open. "You mean you just came here for lasagna?"

"Fine." I huffed and crossed my arms over my chest, squeezing them tight against my body to ease the ache that surfaced whenever I remembered my parents rarely made so much as a guest appearance in my happiest childhood memories. "She was Russian, and I guess in her sixties."

"What was her name?"

"Baba."

He tilted his head, and my jaw tightened as the memories pecked away, like starved birds at my muscles and ribs, relentless in their attempt to reach my heart.

"I mean, I don't know, I think it was Anna," I said, my voice clipped. "I was a kid. The Baba thing...It's short for Babushka. Grandmother."

He smiled. "So, she didn't sleep with your dad and get shipped back to Moscow, I'm assuming?"

I chuckled in spite of myself. "No. My mom just decided I didn't need her anymore when I turned twelve."

Peck. Peck. Peck.

I pressed the heel of my palm against the birds, trying to crush their tiny bones, but they refused to die.

"And then what?"

I inhaled sharply through my nose and waved my hand in the air. "And then the housekeeper started picking me up from school. Look, Christian, what are we doing talking about this? I really want to have sex with you before I go home, and you keep asking about my goddamn nanny."

He leaned forward, his eyes wielding an inescapable gravitational pull on mine. "Because I care about more than just fucking you, Denise."

"Why?"

The way the word penetrated the space between us as it shot from my mouth, and the way my brow furrowed and my nostrils flared, it was as if I was asking him why he hung toilet paper under instead of over, or why he liked Pepsi better than Coke. Disapproving. Judgmental. Like there were some things I would never understand. Some things that would never make sense.

His lips parted, then pressed together as he narrowed his eyes.

"What?" I asked, straining to break loose from his focus.

"I'm just...Did you really ask me *why*?"

My throat constricted. "Yeah. I mean, I told you this isn't going to be anything more than—"

"Let's go sit on the beach."

"I'm not sitting on the beach with you."

"Christ." He blew out a breath and shook his head. "Okay,

Denise, let's go *fuck* on the beach. Is that better? Will that make you go?"

"Fine," I said, pushing myself off the couch and immediately starting down the worn brick pathway dusted with sand. I turned back to him, trying to appear as inconvenienced as possible. "But you mention one thing other than how good my pussy feels or how hard you're gonna come, and I'm fucking leaving."

———

"How is this wine almost gone?" Green glass clanked against ceramic as I filled a mug with the remainder of the bottle. "And how am I just realizing this says *Reagan Bush '84*? I didn't peg you as the conservative type. Did it come with the house, or do you like feeling ironic when you drink coffee?"

He laughed. "Both."

I raised one eyebrow, taking a sip before working the bottom of the mug into the sand and tipping my head back.

Was I drunk or were there a million different stars in a million different patterns above me? I remembered there were some you could see best in the spring. Ursa Major. Leo the Lion. Hydra the Sea Serpent.

"That's a snake with a lot of heads, so I don't like it," I tell my mother. Baba draws the curtains, and I switch on the flashlight. Baba gasps and claps. My mother stares at us until she realizes she's supposed to smile, which she half manages as she instructs us to clean up the mess we made.

I am eight, and the mess is my third grade science project.

"What are you thinking about over there?"

"Huh? Nothing," I snapped, raising my head.

Christian sighed. "You're still mad at me for not sticking to the script, aren't you?"

I snorted. "You're ridiculous."

"But it's not like 'I fucking love how you ride my dick' is an insult, right? I mean, you kept saying 'uh-huh' over and over again, so I thought—"

"You're lucky that your *actual* dick made up for you talking about it," I interrupted, giving him a sideways smile as he snickered. "*And* that I'm still here. Although, I think that's mostly because the wine is really good. But since that's gone"—I brought the mug to my lips, finishing it off with an exaggerated sigh of satisfaction—"I should go."

Christian shook his head. "You think I'm gonna let you drive home after you drank a bottle and a half of wine? No fucking way, Denise."

"I told you when I got here that I wasn't sleeping over, Christian. And I've already stayed way too long. So, yeah... you're gonna let me drive home."

I took a deep breath, preparing to stand, but his stare burned my already flushed cheek, and I whipped my head to the side. "What?"

He shrugged. "Nothing. You're right. You should go. So...go ahead."

"I am."

"Okay, then do it."

"I'm going to."

"Fine."

"Fine."

I pushed myself up from the sand. My left knee wobbled, but I managed to steady myself before turning toward the house and flashing him a satisfied smile. "See. All good."

Two steps forward. One step back. Ass in the sand.

I huffed, planting my hands on either side of me and glaring at him as he shook with laughter. "This isn't funny, Christian. You can't give me a goddamn sobriety test in the sand. And this is *your* fucking fault for plying me with wine."

"Actually, this is *your* fucking fault for *asking* for more wine," he reminded me. "You could've left a long time ago."

He wasn't wrong. I had every intention of leaving after we had sex—of going home, opening another bottle of wine, and watching that new show with Kyle MacLachlan I'd taped, trying to decide once and for all if he was weird or hot or both. But none of that happened because we started talking about something I couldn't even remember, more wine appeared in front of me, and I forgot myself—something Christian had a tendency to make me do.

He tilted his head and grinned. "Am I wrong?"

"But I—"

"But you were having a good time and wanted to stay?"

I shoved my toes into the sand, digging in frustration until my feet were partially covered.

He sighed, his grin fading into a half smile. The moon revealed a gentle concentration in his eyes, almost like I was a puzzle he was trying to solve. Not because I was a challenge or something to pass the time—but because he wanted to see beyond the pieces in front of him.

I looked away, wishing I could tell him there was no point. That it was an impossible feat because the pieces were all that existed.

I was not the rainbow.

I was not the sunset.

Just scrambled, broken parts that would never fit together to be the picture on the label.

"Am I...right?" he asked.

"It's not—" I gathered my hair and twisted it over my shoulder. "It just doesn't matter, Christian. Because who are you even? Some guy I met at a bar who I fucked and had a couple decent conversations with, and now you think this is *something* when I've told you it's not."

He held his hands up. "Look, I know the flowers might have

been a little over-the-top, but I honestly don't think this is anything right now except two people who seem to have a lot of shit in common. And since I haven't met anyone like that down here, it's...cool."

"*Cool?*" I released my hair, which was immediately whipped into a frenzy as the wind picked up. "You think it's *cool?*"

"Do you want it to be more than *cool?*"

I blinked, opening my mouth, then closing it before something even more confusing tumbled out. Why had I said that? In that way? Like I *did* want it to be more. Like I was offended he'd slap such a juvenile label on whatever *it* was—which, it wasn't anything—so why did it matter? And since it wasn't anything, it could be nothing for one more night...couldn't it?

Shit. Maybe I am drunk.

I rolled my eyes. "Whatever. I'll stay. For fifteen minutes."

"Thirty," he countered.

"Anyway, tell me more about this place," I said, ignoring him and nodding toward the house. "Why did your parents buy a vacation home in Santa Monica? Why not Malibu or Newport Beach or something?"

"It's not really for vacations. I actually don't even know what it's for anymore."

"What do you mean?"

"I mean, it's the house my mom grew up in. My grandfather bought it for my grandmother so she could take the kids and move down here." He chuckled. "Clearly a very happy marriage."

I cocked my head, studying the ivory stucco and clay roof decorating the outside of the quaint Spanish colonial. "Don't get me wrong, it's beautiful. But if he had money...It just seems a little modest for someone who was uber-wealthy."

He shrugged, picking up a handful of sand and slowly releasing it from his fist. "My grandmother wasn't a flashy lady.

She just wanted to get away from my grandfather's nouveau riche bullshit."

"Let me guess," I said, clicking my tongue. "Your mom didn't like that."

Christian nodded, taking a swallow of the beer he'd been nursing. "Correct. She missed her mansion and maids and ponies and whatever the fuck else, so when she finished high school, she moved back to Washington and married the man my grandfather told her to." He winked. "Of course, my disinherited uncle who lives on a commune in upstate New York told me this story while we were smoking a joint in the garage one Christmas, so take it for what it's worth. But it's not so hard for me to believe."

I raised my chin toward the house. "And no one sold this place?"

"Nope. Not my grandfather after my grandmother died, and not my mom after she got it in the will. She kept it up, even though she never came down here." He paused, considering. "Maybe she did, and I just didn't know it. That would explain the Reagan mug, at least."

I laughed. "Or maybe there's some psychological reason she doesn't sell it."

He flashed a cheeky grin. "Is that what your friend Siobhan the shrink would say?"

"That *is* what she says," I offered, much too quickly, before snapping my mouth shut.

But it was too late. He knew he had the fish on the line, and his mouth curved into a curious smile.

"About...what, exactly?"

I waved him off. "Nothing. It's nothing. Just...my parents owned this house in Ojai."

Oh, it's nothing, so let me go ahead and tell you everything. What the fuck?

"Oh yeah? Did your mom get sick of your dad's shit and run for the hills?"

"No, it's just, uh..." I trailed off, my stomach all of a sudden unsettled, my arms shaky. "We used to go there when I was a kid. Before my mom left. And actually, it was, um...it was one of the few places I think my parents might have been happy."

"Oh," Christian said softly.

"I mean, it never lasted once we got back home. I guess it had to do with my dad not stressing about work, and my mom not trying to impress anyone when we were there."

"So they're divorced?"

I looked off to the side, my eyes stinging from the salt being carried off the ocean. At least that's what I told myself. "Yeah. I thought my dad sold the house after the divorce, but he didn't. He gave me the keys when I graduated from college and said it was mine. I could sell it, keep it, he didn't care."

"What did you do?"

"I haven't sold it, but I should, right?" I said, still staring into the distance. "I mean, I haven't been back. But he gave me the name of the guy he'd always paid to maintain it, and I just... keep paying him."

"Maybe one day you will go back."

I nodded. "Maybe."

My eyes drifted to him, and I immediately wished they hadn't. It was like looking into a mirror but with no makeup, no good angles, no soft lighting—nothing to trick you into forgetting what was real.

I attempted a laugh, hoping it might break the glass, but the sound that exited my throat was weak and scared. "Well, *that* sobered me up, so, I should...I mean, I really do need to get some work done tomorrow morning. I'm fine to drive."

Christian sucked in a breath, as if he was preparing to protest, but his face unexpectedly fell, and he nodded. "Okay, yeah...if you're sure you're all right."

What? That's it? Didn't he want me to talk about my life, and now he's just fine with me leaving?

"Don't *you* ever have to, like, work or something? Or did you just take the trust fund money and run?" I blurted out like a petulant child.

Christian bobbed his head from side to side, sucking air through his teeth. "I mean, I guess I ran. But the money was more like 'take this and beat it so we don't have to deal with you.'"

I winced. "Sorry, I...I don't know why I said that."

"Forgiven."

He tipped his head back, gazing at the sky the way I had earlier, and an anchor dropped in my stomach as a movie played in my head about a little boy whose mother hadn't cared about his science project, either.

I sighed, pulling my feet out of their sand shoes and criss-crossing my legs. "If it makes you feel any better, my dad only likes me when I do what he thinks I should do. Which is better than my mom, I suppose, who doesn't like me no matter what I do."

He raised his head and smiled softly, the stars still in his eyes. "And if it makes *you* feel any better, I think they're crazy."

"*You're* crazy," I muttered, rubbing my hands over the goosebumps erupting on my bare arms. Whether they were from the way he looked at me or the breeze that rippled off the ocean, I wasn't sure.

"Come here," he said.

I want to.

"I'm good."

I really want to.

"Come on, you're cold and—"

I snorted. "And what? You can warm me up if I sit in your lap and you wrap your arms around me, and I lean against your chest, and your fucking amazing hair gets tangled up with mine while we stare at the moon and talk about how I wanted to be a roller disco queen when I was a kid and you wanted to be David Lee Roth?"

Oh my fucking God, I had no idea any of that was in my head.

I swallowed, hoping to capture any more subconscious thoughts on the verge of escape. "I'm guessing."

"It was actually John Lennon."

"What?"

"I wanted to be John Lennon."

"Oh."

"So can we go back to the roller disco queen thing for a second?"

"Actually, we can skip all that, and I'll go inside. To get warm. In the house."

And then I'll leave.

"As in...you're going to stay in the house?"

"Yes."

Or maybe I won't leave.

"So, you don't have to go to the office tomorrow?"

"I mean, I might have to. I dunno. I can't...remember."

What?

"So...yeah. Inside." I sprang from the sand like a pogo stick before I said anything else, and Christian looked up at me, the dimple in his cheek twitching along with his cautious smile. I wanted to lean down and kiss it and tell him how it made me feel like myself and somebody else all at once. But instead, I gave him a quick nod and began plodding through the sand so fast that my calves immediately began to burn.

"There's more wine in the cabinet by the refrigerator," he called from behind.

I made a thumbs-up gesture over my head, refusing to look back. "Don't forget my Republican mug."

"Are you feeling ironic right now, Denise?"

He laughed, and I couldn't help but smile as I pictured him

in a mop top and Beatles suit alongside me in my hot pants and gold glitter roller skates.

I have no idea what I'm feeling, Christian. No fucking idea.

I didn't have to open my eyes to know I wasn't in my apartment. The salt air I inhaled as I slowly rolled onto my back and stretched my arms over my head reminded me that I never had quite gotten around to leaving Christian's house the night before.

I twisted to my right, the gentle pull of my tired muscles pushing a soft moan through my lips.

"Are you dreaming about me?"

The sound of his voice ignited a soft hum in my center that vibrated through my body, its warmth tempering the cool breeze drifting through the open window.

"Why would I be dreaming about you?" I murmured.

"Because you're smiling"—his hand slid under the sheet and gripped my waist before finding its way to the top of my thigh—"and you're moaning."

I opened my heavy lids and caught his fingers before they made it to their intended destination. "I really would like to be able to walk normally by tomorrow."

He laughed softly and propped himself up on his elbow. I wanted to touch the dark waves that spilled over his shoulders. To reach up and push them back from his handsome face. But I'd already done too much by staying over. I couldn't rationalize any more of...that.

Whatever *that* was.

"Not that I'm complaining," I continued, yawning. "Although I would've preferred to meet your bandmates when I *wasn't* getting fucked on the kitchen counter."

Christian's elbow gave, and he collapsed onto his back. "I swear, they were supposed to be in Joshua Tree all weekend."

I fought the urge to run my hand along his bare chest. "Yeah, I really enjoyed the fifteen minute discussion about how they came home early because one of them dropped too much acid and decided to hug a cactus...*because it looked lonely*."

He chuckled. "Jordan's the sensitive one in the group."

"I mean, I didn't see the damage since I was hiding my face in humiliation, of course," I added, picturing the three flannel-clad, long-haired dudes arguing with each other as I stared down at the floor, pretending I hadn't just had my dress hiked up and my legs spread. "But I'm super excited that the hot emergency room intern gave him her number. That'll be a great story for the grandkids."

He raised his brows. "Our grandkids?"

"Christian."

"Oh, you meant Jordan and the doctor."

"Yeah, there's no way in hell I'm having kids. And after what you've told me about your family, you can't possibly want them, either," I insisted, poking him in his bare chest.

"I don't know. Maybe one day."

I scoffed. "You don't think you're gonna break them just like our parents broke us?"

"I kinda wonder if it's a way to"—he paused and shrugged—"change shit, I guess."

"Well, you're a better person than I am."

He turned on his side, gently brushing the hair from my forehead before rounding his hand down to my jaw and resting his thumb on my cheek. "I think you're a better person than you think you are, Denise."

I held his silvery gaze for a moment before flicking my eyes away. He was beautiful. So beautiful. And I hated whatever was inside of me that made it so fucking hard to look at him.

"I, um...I should go."

"Wait," he said, reaching for me as my feet hit the floor. "We could have breakfast...or lunch...or brunch."

I glanced over my shoulder and smiled. *Brunch.* It was cute, the way he said it, and I imagined us sipping Bloody Marys as a waiter in a black suit and white apron delivered our eggs Benedict and elegantly powdered French toast. But I couldn't have brunch with him. The more time I spent with him, the more he'd think this was going somewhere when it was clearly—

Oh my God, brunch.

My mother. Hawaii. Layover.

BRUNCH.

"Holy shit, what time is it?"

"I dunno, I think, like..."

I didn't have time for him to think.

My insides buckled as my eyes darted around the room for a clock. I spotted my gold watchband across the room and dashed from the bed to the dresser, snatching it up. "Holy, holy shit," I repeated.

Five minutes after one.

"Oh my fucking God. I'm supposed to meet my mom for brunch."

"What?"

"My mom and her husband. They're in town," I said, pressing my hand to my forehead and scanning the room for my clothes. "I'm supposed to be there *now.*"

"The same mom you called a bitch a couple of nights ago?"

I hurried back to the bed, rifling through the sheets for my underwear. My heart beat in every part of my body as I rushed to the corner where I finally located the lacy red bikinis, nearly tripping over myself as I tried to step into them while hopping into the bathroom.

"Yeah, I can't discuss this right now. Do you have any toothpaste I can just, like, eat or something?"

"Drawer on the right," he called from the bed. "And you can use my toothbrush. I mean, you've had your mouth on my—"

"Okay, thanks." I swiped the toothbrush off the counter and squeezed a glob of white paste onto the head.

Is this gross?

Fuck it.

"Do you have a hairbrush, too?" I asked, my words garbled around plastic and bristles.

"Also in the drawer. Just take whatever you need in there."

I spit into the sink and yanked at my tangled hair, examining my raccoon eyes in the mirror, then discarded the brush and splashed water on my face, hoping that would suffice.

I looked up to see Christian's reflection offering me a towel, which I took.

"If you hate her so much, why are you going?" he asked.

"You don't understand," I said, scrubbing the cotton over my blotchy skin. "I know she doesn't want me there, and I don't wanna be there, but it's like...a *thing*. It's almost like I have to show up to remind her what a shitty person she is. That she can't pretend I don't exist. Because I do exist, even if it's just to piss her off."

"But if she doesn't want you there, she didn't have to tell you she was coming."

I rushed past him, grabbing my tank dress, which lay crumpled at the end of the bed. "Well, maybe she has a conscience somewhere inside that big head of hers, and it's guilty." I shimmied into the ribbed fabric and frowned down at my nipples, wishing I'd worn a bra. "Anyway, thanks for dinner and... everything."

I headed for the door, stopping abruptly before stepping out of the room. I turned to Christian, who was sitting where my dress had been, and hurried back to him, placing a quick kiss on his lips. "I had a really good time."

I was out of the bedroom without time to think about what

I'd done, grabbing my purse and fumbling through it for my keys as I shoved my feet into my sandals. My chest was tight as I tore through the back door to the driveway, but I couldn't exhale.

"Denise, wait!"

I turned, gripping the car door handle.

Christian was standing outside, barefoot, in unbuttoned jeans. "You're not broken. You're fucking amazing."

My lungs contracted, and a steady stream of air forced my lips to part. *Finally, a breath.* I managed a fragile smile, folding myself into the driver's seat, wondering how long I could feel just a little bit whole before I let my mother shatter me once again.

14

OCTOBER 2009

"Hello?"

I cough, trying to clear the emotion trapped in my throat. "Hey, it's, um...it's Denise."

Silence.

This was a bad idea. I knew this was a bad idea.

"I, uh...Yeah, sorry, I actually shouldn't have called, so I'm gonna—"

"No, Denise, wait." Christian's voice is like a gentle hand on my shoulder. "I'm just...surprised. To hear from you, I mean. How was brunch?"

I suck in a shaky breath. "Can you come over?"

"You want me to come over?" He pauses, waiting for a response that I can't manage. "I mean, yeah. Yes. Are you okay?"

I hesitate, wiping my palm over my damp cheek before speaking. "She makes me feel like I was a mistake. Like I am a mistake."

"I'm on my way."

"Mom. Light's green. *Mom.*"

My eyes narrowed, the space in front of me blurring as Christian's voice faded into another. I pressed my foot against the gas pedal, sending the SUV peeling through the intersection like I was trying to outrun something...or some*one*.

"Jesus," Lucas muttered, side-eyeing me as he gripped the handle above the door.

I blinked and shook my head. "Sorry. Just, um...thinking about work...stuff."

It had been over a week since the show, and Christian hadn't replied to my email telling him to stay away from Lucas. And when I'd asked as casually as possible if they had done any more writing with him, Lucas said Christian had been sick. My blood turned cold at the thought that "been sick" was code for *relapsed*, but I couldn't probe further without seeming abnormally interested, so I convinced myself that it didn't matter as long as Christian had done as I'd asked. But my stomach still churned, and I found myself lying awake at night, wide eyes locked on the ceiling as my thoughts floated along with the watery shadows from the pool just outside our bedroom. And as the days went by, I realized I wasn't just worried about what he could possibly say to Lucas. I was worried about *him*.

Which worried me even more.

"You think about work too much, *Mami*," Lucas said, finally letting go of the grab handle. "It's just a job, you know."

"It's not 'just a job,' Lucas," I countered. "It's a company. With your grandfather's name on it. With *my* name on it."

"Yeah, but you and Dad have enough money. You could just, like, quit and do something you love."

I shot him a pointed glance. "Are you high again?"

The dimple on his right cheek punctuated his smile. "No! I'm serious. It's like me with music. I love it. It's all I ever wanna do. You've gotta have something that you love like that, right?"

Huh.

I'd never asked myself that question because I supposed it never really mattered. If I wanted to hold the interest of the only parent who ever expressed the slightest bit of it in me, following in his footsteps was the only option. Plus, it was the only thing I'd ever felt like I was good at because it was the only thing my father had ever *told* me I was good at. So why even entertain the idea of anything else?

"I love what I do now. What your dad and I do together," I said, flipping my blinker on. "This is it, right?"

Lucas hummed an "Mm-hmm," and I turned into the nearly empty lot in front of a greige stucco building.

"And I'm glad you're doing what *you* love, I just..." I sighed, shifting the car into park and smiling at him to make up for almost mentioning college. "I'm just proud of you. You have a ride home?"

"Yeah, Mia can give me a lift." He headed to the back of the SUV and unloaded his guitar while I sent a quick message to Marcos asking if he wanted me to pick up something for dinner on the way home.

"Have a good rehearsal," I called out of my open window as he strode toward the building, jeans and T-shirt slightly baggy on his tall, thin frame.

"Thanks. The mechanic said my car should be ready tomorrow." He turned and gave me a quick wave, then jogged up the stairs and opened the door.

My phone dinged with Marcos's message telling me he wanted something greasy. I chuckled and typed out *47-year-olds need to watch their cholesterol...will pick up something healthy* before hitting Send and tossing it back in my purse. But my smile quickly fell as I looked up and saw a man in a black leather jacket walking down the steps of the building. His eyes flicked to me, and I gasped.

Anger and relief collided in my body, the friction from the opposing forces causing heat to burn my face and my vision to blur.

He's okay. Thank God he's okay.

But he's still here. Why the fuck is he still here?

I immediately pressed my fingers against my lids, thinking that when I removed them and opened my eyes, there would be only a faint image dissolving into nothingness. But the phantom was real, deflecting his gaze and staring at his phone like he hadn't just been staring at me.

What was he thinking? That I'd just drive away and he would make a phone call or shoot some drugs or whatever he'd come outside to do, then go back inside and hang out with my son like he hadn't fucking ruined me nineteen years before?

I drew a long inhale through my nose, stretching my fingers long and pursing my lips.

Fuck. That. Shit.

I stepped out of the car, conscious not to slam the door. I didn't want to draw attention to us; I simply wanted to look Christian in the eyes and tell him to stay the hell away from Lucas.

"What the hell do you think you're doing?" I hissed, my heels clicking along the few steps it took to reach him. "Did you not get my email or are you just fucking ignoring everything I said?"

He blinked and rubbed his lips together, then slowly looked up from his phone. His focus fixed on something—or maybe nothing—in the distance. "I got it."

"Then why the *fuck* are you here?" My hand trembled as I fought the urge to reach out and shove him as hard as I could. So hard that the asphalt would crack, the earth would swallow him up, and I'd stop staring at the ceiling every night.

The muscles in his throat constricted as he forced his eyes to center on me. "I'm here because I'm not leaving."

"Wha—" I heaved. The sound of someone who had been kicked in the stomach. The sound of vomit being forced up through an esophagus. "What do you mean?"

"I mean, I can't leave, Denise," he said. "I tried. Even booked a flight home. But I couldn't do it."

"Then fucking rebook it and try again," I demanded, my words as tight as my jaw.

Christian shook his head, dropping his gaze to the ground. "I was going to email you. But this is better. In person is better."

I swallowed, the back of my throat burning as I attempted to keep my insides from spilling out.

He lifted his eyes—needles pinning me like a butterfly. "I need you to tell me something, Denise. And I need it to be the truth."

No. No, no, no.

His voice was much too calm. Measured. Like he'd been rehearsing lines from a script for weeks, while I was expected to improvise. I stared into the spotlight, blinded and melting into myself as the audience leaned forward, holding its collective breath. My thoughts were lasers. Strobes. Strings of colored lights, all blinking out of time.

It wasn't fair. No one had told me what to say. No one had told me what to do.

I'm not ready for this scene.

A voice said, "I have to go." When I realized it belonged to me, I turned and hurried to my car, the sound of blood pumping through my veins too loud for me to hear him follow.

"Denise." Christian pressed his hand against the door before I could open it. "Please."

Tears welled in my eyes. I refused to look at him.

"You need to tell me if..." He paused as his voice wavered from its controlled cadence. "If he's mine. If Lucas...is my son."

I had imagined those words being spoken as soon as Christian's eyes landed on Marcos that night at the club. A double take. A slight furrow of the brow. A quick glance at me, then Lucas to confirm that while the kid didn't look all that much like the people claiming to be his parents, he sure as hell looked familiar. But in all the hours I'd lain awake at night, thoughts swimming back and forth like fish in a tank, I hadn't imagined how the words would actually sound outside of my head.

This is how it feels to be stabbed, I thought.

My eyes went wide, and I pressed a fisted hand into my stomach as the noise from the traffic on La Brea condensed into a high-pitched hum. The air became thin. My mouth was dry.

Pain eclipsed by disbelief.

"Denise."

I could feel his eyes on me, begging me to look up at him and see the emotion that I heard in his voice etched on his face. But I knew if I did, he would see that same emotion on mine.

"You're..." I cleared my throat and blinked deliberately. Once...twice. "That's insane, Christian. Now fucking move."

His hand slid slowly down the door to rest at his side, and I grasped the handle, staring at the ground, waiting for him to step back so I could retreat behind the armor of my car.

"But he's..." he began, his voice just above a whisper. "He's eighteen."

I hated that he knew that. That he could stand there and talk to me about Lucas like he knew anything about the son he'd said he didn't care about.

"*Move*," I said, pressing my nails into my palms so hard that my arms quivered.

"But that was...that was when we were together."

My head jerked up before I could stop it. "You think I couldn't have fucked someone else while you were shoving needles into your arms? Passing out in your own fucking vomit?"

My eyes burned into him, chest pumping up and down, afraid if I looked away he would know those words hurt me just as much as they were meant to hurt him. I waited for him to shrink into himself—to hang his head, walk to his car, and drive straight to the airport, never to be heard from again. My chin lifted and nostrils flared, an instinctual attempt to protect myself and dam the rising tears. Guilt over what I'd said, the thought of him leaving, the thought of him not leaving...I wasn't sure what they were for.

He raised his arm, and my gaze dropped, following its path until his hand landed gently on top of mine. A soft gasp of air forced a slight part in my lips.

"I remember, Denise. That day. At the house. What you told me."

The knife plunged into my stomach again, and I tightened my grip on the door handle.

"I just...I assumed you'd had an...I didn't know you actually..."

I tried to fight the magnetic pull drawing my eyes back to him as a tear slipped onto my cheek, but it was too strong. I wanted to tell him he was wrong. That he was fucked up and imagined it all, and if he didn't stay away, I would get a lawyer, call the police, do whatever people did to make sure lunatics could never come near them again. But all of those words got caught inside, and I said the only ones I could manage. "I'm not talking about this here."

His brows lifted, then furrowed, the hurt in my voice erasing his last kernel of doubt. "Can we...go somewhere?"

I shook my head, terse movements that matched the shaking in my limbs. "Not now. I'll figure something out. You can't...you can't say anything to him."

He nodded and stepped back, his fingertips trailing along my skin as he removed his hand. My body tingled.

Leave. Leave now.

I yanked on the handle and leapt into the driver's seat of the car, slamming the door shut before speeding from the parking lot and turning onto La Brea. A horn blared, and I righted the SUV, gripping the steering wheel. My heartbeat traveled from my fingers, up through my arms, to my brain where my thoughts echoed so loudly they became all I could hear.

What have I done?
What have I fucking done?

———

"Oh my *God*, Mom! Finally!"

I slipped my heels off, dropping my tote bag and purse at the bottom of the staircase. The black and white marble tile checkerboarding the foyer was cold against my bare feet, sending a shiver through my bones as I lumbered to the kitchen.

"I am so freaking hun—" Lola was a blur as she swiveled her barstool toward me. "Where's the food?"

Marisol glanced up from the open textbook on the table in front of her, and I blinked, squeaking out the beginning of a thought that hadn't fully formed.

"Dad said you were getting dinner," she explained.

Cholesterol. Something healthy. Right.

"I, um..." I paused and put my hand to my head. "The traffic. Traffic was crazy. I...didn't get it."

Lola groaned. "I am literally dying of starvation, and we have, like, *nothing* to eat in this house."

"Yeah, I, uh...I can go get—" I pivoted, nearly tripping over my feet.

"Whoa, babe."

Strong hands gripped my shoulders, and I looked up. My reflection was watery and translucent in Marcos's eyes, reminding me that while the shell of my body had somehow made it home, everything that had been inside it lay spilled across a parking lot off La Brea Avenue.

I immediately dropped my gaze. "I forgot the food. I have to go back out."

"Hey," he said, gently cuffing my arm as I attempted to navigate around him. "Don't worry about it. Let's just order pizza. I worked out, so I'm pretty sure my cholesterol is low right now."

"Oh." I scanned him from the feet up—tennis shoes, socks, shorts—stopping at the top of his T-shirt, slightly damp with sweat. How long had it been since I'd texted him about dinner? It seemed like five minutes and five years ago, all at once. "No, it's fine. I can go—"

"Pizza," Lola and Marisol said in unison, and I startled.

"You all right?" Marcos asked.

"I..."

Tell him everything is fine.

Tell him.

"Yeah. My nerves are just shot. From driving, I mean. There was a wreck. On La Cienega. Near that Starbucks."

It doesn't matter. Stop making up shit that doesn't matter. Everything is fine. Everything is fine.

I took a deep breath, trying to fill my hollow core with life, then smiled, finally allowing my eyes to find his. "I'm good. Pizza's good. As long as you worked out." I laughed and leaned into him as I stood on my toes, placing a quick—but not *too* quick—kiss on his lips. "I'm just gonna go change outta these clothes so I can relax."

He squeezed my waist and winked before I walked out of the kitchen at normal speed, like it was a normal night, and I was a normal wife and mom who'd just arrived home from work. Once I reached the staircase, I snatched my purse from the ground, hurrying up to our bedroom, then bathroom, shutting the door behind me. My fingers pulsed as my palms pressed onto the vanity countertop and my lungs worked for air, each inhale telling me one thing, each exhale telling me the opposite.

Hands trembling, I gathered my hair into a ponytail and washed my face, the cold water calming my breath and bringing me back into myself. I looked past the reflection in the mirror, focusing only on what I had to do. Christian wasn't going to leave until I talked to him, but that didn't mean he could force my hand any further. I'd be prepared next time. I'd figure out a way to get him out of my life—out of my son's life—for good.

And there was no need to tell anyone about my lapse in judgment. Our entire family knew that Marcos wasn't Lucas's biological father; it wasn't like I was keeping some diabolical secret from them. So why should Marcos have to worry for one second about sharing the son he loved more than life itself with the man who'd said he didn't want him?

I could figure it out.

I *would* figure it out.

All I had to do was stop feeling and start thinking.

15

APRIL 1990

"Janine can do more than a million," I insisted, opening the folder Marcos had just handed me. "Was that really her final offer?"

He shrugged and loosened his tie before tossing his suit jacket on the conference table. "I mean, is anything ever a final offer? We can all be persuaded."

"Did you tell her Roger is putting up five?"

"I told her he was putting up *ten*. Which obviously isn't true, but she really fucking hates him, so I was hoping for a big win there."

"And you told her who they got to play the lead?"

"Yep."

"Hmm." I tapped my pen against my lip before pointing it at him. "You obviously showed her your boobs, right?"

"I did." He sighed and flopped into the chair beside me. "She said she'd seen better."

My lips twisted as I eyed his chest, covered by a white button-down that had wrinkled slightly during the workday. "Eh. Yeah."

"Maybe you can show her yours?"

I bobbed my head from side to side in consideration.

He chuckled and said, "I'll figure something out," before nodding to the papers scattered across the table. "What's all this?"

"Just trying to get all this contract stuff together for the lawyers to look through for that documentary I'm working on." I yawned and stretched my arms overhead. "About to cross the finish line."

"You should be proud, you know," he said, leaning back in his chair and propping his ankle on his knee. "Your dad didn't think anyone would wanna buy into that. But you believed in it, and they did. Big time."

"Tom Abbott has no time for explorations of the second wave of feminism." I twirled my hand in the air. "And thanks. I just wish my—"

No. Marcos didn't need to hear about the little girl who required her daddy's approval before she could allow herself to be proud of her accomplishments.

I was grown. I was tough. That was the only Denise he would ever know.

"Anyway," I continued, clearing my throat. "Not too bad for a chick who didn't go to USC, right?"

"You went to a great school."

"Yeah, but you know my father," I said, shutting the folder he'd handed me and sliding it to the side. "Although, I probably would've taken the top spot in the graduating class if I'd gone there, so I guess it's good for you that I didn't."

He laughed. "I was two years ahead of you in college."

I arched an eyebrow and gave him a crooked smile. "I would've found a way."

"I have absolutely no doubt you would have." His lips mirrored mine, but there was warmth in his eyes that tempered my competitive streak.

I first met Marcos when I'd come home for summer break

between my sophomore and junior years. He'd arrived in LA from Miami four years prior with a full scholarship to my father's alma mater, and he'd no sooner been hired than I immediately pegged him as my rival. My mother had officially become a lost cause, and I didn't have the attention of my dad outside of work. There was no way I was going to lose that to some frat boy in a pink Lacoste shirt.

I watched him with narrowed eyes and a clenched jaw as he did *real* work, while I was relegated to intern duties, alphabetizing folders of client information. Though his olive skin, sexy smile, and fantastic fucking physique made it hard not to think about the metal file cabinets clanging as he ripped off my clothes and banged me up against them, I forced myself to meet his annoyingly polite demeanor with icy stares or flat-out dismissals. I couldn't wait to graduate so I could give him the cold shoulder full time. Maybe he'd beat it once he was forced to acknowledge that my father was priming me to take over, not him.

It took me nearly three years to realize he wasn't going anywhere and admit to myself that he was actually a nice guy—super smart and in no way trying to outshine me, though when he asked me to dinner the first couple of times, I was certain he was positioning himself for power. A sleazy plan to woo the boss's daughter for an eventual takeover. But the more we worked together, the more I found there wasn't a shady bone in his body. There was a level of mutual respect between us that I'd never had with a man before. Not only that, but he genuinely seemed to *like* me.

I supposed I had somehow fooled him, too. And I wasn't going to ruin that by letting him get to know me outside the office.

"So," Marcos began, sitting forward in his chair, "what are you doing this weekend to celebrate your deal closing?"

"Oh. I, uh...I don't know." My stomach twisted as my mind

flashed to Christian. I hadn't seen him in the two weeks since I had brunch with my mother and her husband. In the thirty minutes it had taken him to get to my apartment after my phone call, I'd managed to pull myself together. It had been stupid to call him crying. I only needed one thing from him, and it didn't involve talking about feelings. So, I'd showered, put on makeup but left my hair damp, and answered the door wrapped only in a towel. But as soon as I saw his face, I fell apart again. I changed into my pajamas and let him wipe away my tears and hold me until morning. Then I put on my pinstripe armor, told him I'd see him around, and got in my car to head to the office.

I hadn't returned any of his calls since.

"I'll probably just stay in. Hang out with girlfriends. Nothing big," I said, pushing the heel of my palm into my midsection, trying to relieve the ache. "What about you?"

"Oh, tons of fun," he said. "Señora Navarro flies in tomorrow. She's concerned that I haven't found a wife yet and needs to figure out why."

"She really wants those grandkids, huh?"

"More than she wants the CIA to try poisoning Castro's cigars again."

I laughed, removing my hand as the pain subsided. "Well, you're her only hope, based on what you've told me."

He sighed. "It appears that way. My brothers have made it clear they have no interest."

I offered a sympathetic smile, and Marcos raised his brows.

"You wouldn't want to get engaged, would you?" he asked.

I chuckled again. "I'm good, but thanks for always thinking of me."

"That's it, Denise. I give up." He stood and picked up his jacket. "You're a riddle I'll never solve. A code I'll never crack. A—"

"All right, all right, I get it." I waved him away. "Now go, so I can get this shit done."

He smiled as he backed out of the conference room. "Deal's in the bag, Denise. Just dotting i's and crossing t's at this point. Congratulations."

I nodded, my lips turning up slightly and my eyes softening. "Thanks, Marcos. I appreciate that."

———

I carried the smile with me all the way to drop the files at the attorney's office before they closed. But when I got home and the realization that I truly didn't have anyone to celebrate with set in, it faded. Beau had to work, Siobhan was immersed in her dissertation, Eva was in Chicago, and the rest of my girlfriends were out to dinner with their husbands or husband-candidates.

I kicked off my heels and sank into the couch, hitting the Play button on the answering machine.

First was Neil, from "like, a couple months ago at The Roxbury" who was sorry he was just getting around to calling, but he'd been raiding some "megacorp" in Houston.

No clue.

Then Matt, an out-of-work bassist (*Drummer? No, bassist.*) and overall nice guy who was really good at sex but talked way too much about nothing and never wanted to leave.

Not worth the trouble.

I sighed, rolling my head along the back of the sofa just as the phone rang. I instinctively reached for the receiver but decided to screen, in case it was Neil or Matt calling again. My eyes drifted to the end table when the machine beeped.

Silence. *Definitely one of those guys.*

"Um, hey. It's Christian. Again."

The pain in my stomach returned, causing me to flinch and hold my breath.

"I, uh...I don't know if maybe I did something wrong last weekend. All the noise in my head keeps telling me I must have, but then I think maybe the noise in *your* head is telling you things, too. I have no idea if that makes any fucking sense, but I...I just like hanging out with you, Denise. We're opening a show tonight at Remi's. I'll put your name on the guest list, you could come if you want, but, uh...I guess if not, just give me a call tomorrow. You can tell me to fuck off. Just tell me *something.*"

More silence, then a deep breath and a quiet "Okay" before a click.

My stomach clenched again, the contractions moving up to my ribs, deep into my lungs. I massaged my chest. The truth was, there *was* noise in my head. Noise that had been there long before I'd met Christian. It had quieted when I'd been with him the previous weekend but gotten louder as I drove away from him Monday morning. A strange development that I didn't like to think about.

His voice echoed in my head, that last "Okay" before he'd hung up. Was he wondering if he'd said too much or not enough? It was a simple word, and he'd barely spoken it at all, but I heard the hurt in it. Normally, I would've told myself I didn't care until I believed it. But I couldn't shake the feeling I'd had the morning after he first slept over—the same one I'd had when I kissed him before I left his house on Sunday. The feeling that he...*mattered.* A feeling I didn't understand, but one that persisted, nonetheless.

I owed him an explanation. A sincere it's-not-you-it's-me.

You're amazing, Christian. Truly. But I'm better off alone. You deserve someone who wants something more.

Yes. That's what I had to say.

I decided I'd tell him in person, making sure to squeeze his hand before I left so he'd know it wasn't all a lie. Even better, I'd go to his gig. A show of support. A talk with him afterward in a public place so we could go our separate ways, and no one would linger at the other's door.

I sprang from the sofa, a renewed sense of energy buzzing through me as I hurried to my bedroom, changing into jeans and a plain gray tank. *No need to get all dolled up.*

I scooped my hair into a ponytail and washed the workday makeup off my face, doing a double take before I cut the bathroom light.

Maybe just a swipe of mascara.

I went back to the living room and called Remi's to see what time the music was starting, but the guy laughed and told me whenever the bands felt like playing. When I muttered a grumpy "Thanks a lot" he huffed out "Probably nine," so I heated up leftover takeout and watched half of a terrible movie before tugging on my leather jacket and a pair of Vans. I stopped at the door, considering going back to my bedroom for a final check in the mirror, then telling myself out loud that it didn't matter—which didn't stop me from opening my compact in the car and running a wand of pink gloss across my lips.

It looks natural, I thought. And somehow, that made the effort okay.

16

APRIL 1990

I 'd been to Remi's only once before when Eva dragged me to see some obscure band because her dickhead ex-boyfriend didn't want to go with her. It smelled like sweat and smoke and a distinctly unpleasant combination of hot dogs and tacos that was impossible to escape, given that the club was the size of a postage stamp.

My name was on the guest list, just as Christian said it would be.

"I know the opening band," I explained to the uninterested bouncer before ducking inside to escape my own awkwardness. I wasn't used to being so stripped down. It was almost like I didn't know how to act without red lipstick and a push-up bra.

I pushed through a cluster of people who acted as if they were cemented to the floor, quickly ordered a beer (the only alcohol they served), then dissolved back into the crowd. Given my mission for the evening, I wanted to remain as invisible as possible. So I settled against the wall where I was shielded by girls in cutoff jeans and ripped black tights, and guys in layered T-shirts and Chuck Taylors.

With my body no longer in motion, there was plenty of

energy to fuel the thoughts in my head. Maybe this wasn't the best idea. What if his band sucked? What if his band sucked, *and* I was giving him the boot? Was I really gonna kick him while he was down? Why didn't I just leave a message on his machine when I knew no one was home like a normal person?

Shit.

One of the guys in front of me stepped back, interrupting my spiral as he squeezed into the tiny space next to me.

"Hey," he said.

My mouth twitched into a weak smile, and my eyes flicked away.

He leaned closer. "It's crowded, huh?"

I took a swallow of beer and nodded, still looking in the opposite direction.

"It usually doesn't get packed till later, but the opening band tonight is *insane*," he continued, now talking directly into my ear. "You seen Soulever before?"

Jesus Christ. The inability of men to take a hint really was a universal truth.

I crossed the arm closest to him over my chest, trying to retain what little of my personal space I had left. "Actually, I'm just here for the music, so if you could, like—"

"Yeah, I know! They're *so* good, right?"

Not even remotely related to what I'd said.

Still, the comfort I felt hearing that Christian would be performing to a crowd of enthusiastic fans sent a cool wave of relief rippling through me...until I felt hot breath on my skin once again.

"My friend is closer to the stage if you wanna come up there with—"

"No," I shouted over the power chords ripping through the speakers. "But you should go. Sounds like they're gonna start soon."

"Can I find you later?"

"Absolutely not."

He grinned, saying "Cool" before pushing his way forward, failing to glean the key word in my reply.

I rolled my eyes and took another sip of beer, wishing it was a vodka cran. Or vodka and any kind of juice. Even just a fucking lemon squeezed into it.

What kind of club can't be bothered to stock a couple of bottles of Absolut and some Ocean Spray?

Seriously, this is ridiculous.

Why am I even here?

I should just go. I'm gonna—

A sudden burst of energy from the crowd sent me to my tiptoes, and I craned my neck as the guys who'd interrupted the kitchen counter sex the weekend before walked onstage. My face burned, at first because I was embarrassed by the memory, but then because I remembered how good it had been before they'd barged in. How good *all* the sex had been. Did I really want to never do that with him again?

Maybe I'm being rash.

Maybe we can work something out.

Set some ground rules.

No. It needs to end. Here. Tonight. That's all there is to—

Oh my God, why did he have to come out here with his fucking shirt off?

"I feel like an idiot coming out here with my fuckin' shirt off, but it's hot as shit in this place," Christian said into the microphone, sweeping the dark hair out of his face.

"It's fine!" some chick yelled from the audience.

If she'd been standing beside me, I would've punched her before I had time to realize that defeated my whole purpose in being there. I was there to end things (whatever those things were), not throw down like some jealous girlfriend.

Girlfriend?

Lover.

I mean lover.

Goddammit.

Stop looking at him.

But I couldn't. That chest, that stomach, that entire perfectly thin but toned body that was already a little bit sweaty. And that gorgeous hair and that gorgeous face. *Fuck. Me.* He was the sexiest thing I'd ever seen.

My feet flattened against the floor as he thanked the crowd for coming, and a heavy bassline thumped out of the speakers and into my chest. It was followed by a loud guitar, a powerful drumbeat, and an even more powerful voice. A voice that belonged to a man who could fuck you on his kitchen counter and make you feel like the dirtiest slut on the face of the earth, then kiss you for hours and make you feel like the most beautiful woman in the whole, entire world. Dominant and aggressive. Vulnerable and warm.

As bodies bumped against me, and one song turned into another, I kept my eyes fixed on the stage, catching glimpses of Christian as he gripped the mic and leaned forward into the audience.

When he'd told me about his band and their sound, I figured their songs weren't about chicks and cars and fucking chicks in cars. But I was still surprised. How could someone be so...*unguarded* in front of all these people?

Christian was singing about his life to two hundred strangers, and I couldn't even bring myself to speak the whole truth about mine to a single person I knew.

Except for him that night on the beach. And the next day after I'd seen my mother.

The music stopped, and I blinked, unsure exactly how much time had passed.

Was it over? Were they done?

I wasn't ready.

"Okay, so, we have a couple more songs, but I just wanna say thanks again for coming out."

Two more songs. I choked down the rest of my warm beer. *Time to get my shit together.*

"And I don't usually talk too much up here because...I don't know, it's just better for me to sing. But I can't get this off my mind, and I haven't been able to write down my thoughts into something we can play yet."

I peered through the tiny space in front of me, watching as Christian wiped the sweat from his brow and ran his hand through his hair.

"So, you ever know someone who's...well, who's just fuckin' *down* on themselves? Like, they think they're bad fuckin' news. That they're a mistake. But when you..." He trailed off, his gaze hovering above the crowd, his smile shining a sliver of light on a memory before being dimmed by clouds. "When *you* look at them," he continued, "and when *you* talk to them, you see the exact opposite, and you wonder how the hell they would ever think they were anything less than perfect."

A mistake.

He paused, and the crowd raised their hands and voices in agreement.

"But the thing is, you actually know how, because *you've* felt that way before. And maybe you still do because for a long time, people told you that you *were* those things. And they did that shit for so long, you ended up believing it."

This was a mistake.

He took a deep breath and turned, lifting a shiny black guitar off its stand and strapping it over his shoulder. "Anyway, fuck it. This song is old, but Denise, if you're here, or even if you're not here, this is for you."

No.

Why did he...

No.

I have to leave. I have to go. I have to leave.

I immediately turned and began untangling my way through arms and legs and bodies. I couldn't tell if they were yelling at me or yelling the song back at Christian. A girl pushed me, sending me straight into someone else's chest. The person beside him thrust his elbow in my direction, and I managed to regain my footing, duck around him, and break through the wall of people blocking my path to the exit. I looked back to where I'd been, then up to the stage as Christian's eyes darted to the fight that was breaking out.

Go.

A man grabbed my arm before I could make it out the door, and I gasped.

"You can't leave with that."

My gaze shifted to his hand, then to the empty beer bottle still in mine. I shoved it into the bouncer's outstretched palm and took off down Hollywood Boulevard, trying to ignore the shoeless old man at the corner of Vine shouting from behind me.

"Everything catches up with you in the end, baby."

————

One. Two. Three. Four.

Was counting the number of times the colon flashed between the numbers on an alarm clock the same as counting sheep? Why was it even sheep in the first place? Why not cats or dogs or something that wasn't an animal?

Something like, reasons to run out of a club when a guy you had sex with once...twice...ten times dedicates a song to you?

I groaned and flipped over in my bed, punching the pillow before my head plunged back into its feathers.

I'd crawled under the covers as soon as I'd gotten home, determined to go straight to sleep and forget about the night, but an hour of tossing and turning was all that transpired. The images of Christian were too vivid, the words he'd spoken too loud.

"...you wonder how the hell they would ever think they were anything less than perfect."

Perfect?

Right.

Sure.

All he knew about me was that I was once a little girl who grew up in a big house with her disinterested parents and *Oh, isn't that sad?* He didn't understand that girl could've done better. That she could've *been* better. That there were clearly so many things wrong with her, even her own mother and father couldn't pretend otherwise.

You can be an asshole and still be right, after all.

I kicked the sheets to the end of the mattress and marched into the bathroom, flinging open the medicine cabinet to scan the shelves for something to knock me out. What if I took four Advil instead of two? Was drowsiness a side effect of Midol? Why was every medication I had for cramps and bloating anyway?

I sighed and shut the door, my frown greeting me in the thin metal-framed mirror.

"What is wrong with you, Denise?" My mother's breath, a potent mix of tobacco, gin, and peppermint, is warm against my ear. "The least you could do is smile when I introduce you to the most famous late-night show host on the goddamn planet. Joanna, hi, so good to see you! You look absolutely stunning!"

She moves on to charm another party guest as I squint, blurring the lights on the Christmas tree. I wonder how a fifteen-year-old girl is supposed to look when her mother is moving 2,017 miles away— the exact amount I calculated when I pulled the map from the glove compartment and spread it across the hood of my father's Aston Martin the night before.

"I'm sorry," I say.

If she hears me, she doesn't give any indication. I turn and hurry up the stairs to my bedroom, where I lock the door, stand in front of the mirrored closet, and force myself to smile.

Is this better? If I try again and get it right, will she stay?

My chest tightened as the memory melted into itself, replaced by a similar but more concrete image—cheeks straining, lips stretched, teeth clenched. The eyes still refused to lie, but I had learned over the years that people usually saw what they wanted to see. What was easier to see. Most didn't have the time to ask what was wrong. And even if they did, none of them had the time to actually care.

None of them except Christian.

"Enough," I said, letting my face fall before trudging down the hallway to the kitchen, where I stared into the dimly lit refrigerator. A corked bottle of white wine, half a block of sharp cheddar, and a jar of pimento-stuffed olives stared back. I plucked each item from the shelf before heading to the living room and placing my snacks on the coffee table. Soft light glowed from the small lamp to my right as I sank into the sofa, unwrapped the plastic on the cheese, and took an overzealous bite.

Am I eating because I'm annoyed, or am I annoyed because I'm eating?

I tossed the block on the table and reached for the wine when a faint knock at the door caused me to gasp and suck the hunk of cheddar down my windpipe.

Shit. Oh shit.

I placed my hand over my mouth and sputtered.

Another knock. Louder this time.

Another cough. Also louder.

Oh my God, is this how it ends? Death by murder while choking?

I pounded my chest with my fist as I stumbled toward the door, all my energy focused on expelling the cheese from my trachea. If they weren't a murderer, maybe the person outside could help me. If they were, well, I was going to croak anyway.

I unlocked the deadbolt, twisted the knob, and pulled the door toward me, hunching over as my body lurched forward. Finally, an orange chunk landed at my feet, and I sucked a stream of air into my lungs.

I'm okay.

I'm okay!

"Holy shit, are you okay?"

A hand grasped my shoulder, and my focus shifted to a pair of worn black boots.

"Fuck." My voice was a weak rasp as I slowly straightened my spine and massaged my throat. "I mean, yes. I'm fine."

"Are you sure?"

I nodded and pushed my hair from my face, noting the concern in Christian's eyes. "Yeah, I'm, uh...I just choked. What are you...Why are you here?"

"I saw you at the show."

At the show? He couldn't have seen me. But shit. The fight. During the song.

"Oh."

"Why did you leave?"

I blinked and licked my lips, which were suddenly dry. "I, uh...I was out that way to meet a friend. For a drink. And I had to go. To meet my friend." I crossed my arms over my chest. "For the drink."

"Bullshit."

The door clicked shut, and my gaze centered on him as he moved closer. *"Excuse me?"*

"That story is bullshit."

I laughed sharply. *So much for hand squeezes and polite it's-not-you-it's-me's.* "Tell yourself whatever you want, Christian, but I—"

"You left because you're scared of your feelings and the

person you really are and all the other things you never let yourself think about because it hurts too fucking much."

The weight of his words threw me off balance, and I stumbled backward. I opened my mouth to scream *How dare you? How fucking dare you?* But nothing came out.

His eyes pleaded with me. *Just say it, just say you're scared, and we'll figure it out.* But he was asking the impossible.

My throat was raw and thick. My nose stung.

"You need to go," I choked out.

"You don't want me to go."

"Leave."

Christian drew in a breath and threaded his fingers through his hair. "Denise, I—"

"I said, I want you to leave."

He shook his head. "You're lying."

"I'm not..." A tear rolled down my cheek.

"You're not what?"

"I'm..." I swallowed and cast my gaze downward.

The creased leather of his jacket was soft against my shoulder, the palm of his hand cool against my cheek.

"I'm not a good person," I whispered.

"Did you not hear what I said?" he asked, the pull of his eyes like the moon on the tide.

I started to speak. To tell him to stop, that everything he thought I was, was wrong. But his thumb, salty from the tears, brushed over my lips and silenced all the noise.

"You're perfect, Denise. Absolutely fucking perfect."

17

MAY 1990

"Hey," I said, flopping into the booth across from Christian. "Sorry I'm late."

"No worries. I made friends."

I arched an eyebrow as he took a sip of his beer and grinned.

"It's amazing how many women feel sorry for a guy sitting by himself, looking like he's been stood up."

"Oh yeah? Where are these women?" I turned in my seat, craning my neck. "'Cause I have a shit ton of work to do, so maybe *they* can come have dinner with you, and *I* can go back to the office."

"Wait, wait, wait." He laughed, reaching across the table to stop me from sliding off the vinyl seat.

I pursed my lips, trying to hide the excitement I felt as his fingertips brushed my bare arm.

"They left when I told them I was only into girls named Denise who pretend they have better things to do than hang out with me."

"And that made them leave?"

He shrugged. "I might've said girls named Denise who

149

pretend they have better things to do than hang out with me *and* give really good head."

"Oh. Well." I settled back into the booth, my mouth slowly curving up. "There's no way they're gonna beat me at that."

"That's exactly what I said!"

I rolled my eyes, still fighting my smile. "You're hilarious, Christian."

He laughed again, causing my face to break as I nodded to the server approaching our booth. "Did you tell the waitress, too? Does she know about my superpower?"

"I did." He lowered his voice and leaned in. "She said she thought she could take you, so I think you should fight her. Right here. But, like, take your shirt off first."

"Oh, shut up. *Hi*, how are you?" I looked up and greeted the pretty blond girl who placed a beer in front of Christian and took my drink order.

He raised his brows after she left for the bar. "A double vodka cran *and* a Diet Coke?"

"So I don't fall asleep," I explained, plucking an elastic band from my purse and gathering my hair into a makeshift bun.

"I know I'm boring," he said. "I'm gonna work on that."

I smiled. "It was just a long day. But it's fi—"

"Tell me about it."

"Oh." My eyes shifted to his hand as it covered mine on the table. "It's nothing. It's fine. Really." I took a deep breath, muscles tensing as I fought the urge to pull my hand back. "Seriously, it's not a big—"

"Come on," he insisted.

I wasn't used to talking about my day. Not honestly anyway. Telling someone that it hurt my feelings when a producer called me an amateur and asked me to go get a man who knew how to close deals wasn't exactly on the top of my list of things to do. I'd usually spin it with an indignant "He can go fuck himself," though my brain would replay everything I'd done while I secretly wondered if he was right. Was I really just a silly girl who should be in the corner taking notes while men made the important decisions?

I tugged at my long bangs, a curtain to hide the emotions that always seemed to make a guest appearance on my face when Christian was around. "There's just this one guy we work with from time to time, and he just...he thinks I'm not *qualified* to handle his deals, whatever that means."

"Well, he can go fuck himself."

I chuckled. *My thoughts exactly.*

Christian leaned against the back of the booth, his palm gliding over my skin before slapping the wooden table. "You're the smartest woman I know. The smartest *person* I know."

"You've known me for a month and a half."

Not that I'm counting.

Oh my God, am *I counting?*

"Or something." I cleared my throat. "Anyway, fine, I'm smart. I know that. I just...I hate how he makes me feel. That he makes me feel at all. It's fucking annoying." I shook my head and flipped open the menu. "Anyway, do I want the bacon cheeseburger *and*—"

"Denise."

"The mozzarella sticks? And you can save the it's-okay-to-have-feelings-and-talk-about-them shit because I don't need to do that. I'm smart. He's an asshole. End of story."

He sighed, holding his hands up in surrender. "All right."

"Here you go," the waitress said, placing my drinks in front of me. "Are you guys ready to order?"

I told Christian to go ahead, and by the time she turned back to me, pen poised over her notepad, I'd decided I didn't have much of an appetite and ordered the house salad.

Christian's eyes widened. "Wha—go tell her you want the fucking bacon cheeseburger and the mozzarella sticks."

"I'm not that hungry," I said, unwrapping the silverware from my napkin. "I want the salad."

"Every time you get worked up, you're all of a sudden 'not that hungry,' and you order a salad."

"*Every* time?" I scoffed. "You act like we've been together for a year, not a month."

"But it's tru—" He stopped and tilted his head. "Did you say we're together?"

"What?"

"You said we were together."

"I didn't say that."

Fuck, I think I said that. Why did I say that?

He flashed a victorious grin, the dimple in his cheek practically begging me to kiss it. "Oh, I think ya did."

I blew out a dramatic I-don't-have-time-for-this breath and took an equally dramatic sip of my drink. I didn't need to label whatever it was we were doing. *Yes*, I'd seen him every week since he showed up at my apartment after his gig. *Yes*, several times a week. And *yes*, he was right—I did order a stupid salad when I was frustrated. And it just so happened that I'd been frustrated a lot since that night on the beach when I lost myself talking about my past and listening to him talk about his.

"Well, I didn't mean *together*," I explained. "I meant... hanging out."

"Oh, like hanging out...*to-ge-ther*," he said, waving his finger back and forth between us.

"You know there's a difference between *being* together and hanging out togeth—" I stopped myself before I sounded any more like a fourteen-year-old boy trying to convince his buddies that even though he'd been at the soda shop with Sally every day after school, that didn't mean she was his *girlfriend*.

"What I'm trying to say is," I continued, stirring the straw in my Diet Coke, "this is...fun. But you should, you know...also do this with other people."

I flinched, the weight of those words hitting me harder than I'd imagined as I thought of the girl at the show who'd commented on him not wearing a shirt. I wanted to punch her all over again.

Christian's brows turned in as he gestured across the table. "Why do you look like you're about to fuckin' clock someone?"

"What?"

Shit, I thought, dropping my gaze and unclenching my jaw along with the fists I'd unconsciously made. "Look, Christian. We have sex and eat cheeseburgers. That's not exactly what I'd call being togeth—"

"I wouldn't say that," he interrupted, shaking his head. "You've been eating an awful lot of salads, actually."

"Oh my God, forget it." The utensils clanked as my head hit the table, elbows splayed out to the side.

He laughed, and I peered up.

That fucking dimple. Why.

"It doesn't have to be this hard, Denise."

I sighed and raised my head, chin cradled in my hands. The truth was, I hadn't been doing "this with other people," either.

"Here's the thing," he began. "I don't really wanna have sex or eat cheeseburgers with anyone else, but if you do...I mean, it's not like I *want* you to want that, but..." A shadow flickered over his face. "*Do* you want that?"

I reached for my vodka, downing the rest of it in hopes that I'd drown the very thought of answering him with anything other than a yes.

I remembered the way he'd smoothed my hair, tucking it behind my ear after the brunch with my mother. His thumb catching the tears that burned my lips the night after his show. What he'd said onstage and again in my apartment. "*You're perfect.*" I didn't know the words to describe how he made me feel. Safe...valued...*seen*? I hadn't felt all those things all at once before I'd met Christian, and when I imagined never feeling them again, my heart dove into my stomach.

"I don't want that," I said, my voice barely above a whisper.

He leaned forward, flecks of silver glistening in his eyes. "Did you say..."

"I said I don't want that."

"Oh, I'm so sorry."

I blinked and turned my head to see the wide-eyed waitress balancing a tray of food on one hand and my salad in the other.

"Did you not order the house salad?" she asked.

"Oh. No," I said, quickly. "I mean, yes, I did order the salad."

Her face relaxed as she placed the plate in front of me, then handed Christian his food.

"Can I grab you another drink?" she asked, pointing to my empty cocktail glass.

"Please." I smiled softly, glancing at Christian from the corner of my eye. "And I hate to bother you with this, but can I also get the bacon cheeseburger and some mozzarella sticks?"

18

OCTOBER 2009

"Your destination is on the right in point-three miles. Your destination is on the right."

Shit.

I hit the brakes on my SUV and swerved into the driveway, stopping abruptly at an ornate iron gate. My chest pumped furiously as I gripped the steering wheel and stared into the tunnel of trees ahead of me. Memories collided, dominos toppling behind my eyes, reminding me of each poor decision that led to another.

How could I have been so stupid?

I'd battered and bruised myself with those words in the days after I left his house for the final time, my only comfort in knowing that after so many wrong choices, I'd finally gotten one thing right.

Maybe *I* deserved Christian, but my child didn't.

He deserved better.

He *still* deserved better.

I just had to convince Christian of that.

I'd emailed him the day after I sped out of the parking lot, having spent the night before talking myself out of telling him it wasn't true, that I'd made it all up to get away from him in the moment. I knew he'd see through it, and I would eventually cave once again. My only option was to make him understand that if he was truly sorry for what he'd done, if he really meant what he'd said on the Venice boardwalk, he'd leave Lucas and me alone.

So I'd gotten up that morning, a week later, and gone to the gym, then pretended everything was normal over coffee and a bagel as I told Marcos I needed to find a dress to wear to the annual fundraising gala at Lola's school.

"I know it's four months away, but I can't wait till the last minute."

I hated lying, but I promised myself it would be the last time. If Christian refused to listen, I'd tell Marcos everything, no matter how much it would hurt him to think he might lose Lucas. Which he wouldn't. Lucas loved him, that would never change, and it would all be okay in the end.

But hopefully it won't even have to have a beginning.

I took a deep breath and reached through the open window to punch in the gate code Christian had sent me. Tires rolled timidly over the cobblestone pavers, past the sweeping Mediterranean mansion to a guest house, where I was lifted from the car by an unseen force and carried down a path carved between scarlet fuchsia shrubs. The sound of my knuckles rapping against the wood of the arched door startled me.

How did I get here?

I yanked my hand back and hooked my thumb around the strap of my purse, glancing over my shoulder, wondering if I could make it back to the car before he answered. There had to be another way to do this.

Maybe I can get a restraining order. I know the right people in the right places. It can be discreet and—

"Hey," Christian said, wedging a hand into his jeans pocket. "Hi."

"Hey." I fought the urge to drop my gaze to the ground.

I pretend to be tough all the time. Work, life...it doesn't matter. This is no different.

He met my stare before shaking his head. "Sorry. Come in," he said, stepping aside. "You...want to come in...right?"

I crossed my arms over my chest, offering a curt nod before following him down the tile hallway.

"Do you want anything to—"

"I'm good," I said, my voice indicating otherwise as I stepped into the impeccably decorated living room.

Christian extended his hand toward the couch. "You wanna sit or..."

I nodded and perched on the edge of the sofa while he took a seat in the chair opposite me. My eyes circled the room— natural rugs, reclaimed wood, ivory upholstery—before landing on a stack of large hardcover books on the coffee table. Versace, Valentino, Lagerfeld. One was opened to a page scribbled with *To Tasha, my muse...Love, Gianni.*

My muscles tensed. *Tasha? Who the fuck is Tasha?*

"My friend who owns the house," he began, pointing to the books. "His wife, Tasha, was a model."

"Oh," I said, unnerved by the brief rush of relief I felt. I cleared my throat and flicked my eyes from the table to him. "I mean, great. Whatever. You're not Lucas's father."

The words tumbled out so quickly that I faked an awkward cough to give myself time to think of what to say next. "I'm only here to talk about that."

Am I telling him that or myself?

His brows turned in. "But I...I thought you said—"

"It doesn't matter what I said. He has a father. Who loves him. Who does all the things that fathers are supposed to do."

"But he's, uh..." Christian pinched his chin, running his

fingers along the dark bristles of his goatee. "You told me he's mine."

"If your criteria for 'mine' equals contributing chromosomes to his DNA, then yeah, I suppose he is." I pressed my lips together. "But that doesn't quite do it for me."

The relief on Christian's face was layered with shame as he sank back in his chair, eyes narrowed, staring out the glass doors behind me. "He looks like me. He looks so much like me."

"It doesn't mean anything, Christian," I insisted. "It doesn't mean anything except that you were there when I got pregnant. That's it."

"Yeah, but...what do I do now?" He blinked, snapping out of his daze.

"You're asking me what to..." I laughed sharply. "I've told you what to do, Christian. Go the fuck home and forget you know any of this. Because it doesn't matter. You're not part of his life. You will *never* be part of his life."

"But I..." He paused, a light switching on behind his eyes. "I want to be, Denise. I want a chance to be the person now that I should've been then."

As if he deserves another chance at anything.

"And what would you like to do? Be in the room when Lucas is born? Oh, wait, that already happened. Maybe coach his Little League team? Darn, he quit ten years ago."

"But did you..." He leaned forward, elbows on his knees, hands steepled together. "I mean, after he was born....did you ever think about trying to find me?"

"You're really going to ask me that? After what you fucking put me through? After what you said?" I glared at him. "After you spent zero time trying to find *me*?"

"I know, and I'm sorry. I just want to make things right."

"He doesn't need you to make anything right," I snapped. "And it's really fucking selfish of you to think that he does."

Christian deflated against the back of the chair with a long exhale, massaging the faint lines along his forehead as he nodded.

I swallowed, my head bobbing slowly, cautiously. "So you... understand, then."

"Yeah."

"You'll stay away from him. And you'll go home." I winced, a sharp pain stabbing the top of my rib.

His hands slid down his face, fingers interlacing just below his chin. "I...I don't know how to do that."

My nails curled into my palms, muscles shaking as I fought the urge to throw every pretentious fucking coffee-table book at him. "If you want me to believe you're sorry for any of what happened between us, you'll stay the hell away from him. And if you don't, I swear to God, I'll—"

"He's my kid, Denise!" Christian sprang from his chair. "And he's eighteen now. Shouldn't he have a say in this?"

Images of that last day at his house flashed loud and red behind my eyes, and I snatched my purse off the sofa before standing. "No. No, he shouldn't. He just graduated from high school. He still lives at home. He's a *child*, Christian, and I'm not going to let you do this to him."

"No, wait, sit down." He cupped his hand over his mouth, shaking his head as I clasped my purse against my body. "I'm sorry, I just...I don't know what do because it's another thing I fucking ruined. As if ruining you and me wasn't enough."

My breath caught in my throat. "That's not...We're not talking about us, Christian."

He gripped the top of his head, sighing as he collapsed back into the chair. "I don't know how to *not* talk about us, Denise. And I definitely don't know how to not *think* about us because until last week, I was sure that losing you was the biggest mistake of my life." His voice was fragile, as if he could shatter at any moment. "Then I found out I lost our son, too." He paused, sucking in a shaky breath. "But I don't even have any memories of him to hold onto like I do of you, and I honestly don't know which fucking hurts more."

A wave crashed out of nowhere, knocking me backward into the soft down of the sofa cushions. The inside of my nose fizzed and stung, and I strained to look past him, focusing on the waxy green leaves sprouting from the plant in the corner of the room. Letters scrambled in my brain too quickly to form the right words.

"But you..." The tear balancing on the bottom of my lid slipped as I shifted my eyes to Christian. "You said you didn't care about him."

Or me.

I shook my head. "How am I supposed to believe you do now?"

"I don't..." He sniffed and cleared his throat. "I don't know. But I will do whatever it fucking takes to make that happen."

I bit my lip, held my breath, blinked and blinked again— anything to keep more tears from falling. But they fell anyway. "I need to talk to my..."

Husband.

It was what I needed to say for Lucas, for Marcos, but the word was a rock in my chest, too heavy to lift.

"I need to think about it."

I swiped my fingers under my eyes, black streaks staining my skin, and shoved my purse under my arm before shooting up from the sofa. "I have to go."

"Wait. What are we gonna...What do you want me to do?" Christian followed as I hurried through the living room to the hallway, his voice breathless and urgent.

"I don't know." I gripped the knob and opened the front door, my palm slick against the metal.

"But we'll talk again?" he asked.

No.

"Yes," I said, turning around, a knot forming in my throat as I met his glossy eyes. "But if you tell him, I'll—"

"I won't," Christian promised.

I nodded and darted down the path of fuchsia bushes, smooth, thin branches bending toward me as their red trumpets sounded a warning that echoed in my head all the way home.

19

JULY 1990

"So, that girl in the picture on your fridge," Christian began, handing me a Diet Coke before sinking into the sofa with a bag of Doritos. "Is that Eva? The best friend from college?"

"Yeah." I drew out the word, assessing him from the corner of my eye as I popped the top of the aluminum can.

"Why are you always so suspicious?" he asked, his words garbled around the chips he'd crammed into his mouth.

"I'm not suspicious."

My tone was defensive, causing him to raise his brows.

"Fine." I huffed. "I guess I'm just used to everyone having an angle, okay?" I pressed my back against the armrest and pulled my knees into my chest. "Like, who's that girl on the fridge, what's her last name, excuse me while I call four-one-one for her phone number so I can find out all your secrets and what you've told her about me."

"What *have* you told her about me?"

My insides buzzed. "What?"

"Right." He chuckled. "I'll take that as *I haven't even told her you exist.*"

I ran my tongue over my teeth, looking at the ceiling as I tried to conjure up even the most marginal of excuses. "I mean, I'm going to. She's just really busy at work, and she's dating this new guy and...stuff."

Dumb. So fucking dumb.

"I hear *you're* dating a new guy," he said through another mouthful of chips. "Really hot. Good manners."

My lips shifted into a half smile. "Is that so?"

He nodded and wiped his mouth with the back of his hand as he chewed.

"Whatever," I continued. "I'll tell her. I will."

Will I?

Every time I thought about it, there was a strange twist in my stomach, like telling Eva about Christian and me would mean it was real, and I hadn't quite let myself believe that. It was sometimes easier to imagine that I'd ducked out of my life for a minute and nothing about my actual existence had changed. I could just step back into reality whenever I wanted, pretending like it had all been a dream.

Christian took a long swallow of his Coke, then motioned toward the kitchen. "I just don't wanna end up like the guy whose face *literally* got cut out of that picture of you and her."

I laughed and nudged his hip with my foot. "Don't be a motherfucking asshole like her ex-boyfriend, and you won't."

"Noted." He cleared his throat and turned toward me, resting the bag of Doritos on the edge of the sofa against the wall. "So, uh...speaking of past relationships..."

I recoiled my outstretched leg. "Oh God. Have you been talking to Beau?"

Beau was the only one who knew Christian and I were together, and that was only because I'd had no choice but to confess. The same guy coming and going from the apartment over the past several months had Beau "all atwitter." What if he'd run into Christian outside the building and invited him over for a drink because "I never get to meet any of Denise's men. It's usually such a revolving door around here!"? I imagined forced laughter followed by an awkward silence as they both realized what he'd said.

"What do you mean?" Christian asked.

"Nothing," I said, shaking my head.

I supposed it didn't matter that I'd slept with half of Los Angeles without calling them back. I just didn't necessarily want Christian to know there had never been an *ex*-boyfriend because there had never been a *boyfriend*. It felt...private—not like something I was ashamed of, but the fact that he was the first didn't need to be a bigger deal than it actually was. I'd learned the hard way about expectations and disappointment that night at the hotel off Highland when I was fifteen, and it wasn't a mistake I was going to make again.

"Hey, we should put the movie on." I snatched the remote from the coffee table, hoping for a change of subject. "I've gotta return it tomorrow."

Christian glanced behind him as the television sprang to life. "Yeah, okay, I just...I've been wanting to ask you if—"

"I'm into anal? Yeah, let's go, let's do it."

Not exactly on my agenda for the day, but what man turns that down in order to have some long, drawn out relationship conversation?

"No, I..." Christian's forehead wrinkled, then immediately released as his lips parted and a tiny puff of air escaped. "Wait, really?"

Not really. But still better than unearthing my past.

"Uh...sure." I tossed the remote in front of me, ready to push myself off the couch. "I'll meet you in the bedroom."

Christian gently clasped my ankle before I could swing my legs off the cushions. "Not what I wanted to ask, but good to know for the future." He gave me a cheeky grin and glanced at his watch. "*Near* future."

Awesome. Not only had my escape plan failed, but I'd agreed to something which typically required at least six shots of tequila before I'd even consider it.

I looked at my Diet Coke and grimaced.

"But before you put that idea in my head, which I now cannot erase to save my fucking life"—he blew out a breath and shook his head—"I wanted to ask you about...I mean, I feel like we've talked about a lot of things in our past, but not about the whole relationship...thing."

I opened my mouth, then closed it as he raised his hand like a white flag.

"And we don't have to," he added quickly. "I just want you to know I haven't really done this since...Well, I just haven't really done this that much."

He hasn't?

Christian had always seemed so calm and confident, I'd assumed this was old hat for him. Was it possible that this was yet another piece of our pasts we shared? That if this territory was as unfamiliar to him as it was to me, maybe there *was* something special about us?

"So what I wanted to ask you without being completely fucking weird is if you maybe want to...meet my brother?"

A bolt of electricity shocked my brain. "In Sea—*You want me to go to Seattle*?"

Christian's eyes widened. "No. What? Shit. No. He's coming here. In a few weeks."

My shoulders began to relax. "Oh."

"I'm just asking because he worries about me, and I want him to know that things are good. That *I'm* good."

I cocked my head. "Why would he worry?"

"No reason." The muscles in his cheek twitched. "I mean, there's no reason for him to worry. I think it's just, like, big brother-little brother shit, you know?"

I nodded, reminded of how much I cared about Eva, the

closest person I had to a sister. I would have done anything to make sure she was happy and got all the wonderful things she deserved, even though she was more than capable of taking care of herself.

"If it's too much, we can forget it," he added. "But you're one of the things that make LA good for me, and I want him to know that. To see that."

My eyes flicked away as my face warmed, and my chest constricted. I wasn't sure if my heart had suddenly outgrown it or I was about to hyperventilate, but as my gaze reconnected with the warm gray of Christian's, the tension released and a smile slowly spread across my face.

"Fine," I said, settling back into the cushions. "But I have a stipulation."

"Anything."

"I agree to meet your brother, and you agree to forget that this"—I smacked the side of my ass—"was ever even an option tonight."

He arched a brow. "I thought you said you were into it?"

"I was trying to distract you."

He pointed to the crotch of his jeans. "But now my dick is hard, and you're going to have to distract me from the distraction."

I laughed and tossed a throw pillow at his head. "Shut the fuck up and eat your Doritos."

20

AUGUST 1990

I glanced at the gold bracelet watch on my wrist.

Five sixteen p.m.

Dammit.

If I didn't leave soon, there was no way I would make it to Christian's house by six. I'd planned to meet him and his brother there, then head to dinner with them in Venice. The day was so busy, I hadn't had a chance to call him and make sure Carter's flight got in on time and our plans were still intact.

I snorted. *Carter.* When I'd first heard his name, I immediately pictured a guy on his forty-foot sailboat, surveying the open waters ahead, while the sweater tied around his shoulders flapped in the ocean breeze along with a few blond strands that had been freed from their hair gel prison.

"Am I right or am I right?" I'd asked Christian, grinning.

He'd chuckled and told me I'd gotten the hair color wrong.

I knew the type all too well. Had he lived in LA, I would've been nervous that I'd casually flirted with him over martinis at The Polo Lounge before noticing the indentation on his finger where a wedding ring belonged.

Despite all my preconceived notions, he wasn't actually an asshole. At least that's what Christian told me. "I think Carter just found it easier to go along with everything my father planned for him in life," he'd said, shrugging. "He's the heir, I'm the...you know how it goes."

He'd laughed, then I'd laughed, but I wasn't sure either of us meant it.

"Denise."

My breath caught at the sound of my own father's quiet yet painfully intimidating voice. Certain I'd done something he disagreed with, shame flamed my cheeks. It wasn't that he constantly corrected me, but the indignity I felt when he did consumed me. I'd lived in fear of disappointing him since I was a little girl.

I paused before looking up from the flashing green cursor on the computer screen, my ears hot and humming as I squeaked out a shaky "Hi."

He folded his arms over his chest, single-breasted suit jacket buckling at the elbows. "Hal called today."

My shoulders tensed. *Great. The fuckwad producer who stares at my tits while telling me to go find a man for him to talk to.*

"He said you had funding secured for his next project an hour after you met with him on Tuesday."

I cleared my throat and tucked a piece of hair behind my ear. "Yeah. I mean, I just need to get the final paperwork done, but it's...Did someone back out or something?"

My father shook his head. "He was actually quite impressed. Said it was almost like I had a son, not a daughter." His mouth twitched, then he blinked as if he found the urge to smile surprising.

My eyes widened. "Oh."

"That guy's a real prick," he said, his face still fighting emotion.

I coughed out a laugh of astonishment. "Uh, yeah. He is."

"Keep up the good work." He uncrossed his arms, then rapped his knuckles against the doorframe before turning into the hallway.

My shoulders immediately rolled down my back, and I closed my eyes, pulling in a long breath. Relief followed by a shot of confidence.

Tom Abbott thinks I'm good at my job. I am good at my job. But if he thinks I'm good, then I'm really good.

"All right, when's the article coming out?"

My eyes snapped open, and Marcos chuckled.

"Shit. Sorry. Didn't mean to scare you."

I pressed my palm to my chest and exhaled. "Hey. Hi. What, uh…what article?"

"You know, the one with the picture of you and your dad, back-to-back, arms crossed as you're both staring into the camera. I think the title is 'The Most Powerful Father-Daughter Duo in Hollywood.'" He highlighted the imaginary headline with his hands.

I twisted my lips into a victorious smile. "You heard about Hal, huh?"

"I was with Tom," he explained, stepping inside my office and leaning against the glass window. "He called Hal a prick as soon as he hung up the phone. Which he is. A prick."

"Biggest one I've ever met," I said, cutting the power to my computer and pushing my chair out from the desk with a surge of self-assurance. "Which means I need to go for a cocktail to celebrate."

Over the past several months, I'd found a certain sense of freedom in finally allowing my outsides to match what was within. It still felt like too precarious a thing to practice with just anyone, though, so I kept my response to Marcos cool, nonchalant. *Of course, Hal realized I'm fucking brilliant. He had to eventually, didn't he?* But with Christian, taking off the mask became easier every day, which is why I couldn't wait to get to his house and let a whole goddamn universe of rainbows and hearts and unicorns spill out of me. The thought of him picking me up and swinging me around like we were in some delightfully silly rom-com made me so ridiculously embarrassed that I almost giggled.

Marcos grinned. "Cocktails sound great. Where are we going?"

"*I'm* going to Venice to meet"—I swung my purse over my shoulder—"some friends."

"Fine," he said, letting out a long sigh. "I was trying to get out of a set up, but if you don't wanna help…"

"Oh." My insides stiffened, and the corners of my mouth turned down. *Weird.* I instantly forced them up, along with the pitch of my voice. "Well, who knows? Maybe she'll end up being the girl of your dreams."

What the hell? Did I just squeak?

He gave me a knowing look, then shrugged as he pushed himself off the window. "Maybe she will," he said, returning my smile and winking before he left the office.

I shook my head and blinked to clear the specks of jealousy that clouded my vision.

Don't be ridiculous, I told myself as I flipped off the light and headed to the elevator. *Marcos can do whatever he wants.*

———

A rush hour drive from our office in Century City to Santa Monica would've normally sent me out of my skin, but traffic was surprisingly light. I didn't want to purposely clip anyone on the 10, and the songs were so good I didn't have to tell the radio to shut up once.

I pulled into the driveway and shifted my car into park, grabbing my purse and dinner outfit so I wouldn't be stuck in a suit all night. My heels clicked against the worn brick path leading to the door, where I rang the bell, standing taller, ready to shake hands with Carter and tell him how wonderful it was to meet him before excusing myself to change. I'd ask Christian if he would mind helping me with the zipper on my dress, and once we got to his bedroom, I'd squeal and jump into his arms, relieved I could finally be myself.

I hit the bell again, then pressed down on the lever and pushed on the door handle, thinking maybe Christian was running behind and just hopping into the shower. That time had gotten away from him while he and Carter were catching up.

Locked.

When I reached for the bell again, the door opened, and Christian's bandmate, Jordan, stood in front of me wearing only a pair of long baggy shorts, rubbing his eyes.

"Hey," he said, his voice low and gravelly. "What's up?"

I narrowed my gaze. *What's up?*

"I, uh...I'm supposed to go to dinner with Christian and his brother." I tried not to let the irritation I felt seep into my voice. Jordan wasn't a rude guy, he just wasn't the brightest bulb in the box. He'd once hugged a fucking cactus in Joshua Tree, for Christ's sake.

"Oh, yeah," he said, nodding his head slowly. "I think Carter's flight might be late or something. I haven't seen Christian for a while. He said something about not feeling good earlier, so he must be in his room."

He stood in the doorway, still bobbing his head up and down, long dirty-blond hair falling over his shoulders.

I raised my brows. "So, can I come in, then? See if he's in there?"

"Shit. Sorry, yeah."

He stepped back, scratching his chest and yawning, and I muttered "Thanks" as I passed through the foyer and living room to the primary suite. The door was closed, so I knocked, thinking Christian had probably meant to call and let me know Carter's flight was delayed but had fallen asleep fighting off some twenty-four hour bug.

When there was no answer after the second round of knocks, I turned the knob hesitantly, wanting to respect his privacy. Hinges creaked as I peeked around the door, saying his name before opening it all the way to find an unmade bed with no Christian in it. My eyes shifted to the bathroom door, which was also shut.

Oh God, I thought, backing out of the bedroom before I heard something I didn't want to hear. *Just let the man have the stomach flu in peace and call him later.*

Unless...was I supposed to stay? I wasn't exactly up to speed on relationship rules when it came to, well, anything, much less illness.

No. No one wants someone hanging around while they puke. Just tell Jordan to slip him a Sprite later and—

A loud thud startled me, and I froze.

Shit. Did he fall?

Another thud sent me tiptoeing toward the sound, my brain buzzing with worry that I was somehow still invading his personal space. I placed my purse and change of clothes to the side and tapped my fingers softly against the solid dark wood before leaning my ear against it. "Christian?"

No answer.

"Christian, it's me."

Still nothing.

Fuck.

I sucked in a deep breath as I turned the handle and pressed forward with my shoulder, averting my eyes. "Christian, I'm coming in, I want to make sure you're—"

One hand slipped from the gold metal knob as the other covered my mouth in slow motion. My eyes widened and began furiously darting around the room.

Yellow liquid splattered across the toilet. Christian splayed out, back against the tub. A thick piece of...What is that beside him? Did he throw that up? And what the hell is...Fuck, is that a needle? A syringe?

A voice said "Jordan, Jordan" much too quietly for Jordan to hear. When I realized it was my own, I forced his name from my lungs, stronger and louder, as I hurried over to Christian, my knees hitting the tile floor so hard that I thought my bones might shatter. "Christian, what's...Are you sick? Did you get sick? Did you take something? What did you take?"

His head wobbled in my hands, lids fluttering before opening halfway. Two tiny black dots in a sea of gray.

Something's not right. His eyes aren't right.

"Can you...can you hear me? Can you stand up?" I kicked off my heels and scrambled from the floor before hooking my elbows under his armpits in a futile attempt to lift him. "Jordan!"

I fell back down on my knees, fear beginning to choke and blind me as I pressed my hands to his cheeks. I pushed his hair from his face, dried bile mixing with sweat. "Oh my God, I don't know what to do. I don't know what to do. Somebody fucking help me!"

Christian wheezed then coughed, his lids still heavy. "It's fine. It's fine," he mumbled.

I gasped, tears spilling over as I searched his face. "Are you okay? What happened, did you get sick, what—"

"Denise, did you call—" I turned my head to see Jordan standing in the doorway, eyes fixed on the syringe beside Christian. "Oh, man. What the fuck." He covered his face with his hands and shook his head. "What the fuck, what the fuck, what the fuck."

I gripped Christian's shoulders as he attempted to push himself up from the floor. "Don't get up. We need to get you to the hospital. Jordan, we need to get him to a hospital or call 911 or—"

"No, we don't." Jordan sighed loudly, letting his hands fall.

Christian tipped his chin up just slightly, exchanging a brief look with Jordan before pulling his knees to his chest and letting his head hang.

My eyes ping-ponged back and forth between the two of them. "I don't...He's sick, Jordan. Is he diabetic? Is that, like... insulin or something?"

Jordan walked over to us, snatching up the amber tube I'd thought in my panic was something Christian had thrown up. "More like heroin or something."

Had I not been on the floor already, the word would've brought me to my knees. "*What?*"

"I'm fine," Christian said, his voice faint and raspy. "It's fine. It was just one time.

The air was all of a sudden thick, too thick to breathe. My heart thumped in my chest, my neck, and my jaw as my eyes circled the room, searching for a way to wake myself up from what had to be a bad dream. Something silver glinted on the bathroom counter, and I squinted. A spoon. And a lighter.

My stomach dropped.

No. This can't be real. This can't be real.

I slowly crawled backward, grabbing the edge of the bile-splattered toilet to stand.

"You should go." Jordan leaned down to retrieve the syringe, then turned to me. "I'll handle this."

My hands shook as they wiped at the tears falling down my face and the snot dripping from my nose. "Is he okay?" I whispered.

"You need to go, Denise. I'll make sure someone calls you."

Someone?

I inched along the wall to the door, as if any wrong move could set off a land mine.

Christian muttered, "I'm okay, baby," as a watery image of Jordan nodded for me to go.

I snatched my purse and change of clothes from the floor before running out of the house, not realizing I was still barefoot until my skin pressed into the ridged rubber of the brake, and I shifted my car into reverse.

21

____

AUGUST 1990

I stared at the television, my thumbnail practically gnawed to the quick, as Letterman faded into an infomercial. I pressed the Off button on the remote, the only light in the room now a faint glow from the floor lamp in the corner.

One thirty.

Seven hours since I'd left Christian on the bathroom floor.

Six and a half hours since I'd walked into my apartment and curled up on the couch, waiting for the phone to ring and "someone" to be on the other end.

It had been too long. I'd picked up the receiver so many times, wanting to call the house, wanting to call an ambulance, wanting to call the police without somehow landing Christian in jail. But wouldn't that have been better than...

Fuck. I can't think it. I can't even fucking think it.

I'd thought about calling Eva. Of course, I had. I just couldn't figure out what to say. She didn't even know Christian existed and that would've been a hell of a way to tell her.

Hey girl. So, no big deal, but I forgot to mention that I'm dating someone, and oh, I just found out he might be a heroin addict. I know! So crazy, right?

Was he an addict? I didn't even know what was going on, not really. I needed more information before I could say anything to her. The way Jordan had reacted, obviously concerned but oddly calm, made me think it wasn't the first time he'd witnessed that scene. But could Christian have hidden something so obvious from me for nearly *five* months? This wasn't a bump of coke when no one was looking. This was needles and spoons and could he even have pretended to be normal on fucking *heroin*? We'd spent so many days and nights together, and he'd never once seemed off. He barely even drank —sometimes a beer or two if we were home, maybe a couple more if we were out. No prolonged trips to the bathroom, no ducking out of restaurants or bars to make shady calls from shady phone booths.

Nothing made sense, and I wondered if Eva could help me at least try to sort it out. She'd worked in the music industry, been on tour buses and at backstage parties, and seen some crazy shit go down.

But no, I thought. *No. I can't tie up the line. What if Jordan calls? What if—*

The phone trilled, and my stomach immediately tied itself into a knot. I picked up the cordless receiver, and a shaky finger hovered over the Talk button before pressing it.

"Hello?"

"Did I wake you up?"

I squeezed my eyes shut, and a rush of air left my lungs. My bottom lip quivered, and I took a moment before answering to make sure I could speak without breaking down. "No, I...I couldn't...I mean, I'm not..."

I didn't know what to say. What to ask. So I waited, hoping he would fill in the empty space.

"I'm so sorry." Christian's voice cracked, followed by a series of tiny gasps. "I am so fucking sorry."

I cupped my hand over my mouth and dipped the phone

below my chin, trying to silence the sobs that shook my body from the sound of his tears and the fact that he was still alive to cry them.

"Can I, um...can I see you? I'm at a pay phone down the street. I didn't want to freak you out, so that's why I called. Why I'm calling."

I swallowed hard, trying to process the fact that he was anywhere but under the watchful eye of his roommates after the condition I'd seen him in. "What are you...You should be at home, Christian. I saw you, on the floor, and you weren't okay, you weren't—"

"I'm okay, baby." He sniffed. "I'm okay."

The same words he'd said to me as he sat on the cold tile, head too heavy to lift, sent a chill up my spine. I wiped my cheeks with the palm of my free hand while questions catapulted from one side of my brain to the other.

If I say yes, will he come over and tell me everything is fine, only to end up on my bathroom floor later tonight? If I say no, will he go home and end up back on his?

Part of me wanted to see him so I could understand. I knew him, I knew who he was inside, and there had to be reasons. The other part wanted to scream at him, shove him, hit him as hard as I could because maybe I actually didn't know him at all. And maybe I was stupid for ever believing I did.

An engine started and a door chimed in the background. My chest tightened as I imagined a gas station phone booth, a man slinking up to Christian and opening a trench coat lined with long, shiny needles.

"Yeah," I said softly. "Come over."

Five minutes later, he was standing at my door, arms outstretched as the porch light cast a yellow halo above him, asking me without words to forgive him. His hair was damp, as if he'd just showered, and his eyes were red and tired. The skin beneath was swollen and dark.

I glanced down at the crook of his left elbow, covered by a flannel. "That wasn't the first time...was it?"

He rubbed his lips together, then shook his head. "I'll tell you everything."

That last word should've knocked me over, but I supposed that somewhere inside of me, I already knew there was more to the story. So, I nodded and shuffled back to the couch in the crumpled pantsuit I had yet to change out of and sat down, hugging my knees to my chest, as if that would somehow protect me from "everything."

———

"I met Andie when I was twenty." Christian sat in the chair across from me, hands planted on his legs. "Me and Jordan had just gotten the band together, and we were playing at this hole-in-the-wall club downtown. I walk offstage, she grabs my hand, and the next thing I know, I'm at her apartment, and there's a needle in my arm."

I could see the tension in his muscles as the past replayed in his head. "She wasn't a bad person. She was in just as much fucking pain as I was, but neither one of us knew how to deal with that. So, we both did what we could to try to forget it."

I sniffed and ran the back of my hand under my nose. "And she was...You were...together?"

"Yeah. We, uh...I thought I was in love with her. I mean, I was, as much as I could've been. We did other stuff, normal stuff. So, it wasn't *all* the time, you know?" His gaze dropped to the floor before slowly drifting back to me. "Until it was, I guess."

"So, how did you...How are you here and she's..."

He took a deep breath, then laced his fingers together, bringing them under his chin. "She died. On her birthday. Three years ago today."

"Oh my God." I steepled my hands over my mouth. "Did she over—"

He swallowed and offered a quick bob of his head as an answer. "But that's not...It's not an excuse. It was awful, of course it was, and it should've never happened, but that part of my life is behind me. I came to LA for rehab, and I stayed here to get away from that scene. The guys in the band, they were never really into that shit, and they followed me down after I got out. I swear, I hadn't touched a single drug in over two years. I don't know what happened. Maybe Carter canceling his trip at the last minute when he knew what today was..." He shook his head. "I need you to know it's not gonna happen again, Denise. I swear, it won't. And I'll do anything to prove that to you." He gripped the top of his head, frustration and desperation turning his knuckles white. "Please believe me. Please."

My eyes fixed on the wall behind him.

"Say something," he pleaded. "Even if it's to tell me to get the fuck out, just say it because I can't stand to see you like this, especially when it's all my fucking fault."

Thoughts floated in my mind like snowflakes, each one with its own complexities, melding together and creating a thick blanket that made it difficult to find a path forward.

I had a million things to say. A million things to ask.

I'm sorry your girlfriend died.

I'm sorry for everything that happened.

But how could you fucking do this?

And how am I supposed to believe you ever again?

My gaze shifted to him. "Why didn't you tell me?"

He sighed, a sound of relief that I'd finally spoken, coupled with regret that he'd kept his secret from me. "I wanted to. I did. It's just that...you've got your shit together, Denise. I mean, I know we both have all the baggage with our families and stuff, but you've got this great job, great apartment, great *life* that you built for yourself, and you did it on your own. I got so fucking lucky that you took even two seconds out of it to talk to me. How could I give you any reason to question that?"

It wasn't a great life without you.

"It's, like, you know that saying? The one about women wanting to be her and men wanting to be with her?" he asked.

I gave him a cautious nod.

"That's you, Denise. You're *her*. And I'm some trust fund kid on smack who can't get a goddamn record deal to save his fucking life."

His words reached into my chest and squeezed my heart, flooding my body with blood and raw emotion.

"No," I said quietly, shaking my head, the force increasing as my voice grew louder. "No. That's...that's your parents talking. You told me the very first night when we ate Chinese food on this couch that they don't get to say who we are."

He shrugged, muscles tensing as if trying to prevent his body from collapsing in on itself. "Some days I believe that, and then I get another door slammed in my face and I remember the only reason I'm not living on the fucking streets is because of people who paid me to stay out of their way."

I shuddered as I pulled in a tiny breath. *That could've been me.* If I had taken a second to consider any options other than working for my father. If I had allowed myself to think about anything that didn't align with his plans for me. If I hadn't been so eager for him to approve of everything I did and everything I was.

Christian had taken a risk that I hadn't been strong enough to take. He'd shown his family, his friends, the fucking *world* that he wasn't afraid to be himself while I pretended to be only those things I thought were acceptable. The obedient daughter, the successful businesswoman, the girl who would leave you lying on the bed, no strings attached—wanting so badly to be wanted but afraid of wanting anyone back.

Except him.

I couldn't fool him. And I didn't have to. Because as hard as I tried to hide from Christian, he saw the real me. If I left him now, I'd be doing the exact same thing that I lived in fear of people doing to me. If I abandoned him, I'd be abandoning myself.

"We're not so different, Christian." I unhugged my knees. "You're just a lot fucking braver than I am."

"I wasn't brave today." He raised his eyes to meet mine. "But I love you, Denise. I really fucking love you. And I've been wanting to say that since you ordered that stupid fucking salad at Barney's when you wanted the cheeseburger and mozzarella sticks."

I choked on tears and laughter. "That's very romantic."

"It's very true."

"I..." I cleared my throat, trying to release the words that were stuck. "I've never said that before. Not to someone other than a friend."

"You don't have to say it."

"I do, though."

"No, it's okay, I—"

"I mean, I *do* love you." I smiled, the heaviness in my heart lifting. "I do."

Christian dropped his head into his hands as his shoulders shook, and I immediately pushed myself off the couch, curling onto his lap and lifting his chin. *This is where I belong*, I thought as I held his face in my hands, gently kissing the damp lashes that framed his beautiful, sad eyes.

"It's you and me, okay?" I said, my thumbs tracing the top of his cheeks. "But I can't do this again. I can't. So I need you to promise."

"I promise, baby," he said, pressing his forehead to mine. "I promise."

22

NOVEMBER 2009

"Babe. Dee. Denise."

I blinked, a slight shake of my head snapping me from my thoughts. "Huh?"

"You're staring into space."

"Am I?" I looked down at the book in my right hand, the words slowly coming into focus, though I had no idea what I'd read before my eyes drifted to the specks of sunlight flickering on the wall.

Marcos chuckled, tousling his freshly washed hair. "I said your name, like, three times. You all right?"

"Yeah." I straightened my back against the headboard of our bed, tossing the book aside. "I think last week took it out of me. I swear, I had a million meetings."

More like a million memories of Christian.

I still hadn't emailed him after the previous Saturday at the guest house, and I worried time was running out. That he would get impatient, take Lucas aside one night after practice, and single-handedly turn my entire fucking world upside down.

As I watched Marcos sort through a dresser drawer, I once again considered confessing.

Just say it. Say it quickly, don't think about it, just let the words come out.

But I couldn't. And they didn't.

Tomorrow. Maybe I can tell him tomorrow. Sundays suck anyway. Why ruin a perfectly good Saturday?

I stretched my arms overhead and rolled my neck, pretending to let go of whatever I had on my mind. "Anyway, thank God it's the weekend." I eyed the towel wrapped around his waist as my mind conjured up a distraction. "And, I mean, since it *is* the weekend..."

He glanced over his shoulder, and I arched an eyebrow, slowly sliding my right hand under the covers and biting my bottom lip.

"Really? Twice in less than twelve hours?" he said, turning to face me. He smirked as he fixed his eyes on the movement beneath the sheets.

My hand dipped into my underwear, and I traced the edge of my tank top and the skin just above my breasts with the tip of my finger. "This week just made me so tense."

Not a lie in itself.

"And you look so hot right now."

Definitely not a lie in any shape or form.

Throughout all the years I'd known Marcos, I recalled only one time when he could have been considered even the slightest bit unattractive. He'd gotten seasick during a Caribbean vacation, turned several shades of green, and thrown up over the side of the chartered boat for the two hours it took to get us back to shore. Despite his unfortunate situation, he was still cute in the most vulnerable of ways, insisting between vomiting episodes that he didn't get seasick and that the shrimp cocktail must've been bad.

"Oh yeah?" he asked, his smile growing bigger. He approached the bed, making a pit stop to lock the door before sitting beside me.

My breath quickened as I began to enjoy what I'd started. "Mm-hmm."

He bobbed his head to the sheets. "You want me to help you out with that?"

I slipped my hand and my bare legs out from under the covers. "I kinda wanna do something else first," I whispered, tugging him toward me and dropping my gaze to his crotch before our lips touched.

"Did I forget that today's my birthday? Or...shit, is it our anniversary?"

I eased onto my knees. "Neither," I said, my palms sliding up his thighs before landing on his waist and breaking the twist that held the towel in place.

Good God.

The fact that the sight of him still made me as wet as he was hard after all the years we'd been together never ceased to amaze me. But then again, there was nothing *not* sexy about the man I'd married. The man I loved more than life itself, and who probably loved me—or at least the person he thought I was—even more than that.

I need to tell him. I need to tell him tomorrow.

He'll be fine. He'll know what to do, and it'll all be fine.

Now focus.

I grasped his dick, firmly but gently, then tossed my hair to the side and ran the tip of my tongue along the shaft. He moaned as my lips circled the tip, a throaty *"Fuuuck"*—the kind that made it all worth it—escaping as I took him further into my mouth.

He placed his hand on the back of my head, his hips pulsing slightly. I twisted my hand, sliding it up, then down. My pussy ached as I imagined him inside me like he'd been the night before, and when he groaned "That's so fucking good, baby," I raised my eyes, slowly...deliberately.

And your cock is so fucking hard, Christian.

Christian?

Long hair melted into short. Gray eyes into hazel. And I gagged.

"Dee?"

I jerked back, hunching over, pounding my fist against my chest while I convulsed like I'd choked on a goddamn bone.

No pun intended.

"Denise," Marcos said, scrambling to the floor and rubbing my back as his eyes searched my face, which I was sure was red as a beet.

"I'm okay," I croaked, squeezing my thighs together so I wouldn't pee my pants and make the scene somehow even more horrifying. "I'm"—*cough, cough, cough*—"I'm okay."

I managed to catch my breath. "Fuck. I'm so sorry."

Marcos smiled as he sat on the floor across from me. "Wow. I haven't had anything like that happen since this girl I dated in college got drunk and threw up all over my—"

I groaned, cutting him off. "Oh my God, *shut up.*"

Laughter sputtered from between his lips, and I coughed one last time before falling into him. My body convulsed again, this time because it was impossible to pretend some hammered sorority chick yacking on his dick wasn't hilarious.

I blew out a breath, resting my forehead on his shoulder. "Maybe you should get a penis reduction."

He chuckled as he stroked my hair. "How about I take you to dinner tonight instead?"

"Wait, is it my birthday? Or did I forget our anniversary?" I asked, my voice muffled by his chest. I pulled back, lifting my chin and winking. "That actually sounds really good."

"Perfect. Then we can come back here and try that again."

I scrunched my nose. "You sure I should do that on a full stomach?"

He shook his head, pressing his smile against mine. "Goddamn, you're cute."

23

NOVEMBER 2009

"And after *all* that, he called his friend who knows the owner of Nobu and got us this fantastic table on the deck."

Eva snickered. "Then you finished the job when you got home, of course."

I tapped the tip of my pen against my desk, lips curling into a sly smile. "I didn't think it was fair to make him wait."

"So, while he was driving?"

"God, no. He could've gotten distracted and wrecked the car."

Her sharp gasp made me feel so scandalous that I squinted through the glass window of my office, making sure no one was loitering outside the closed door.

"You gave him a blow job in the middle of the fucking Nobu parking lot?"

"It was nine thirty at night, Eva! And we were parked off to the side, not in the middle." I chuckled to myself. "It was dark... ish."

"Oh my God," she said, emphasizing each word. "You will never not be Denise, will you?"

I began to laugh out loud but only for a second. My stomach sank, my mind twisting her words. *Meeting with Christian, hiding it from Marcos...I am the same person I've always been.*

I hadn't told Marcos on Sunday like I'd planned. I supposed I hadn't really *planned* anything anyway. I'd just done or said whatever I needed to in order to distract myself for another couple of days as I held onto the hope I could fix it all myself.

I cleared my throat, then went quiet.

"Oh shit, did someone come in your office?" she asked.

"No, I..." My pulse picked up as I tried to work up the courage to tell her about Christian, and I pulled in a deep breath.

Say it.

"Okay," I managed, releasing all the air from my lungs. "This is gonna sound crazy, but I, uh..."

Just fucking say it.

"What's going on?" Concern crept into her voice.

"It's just that I...remembered I have to be at Marisol's school. They're, um...they're doing this early Thanksgiving... thing."

"Oh." She was silent for a beat. "Okay, well, are you sure that's all—"

"I'm actually already late," I interjected. "But give the boys and Eric a hug for me. I'll call you later, okay?"

Eva sighed. "All right. Love you, babe."

After a hurried "Love you, too," I ended the call and slid my cell across the desk, out of reach, like it was contaminated. An evil device that made me lie to people.

I clenched my jaw and drummed my fingers on the desk, resisting the urge to strangle myself for not telling Marcos the weekend before. But as much as I regretted my actions—my *inactions*—I was going to have to deal with them. He was the perfect husband, and I'd gotten lucky that he somehow thought I was the perfect wife. I couldn't give him any reason to question that. Even if he understood why I'd kept it from him, that I wanted to protect him from even *one second* of worry or hurt, he would think just a little bit less of me each day—until eventually, the rose-colored glasses he'd always seen me through would finally fade, and all my flaws, everything that was wrong with me, would suddenly become crystal clear.

There had to be a way to get Christian out of my life, out of Lucas's life, without Marcos knowing.

I tapped out an internet search on the keyboard—*diners in... Monrovia*—then copied the address of a place that looked neither particularly good nor bad and pasted it into a new email to Christian, asking him to meet me there at 3pm the next day.

This time we'd be on neutral turf—in public, but far enough away that I wouldn't be in danger of seeing anyone I knew. Somewhere he wouldn't get overly emotional. Somewhere I wouldn't do the same.

I hadn't been prepared for battle the last time I'd seen him. I hadn't been able to steel myself against his pleas, insisting there was no way in hell Lucas would want to be a part of his life after he found out it was Christian who'd abandoned him.

But this time, I'd be ready.

"Sorry I'm late." I tossed my purse on the vinyl seat, then slid into the booth across from Christian. "Traffic."

"It's fine. I'm just glad you wanted to meet." He raised the pebbled plastic glass in front of him and took a sip of his drink. His hand was trembling. "It's kind of a drive out here, isn't it?"

My jaw tightened. *Game on.*

"Oh, I'm sorry, Christian," I began, flipping my sunglasses on top of my head. "It's not often people want to come back into my life after nearly twenty years and completely fuck it up. So forgive me if I'm not comfortable with having this conversation in the middle of Sunset or wherever the fuck would've been more convenient for you."

He froze, the ice in my stare penetrating his skin, then cleared his throat and gingerly placed his cup on the table. "I wasn't...I didn't mean..."

I forced a tiny smile as a brassy-haired waitress with a pony-tail and curled bangs appeared.

"Hey, hon, can I get you something?"

"Just a water would be great."

"Nothing to eat?" she asked.

"No, I'm good, thanks."

I was starving. So much so that my stomach growled at the mention of food, and I coughed in an attempt to cover it up. My hunger instincts had finally overcome the nerves that buzzed through my body all morning, making breakfast and lunch impossible. My insides churned when I'd asked my assistant to cancel my afternoon meetings, spinning a story about a forgotten doctor's appointment. I tacked "and a bunch of errands" onto the end while recounting it to Marcos, wanting to throw up when he told me to take my time, he'd make dinner.

But I wasn't there to break bread with Christian. I was there to get him out of our lives.

The waitress nodded. "What about you, hon? You want something?"

"Can I get a cheeseburger and fries?"

Did he just look at me? Did he just fucking look at me?

He handed the laminated menu to the waitress, telling her "Thanks."

That asshole.

I fucking loved cheeseburgers. But, of course, he already knew that.

"Ma'am," I called after her. "Can I actually get a house salad?"

I crossed my arms, settling against the back of the booth and arching a brow. "Changed my mind."

Christian sighed. "Look, Denise. I can already tell you're not exactly happy to be here, and I get that. But you don't have to pretend to want some shitty diner salad when—"

"I don't know what you're talking about." I pressed my lips into a thin line.

"I'm talking about the fact that you always order a salad when—"

"Don't act like you fucking know me *always* anymore, Christian." My utensils clanked against the Formica as I unwrapped them from the paper napkin bundle.

"Okay." He held his hands up before clasping them together on the table. "I just thought after I saw you last that maybe you were wanting to talk about how to tell Lucas." He paused. "Or that you were at least thinking about things."

"Yeah, well..." I flashed a two-second smile at the waitress who returned with my water. "I did think. And if you're under the impression that Lucas knowing will do anything but hurt *everyone* involved, you're wrong."

Christian's face fell as he slumped against the back of the booth.

My chest squeezed. "I'm sorry."

Shit. This is war. Don't apologize for striking the enemy.

"I didn't mean I'm sorry I said that," I added, attempting to correct my tactical error. "I meant, I'm sorry you don't under-stand how much it would hurt him." *True.* "And how he would never be able to forgive you if he knew." *Maybe.*

The silver in his eyes faded to a dull gray as he stared at his hands, running one thumb over the other.

"Why would you want to do that to him?" I asked, cursing

my voice for rising at the end. I hadn't wanted it to sound like a question that required any consideration.

He lifted his gaze. "Does he know your husband isn't his—"

"Yes."

"And has he...has he said he doesn't want to know who I am? Who his real father is?"

"*Marcos* is his real father."

"Right." He sighed and nodded. "Who his...*biological* father is, then."

"He's never asked for a name."

"But has he ever asked *about* me?"

Once, when he was ten and a kid told him he didn't look like his dad was Cuban. And then when he was thirteen and just...curious, I suppose.

I reached for my water, taking a long swallow. "Here's the thing, Christian. I honestly don't know why you would even want to do this to *yourself*. I'm telling you, he won't forgive you. He won't want anything to do with you."

He flinched. "Did he say that?"

"What?"

"That he didn't want anything to do with...whoever his father is?"

Dammit.

If I said yes, he would assume Lucas had given more than a fleeting thought to him over the years. If I said no, he would assume Lucas was more open to the possibility of a relationship than I had let on.

Don't look rattled. Think...think...

"We told him when he was *eight*," I explained, my tone sharpening. "He said 'Okay' and asked if he could go upstairs and play with his Legos."

"But don't you think now that he's older he would want to decide for himself?"

I don't know. I don't fucking know.

"I can't be around him all the time, writing songs and talking about music, while I'm keeping this from him." He massaged his brow. "I feel like I'm constantly lying, and it's fucking eating away at me."

Lying...lying...lying. The word echoed in the canyons of my brain.

"Then leave," I said quickly.

He tipped his head back and sighed. "Look, if you tell him, and he decides he doesn't want anything to do with me, I'll go. But if he does...He's just so fucking talented, Denise. I know he didn't sign the record deal, that it's technically Mia's thing, but he's good—*really* good—and he needs to be a permanent part of her band. I can make sure the label doesn't try to push him out for some guy who's flashier onstage or who has more experience."

I took a deep breath.

"He told me music is all he ever wants to do, and after all the mistakes I've made..." Christian shook his head. "This is the least I can do for him."

I remembered driving him to practice the day I'd confronted Christian, Lucas's silver eyes sparkling as he'd said those same words: "It's all I ever wanna do."

"I know I can't replace your husband."

My heart skipped a beat.

"I mean, as Lucas's father. But I *can* do everything in my power to make up for the past. For what I did to both him *and* you."

And then my heart exploded.

"I can't..."

I can't understand why you didn't choose me. Why you didn't choose him. Why you didn't choose us.

I curled my fingers against my mouth and shook my head. "No. I can't do this. I don't know if you're clean, if you'll stay clean. I can't risk that. Not with Lucas. I'm not going to let him get mixed up in that shit or let you leave him...again."

He winced. "I know, but I've been sober for seven years, Denise. I haven't even had a *drink* since then. I go to meetings, I have a sponsor." He bounced his knee under the table so hard his body shook. "What if we, um...what if we take time for you to see how my life has changed. For me to prove it to you. I just need you to give me a chance. Things are different now. I promise. "

I sighed, shaking my head. "You make an awful lot of promises, Christian." I tried to sound angry, accusatory. But the sadness inside of me was too big to hide.

He squeezed his eyes shut, bracing himself before reopening them. "I know. And I broke a lot of them in the past, but—"

"You broke all of them."

"But I'm not gonna fuck this up. I *can't* fuck this up." A tear dropped onto his cheek, and he quickly brushed it away. "Because this is my *son*, Denise."

Fuck.

My battle plans didn't make sense anymore, his offense not what I'd expected, and I began to question everything.

Was I being fair to Lucas? Should I give him the opportunity to make up his own mind? I had no doubt Christian could help him with his music, even open doors for him if he ended up not being a permanent part of Mia's band. I would have to tell Marcos first, of course, but I had to make sure Christian was really sober before I crossed that bridge. I couldn't ever know for certain, I supposed, but maybe I could feel better about it, like at least I wasn't putting Lucas directly in harm's way.

The waitress slid Christian's plate in front of him, my salad in front of me. I stared down at the wilted lettuce and wrinkled tomatoes.

I can't think. I'm not thinking straight.

My stomach rumbled, ached.

"I'm so sorry to ask," I said, stopping the waitress in her tracks. "But could I also order a cheeseburger?"

———

"It's not bad, huh?" Christian gestured to my burger as he finished his own and tossed the paper napkin on his plate.

I nodded while I tore into my food, trying to maintain some level of decorum by covering my mouth with my hand. "Definitely better than I expected," I said, swallowing and taking a sip of water. "But even a shitty cheeseburger would taste good right now."

I set my drink down and rolled my shoulders back, the ache in my stomach and the fog in my brain subsiding, though the heaviness in my chest remained. As much as I wished Christian hadn't reappeared in my life, there was no changing the fact that he had. Lucas was going to find out the truth one way or another. Christian wasn't going anywhere (with what he could do for Lucas and his music, was it selfish of me to want him to?), and it was only a matter of time before he told Lucas the truth himself. I had to do it on my own terms and make sure I wasn't blindsided by his unpredictability. I wasn't going to let that happen again. I was already embarrassed enough to tell Marcos I'd been mixed up with a drug addict in the past. What if he was *still* a drug addict, and I let the son who Marcos raised get mixed up with him, too? *No.* I had to make sure he was clean before I went down the path of telling my husband. Once I was certain, we could figure things out together.

"I'm sorry, Denise," Christian said, studying my down-turned mouth. "I'm sorry that I'm asking you for this after everything I did. But being able to get to know Lucas as his fa—"

I narrowed my eyes, watching as the word he wanted to say lodged in his throat.

"It would mean the fucking world to me," he finally managed.

"Yeah, well, I wouldn't be doing it for you, Christian," I said, my voice sharpening. "I only care about being fair to Lucas." I fixed my gaze on him. "I don't owe you anything."

His eyes flicked down to the table. "I know you don't."

"But I do owe Lucas the opportunity to make his own decisions."

"So, then..." He lifted his chin. "You'll give me a chance?"

"I..." I paused, avoiding a direct answer to his question. "Telling him isn't going to be a five minute conversation and all of a sudden everything's sunshine and rainbows, you know."

He nodded. "I know."

I leaned against the back of the booth, arms folded over my chest, head cocked. "Do you really, though? Because you've never seen your child hurting before. It is a whole new level of pain that I cannot begin to describe to you except to say, you would do anything—and I mean, *anything*—to take it all away from him."

"I can't imagine what—"

"I'm not done," I said, tilting forward, elbows resting on the table. "I need you to understand that Lucas *will* be hurt. And he'll be angry and confused and feel every fucking emotion a human can feel. He'll ask what happened all those years ago, and I'm not keeping that from him."

"No, you're right." He sucked in a deep, shaky breath. "He... he needs the whole truth."

"But I have to know that you're clean first, Christian. And if you're not, I'm begging you, please don't do this to him. Just go home now, and don't do this." My steely tone began to crack as my vision grew watery. "I love that kid more than anything in this fucking world, and he doesn't deserve to think he's going to have a relationship with you if the only thing you care about is getting high."

"I know, Denise. I want you to see that my life is different now. That I'm sober and have been for a long time. I'm not going back to where I was."

I nodded, blinking back tears. "Maybe I can come to band practices or something. No, that's weird, Lucas will think that's weird." I inhaled, trying, but failing, to slow my thoughts. "I don't know, maybe we can meet out here again for lunch or maybe somewhere else. I have to think about what makes sense."

I wasn't sure *anything* made sense, considering I was putting my trust in someone who'd given me all the reasons in the world not to. He'd fooled me before, and there was a chance he could do it again. But I couldn't let him into Lucas's life any further without at least trying to find out if he was truly clean and committed to staying that way. I wasn't the girl I'd been back then, blinded by emotion, all her defenses down, so desperately needing for him to be the person she'd thought he was. I just hoped that was enough, though I knew that no matter how it turned out, the time before he'd come to LA was gone, and I wasn't going to get it back.

"I don't want to wait too long to tell him," I continued. "I just...I need to do this first."

"Yeah, I understand."

"Okay." I quickly glanced at my watch, the exact time not even registering, then pulled my wallet out of my purse and tossed a twenty on the table. "I have to go, but I'll email in a couple days."

"Denise, no, I got this." He picked up the money and tried to hand it back, but I waved him off.

"You can't say anything to him, Christian. I need to be the one to tell him. Me...and his dad." My stomach dropped at the thought of confessing everything to Marcos.

"I won't. I promise."

"No," I said, grabbing my purse. "No more promises."

I gave him one last look before hurrying through the diner to my car, where I quickly pulled out of the parking lot and drove west, chasing the late afternoon sun as it slowly fell from the sky.

24

———

SEPTEMBER 1990

"Should I wear this"—I tucked a hanger displaying a plum minidress under my chin, then replaced it with a slightly more modest one in black—"or this?"

"Whichever one is sluttier," Christian said, his voice muffled by the pillow covering his face, shielding him from the overhead light I'd flipped on.

I twisted my mouth, holding them both out in front of me. "I think they're both medium to high on the slut scale, depending on your tolerance."

He tossed the pillow to the side and propped himself up on the bed. "I like the purple."

"*Plum.* Or maybe eggplant. Either way, that probably isn't the look I should be going for when meeting your brother."

"Oh, he'll love it."

I scrunched my nose at Christian, who was shirtless and grinning with the sheets twisted around his waist.

"Honestly, Carter probably won't even notice," he said. "He doesn't think about anything besides work and money. But other guys will."

"And that turns you on?" I asked, doe-eyed, lashes flutter-

200

ing. As if I had no idea that few things incited a raging hard-on faster than a man thinking about how many other men wanted to fuck his girlfriend.

He puffed out an exaggerated breath. "Are you kidding? Knowing that the entire room is staring at your tits, but I'm the one who gets to touch them? Staring at your ass, but I'm the one who gets to fu—"

"Yeah, I told you, that's not a regular thing," I said, hanging the dresses back in the closet.

"It's so hot when you're the boss of me. Come back to bed."

I stepped into a pair of black underwear and clasped the front hook of a matching bra. "We have to be at the restaurant in an hour and a half."

"I'm still basking in the glow of surprise afternoon sex."

"You can bask in the shower."

I leaned closer to the mirror above my dresser, Christian's reflection coming into focus after I secured a pair of jeweled pendants to my ears. He was frowning, his gaze pointed somewhere between me and the floor.

"What's wrong?" I asked, turning to face him.

"Huh?"

I walked to the end of the bed and sat down. "You went quiet and were staring."

He blinked. "Oh. It's nothing. I just, like, zoned out. Anyway, I should go shower."

"Uh-uh," I said, grabbing for his leg as he tried to escape. "You don't get to give me the we-need-to-talk-about-our-feelings speech ever again if you don't tell me what's up."

"Fine." He sighed and situated himself on the mattress, back resting against the headboard. "It's just that I think I'm kinda...nervous or something. I mean, Carter's my brother, we're part of the same dysfunctional family, but I still feel like I have to...impress him, I guess."

I squeezed his calf through the covers. "Christian. Shall I

tell you the story of me and my father for the five hundred thousandth time? You *know* I know how that goes. ''

He nodded. "I just want him to see that I'm successful. That I'm not the fuckup everyone thinks I am."

"Well," I began, crawling farther up the bed and sitting on my knees beside him, "I'd say that record contract you signed last week should give him a clear indication that you're doing pretty okay."

He smiled as his fingertips traced the curves of my breasts and my hips. "That *is* kind of impressive, isn't it?"

"Very impressive." I leaned forward, my lips meeting his. "And I'm so proud of you."

Ten years after Christian had started writing songs, and five years after he and his friends had put the band together, the right guy from the right label had shown up at the right show. *Finally.* There was talk of albums and tours, the record company proclaiming that Soulever had brought the Seattle sound to LA, and now it was the rest of the country's turn.

Over the past week, Christian had been ecstatic ("This is everything I've ever wanted!"), then stressed ("But what if I fuck it up?") before eventually landing somewhere in between. But he assured me he was going to extra 12-Step meetings and had daily calls with his sponsor to intercept thoughts of using drugs to relieve the anxiety. The image from the bathroom that had been branded on my brain a month and a half before had begun to heal, less raw and red each day. Though I wasn't sure something like that ever really disappeared, the effort he was putting into his sobriety made it hurt much less. He drank Coke instead of beer at a celebratory dinner hosted by the label, and I toasted him with a diet one in solidarity.

"I'm a rockstar's girlfriend," I'd said as our glasses clinked.
Backstage passes and big sunglasses.
How did that story go again?
Once upon a time, a fifteen-year-old girl met a boy—no, a man

—who made music. He told her she was special, and she believed him. Then he took her virginity, leaving her to cry in the bathroom and all the way home. When she went to sleep that night, she wished she was one of the dolls tucked away in the corner of her room. The kind she used to make believe with when she was a little girl. Pretty enough on the outside that people wanted to play with her. Hollow enough on the inside that she didn't care if they did.

I smiled, the memory fading as I brushed a few long dark waves from Christian's face. *Funny how one person can change everything.*

The phone rang, snapping me out of my lovestruck haze. "Should I answer?"

He shook his head. "Nah."

"What if it's my dad about work? Or what if it's Beau, and there's an emergency at the club?"

"What, like, they ran out of blue eyeshadow for the drag queens?"

"I'm gonna get it." I leaned over him to grab the receiver from the nightstand. "Hello? Hey, babe."

Christian heard the voice on the other end and mouthed "Babe?" while looking theatrically offended.

I chuckled, then cleared my throat, turning my attention back to Eva. "No, nothing's funny. I'm just...hanging out. How are you?"

His fingers traveled across my waist, slowly working up speed as I attempted to shove them off with one hand while holding the phone in the other. "No. No, I'm not laughing."

There was no universe in which I wasn't, but I maintained my innocence until I couldn't take it any longer. I fell on my side, yanking the phone cord and sending the base crashing to the floor.

Christian and I both gasped.

"Eva?" I sputtered, sweeping my mussed hair back as I tried to catch my breath. "Sorry, I dropped the...Are you still there?"

"Denise!" she shouted, the volume of her voice such that it could have been heard on Mars. "You cannot hide this from me anymore, okay? Every time I call, you're either not home or you're too busy to talk. So tell me who's over there and how long you've been seeing him!"

I pulled the receiver away from my ear, slapping my hand over it, eyes growing wide as I looked at Christian.

"You still haven't told her?" he whispered.

"I was going to call her tomorrow, I swear."

He shot me a sideways glance.

"I was." *Mostly true.* It was definitely on the Sunday agenda, but if I all of a sudden needed to get my nails done or there was a really good show on television, I wasn't opposed to rearranging the schedule. I wanted her to know, I truly did. But I kept putting milestones on the relationship, then pushing them out every time the date would arrive. *I'll tell her when it's been three months...when it's been four...no, five.* It had gotten to the point that I wasn't particularly scared of talking to her about Christian, but I *was* painfully embarrassed about how long it was taking me to do it.

"You could tell her now," he suggested.

"*Now?*"

Eva huffed. "Denise! I'm not fucking stupid!"

Christian raised his brows.

"Okay, okay, but go shower," I said. "This is, like, girl talk or whatever."

He winked and hopped out of bed, placing the phone base back on the nightstand. "Don't forget to tell her about that one time you let me fuck you up the—"

"Go," I hissed through gritted teeth, shooing him away as I pressed the receiver to my ear.

"All right, babe," I continued, taking a deep breath. "Let me have it. What do you want to know?"

She asked her first question, and my stomach whirled.

"His name?" I repeated. "His name is…" He not-so-subtly peeked his head around the bathroom door, and I smiled. "Christian."

———

"So, Denise," Carter began, taking a sip of red wine. "Christian told me you work in the film industry. That must be exciting."

"Oh. No." I laughed politely and waved him off. "I'm on the business side of things. Long hours, always a fire that needs to be put out. Not very glamorous."

He placed the glass down. "Sounds like a pretty prestigious job, regardless. And you got your degree in…"

"Uh, finance, actually." I took a bite of my salmon then dabbed the corners of my mouth with a black cloth napkin.

"I was an economics major," Carter said. "Then, of course, I got my MBA. Do you ever think about going back to school for that? Because you should. Can really make a difference when it comes to moving up the corporate ladder—which, you know, with a musician, you may be the one bringing home the bacon, so to speak."

I turned my head to Christian as Carter cut into his steak, my expression asking *What the fuck is this conversation?*, his responding *Par for the course.* Not only did Carter look exactly as I expected—neatly-trimmed hair, starched button-down, casual sport coat, and pressed khakis—but true to Christian's words, he did not, in fact, appear to think of anything other than work or money.

"Ah, well," I said, shifting my focus to Carter as I sipped my water. "Good thing I like bacon."

Carter gestured toward his brother with his knife. "I always tell Christian it's not too late to go back. He only went to UDub for a semester, so he'd have to start from the beginning, but he's still young."

Christian inhaled, the muscles in his leg tensing against mine, and I fumbled for his hand under the table, giving it a squeeze.

I've got this.

"You know," I began. "I was reading a really interesting article the other day about that guy...Oh, what is his name? That computer guy. I think he's actually from Seattle."

Carter took another sip of wine. "Bill Gates."

I clapped my hands together. "Yes! I was shocked at how much he's worth now. I think it's two, two-point-five billion?"

"Two-point-five," Carter answered, not missing a beat.

"That's a crazy amount of money, isn't it?" I shook my head in mock disbelief. "And to think he never finished college."

Carter's brow furrowed with a hint of realization. "Well, you know, he's in a unique industry, so—"

"Oh my gosh, Carter!" I pressed my palm to my chest, swiftly changing the subject. "I feel so rude talking about all this when I haven't even congratulated you. I heard you and your wife had a baby girl a few months ago. I can't remember what Christian said. Is this your first or second?"

"Second. Our son is almost three. And you really should see him now," he said, tipping his glass to Christian before looking back at me. "Christian left when he was a baby."

"Yeah, I, uh...I want to. It's just not that easy for me to go back," Christian replied, reaching for his water. "But I'm sure we'll have tour dates there. You could even bring him to the show, put those little earphones on him."

"Right. The whole"—Carter swirled his wine—"record contract thing. Did you get a lawyer to look over all the paperwork?"

Christian sighed, setting his fork down on his plate. "Don't worry, Carter. We have a manager. She takes care of all that. Everything's fine."

"I'm just saying, there's always someone who's out to screw someone else."

"Yeah, but we trust her," Christian said, his tone indicating he was ready for a new topic. "Anyway, we go into the studio next week. They want the album out by early spring, so it'll be tight but—"

"I guess you never know." Carter shrugged. "Could turn into something."

"It's a real studio, Carter. Where we're making a *real* album. To be sold in *real* stores."

"Right, of course. I just meant it's a hard business. Only a few spaces at the top and lots of people fighting to get there. Not everyone can be Phil Collins."

"Well, that's good to know because we're actively trying to *not* be Phil Collins," Christian deadpanned.

I brought my napkin to my mouth to keep from spitting the asparagus I'd just taken a bite of across the table.

Carter cleared his throat, finally seeming to pick up on the fact that he'd been disparaging his brother for the past twenty minutes. "Well, whatever the case, I think it's great. Seriously. Cheers, man." He lifted his glass, then finished off its contents. "Do you, uh...do you want me to tell—"

"Do you think they'd care?"

Carter let out an awkward laugh, stopping when he realized Christian wasn't trying to be funny. His eyes darted around the restaurant, and he coughed twice, a sure sign he had no idea how to answer the question I assumed was about their parents. The waiter sliced through the silence by asking if he could bring more wine or water, and Carter excused himself to the restroom.

Christian immediately released a long breath once he was gone.

I turned in my seat, sliding my hand along his back. "You okay?"

He nodded. "I'm fine. Carter just…He doesn't understand why I can't be like them. I actually think it's easier for him to not even try because then he might start to question himself."

It made sense. I'd been putting my head down and doing what my father expected of me for years. I said I liked my job, and maybe I really did. I never gave myself much of a chance to think about it one way or another because I was too busy trying to make sure I had Tom Abbott's stamp of approval.

"He'll see once the album comes out," Christian assured me. "And that Bill Gates bit was fucking brilliant, by the way."

I chuckled. "It was as much for me as it was for you."

For us. We're an us.

"Oh, we should order dessert so I can get a few more digs in before leaving. I'm sure I can think of something about Phil Collins, and also, I really fucking want cake," I added, grinning.

He smiled softly and shook his head. "How are you even here? With me?"

"You ambushed me at the Whisky when I was hungover and vulnerable and then wouldn't leave my apartment."

"Such a damn fairytale."

I snickered. "Hopefully without an evil bitch in the kitchen poisoning my cake."

"No one's gonna fuck this up, baby," Christian said, cupping my cheek. "I promise."

25

OCTOBER 1990

I gasped and sprang from the couch at the sound of someone outside my apartment.

"Finally," I said, opening the door. My face immediately fell as Beau bent down to retrieve the keys he'd presumably dropped. "Oh."

He screeched and popped up, slapping one hand over his heart. "Jesus, Denise! You scared the shit out of me."

I sighed and slouched against the frame. "Sorry."

"Why do you all of a sudden have the ears of a fucking German shepherd?" he asked, taking a drag off his cigarette. "Did you hear me all the way from your bedroom?"

I smoothed my hand over my hair, sure it was mussed from rotting on the sofa all night, picking up the phone every hour to make sure there was still a dial tone and the lines hadn't mysteriously gone down. "No, I wasn't sleeping."

"Really?" He narrowed his eyes. "But you're in pajamas and your face looks...squished."

"Thanks, Beau. Truly." I gave him a go-fuck-yourself look before continuing. "Anyway, I was just watching TV...or whatever."

His expression turned coy as he batted his eyelashes. "*Oh. Are you waiting for your lover?*"

"Please. You know me. I don't stay up till all hours waiting for a *guy*." I blew a raspberry and rolled my eyes, but it was all too theatrical.

"Mm-hmm." Beau crossed his arms. "Well, you opened the door at 2 a.m. like it was the rapture and Christ was comin' to take you home. And since you and I both know we ain't going *nowhere* when that day arrives, I'm pretty sure you were expecting someone else."

I reached for his cigarette, taking a puff before handing it back. "I have no idea what you're saying to me."

"You're smoking." He pursed his lips. "I'm coming in."

My shoulders dropped. "Fine," I said, drawing out the word as I motioned for him to extinguish the butt before stepping inside.

Beau settled into a chair while I flopped on the sofa.

"So," he began, crossing his legs and twirling a piece of short sandy-blond hair. "Tell me your troubles."

I pulled a throw pillow onto my lap and groaned. "Ugh, I don't know. Christian said he was gonna try to come over after the band got done recording tonight, but I haven't heard from him."

"Hmm." He tapped the tip of his nose. "I'd recommend no blow jobs for at least a month as punishment. That should teach him a lesson."

I chuckled, but it was hard to hide the sadness in it. "I'm annoyed that I'm annoyed about it, you know? He said he'd *try* to come over, not that he definitely *would*. Plus, I don't keep tabs on guys. That's not me. I'm sure he got caught up and lost track of time, but after what—" I snapped my mouth shut. I hadn't told Beau about finding him in the bathroom. I hadn't told *anyone*.

"After what?"

"After what...what?"

"You were going to say something, and you stopped." He raised an eyebrow. "Did something...happen?"

"No," I insisted much too loudly. "What do you mean, 'Did something happen?' Nothing happened."

"Yeah, so, you know that saying about the bitch who doth protest too much?" Beau cocked his head and pointed at me. "That's you. You're the bitch."

I dropped my eyes and rubbed the piping on the pillow between my fingers. "I mean, nothing *really* happened. He's just been so busy with the album, we haven't seen each other as much as we normally do."

After Carter's visit, Christian and the band had gone straight into the studio. On days they weren't recording, he was rewriting and tweaking and generally obsessing over the tracks so that even when we were together, he seemed far away. My mind immediately went to the worst-case scenario, but I tiptoed around my concerns by simply asking if the stress was getting to him. As if he'd read my mind, he promised me he was going to meetings, calling his sponsor. And so, even though my breath caught occasionally when he stepped away to the bathroom, I believed him. I *had* to. After spending my entire teenage and adult life as the exact opposite of a nagging girlfriend (or a girlfriend at all), I hated the idea of playing twenty questions every time I saw him.

"Ah, young grasshopper. This happens in relationships. The newness wears off, you settle into your lives, people get busy. Totally normal." Beau paused, his face twisting as if he wasn't totally convinced. "Although..."

"What?" I asked, struck by a bolt of panic as I looked up from the pillow.

"Well, I do think he should've called you tonight. So, I stand by no oral. For him, I mean. He should have to do extra"—he scrunched his nose and gestured at me—"whatever it is straight guys do with women down there."

I laughed—sort of—and he took a deep breath.

"Okay, Denise. What is it you're not telling me?"

"Nothing. It's nothing."

He raised his brows.

"Fine," I said, closing my eyes and massaging my lids before reopening them. "It's just that he kind of had, like, a little drug...thing. In the past." I emphasized the last part because technically, it was.

"What kind of 'little drug thing'?" he asked, leaning forward in his chair.

"It wasn't a huge deal. He just, you know, did them." I cleared my throat. "But, I mean, he's fine now."

"Like, was he a stoner, or was he shoveling six feet of snow up his nose on a regular basis?"

"No, no, nothing like that." *Not exactly a lie.* "I think he just maybe did...heroin or something?" My voice lifted at the end, a question for him to answer, hopefully with an *Oh, that's nothing to worry about* so I could stop making up shit in my head.

Instead, Beau recoiled. "*Heroin or something?*"

Dammit.

"Yeah, but it's totally done. Since he came down here, he's been, you know...He's good. And he didn't even have a *problem,* problem with it, really. I just want to make sure he doesn't fall back on that if he's stressed."

"You're being weird, Denise."

"I'm not being weird."

"Mm'kay, but you are."

"I'm not. It's stupid. It's, like, he should be worrying about me sleeping with ten other men because I did that once upon a time, but he isn't because I don't anymore."

"He's taken all the fun out of you."

"It's sad, I know. Anyway," I began, pushing myself up from

the sofa and trudging over to Beau, "I gotta be at work tomor-row, so time for bed." I leaned down, my arms circling his neck as I kissed his cheek. "I love you."

"I love you, too. And I'm sure your man got busy with his music. Just remember, though..." He clasped my arm as I pulled away, a serious shadow falling over his face.

Oh God. Here it comes. He's gonna tell me to be careful, that Christian could be hiding needles in my apartment and that—

"No blow jobs. For *at least* a month," he stressed.

I smiled and nodded, rubbing the side of my face. "Perfect. My jaw could really use the rest."

He stood and booped me on the nose before gliding to the door. "I knew my little whore was still in there somewhere."

———

I tapped the end of a ballpoint pen against the celebrity gossip magazine in my lap. "What's the hardest bone in the human body?"

Christian snickered. "Are you serious right now?"

"What?" I asked, oblivious to the innuendo until I looked up to see him smirking. "Oh, *come on*. And it's five letters, not four."

He balanced his acoustic guitar on his knee and began counting on his fingers. "P...e...n...i—"

"*That's* the bone you think Billy Idol broke during a motor-cycle accident in Hollywood?" I asked, reciting part of the cross-word clue.

He chuckled, squinting in the late morning sun blanketing the patio outside his house. "Yes?"

I rolled my eyes. "You're twelve."

"Like you weren't asking for it on that one," he said, smiling and giving his guitar a strum. "Also, I think you're the only person who does those crossword puz—"

"Oh my God! F...e...m...u...r." I placed each letter in the appropriate box, grinning victoriously at him when I finished. "It's femur. And I do the crossword puzzles because it makes me feel like I'm using my brain after reading a bunch of crap."

"You don't *have* to read the crap, you know."

"Well, I need *something* to do while you stare at the ocean and play that thing." My tone was playful, but I wasn't sure my mood matched it.

"There's just one part of this song I can't get right." He sighed and gave the guitar a final strum before laying it across his lounge chair. "But it's fine. No more music stuff. Today is us. *Just* us."

I swung my legs over the side of my chaise to face him, offering a sympathetic smile. "The album's gonna be amazing. And look, if you really feel like you need to work on it..."

He shook his head. "No. I hate that I got stuck in the studio on Thursday. And you drove all the way over here last night just for me to crash thirty minutes after you walked in the house."

"It's okay." I flipped my sunglasses on my head, tossing the magazine and pen aside. "I had my crap to read. And you made up for it this morning."

"Good. And sorry about...you know." He cringed. "I think I'm just exhausted. But I'll relax today."

I pushed myself up and walked over to him, straddling his lap and wrapping my legs around his waist. My arms circled his neck as I looked into his eyes. "I'm not complaining."

After all, when did a girl *ever* complain about a guy who had Christian's skills using his tongue instead of his dick? Besides, that shit happened with guys for all sorts of reasons. If they were stressed out or in their heads about something or drunk or...

I blinked at the thought.

He hadn't been drunk...had he? There was no way. He hadn't smelled like alcohol, wasn't stumbling around the house.

People couldn't hide being hammered. But could they hide being...

No.

I'd seen him on heroin—sick, barely able to look at me, barely able to speak.

He's worried about the album right now. It's just stress. He's worn himself out from singing and playing and recording and trying to make it all perfect.

"So, I was thinking," Christian said, threading his fingers through my hair, brushing it away from my face. "You'll come see me when we go on tour? I know it's not happening tomorrow or anything, but it'll be here before we know it."

We'd briefly mentioned the inevitability of a tour after they'd signed the record contract, but it hadn't really sunk in at that point that he'd be away for months at a time. After the other night when I'd waited up for him, though, I realized how much I was going to miss him. Not only that, but I wondered if he would be okay on the road and able to stay sober. Even though he'd said that his bandmates were committed to doing what they could to help, I wanted to know more. But this wasn't the time for a detailed discussion about any of that. He needed a day to unwind, not figure out the future.

"Of course I will," I answered. "But we don't have to talk about that now, let's just have a fun—"

"But you will, right?"

"Yes." I smiled. "Just don't make me sleep in some tiny little bunk while the other guys are all snoring or fucking some chick so loudly that I wake up in the middle of the night. Because then I'll realize I've gotta pee, and I'll have to use the totally disgusting bathroom, and the bus will keep running over potholes while I'm hovering over the toilet seat. And *then*—"

"Wait a minute, wait a minute, wait a minute. This is all very specific."

"Oh." My brows pinched together as I cleared my throat. "That's just a story Eva told me. I've never been on a tour bus in my life."

His narrowed eyes broke my exaggerated serious face.

"Okay, maybe I've been on, like, *one*." I winked. "But only yours from now on."

"I love that you're so fucking wild, but so fucking mine."

Our lips met, and I felt him harden beneath me as he slid his hands from my hips to my ass.

"See, I can already feel how relaxed you're becoming," I teased between kisses.

His mouth moved to my neck. "Let's go inside."

I whispered "Okay," and as I pulled away, my stomach let out a long, angry growl.

He placed his hand on my belly and chuckled. "Maybe we should feed you first."

"Right," I said, leaning my forehead against his. "I mean, I know that was super sexy and not a mood killer at all, but food is probably a good idea. Where should we go?"

"I'm not that hungry, so you pick."

I lifted my head. "What? How can you not be hungry? It's almost noon, and we haven't eaten since we woke up." I slid my hand down his back, slipping it through the loose waistband of his jeans. "I know you've had a lot going on, but you need to eat, Christian. Your pants are practically hanging off you."

"I know. I just get so focused, I forget, I guess."

"Come on." I unhooked my legs from around him and stood, reaching for his hand. "You'll be hungry once you see my cheeseburger."

"You single-handedly keep the beef industry afloat," he joked, pushing himself up from the lounge chair.

I smiled. "Cheeseburgers are the perfect food, and I love..." My eyes dropped to a small, clear plastic bag that had nearly worked its way out of his front jeans pocket. "Careful, you're gonna lose…What is that?"

"What's what?" he asked, eyes following mine.

My insides tingled as I pointed to it. "That."

"Oh," he said, quickly stuffing it back in. "I, um, threw all my guitar picks in this the other day when I went to the studio. You know how they fall out of my pocket all the time, and I leave them everywhere. I figured this might help."

"Well, where are they?"

"What?"

"The picks."

He grinned. "I guess I left them everywhere anyway."

My pulse picked up, and I fixed my wide eyes on the ground, certain that the panic I felt inside was starting to show on my face.

"Hey," he began. "What's wrong?"

"Nothing, it's just…" I lifted my gaze. "Are you lying to me?"

His brow creased. "*What?*"

"Are you lying to me?" I repeated. "Like, I'm not stupid, Christian, I know what comes in baggies, and I—"

"You mean you think it's…" He sighed. "Baby. No. I had guitar picks in here, not drugs."

I was silent.

"Denise. I swear," he said.

"Let me see it."

"Fine. Here," he said, irritation tainting his voice as he shoved it at me.

My hands trembled as I opened the baggie. But there was nothing in it. No traces of powder, or whatever the fuck heroin looked like. At least nothing I could see in the bright sun.

This is silly. What am I going to do? Go inside and examine it? Send it to a lab? He's looking right at me, he's talking to me, normal eyes, normal voice. He's obviously not high right now, and I've been with him since last night. I have to trust him. If I want this to work, I have to trust him.

I chewed my lip and nodded. "I'm sorry. I don't know why I thought...Sorry."

He pulled me into his arms, and I leaned into my safe place, the warmth of his chest comforting me.

"It's all right. I get it," he said, softly stroking my hair. "But everything is fine. Everything is good. *I promise.*"

26

NOVEMBER 2009

"Let's go, Lola!" I called from the foyer. "We're watching a soccer game, not walking the red carpet."

"Oh my God, I'm coming," she said, eyes locked on her phone as she idled down the stairs. "You don't have to freakin' yell." When she reached the bottom, she crossed her arms and studied my full face of makeup. "I thought this wasn't the red carpet."

"It's not, but I'm old and need help. You're young and have beautiful skin."

"Whatever. Are we going?"

"Yes, your sister's already there for warm-ups. Where'd your dad go? Marcos—" I yelped as I turned to find him standing behind me. "Oh."

"Lola. That shirt," he lamented, shaking his head at her crop top.

I bit back a laugh. *Like mother, like daughter.*

Lola clenched her jaw. Her brown eyes, framed with long, thick lashes, were wide and pleading. "Mom."

I wanted to compliment her on her mascara application but

thought the better of it. "It's fine, she looks cute. We need to leave, or we'll be late."

"Okay, okay," he said, holding his hands up as he walked toward the front door, Lola and I following.

"Where's this thing at anyway? And where's Lucas?" Lola asked as she shut the back door of the SUV.

"It's in Northridge. And Lucas is at work," I explained, clicking my seat belt into place as Marcos pulled out of the driveway.

She groaned. "*What?* Why doesn't he have to go?"

"I just told you, he's working."

"That's so not fair. I have other shit to do, too."

I twisted in my seat and narrowed my eyes at her. "Lola."

"Well, I do," she insisted. "Jasmine asked me to go to the mall."

"Enough," Marcos warned, slowing as we approached a stop sign. "We're going as a family to support you sister."

"But she plays soccer *all* the time, so why do I have to—"

"Seriously, Lola. We're done talking about it," I said.

Her nostrils flared as she huffed and slumped in her seat. I turned back around, giving Marcos a sideways smile and rolling my eyes. He chuckled and reached across the console, clasping my hand—a subtle celebration of the teamwork it took to raise three humans and a harsh reminder of what I was keeping from him.

Soon. You can tell him soon. You just need to figure things out. Make sure Christian really is sober, and Lucas is safe.

I flipped the radio on to drown out my thoughts during the drive. By the time we got to the field and I saw Marisol—high ponytail swinging behind her as she laughed with her team-mates—all I could think about was how proud I was of my baby girl. When she saw me standing near the sideline, she gave me a wave while I snapped grainy pictures with my cell.

"Mom, come on, you're being embarrassing," Lola whined.

"I'm coming, I'm coming," I said, taking one more photo before following her and Marcos up the bleachers.

As soon as we sat down, she began texting again.

"Lola, put that damn thing down for two seconds," Marcos demanded. "The game is starting."

She expelled a long, dramatic sigh and shoved the phone into her jeans pocket. "Fine. Which one is she?" she asked, staring blankly at the field.

"The one that looks like your sister," I deadpanned.

"The *best* one," Marcos added as the opposing team took possession after kickoff. "They practiced this the other day. Just watch."

A member of our team managed a steal, then kicked the ball to Marisol, who turned and sprinted toward the goal. Marcos and I stood, clapping hard and shouting her name as she faked out an opponent, dribbled around her, and launched a powerful shot past the goalie. Marcos slapped my raised hand in a high five as the crowd cheered.

"Oh my God!" Lola hopped up from her seat.

I was about to tell her to sit down and shut up, I didn't care if we were cramping her style, but she squealed and clapped with a level of enthusiasm I hadn't witnessed from her since she'd seen Chad Michael Murray at Taco Bell in 2006.

"She got a...whatever that's called. Go, Mari!"

Lola leaned into Marcos, and he pulled us both close as we watched the celebration on the field. I glanced over at her as Marcos kissed her head, then turned to me.

"Did you teach her that?" I asked, smiling up at him.

"Mostly her coach, but we may have run through it a few times in the backyard." He winked.

"You're incredible," I said, giving him a peck on his lips before we sat back down.

I threaded my fingers through his and took a deep breath. Any world where he wasn't my husband and the father of my kids seemed so wrong that I couldn't believe it had ever even been a possibility. But it had, and while Christian was once just a memory, the past month had made him a constant reminder of a life that could've been. The shame of having to tell Marcos about him, about how stupid I'd been for staying with him after I knew about his problem and all his lies...It was almost too great to bear.

But I have to tell him, I reminded myself. *And I will. Soon.*

"She's really good." Lola beamed over at us, her bright eyes tugging at my heart. "But, like, how many more do they have to score before it's over?"

Marcos and I dropped our heads.

"You can go to the mall later, Lola," he said as she dug for her cell.

"*If* you watch the rest of the game without looking at your phone," I added.

She groaned, pushing the device back in her pocket as I fixed my eyes on the field. I nudged Marcos and smiled.

Teamwork, indeed.

———

"Here's to two goals, *mi niña*." Marcos raised his glass, clinking it against mine and Marisol's.

I shot Lola a look, and she huffed before reluctantly lifting her drink to ours. "You guys are seriously so embarrassing."

Marisol tentatively glanced around the restaurant, a silent assessment as to whether or not she should find us as humiliating as her sister did. I had no doubt she would, once the teen angst set in, but I was hoping the peace between us would last for another six months or so.

"Oh, come on." I gently prodded Lola with my foot under the table.

She took a sip of her soda, then sat it down, turning to her left. "You did good out there, Mari. I'll celebrate by buying you something at the mall *if* I have time, since I probably won't get there till right before it closes."

Marisol's eyes went wide. "Oh, what are you going to get me?"

"Lola, it's one thirty. The mall closes at nine," Marcos said as I thanked the waiter, who placed our pizzas on pedestals in the middle of the table.

Marisol reached for a piece of the pepperoni. "Can you get me a new iPod? I want the Touch one."

My brow furrowed as I placed a veggie slice on my plate. "You have the Touch one."

She brushed away a couple of the stray strands of dark hair that had fallen from her ponytail. "Yeah, but it's, like, a year old."

My face crumpled. *Maybe I don't have another six months.*

"Oh, so, girls," I began, changing the subject. "I talked to your grandfather a few days ago. He and Gigi are coming over for Thanksgiving."

Marisol grinned, lavender braces on display. "Can I ask *them* for a new iPod?"

"No," Marcos answered, not missing a beat.

"But," Lola began, tearing a piece of crust from her pizza, "we usually go over there."

"Their kitchen remodel is taking longer than expected," I explained.

Lola cringed. "So, are they, like, bringing food, or…"

"Why does everyone always think I can't cook?" I asked, turning to Marcos and Marisol for backup.

They both looked at the ceiling.

"Well, just so you all know, I *can.*" I took a bite of pizza, then swiped my napkin across my mouth and winked. "But I figured it would be easier to call the caterer, so I went ahead and did that. They're squeezing us in."

Relief washed over Lola and Marisol's faces, and Marcos put his arm around my shoulder, pulling me closer as he chuckled.

The fact that I was even talking about having a happy holiday meal with my father and his wife still astounded me, even though it had become an unexpected tradition when Gina entered the picture twelve years prior. I hadn't been sure what to think of the woman who'd married my dad four months after they met, but when she called me that first Thanksgiving and asked if there was anything special she could make for Lucas and Lola, I was so shocked I could barely squeak out "Mac and cheese would be wonderful." Since we'd previously been subject to the pretentious whims of my dad's second wife, Kitty, I was expecting Gina to tell me she'd moved our dinner of salmon meunière to 9 p.m. because "that's when Europe eats."

Gina had quickly become the kids' *Gigi*, and with Marcos's mother in Miami and mine deciding that birthday cards and once-a-year phone calls were sufficient, I was grateful the kids had a grandmother close by. Especially one that made my father a little less serious and a little more *Grandpa*.

"And *Abuelita* is still coming for Christmas?" Marisol asked.

"*Sí*," Marcos said, then thanked the waiter for refilling his drink. "You know she can't be without her *niños*."

"And she won't let me near her when she's making the *lechón asado*, so you're safe," I added before turning to Marcos. "Unless you think I should ask again this year?"

He smiled at the girls. "Your mom tried to help *Abuela* make dinner for *Noche Buena* the year we got married."

"*¿Y Abuelita la echó de la cocina?*" Lola leaned into Marisol as they giggled.

"Well, she didn't *literally* kick me out of the kitchen. She just said something in Spanish to your dad, then told me I looked tired and should go rest before midnight mass." I grabbed another piece of pizza. "I got the hint."

"It's okay, Mom." Lola picked a pepperoni off the slice in front of her and popped it her mouth. "You're a badass businesswoman. You don't need to be a badass cook."

I paused midbite, then chewed slowly as I put my slice down and cocked my head. "Is that a...compliment?"

"I mean, duh," Lola said, retrieving her phone from her pocket. "But can we actually hurry up and eat? Jasmine keeps texting me."

My vision blurred with tears as she went back to complaining about how late it would be when we finally got home, and I smiled as Marcos squeezed my knee under the table.

I was still beaming when we pulled out of the restaurant parking lot, and he said something about not wanting to take the 405. I sighed a dreamy "Mm-hmm" as we passed by the Valley strip malls with their Froyo shops and nail salons, palms waving in the background against the bright blue sky.

My daughter doesn't think I'm a failure.

I glanced to my left, in awe of my husband, my kids, and the life that had found me, then rolled my head to the right. Marcos stopped at a light, and outside the window, the strip malls had been replaced by a dull gray building displaying a marquee with crooked plastic letters hanging above its chained doors.

My ears buzzed, a low hum that rose to a crescendo as time rewound, the sky darkened, and the sign sparked to life. In my mind, the doors opened, and a girl stumbled onto the sidewalk, black rivers flowing down her cheeks and over smudged red lips as she furiously rubbed her arms. My fingers curled around the handle beside me and my legs twitched, aching to open the door and run to her, even though I knew she wasn't really there. We'd scream and kick the cinder block building until it crumbled into nothing, then I'd take her home to her warm bed, where she'd be safe from him and his lies.

But I remained inside, a painful belief in self-retribution freezing me in place until the car began to glide through the intersection. I turned in my seat, looking back as her hand reached out before falling limply to her side. My fingertips brushed the window, their prints fading from the glass as she dropped her head and slowly disappeared.

I offered a silent apology, but she knew, just as I did, that it wasn't sincere.

She was stupid to have believed him anyway.

And she'd gotten exactly what she deserved.

27

NOVEMBER 1990

"I have no idea why you're not swinging from the fucking rafters right now." Christian's bandmate Jordan rolled his thumb along the lever of a yellow Bic, touching its flame to the tip of his cigarette. "That show was killer."

"I don't know, man." Christian took a sip of Coke and shrugged. "I mean, it was *fine*. I just think we need to be on another level at this point if we're gonna release an album in a few months and go out on the road."

"Dude, you gotta stop being so fucking hard on yourself." Jordan took a drag off his smoke and leaned against the small vanity behind him, one leg crossed over the other. "We got the record deal. We just played a fucking phenomenal show. We've got everything going for us, so let's just, you know...*enjoy* it."

The fluorescent bulbs in the backstage dressing room flickered, highlighting the worry lines on Christian's forehead. After a few months of lying low, their label had arranged a gig to start getting them in shape for their upcoming tour. The club was out in Reseda, a dull gray cinder block building that looked more like a giant holding cell than a music venue, but it was a popular joint, and they'd sold the place out.

I wasn't sure why Christian was so down on himself, other than that's just what he seemed to be lately. He was clearly bringing Jordan down, too, and while I didn't know the two other guys in the band particularly well, it became apparent that they wanted to celebrate instead of sulk when they'd gotten a ride to a house party in Tarzana right after finishing the set.

"The show was *great*." I nudged Christian, who sat beside me on the worn pleather couch. "We should celebrate. Maybe that party in Tar—"

"Babe," he began, raising his soda can. "I can't go to a party."

"Oh. Right. Yeah, I, uh...I'm kinda tired anyway."

I wasn't exactly thrilled about hanging out in a house that smelled like stale beer and cigarette smoke, either, but his tone sent heat climbing up my chest. I felt stupid for even suggesting it.

"You should go, Jordan," Christian insisted, nodding at him. "I've got my car, and Jimmy's driving all the gear back in the van right now. He'll unload it for us."

"Jimmy, the 'roadie'"—Jordan curled his fingers into air quotes—"who dropped my fucking '59 Les Paul earlier tonight? Awesome."

"Don't worry, man. He's got help with him, he's not gonna break anything. Besides, you're right. We *should* enjoy this. I'm just gonna enjoy it with my woman." Christian offered a smile and a wink.

I rolled my eyes. "There's that rock star energy."

Jordan laughed and ground his cigarette into the ashtray beside him. "All right, dude. Mike and Kurt gave me the address before they left, so I'll see if I can find it."

Christian raised his hand, which Jordan gripped in a see-you-later-brother handshake before heading toward the door, which led to the main floor of the club.

"You're not going out the back way?" Christian asked.

Jordan turned and smirked. "This girl in the front row eye-fucked the shit out of me during the show. I gotta see if she's still here before I go." He paused, then added sheepishly, "Sorry, Denise."

"Oh, no worries. I eye-fuck guys from the front row all the time." I winked as he gave me a thumbs-up and left the room.

"So," I began, leaning over to Christian. "Does the little woman get a say in what we're doing, or no?"

He rubbed my shoulder. "The little woman said she's tired. Does she need me to take her home?"

"Well, I'm not *tired,* tired," I explained, my eyes narrowing in confusion as his words sank in. "And does 'take her home' mean you're not coming with me?"

"Oh." Christian blinked. "I just thought...I thought you wanted to go to bed. Get some rest without me snoring or whatever it is you claim I do." He let out a tiny laugh.

I cocked my head. "Are you okay?"

"What? Of course, I'm okay." He cleared his throat and shook his head. "I mean, you know me, I always think every show could've been better, but it's fine."

My scalp tingled, the initial prick of worry before all my nerves activated. "You're being weird, Christian. You said you wanted to enjoy the rest of the night with me two seconds ago, and now you're talking about taking me home."

His brows angled in, and he gave me a look that told me he thought I was crazy. That *I* should think I was crazy. "Why are you acting like I did something wrong? You said you were tired."

My eyes flicked around the room. Had *I* actually done something wrong? Had my voice been too loud? My tone too irritated?

I took a deep breath in an attempt to sound calm. "Yeah, but I just...I've missed you. I don't want to go home without you."

"Okay, well, you don't have to," Christian said, as if he had been trying to do me a favor by offering me the option to sleep alone. "But I should, uh...I should go tell the owner thanks for having us."

"Oh. Yeah. Just let me get my purse, and I can—"

"You don't have to worry about coming with me, babe. I'll be right back." He stood and grabbed a zip-up hoodie from his bag in the corner, slipping it on while he walked to the door. "And then we'll go home...*together*."

He gave me a smile, and I matched it with a weak one. I slumped against the couch as soon as he left the room, chewing my thumbnail, trying to prevent my thoughts from forming a funnel cloud and spinning out of control. As soon as one was in danger of getting swept up in the rotation, I'd counter it.

Why did he want to drop you off at home?

I said I was tired.

Why did he sound annoyed?

He's stressed about finishing the album.

Why didn't he want you to come with him to talk to the owner?

He probably just wants to say thanks and leave as quickly as possible.

I flicked my wrist to see the time on my watch. Fifteen minutes had passed since I'd started playing the warped game of twenty questions with myself. Maybe the owner of the club was a talker, and Christian couldn't escape. Or maybe some overly enthusiastic fans had stopped him, and he needed a way to politely excuse himself.

Convinced he needed a rescue, I pushed myself off the couch, slung my purse over my shoulder, and headed for the door. The music had been turned down, the crowd had thinned, and as I surveyed the club, I didn't see anyone who looked like they owned it. But what did that person look like anyway? I imagined a short round dude in ill-fitting polyester pants, but what if said owner was actually a tall, thin blond woman in a fits-just-right spandex dress?

Oh God. Am I...jealous?

No. No, I don't get jealous of other women. At least not when it comes to men...do I?

"Hi," I said, shutting off my thoughts for a moment as I leaned on the bar in the back of the room. "Is the owner somewhere around here?"

The long-haired bartender regarded me with suspicion. "What's up?"

"Nothing. Just my boyfriend...He went to go talk to him—or her—and it's been a while, so I—"

"Who's your boyfriend?" The guy raised his chin, his lips curling into a suggestive smile.

"What?"

"Your boyfriend," he said, wiping down the counter. "Who is he?"

"Why does it matter?"

"'Cause I wanna know what kind of guys you're into."

I sighed. "Can we not do this?"

"I just wanna see if I have a shot," he said, grinning.

"Fine," I snapped. "My boyfriend is the guy who sang onstage tonight. And no, you don't."

"Oh shit," he said, laughing. "But, I mean, hey...I'm in a band, too."

"Great. Good for you. Now, have you seen him?"

He shook his head. "No, but I took a smoke break a little while ago. You can ask the other bartender when she gets back."

I pursed my lips in lieu of saying *Thanks for nothing*, and turned, wandering toward the backstage door. He was probably in the man's—or woman's—office, and I couldn't just poke around till I found it and barge in.

As I headed back to wait on the couch, a dim light in a small alcove to the left caught my eye.

The bathroom. He was probably just in the bathroom. He'd been talking to the owner and then stopped in the—

Bathroom.

The memory shocked my brain.

No. No, that's ridiculous. He's sober. He's totally sober. I would know if he wasn't. And this is a public place, anyone could walk in, so he wouldn't...would he?

My thoughts and my actions tugged in opposite directions as I entered the alcove and pressed my fingertips against a wooden door. They pulsed in time with my heartbeat as I held my breath and gave it a gentle push forward. A single bulb buzzed on the ceiling, the only light in the dingy room, and as I peeked around the door, I could see two vacant urinals bolted to the wall in front of me and a rusty sink to the right.

My shoulders relaxed, and I exhaled.

It's fine. Everything is fine. I should've trusted—

A cough echoed off the tiled walls, and I caught the door before it swung shut. I stepped inside, my eyes shifting to the left and traveling down a lone stall I hadn't seen before. The stall door was cracked, the open space at the bottom revealing a pair of black combat boots, angled in a strange position. A gray hoodie lay crumpled beside them.

I inhaled sharply, nails stabbing my palms as I squeezed both hands into fists. *Stay calm. You have to stay calm. Lots of guys wear boots. And hoodies. These could belong to anybody. Like, what guy* doesn't *own a pair of*—

"Christian?"

My eyes went wide, and I cupped my hand over my mouth. *Was that my voice?*

There was no answer. Just another cough.

I stepped forward, the click of my heels against the tile matching the drip of the faucet in the sink behind me. "Christian, is that you?"

I reached the door and pushed it open, causing a broken

lock to clang against the metal. My bottom lip quivered, and a tear slipped down my cheek.

Half of his body was on the toilet seat, while the other half slumped against the stall. His left arm dangled at his side, a black shoelace tied loosely around his bicep.

Christian lifted his gaze to me, his lids heavy. "Hey, baby. I just...needed to relax."

"What did..." I whispered as another tear rolled off my chin. "What did you do?"

"Just a little. It was just a little." He rubbed the side of his head along the stall as he spoke, his words slurred.

"No." I swallowed. "No, you told me you were done."

"I just needed...Why are you sad?"

My breath was the only sound I could hear as I stared at him, wondering how I'd been so stupid. The bag that fell out of his jeans, the clothes that didn't fit him anymore, the food he barely ate. He'd been lying to me for months. *For fucking months.*

I backed away from the stall. "I'm not doing this, Christian. I can't...I'm not doing this."

"Don't be sad, baby. Don't be..." He lifted his arm, reaching for me, but it immediately dropped back to his side. "It was just a little, I promise."

No. No promises. No more fucking promises.

I turned and pushed through the bathroom door, weaving around the small crowd of late-night stragglers to the middle of the club.

What do I do? What do I fucking do?

My chest heaved, eyes darting from wall to wall before landing on Jordan and a girl standing by the stage.

"Jordan," I called, rushing to his side, eyes burning from the millions of tears I wanted to cry. "You have to go get him. He's in the bathroom. You have to—"

"Is this your girlfriend?"

I whipped my head to the left to see the girl staring me down, head cocked and hands on her hips.

"What? No, she's...Hang on, hang on." Jordan took my arm and led me a few steps away from her. "What's going on?"

"Christian. He..." The words came out in ragged sobs. "He told me he wouldn't do it anymore."

Jordan placed his hands on my shoulders, pinning me with his eyes. "Denise, I need you calm down so I can—"

"No, I'm not doing this, I'm not fucking doing this." I broke free from his grip and shook my head. "Just get him home."

"Wait, where are you going, how are you gonna—"

I put my hand out as he stepped forward. "I'll...I'll call a cab. Just please take care of him. Please."

"Okay," he said, sadness coating his voice. "Okay."

I turned, nearly tripping over my feet as I hurried to the bar.

"Do you..." I gripped the wooden counter, steadying myself before wiping my palms across my cheeks. "Do you have a phone I can use?"

The long-haired bartender's brow creased. "You okay?"

"I need to call a cab."

"Uh, yeah," he said, studying my face. "I can call one for you, but are you—"

"I'll be outside," I called over my shoulder as wobbly legs carried me toward the exit.

I stumbled out the double doors, sinking into a shadow and leaning against the cold gray cinder block of the building. Hot tears streaked my face as passersby turned glassy and fluid, each one stopping in front of me, their judging eyes glowing yellow in the streetlights.

This is what you get, Denise, they said in my father's voice before floating down the sidewalk. *This is what you get for feeling.*

28

NOVEMBER 1990

"I'm so sorry, babe," Eva said softly through the phone. "I just wish you would've told me what was going on."

"I guess I knew deep down it wouldn't last, so why bother." I tugged at the covers on my bed, tucking them under my chin. "You've gone through enough over the past couple years, and things are good for you now. I wasn't going to let you miss one second of that happiness whining about this...*drama*."

She sighed. "Okay, first of all, I've never heard you whine once in the entire time I've known you. And second, it doesn't matter what's going on in my life, *that's what I'm here for*."

"I know. But it's..." I swallowed the lump in my throat. "It's not a big deal."

There was a beat of silence before she spoke. "I'm not trying to tell you how to feel, Denise. But I want you to know, it's okay if it is."

"I just think of this as proof that relationships aren't for me," I said, skating around the opportunity to tell her my whole fucking world had fallen apart. "Like, the first one I'm in is with a heroin addict. I think that's a sign." I managed a weak laugh as a tear rolled from the corner of my eye.

"Are you sure you don't want me to come out there?" she asked.

I shook my head, the pillow mussing my hair. "No, I'm fine. Really. And you didn't call to hear about all this. You *called* to invite me to Chicago for New Year's Eve."

"Yes!" she said, her voice rising to a more cheerful octave. "I'm so excited for you to meet Aaron. He's gorgeous, he's smart, he's successful, he's...*everything*. I feel so lucky, Denise."

I scoffed, and Eva gasped.

"Oh God," she said. "I'm going on and on about him when you just...I'm sorry."

"That's not what I meant."

She hesitated. "Then what did you mean?"

"I meant *he's* the lucky one, Eva. *He* is. And don't you forget it."

"All right, all right, whatever," she sang, dismissing me. "But I'm still excited for you to meet him."

"Me too," I said, a tiny smile breaking through the sadness. "I gotta go, but we'll talk soon, okay?"

"I love you. And call me whenever you need me. Even if you aren't sure if you need me, but you think you might. Okay?"

"Love you, babe. And I will." I hung up the phone and curled into a tight ball as a shaky breath fluttered from my lungs.

What was wrong with me? What the hell was wrong with me that I couldn't tell my best friend the truth? That my heart hurt, my stomach hurt, my head hurt, *everything* fucking hurt because Christian had found all the parts of me I'd killed off long ago and brought them back to life—only to abandon them, wounded and bloody and dying an even more painful death than the one before. And despite what he'd done, there was an ache of guilt that gnawed at that hurt. Guilt about not doing more to help him. About not seeing all the signs I should have. About leaving him in that club like I'd never loved him at all. Like I didn't still love him now.

It had been a week since that night in Reseda. I'd walked to the door at least five times before the cab arrived, but when it finally did, I got in and didn't look back. I rested my head against the cold glass window and answered the driver's questions with as few words as possible until I stopped responding altogether. As soon as we arrived at my apartment, the entire contents of my purse spilled onto the floorboard, sending me into hysterics. I fumbled around in the dark until I found my wallet and keys, leaving lipstick and gum and everything else behind as I scrambled out of the car.

I'd spent Monday through Wednesday lumbering into work like a zombie, Marcos offering to take me to get coffee or lunch each day. Anything to lift me out of the mood which I dismissed as "stupid girl stuff." On Thursday, I'd dragged myself to my father's house for a miserable Thanksgiving dinner, then dragged myself home and collapsed back onto my bed, the messages Christian had left on my machine begging for forgiveness playing in my head like they had been all week. One minute, I'd look at the phone and feel terrible about leaving him at the club. The next, I'd want to scream at him until my throat was as raw as the rest of me. At some point, I decided it was for the best to delete them without even listening. He'd entered my life in a fragile, unguarded moment, and now I needed to rebuild the walls that had been torn down.

I rubbed my eyes and looked at the clock on my nightstand. How was it already two thirty in the afternoon? I'd slept through Saturday morning step class, hadn't showered, hadn't eaten. I had to snap out of it. Maybe get some food in my stomach. Not that I had any. I hadn't gone to the grocery store or anywhere after leaving the office because it took all the energy I had just to drive home. Suits hanging at the dry cleaners, prescriptions waiting at the pharmacy, friends expecting me at our weekly happy hour—all ignored for the comfort of my bed.

I sighed and pushed myself off the mattress, hoping that water and whatever I could find that wasn't molding in the refrigerator would help. The apartment was as gray as the sky, as gray as I felt. *If the sun comes out, I'll go for a walk,* I thought, but knew I didn't mean it. I trudged into the kitchen, pulling a glass out of one of the cabinets when a knock on the door caused it to slip from my hand and crash to the floor.

"Shit," I hissed, tears building behind my eyes once again as broken shards scattered across the porcelain tile.

There was another knock, this one louder, and I groaned. I didn't need Jesus, I didn't want to buy anything, and I wasn't signing any petitions. I didn't even feel like talking to Beau.

"Fuck off," I muttered as I made my way to the closet in the hall to grab a broom.

"Denise!"

I gasped at the sound of Christian's voice.

"Denise, please open the door."

My body tingled, a brief, unconscious feeling of relief (that he'd finally come for me, that we'd finally be back together again?) before my mind intervened.

No. Stay here. Go to your room. Go anywhere in this apartment, but do not answer the door.

I flattened my back against the wall and held my breath as the door rattled again.

"I know you're home, your car is outside, and I...Just give me five minutes. Five minutes."

If I stay quiet, he'll leave.

If I just stay quiet, he'll leave.

I squeezed my eyes shut and balled my hands into fists.

But how many times will he come back?

"Go away, Christian," I said, loud enough for him to hear.

"I'm done with that shit, baby. I promise. Please let me in so I can talk to you."

My heart squeezed. *Promise, promise, promise.*

"I love you, Denise." The words came out cracked, strained. "You know I love you. I'll do anything."

My eyes snapped open at the sound of another voice. *Beau.* He'd been out of town, and I hadn't told him Christian and I had broken up.

"Denise? Honey?" Beau called, knocking on the door. "You know I love you, but I cannot have this heterosexual drama happening when I'm trying to get my beauty sleep before the show tonight. Tired hag in drag is not what people pay to see."

Fuck.

"Denise." He knocked again. "Sweetie, are you okay? Do I need to call the boys in blue to help us out here?"

Fuck, fuck, fuck, fuck, fuck.

I shoved my hands in my hair, pressing them into my head until my arms shook. *Of course, that's where Beau's mind would go.* I'd told him that Christian had a *problem* in the past, and he wanted to protect me. But I didn't need the police at the apartment. I was embarrassed that I'd let Christian into my life to begin with, and I sure as hell didn't need anyone watching as I tried to get him out of it for good.

"Goddammit." I gritted my teeth as I pushed myself off the wall and walked down the hall to open the door.

Christian's eyes widened, and I quickly shifted mine to Beau.

"Sorry," I said. "No need to call the cops."

Beau lifted his chin and pursed his lips as he examined me, my face red and blotchy, my hair wild and tangled. A braless disaster in a tank top and sweats.

I pushed down one bunched-up pants leg with my opposite foot. "Really, it's fine. We just had a...disagreement. But I'm over it now."

Beau stared at me, transmitting a telepathic message. *I remember what you told me about his little habit. Blink twice if you're not okay.*

I met his gaze. *It's fine. I'm fine.*

Beau relented. "Mm-hmm. If you say so."

He turned and assessed Christian in his torn jeans, worn Converse, and faded black T-shirt before offering up a disapproving *humph* and sweeping back to his apartment, silk kimono robe flowing behind him.

I leaned against the doorframe, crossing my arms over my chest before tilting my head up to look at Christian. "What the fuck do you want?"

"I had to see you. To talk to you. You won't answer my calls, you won't call me back, so I..." His forearms flexed as he gripped the top of his head. "I just can't stand being without you, Denise. I'm going fucking crazy."

"Maybe you should've thought about that before you decided to shoot up in a goddamn bathroom in the Valley."

"I know it was stupid. I know *I* was stupid. But I swear, I haven't used since then. I'm done for good this time. Just let me—"

"Leave, Christian."

"Can I...can I just explain?"

"There's nothing to explain."

"But there is, and I need to..." He paused as my upstairs neighbor and her dog trotted up the walkway to the quadruplex. "Can I come in? Please?"

I glared at him and inhaled sharply before stepping back and allowing him to pass. I shut the door and leaned against it, recrossing my arms. "So what is it? What do you want to explain?"

He faced me, hands out to his sides, palms facing up. The same pose he'd struck when he showed up after I found him at his house, barely coherent and surrounded by vomit. "I wanted to say I'm sorry. And that I'll do anything to make it up to you."

I rolled my eyes and pushed off the door, poised to open it. "That's not an explanation, Christian."

"No, wait."

I turned around, my hand falling from the knob. "What?"

"The explanation is, I'm a fucking addict," he said, scrubbing his hands over his face. "Drugs are what I turn to when things get tough, and I've been so scared of fucking this whole thing up—the album, the tour...*you and me*—that I didn't know what else to do."

I huffed. "Then you should've talked to me. But you chose to lie instead and say you were going to meetings and you had a sponsor and everything was *fine*."

"I...I didn't think it would get as bad as it did before. I thought I could just do it to relax, keep it under control, and you wouldn't have to know. I wouldn't have to upset you or make you worry. But I know I was lying to myself." He swallowed. "And you."

My nostrils flared as I sucked in a breath.

"But I'm starting treatment next week," he continued. "It's outpatient, so I can still finish the album, but it's five days a week and—"

"No," I said, tightening my jaw. " I don't believe you. You lied to me for months, Christian. *For months.*"

"I can give you the name of the place. You can call them. Or they can call you." His eyes pleaded with me.

I opened my mouth to speak, but closed it, surprised by his offer. *He can't possibly mean that, can he? Will he really give me names and places and—*

No. This is just another lie.

"Stop. Just stop with whatever shit you're making up. Because you know and *I* know, you care about getting high more than me. More than *us*. If you didn't, you would've talked to me and you would've told me what you were going through. But you didn't, so—"

"Because I was fucking terrified of you walking out on me, Denise!" His chest heaved, and his eyes glossed over. "That night, after you found me at the house, you said you weren't going to go through that again, that you *wouldn't* go through that again. And I...I thought if I told you I was struggling, it would all be over."

I winced, covering my mouth with my hand. *No. No, I didn't mean it like that.*

I'd said those things, yes, but I hadn't meant I didn't want him to talk to me, to be honest with me, to feel like he couldn't tell me what he was going through.

"You've got your whole fucking life together. You've got everything going for you," he continued. "You don't *need* anyone, so the best I could hope for is that you wanted me. And why would you *want* a fucking junkie?"

I steadied myself against the door, his voice and the pain inside it nearly powerful enough to send me crashing to the floor.

I did need you.

I do need you.

How can you not see that?

"I could've helped you. I *would've* helped you."

"I just..." He choked on his words. "I didn't want you to leave me. So I hid it. And I lied. And I wish I hadn't, but I was so fucking scared of losing you."

"I'm sorry I left," I said before I could stop myself.

His breath shuddered as he rubbed his eyes with the heels of his palms. "What...what do you mean?"

"The club. I should've stayed and made sure you were okay, but Jordan was there, so I...I left."

"It's okay."

I dropped my head, watching as one tear, then another, splattered on the wood floor.

"You don't need to apologize." He stepped toward me, and my muscles tensed.

"I know, I just..."

Say it. Say what you want to say, what you need to say. Tell him why it hurts so much. Tell him why it's always hurt so much.

"I just wanted you to choose me, Christian," I blurted out as my head snapped up. "For once in my fucking life, I wanted someone to choose me over everything else. But my own parents couldn't even do that because I've never been good enough, so I don't know why I expected you to."

"Baby, I—"

"And I don't know, maybe I should've done more to make *you* believe you were good enough for *me*, that I would do whatever I needed to do to help you. But we're...we're too fucked up, Christian." I took a ragged breath. "Both of us are, and this can't...We can't do this."

He stepped forward again, but I didn't protest.

"I *do* choose you," he said. "I'm choosing you right now, and I will choose you over and over again."

I had been waiting my entire life to hear those words. And I wanted to believe them. I wanted to believe them so fucking badly.

"I love you, Denise." He moved close enough to tip my chin up and run his thumb along my bottom lip. "More than anything in the world."

My shoulders relaxed, and I saw myself floating in his eyes, drifting slowly downward until I landed in their soft, gray feathers. "Please don't make me regret this," I whispered before my lids closed and my mouth met his.

I pressed against him as he threaded his fingers through my hair, my body humming in a way that made me feel like I'd never kissed him before. Like he was at my apartment for the very first time, that very first night, and I was unaware of what was to come. Like the days before I spent my time worrying whether he was okay, or he was high, or he was thinking about getting high. So I fell into him, letting him catch me while I forgot about everything except how no one in my whole fucking world had ever been him, and no one ever would be.

I grasped the bottom of his T-shirt, hands sliding along his warm skin, as he raised his arms so I could lift it off. He turned, guiding me backward down the hall to the bedroom, where he hooked his fingers around the waist of my sweatpants, pushing them and my underwear off my hips. I ripped my tank top over my head, and he kicked his shoes off, stepping out of his jeans before we fell onto the bed, our lips parting with sighs of relief as he pushed into me, slowly rocking his hips against mine.

When he rose to his knees, he brought my ankle to his shoulder and slid his fingers between us. I moaned, and he gripped my waist with his other hand just before my entire body tensed. I closed my eyes and pressed into him, body shaking, hands grasping the sheets so hard I thought I might tear them off the bed.

He gently guided my leg down, then leaned forward. "You are so fucking beautiful."

I sighed, my eyes half open, head swirling, chest heaving. He brushed his lips against mine, and my hands trailed down his back, bringing him closer.

I never want this to end. I never want this to—

Wait.

No. No, no, no.

Panic surged through me, and my eyes went wide.

My pills. They'd fallen out of my purse in the cab, and I hadn't picked up the new prescription, and I hadn't taken one in—

"Christian, I need you to—"

"Fuck, you feel so good," he murmured against my neck.

"Christian, you have to pull out, I—"

"*Fuuuck.*" He pressed himself deep inside and groaned before releasing his weight onto me.

I took a deep breath, then pushed all the air from my lungs. *It's fine. It's totally fine. I've had sex hundreds of times and never gotten pregnant.*

He lifted his chest and smoothed my hair from my face. "I love you so fucking much."

Everything is going to be fine.

I smiled softly as his eyes melted my fear. "I love you, too," I said, twirling the dark waves that hung over his shoulders between my fingers.

"And you're not leaving?" he asked.

"I'm not leaving." I placed my hand on his cheek. "Are you?"

"Never," he said. "It's you and me, remember?"

We lay in bed for the next few hours, his voice filled with hope as he told me about the outpatient program. Afterward, we ordered food and watched TV on the couch, my eyes eventually getting so heavy from the week of restless sleep that he insisted on carrying me back to the bedroom—even though I laughed and told him that was stupid. Then I fell asleep in his arms, wishing I could stay there forever, knowing he was safe and so was my heart.

29

DECEMBER 1990

"Look, Denise," Beau began, planting his hands on his hips. "I know you're feeling crazy right now, and you have every reason in the world. But I'm not going to get another one. It's embarrassing for the clerk to think I have sex with women, and there's no way you peed on"—he counted the white sticks scattered on my bathroom counter—"*seven* of these the wrong way."

"Fuck me." I plopped down on the lid of the toilet and shook my head. I knew that Beau buying four more tests wasn't going to change the results of the first three I'd taken, but still, I'd hoped for a miracle.

He perched on the edge of the tub and patted my knee. "It's gonna be okay, hon. I'm honestly more concerned that you were able to pee that much."

My mind was too scattered for his joke to register, and I dropped my head into my hands. "I mean, clearly, it's going to be okay because I'm not going to have it, I think, but...I just can't believe this happened."

"You...*think*?"

"I think what?"

"You said 'I'm not going to have it, *I think.*'"

I raised my head. "I did?"

He nodded. "Are you considering—"

"What? No. I...I don't even know what I'm saying right now, okay? I just found out I'm *pregnant*, Beau. Why are you expecting me to make sense?"

There had been a moment after the first test when a strange sense of calm settled over me. I'd expected to cry and scream and crumple into a heap on the floor, but as I stared at the double lines, I considered a future different from any one I'd ever imagined. The idea of Christian and I as parents seemed crazy, but that first weekend we'd spent together, he told me he thought having kids one day could be a way to change things, to show them all the love he'd never received. I had already changed so much with him in my life that I couldn't help but wonder if this could be something just as unexpected and wonderful.

No. He doesn't need this right now.

Maybe when he had a few more years of sobriety under his belt. Once he got to enjoy all that awaited him and the band. It wasn't the right time for any added pressures. It wasn't the right time at all.

Beau pursed his lips. "So, I'm sure that was some sort of hormone yelling at me just now, but since I stood in line at the Sav-on tonight, double-fisting Clearblue Easys for you, let's adjust the attitude, mm'kay?"

I groaned. "Oh God, I'm sorry. I just...I feel like such an idiot."

"You're not an idiot, Denise," he said, his tone softening.

"Do you think *maybe* the tests are wrong? Like...*maybe*?"

Beau sighed and gave me a sad smile. "I have no idea, sweetie. Just call your doctor tomorrow and make an appointment. Then you'll know for sure."

Yes. A plan. I need a plan.

"Right." I nodded and tapped my foot against the tile as my mind sprang into action. "I doubt I can get in before I leave for Chicago because Christmas is next week, and my flight is on the twenty-ninth, but yeah...I'll do that. I'll call her and go in when I get back."

His smile turned encouraging. "Good. That sounds good. Is Christian going with you to Chicago?"

"No, he's so busy with the album coming out in February that he's gonna stay here. I, uh...I could go ahead and tell him, though, I guess?" I paused. "I mean, I *should* tell him...right?"

For some reason, I thought Beau might say no, and it could be our little secret forever and always. Instead, he looked at me like I had seven heads. One for each pregnancy test.

"Okay, I know I should," I continued, my leg bobbing in time with my head. "He's just got so much going on, but it's not like we have some major decision to make. I'm going to tell him, and then I'm gonna go and get...un-pregnant." I let out a weak laugh.

"When are you seeing him next?" Beau asked.

"No real plans till Christmas Day after brunch with my dad and Kitty," I told him. "He said he'd come with me if I wanted, but I'm not going to subject him to that. So, yeah, I'll make sure to see him tomorrow, and I'll just get it over with, like, *It's fine, I'm taking care of it, you don't need to worry about it at all.* And then I'll go to Chicago and have fun and forget about it." I stopped, my body forcing me to take a breath. "Shit, I have to tell Eva, but I don't want to ruin her New Year's, of course, so maybe I'll—"

"Denise. Honey. Slow down." His voice was gentle but firm as he squeezed my hand. "This isn't your *fault*, okay? It's not anything you need to apologize for or protect him or *anyone* from."

I wished I could tell Beau the truth—about the drugs, about the club, about the rehab—because then he'd understand that

I *did* have to protect Christian. That I had to let Christian know his well-being was the most important thing, and it didn't need to be derailed by...*this*. He clearly hadn't heard me ask him to pull out that night, and with his sobriety as fragile as it was, I didn't mention it again—just casually told him that we needed to use condoms for a little while because the drugstore had screwed up my pills.

But right now, it was too much to tell Beau about everything that had happened. He'd warn me to be careful, to consider what I was doing...all the thoughts I'd already quieted in my own mind because I loved Christian, and he loved me, and that was all that mattered.

I chewed my thumbnail, my eyes continuing to dart around the room. "I know. He's just got so much on his plate with the album. The last thing he needs is more stress."

"Sweetie, this isn't you stressing him out. This is *life*. This is a *relationship*. This is the two of you leaning on each other, handling shit *together*."

I knew that was how things were supposed to work, but Christian had been strong for me when I doubted myself. When I told him how my parents had hurt me, how I never thought I was good enough to love. *I* had to be the strong one right now. I'd told him I would support him, I would listen, I would be there for him, and he'd promised he'd do the work to stay clean. Showing up at his house blubbering about being pregnant wouldn't exactly be holding up my end of the bargain, unless...Was it possible that he'd actually be...*happy*?

No. There was no way. Surely, he'd agree with me, that there was too much going on, too much he and I both had yet to do.

"You're right," I told Beau to appease him. "I'm just used to handling my own shit, I guess."

He tilted his head. "Everything's okay with you and him, right?"

Everything's fine, just tell him it's all fine. Because it is. And it needs to stay that way.

"Oh, yeah. Things are good. Really good." I let my gaze meet his. "Why would you...Do they not seem good?"

"You just sound...tense."

I opened my mouth to protest.

"Don't get me wrong. I know *this*"—he pointed to the counter—"is a lot to process, but besides that. You sound tense about you and him. I know y'all had that fight and—"

"No, everything's great. But I should, um..." *Change the subject, change the subject.* "I should really try to get some sleep. Making it through work tomorrow is gonna be tough enough as it is."

"Okay," Beau said, rising from the edge of the tub. "But I'll stay if you want me to, and...*ooh*, we could watch *Xanadu*." He pressed his hands to his heart and sighed a dreamy sigh. "Olivia Newton-John on roller skates cures all, sister."

I smiled. "Yes, she does. And you're sweet, but I'll be fine."

"All right, then. Hug, hug, hug," he commanded, waving me into his arms.

I stood and leaned into him as he wrapped me up and kissed the top of my head.

"You know I'll always buy you pregnancy tests, Dee. Even if I bitch about it the entire time."

I laughed against his chest. "I know you will. But I don't plan on making this a habit. I'm not exactly the motherly type."

"Oh, I don't know about that," he said, smoothing my hair. "I think one of these days, you just might surprise yourself."

———

I left work early, trying to beat traffic on the way to Christian's. Twinkling white lights lined the perimeters of buildings and wrapped around the trunks of palm trees, an occasional colored strand thrown in by someone who was feeling rebellious. A glowing plastic Santa with a dented face greeted me when I pulled up to his house, and I chuckled at his attempt to be festive. Finally, something that made me laugh.

After Beau had left the night before, I settled into the couch with the television on, assuming I wouldn't be able to sleep with all the thoughts spinning in my brain. But the cells inside me that were multiplying (or dividing or performing whatever mathematical equations were necessary to create a human) eventually consumed all the energy normally reserved for spiraling, and I woke up to the sun slicing through the curtains, warming my skin.

With Christmas the next week, work was slow, and I'd caught myself drifting off, elbow planted on my desk, chin in my hand, more than a couple times. It was as if once the source of my exhaustion—a bone-level fatigue like I'd never felt before in my life—had been confirmed, my body decided to stop fighting. The idea that I was coming down with a cold or the flu had been tossed in the garbage along with the pregnancy tests.

I cut the engine to my car and took a deep breath, holding it for a count of three before blowing it slowly through my lips. It was an attempt to clear my mind, calm my nerves, but I instantly imagined myself in a hospital, feet in stirrups, Christian telling me to breathe as he wiped sweat from my brow. *Just one more push*, the doctor said. Christian squeezed my hand, and I screamed, and all of a sudden, there was a tiny human in my arms. It was crying, and Christian was crying, and I was crying because the thing I thought I never wanted was now the thing I never wanted to let go.

Hormones, I told myself, shaking my head. *It's just the hormones talking.*

I couldn't be a mother. Not a good one anyway. Sure, I'd probably do better than my own had, but that bar was so low it was on the damn ground. Besides, I'd already made room in my life for one other person with Christian. A *kid* was a whole different ball game.

Before I met him, my plan consisted of eventually taking over my dad's company and possibly marrying some man who was more interested in how much money he made than me. He'd serve his purpose by making a reliable date to events and galas and all the places for industry hobnobbing, as well as fending off all the probing questions I'd get if I never married. We'd go to Europe on vacation once a year where we'd have sex twice, but each time I'd have to pretend I was a girl he'd hired, which sounded fun but would end up being boring just like him. He'd *actually* hire girls the rest of the time, for which I'd be grateful, and I'd find someone (or two or three) more exciting than him. And it would be okay because it was all understood, along with the agreement that there would never be any children.

But the fact that I was sitting in my car in Santa Monica, staring at a plastic Santa with a squashed smile, was proof that plans changed. Was it possible they could change even more? Could there be Christmases with kids bouncing on the bed, begging Christian and me to wake up so they could see what had been left under the tree? I'd done that once to my parents when I was four, and my mother warned me to go back to bed or Santa would never bring me presents ever again. I supposed my dad had felt at least a small pang of guilt when I'd started crying, because he asked me to give him fifteen minutes, after which he poured himself a cup of coffee and massaged his forehead the entire time I unwrapped my gifts.

But Christian and I...we could be different. Of course, my head might hurt from one too many martinis on Christmas Eve, but I'd pop a couple Tylenol and power through, smiling like I was fresh as a daisy because I'd been given the chance to be the mother I'd always wanted but never had. As much as I'd fought him in the beginning, Christian had shown me that there were possibilities. That I was capable of loving and being loved. The fear that I'd end up just like *her* still lingered, though, like cobwebs in the corner of the room. Ones I could never quite reach to sweep away.

But if...just *if*, by some chance a smile replaced the shock on his face after I told him the news, and we talked and decided together that we could somehow make this work...

No, it's not the right time. He'll tell me that it's my decision because he loves me, but no. It's my job to take care of this.

I took one final deep breath and stepped onto the concrete. It was five, earlier than I'd expected to arrive, and the blue sky had darkened to a steely hue streaked with orange as the sun set. I'd told him I might come over, depending on how a work project was going, which was really just a way of allowing for the possibility of a freak-out on my part. But as I stood in front of the door, poised to ring the bell, I reminded myself that I was twenty-six—almost twenty-seven—years old, and this was how grown-ups solved their problems.

Is this a problem, though?

Yes. Yes, it is. And I'm going to solve it. Right now.

I pushed the button and drummed my fingers against the side of my thigh, telling myself to calm down as I glanced back at his car in the driveway to make sure I hadn't imagined parking beside it. He'd told me his outpatient rehab ended at three every day, so I was sure he was home, but what if...

No. Stop. There is no scenario other than he didn't hear the door.

I pressed the button again, and there was a clatter, then footsteps. My pulse slowed.

See, no reason to be worried. No reason at—

"What time is it?" Christian stood in front of me wearing a pair of long shorts and an unbuttoned flannel, no T-shirt underneath.

I blinked, wondering if I'd missed a sentence or two. "Uh... hi?"

"I just...I was, um..." He looked at me, eyes flicking back and forth, before he turned around and walked through the foyer to the kitchen, leaving me to trail behind. "I was looking for something, and I can't..."

Utensils clanged against one another as he rummaged through an open drawer, not bothering to shut it as he moved on to the next.

"Christian, what are you..." I picked up a large metal spoon, a spatula, and several forks he'd discarded. "What are you doing?"

He pulled another drawer out and off its tracks, turning it upside down. I leapt back as the contents plummeted to the floor, coins and pens scattering across the tile.

"Jesus. What are you looking for?"

He continued his search in silence.

"Hey. What's going on? Why won't you answer me?" I tossed the utensils on the counter and followed him to the living room.

"I can't find my..." He snaked his hands between the cushions and the frame of the couch. "Pills. That they gave me."

I nodded. That made sense. The rehab clinic had probably given him a prescription, something to help with anxiety and sleep.

"Okay," I said, stepping closer. "What do they look like, were they in a—"

"No!" He put his hand out to stop me. I startled, and he lowered his voice. "I, uh...I know what they look like. I can find them."

"Baby, I..." I took a step toward him. "You're freaking me out right now. I just want to help."

He ignored me, pulling the cushions from the couch, flinging them across the coffee table. A glass tipped over, and water dripped onto the floor. His eyes were wild with panic, his breathing quick and heavy as the last cushion came off, and he surveyed the room.

I swallowed. *Just ask. Just ask what you want to know.*

"Are you...looking for drugs?"

"What?" He kicked a pillow out of his way as he headed for the chair across the room to scavenge it as well. "I told you. It's medicine. The, uh...the people...at the place...they gave me medicine."

"Then I'm sure we can call the clinic and—"

"You should go, Denise. Just go and, uh...come back later, okay?" He paced the floor in front of me, frantic, as if trying to grab onto thoughts that were firing too rapidly in his brain. "You can come back later. After I find it."

I steepled my hands in front of my mouth. "Look, if you just stop for one second and tell me what's going on...If you just tell me the truth, I can—"

He shoved the chair with his foot, nearly tipping it backward. "You think I'm lying to you?"

My eyes went wide, and I pulled in a shaky breath. "No, I..." *What do I say, what do I say?* "I just think you need your... medicine, and I want to help you, so—"

"I don't want your goddamn help!" He turned, hair swinging in front of his face, chest heaving.

I steeled myself. I was going to help him. I was going to get him through this. Get *us* through this. "Okay, but can you please calm down so we can—"

"Calm down? Are you fucking kidding me?" He shook his head. "You don't know, Denise. You don't have *any* fucking idea what this is like."

I nodded, trying to keep my voice even. "But I can call the doctor. I can call the clinic. Their number is in my purse, I just need to go get it from the car."

He lunged in front of me, blocking the way to the door. "Don't call them."

"What the—" I stepped to my right to walk around him. "Christian, you need to move so I can go get the num—"

He grabbed my wrist, and I looked down as his fingers pressed against my bones so hard they ached.

"What are you—"

"You're not calling them because they won't know who the fuck I am."

"*What?*" The word echoed in my brain. I wasn't sure I'd said it out loud until he answered me.

"You heard me," he spat. "I never fucking went."

No. No, he's just saying that so I won't call, but surely he—

"I was lying to you, Denise. And guess fucking what? I lie to you *all the time*. Like right now. Because you know what I'm really looking for? Heroin. Did you hear that? Fucking *heroin*." He enunciated each syllable of the last word as he glared at me, the sweat on his palm slick against my skin as he squeezed tighter.

My pulse pounded in my neck. There had to be something I could do. I assumed his bandmates weren't at home, otherwise they would have appeared when they heard the commotion. I did have the number for the clinic, and I'd called when he'd first given it to me, only to hang up on the person who answered because I wanted to prove to myself that I trusted him. But I could call them again. Even if it was true that he'd never been there, the clinic was real, it existed, and surely someone there could tell me what to do.

"I, um...I'm going to get someone who can help you. So let go of me, and we'll figure this out togeth—"

"I'm not stopping, okay?" he said through gritted teeth. "Do you understand me? I tried, and *I can't stop*."

"But you can." My eyes begged him to believe me. "I know you can."

"No." His nostrils flared as he shook his head. "*This* is what happens when I don't have it. *This* is why I need it. And I'm done. I'm so fucking done, so just...just go."

My body caved in, and I slumped forward as if I'd been kicked in the stomach. "What do you...what do you mean you're done?"

"I mean, *we're* done. So fucking leave. It's over."

"Christian, please."

He released my wrist and squeezed his hands into fists so tight his arms shook. "Jesus fucking Christ, what do I have to do to make you leave me the fuck alone?"

Think. Think. Just calm down and think. He needs to understand he's making a mistake. Then he'll realize he's not okay, he'll believe I want to help him, and all of this will be over.

I massaged my wrist, hands trembling as I tried to figure out what to do. I was scared for him and scared for me—desperate to convince us both that we were safe, that we could sit down and talk and make things right. I needed him to come back to me, to snap out of the craziness, the pure fucking insanity happening in front of me. I needed to do something, say something that would make him come to his senses.

"I'm pregnant."

His eyes met mine, and, for a moment, I thought I saw *him* again. The man who'd once told me I was the most beautiful woman he'd ever seen. The man who'd said I was amazing and I was perfect.

"Yeah, well, I don't *fucking care*, Denise."

No. No, he doesn't mean that. He doesn't know what he's saying.

But as he laughed sharply, I realized that *I* was the one making the mistake. The mistake of thinking I could save him now, or ever.

Part of me wanted to punch him and kick him and scream over and over again *How could you do this to me, how could you do this to me?* until he realized he hadn't meant any of what he'd said. The other part wanted to fall to the floor and cry, asking him to forgive me for whatever I'd done, for whoever I was, for whatever was wrong with me. But instead, I whispered, "I don't know if I'm keeping it," then cupped my hand over my mouth, staring past him as my body shook with sobs I refused to set free.

"Did you not fucking hear me? I don't fucking care what you do because I don't want anything to fucking do with it *or* you. Now get the *fuck* out!"

He swept his arm forward, sending the lamp on the table beside him crashing to the floor. I flinched, my eyes fixed on the broken pieces of clay as the bulb flickered out, before a cold shot of adrenaline catapulted me to the door.

Tears blinded me as I pulled away from his house and into the first parking lot I found. The neon signs in the window promised bargains on cigarettes and liquor, while a crooked red and green *Merry Christmas* hung on the door. Images of the holiday party where my mother told me I was embarrassing her blinked along with it. I rested my forehead on the steering wheel, inhaling the memory of tobacco, gin, and peppermint as tears wet my cheeks.

"What is *wrong* with you, Denise?" she'd hissed before I ran upstairs to think about the question, certain there was correction, a fix I could make so she'd love me.

But sitting in that parking lot, eleven years later, I knew there was nothing I could do to make myself right. That just like my mother, and just like my father, there would always be something more important than me, something that held Christian's attention more than I ever could, because I wasn't enough.

And I never fucking would be.

30

FEBRUARY 1991

"Happy Valentine's Day," Marcos said as he placed a paper bag and cup holder on my desk.

I looked up from my computer and wrinkled my brow. "What's this?"

"Lunch. Cheeseburgers and fries, to be exact."

I peeked inside, the smell of fried grease instantly soothing my soul. "Oh my God. You went to Tommy's."

"It's your favorite, right?" He slid a chair up to the desk and sat down across from me.

He always remembered my favorites.

I melted into my seat with a grateful sigh and raised my eyes to him. "You didn't have to do this."

He pulled a wrapped burger and box of fries from the bag, placing them in front of me before retrieving his own food. "It's fine. I wanted to."

"Well, since you were so sweet to go get this, I'll eat it." I smirked. "Even though you know Valentine's Day is stupid."

Extra stupid this year, I thought.

"Right. Of course it is." Marcos made little effort to keep a

259

straight face as he unbuttoned, then rolled up the sleeves of his light blue dress shirt.

I remembered how I'd spent the summer I first met him daydreaming about how sexy his forearms would look while he fucked me in the file room, the muscles straining and flexing as his hands pressed into the metal cabinets. This was all before I'd realized he was much too good for someone like me.

"But," he continued as I shooed the image away, "you've seemed kinda down these past few weeks, so I figured I could at least make sure you ate on this day, which just happens to be February fourteenth."

I opened my mouth to protest, to insist I wasn't "down," but instead, my lips met in a smile. "Thank you," I said, lifting the drink marked *Diet* out of its holder.

Of course, he got the drink right.

Food had recently gotten much easier to stomach, something I was grateful for, since I'd lived in constant fear of someone hearing me throw up in the office bathroom for the past couple of months. No one knew about my situation except Beau, of course, and Eva, whom I'd told when I went to Chicago for her New Year's Eve celebration. My business attire had started to consist of blousy shirts fluffed over the safety-pinned waists of my pants and skirts, and I did my best to avoid social gatherings, insisting I was much too busy at work.

I'd picked up the phone no less than twenty times in January to call my doctor and schedule the procedure, but the receptionist's gentle voice made me cry, and I'd either squeak out "Sorry" and hang up or put the receiver down without saying anything. I didn't understand why I couldn't be rational about it. Having a baby now or *ever* didn't make sense. There were so many reasons not to—the career that had been mapped out for me, the safe and solitary life I'd planned, the terrible parenting genes I'd likely inherited from my own mother. Never mind the daily reminder that I'd so carelessly let someone hurt my heart the way Christian had. But I was just past the end of my first trimester, the invisible line I'd drawn between *You can still decide* and *You've already decided*. And every time I thought about ending the pregnancy, images of me holding the baby and Christmas mornings filled with laughter —the same ones I'd seen so clearly when I'd gone to tell Christian the news—flashed like a warning in my mind. *You're going to regret this. You've seen what you can be, and that's everything they weren't.*

Yes, something inside me was broken, but I'd try harder to fix it. And if that didn't work, I'd still do everything in my power to make sure my child got all the love he or she deserved, even if I couldn't ever be worth loving back.

I hadn't spoken to Christian since I'd left his house nearly two months before. He hadn't called, and I hadn't either, and after several weeks, I accepted the fact that neither of us was going to. Part of me wished I would hear from him, while the other part knew it was for the best that I didn't. The hole he'd left in my heart was so big that if given the chance, I was afraid I'd spend an eternity searching for the person I was sure lay buried somewhere deep inside him.

"So I take it you don't have plans for the evening?" Marcos's voice sliced through my thoughts.

I blinked. "Huh?"

"No one's taking you out to a romantic dinner tonight? I'm assuming the whole idea of celebrating Valentine's Day is too ridiculous...right?"

"No. I mean, yes." I chuckled as I picked up my burger. "Totally ridiculous."

"Well then, I'm glad I brought you lunch," he said. "Because you deserve something special today. Even if you don't think you do."

I paused midchew and tilted my head as my brows pinched together. Was how I felt about myself *that* obvious?

"I didn't mean you don't think you deserve something special," he clarified, swiping a napkin over his mouth. "Just that you don't want it."

"Oh." I nodded. "Yeah. It's just so...overrated."

"Valentine's Day or romantic dinners?"

"Both," I said, taking a sip of my drink. "But what about you?"

Marcos grinned, his hazel eyes fixed on mine. "I don't think either are overrated."

I blushed, my muscles straining to swallow the liquid that got caught in my throat. "I meant, uh...do *you* have a romantic dinner planned?"

Why did I ask this? I don't want to know, I don't want to—

"No." His mouth turned down as he studied my face. "And why do you look so happy that no one wants to go to dinner with me?"

I squared my shoulders, trying to appear ambivalent. "I don't look happy. I'm not happy."

Am I?

Maybe I was that horrible kind of person who thought if she was sailing on the sea of misery, everyone else should be on the boat with her. Maybe *that's* what was wrong with me.

"And besides," I added. "I'm sure there are a ton of women who want to go to dinner with you."

You're kind, you're smart, you're gorgeous, you don't do drugs in bathrooms or probably at all.

"Maybe." He shrugged. "But don't feel too sorry for me. The truth is, I didn't ask anyone."

"So, uh..." I cleared my throat. "Still no candidates for the role of the future Mrs. Navarro?"

Oh, for fuck's sake, stop asking weird questions.

"I just had to ask because, you know..." I took a long pull off my drink, thinking of how to explain why those words had come out of my mouth. "You're always talking about how your mother wants you to find someone to, um...settle down with or whatever."

"That she does." He laughed before his expression gained a touch of seriousness. "And I'm starting to feel the same, if I'm being honest."

"Oh," I said, chewing slowly.

"Does that surprise you?"

"I, uh...I don't know." It actually didn't, but I filled the moment of silence with the only thing I could think to say. "I guess it's just that you're a guy, so...don't guys love being single and doing whoever, I mean, whatever they want?"

Jesus fucking Christ. If I thought the safety pin on my pants would hold, I'd crawl under my desk right now.

He cocked his head and gave me a lopsided smile. "Did you just say—"

"No." I shook my head and took a big bite of my burger, shoving some fries in behind it so I wouldn't be able to talk.

I knew Marcos wasn't like that anyway. He hoped for the wife, the kids, the nice house with the landscaped lawn...the whole nine yards, but in a way that went deeper than appearances. He wanted a truly happy family, not one like mine that couldn't even pretend.

He narrowed his eyes, calling a silent *bullshit* on my denial, then moved on. "Sure, that's fun for a while," he said, reaching for his soda. "But at some point, it's like, where's the girl who's fun *and* likes to eat cheeseburgers?"

I scoffed and rolled my eyes, but as hard as I tried, I couldn't keep myself from smiling.

"Oh my God," he continued, looking down at his food as if he'd just realized what was in front of him. "We're eating cheeseburgers, aren't we? I didn't even...Wow."

"Stop." I waved him off before covering my face with my hand as he laughed and winked. "I have friends who like cheeseburgers, you know. I can set you up with them."

I don't really want to, though.

"It's fine, Denise. I'll be okay," he assured me, his laughter quieting as he took another bite of his burger. "This is really fucking good, by the way."

"Tommy's is the best." I smiled. "And thanks. For getting it for me. For remembering it's my favorite."

"Like I said, you deserve it."

I don't, I wanted to say. *I don't deserve it at all.* But instead, I nodded and said a silent prayer to whomever was listening that he'd keep on believing I did and would never see whatever was so wrong inside of me.

31

MARCH 1991

I hung my head, hiding my face until the elevator reached the first floor. My hand trembled as I situated dark sunglasses on the bridge of my nose, hurried through the lobby, and pushed through the double doors. The midday sun instantly warmed my skin as I darted to the side of the building, leaned against the glass facade, and began to cry.

I'd decided to take Beau up on his previous invitation to watch *Xanadu* on Valentine's night. Olivia Newton-John had just tap danced with Gene Kelly, and Beau had just slurped down his third strawberry daiquiri when he paused the VCR.

"I wanted to say something the other night when you told me about Christian's...problem, and I can't stop thinking about it, and it's probably totally fine, but I have to ask you," he said in one breath.

"Oh God." I sucked in a tiny gasp of air as my mind rewound to the prior Sunday when I'd finally confessed to Beau the real reason Christian and I had ended. "What?"

"Just please know I'm not trying to freak you out."

"Okay, but you actually *are* freaking me out right now, so..." My eyes widened, pleading with him to tell me.

He set his glass on the table beside him, then covered his face and blurted out, "Did you get an HIV test?"

I pushed myself up to sit on the sofa. "What?"

He sighed and let his hands fall. "An HIV test."

"I..." *I can't breathe. Oh my God, I can't breathe.*

He turned in his chair. "I know so many people still think *Oh, that's just something those gays get.* Not that I think *you* think that, but—"

"The needles," I said, my voice barely above a whisper. "How could I not have..." I cupped my hands over my mouth and shook my head.

While I hadn't always been the most careful when it came to sex, times had changed and over the last couple years, condoms had become a nonnegotiable. But somewhere along the way, since Christian and I weren't sleeping with anyone else, we'd stopped bothering with them.

"I thought maybe your doctor said something, but then I also thought you probably didn't tell her about...that, and I"— the muscles in his throat constricted as he swallowed—"I just wanted to mention it."

Tears sprang to my eyes. How had this never crossed my mind? How could I have been so fucking careless? "Oh my God, Beau, what if..."

"No," he said, scrambling over to the sofa and putting his arm around me. "No, you're fine, I'm sure you're fine. I'm sorry I brought it up, he probably didn't even ever share needles with anyone else, but maybe your doctor could confirm things? Just to be safe."

I honestly don't know what the fuck he did or didn't do.

In fact, I'd probably never really known him at all.

"I'm so stupid," I said, bringing my gaze to him as the tears spilled onto my cheeks. "And you're right, I have to get tested. I have to, um...I have to call my doctor."

Beau talked me out of dialing the emergency number, so I

called the next day, begging until I got an appointment that afternoon. And, finally, after waiting an excruciating two weeks, I was crying again, this time with relief because the results were negative.

I took a shaky breath, pushed off the building, and started for the parking lot. *This is good news, everything is going to be okay, I'm completely healthy and...Why does my car look like it's sinking?*

I leaned down to get a closer look and groaned, my whole body deflating just like the right front tire had. I looked around the lot and toward the street for a nonexistent pay phone before trudging back inside to call someone to help. The wait for AAA was over two hours, so I tried Beau since he was the only one of my friends who could change a tire *and* already knew why I'd be at the doctor's office. But there was no answer. Unless I wanted to leave my car there and call a cab or a girlfriend (who would immediately compute that doctor plus no happy hours equaled knocked up), I only had one option.

I quickly swiped my fingers under my sunglasses and waved as Marcos approached in his BMW within fifteen minutes of my call.

"Hey, are you all right?" he asked, hurrying from his car and placing his hand on my arm.

I sniffed and nodded. "Yeah, it's just stupid, you know. Like, of all the days this has to happen, right? It's not like we have that presentation on Monday or anything."

"You sounded so upset on the phone, I didn't..." His eyes shifted to the sign on the outside of the building which read *Medical Center*. "I didn't know if something else happened."

"Oh," I said, trying to decide whether concocting a story about why I was there would make things better or worse. "No, I'm fine."

I folded my arm across my stomach to hide the tiny bump beneath the billowy flowered dress I'd recently purchased. If it didn't become *completely* obvious to everyone soon, I would likely blow my own cover by wearing something that wasn't oversized. I couldn't stand looking like I lived on the fucking prairie much longer.

"Yeah. Okay." Marcos hesitated before rolling up his sleeves. "Well, don't worry about this. I'll take care of you." He paused and gave me a smile that wanted to be bashful but couldn't help being sexy. "I mean, *it*. The tire."

Christ.

I let out an awkward laugh, slipping one shoe off and planting my bare foot on the ground as I nervously flounced my dress. "Thanks. Sorry I'm..." I wasn't really sure what I was. A ticking time bomb of emotions on her way to churn butter and ride shotgun on a covered wagon? At least I still had my heels, even if they hurt like hell.

He retrieved the spare and tool kit, placing them on the ground before cocking his head at me. "You *sure* you're all right?"

"Yeah, I'm fine." I shoved my foot back into place. "Just, you know, high heels."

He kneeled down, setting to work on removing the hubcap as the sun glinted off the silver band of his watch, drawing my eyes to his forearms. I hadn't ever imagined their muscles flexing in *this* exact scenario, but that didn't stop the blood from rushing to my—

So it really is true what they say about pregnancy hormones.

"Do you wanna wait in my car?" he asked, placing the hubcap on the ground, then glancing up at me as he unfastened the top button on his shirt and loosened his tie.

The sunlight shifted from his wrist to catch the gold in his eyes, and I swallowed, considering if my feet hurt badly enough to abandon the view. "Uh, yeah. Sure."

I folded myself into the passenger's side and rolled down the window, watching him out of the corner of my eye as he used the thing to get the things off the tire. He placed the jack under the car, pumping it up and down as his shirt strained across his back, and I slowly covered my mouth after several unsuccessful attempts to stop staring.

Oh my God. Stop. Just stop. This is Marcos, and you're going to be a mother *in six months. Think about something else.*

I let go of my breath and surveyed the tan leather interior of the BMW. I didn't know anything about tires, but I'd had to endure years of guys rambling on about their cars, thinking that would get me to sleep with them. The 325is was pricey but not outrageously expensive, sporty but practical enough, and hot (especially in red) but not ostentatious. He kept the inside clean, but it wasn't eerily sterile. There was some dust on the dashboard, a gym bag thrown in the back, a Styrofoam coffee cup in the holder, and a pack of Tic Tacs beside it. For some reason, I found the mints endearing, though I couldn't help but think he kept them there for when minty fresh making-out breath was required.

I wondered if the future Mrs. Navarro would sit where I was sitting one day. If she would like her husband's car or want him to drive something flashier. *Probably the latter*, I thought. I'd seen a few girls meeting Marcos at the office before heading off to lunch dates over the years, and they'd been tall and blond and probably modeled on their days off from just being regular sexy people.

I was sexy once. Never tall, never blond, but I was *sexy. And now I'm frumpy and horny and watching tire porn.*

Fuuuck.

I gripped the center console and stared straight ahead for the next ten minutes, sneaking occasional glances as Marcos finished putting on the spare. When he was done, I composed myself and stepped onto the asphalt.

"Thank you," I said. "You're a lifesaver. Really."

He wiped the sweat on his brow with the back of his hand

and whatever composure I'd gathered fell apart. His skin was smudged with black, and there was a similar mark on his shirt.

"No problem. I'm glad I could do it."

I gave his forehead and chest a clumsy swipe with my thumb. "Sorry. You just had...I think I've got something for that." I dug in my purse, producing a travel pack of Kleenex, which I shoved at him. "You can keep them."

"Thanks," he said, chuckling as he pulled out a couple tissues and began swiping at the grease.

I nodded. "Okay, well, I'll see you back at the office. I owe you one."

He reached for my arm but retracted it, remembering the smudges. "Wait. You can't drive that. I'll take it to the shop, and you follow me in my car."

I blinked. "Oh, uh...you don't have to do that, I can just—"

"Denise." He gave me a look that told me there was no way the rescue was going to end here, then flipped his palm up, waiting for my keys. "Come on. I'm not letting you drive on a shitty spare. I got this."

"Um, all right," I agreed, exchanging my keys for his. "Thanks. Again."

He opened the door to my car, adjusted the seat to fit his tall frame, then immediately turned toward me. "Actually...have you eaten anything?"

I raked my teeth along my bottom lip, trying to recall if I had. *This kid is feeding off my brain cells.*

"I'm taking you to lunch while they put the new tire on," he said before I could answer.

I worried for a moment that the jig was up, that he was overly concerned about me because he *knew*. But then I remembered that Marcos didn't need reasons to be kind—he just *was*.

"Oh, that's really sweet, but you don't have to do that."

"I know I don't have to," he began, smiling and settling in behind the steering wheel, "but I want to."

My face grew warm, and I felt tears rising behind my eyes, yet again, this time because I was grateful. While I had only a few people I could count on, I hoped he would always be one of them.

"Sounds good," I said. "But can I at least buy this time?"

He grinned before shutting the car door. "Maybe."

32

MARCH 1991

I brought the aluminum can to my lips and tipped my head back, hoping the last few drops of Diet Coke would help me focus. It was Friday night, and while other single people our age were heading out to bars, Marcos and I were sequestered in the office conference room, working on Monday's presentation to some potential investors from San Francisco.

My doctor kept insisting I cut back on the caffeine, and I kept insisting on not listening. The fatigue I'd felt during the first trimester had mostly lifted, but I still wasn't up for working long hours. I was tired, grumpy, and craving either two double cheeseburgers with extra pickles and mustard *or* a large pizza with sausage, black olives, and green peppers, *specifically*.

This wouldn't fly once the baby came. No more staying at work till all hours and living off junk food (tempered by the occasional salad) like I had for the past twenty-seven years. There would be no missing important moments with him—or her—and babies didn't eat those things.

Do they? No, of course they don't. Not until they get teeth. Maybe I can still eat that stuff and they can eat...What the fuck do they even eat?

Whatever the case, balancing responsibilities at the job and at the house was something I'd have to get used to.

Shit. I should probably get a house. Kids go outside. They play in yards, not streets, right?

"Can you pass that red folder to me?" Marcos asked.

I slid a manilla file across the table, not taking my eyes off the papers in front of me.

He chuckled. "The *other* red one."

I looked up. "What?"

"I need the"—he motioned to my left—"that one."

"Oh. You didn't say red."

His brow creased. "Pretty sure I said red."

"I'm not stupid, Marcos," I scoffed. "I would've heard red if you'd *said* red."

Wow. Way to talk to someone who changed your flat tire, drove your car to the mechanic, then had to watch you chow down at the Del Taco next door (surely not his first choice for lunch) like it was your damn job.

"Fine. You said red," I conceded without an ounce of emotion in my voice. "Sorry."

"So, can I have it?" He grinned and winked. "The red one, I mean."

I huffed. "That's not funny."

"It was kinda funny."

"It wasn't," I bit back.

His eyes narrowed. "Are you okay?"

"I'm *fine*," I said. "Just like I told you each of the ten times you asked me yesterday."

He raised an eyebrow. "Once at the doctor's office and once at Del Taco is ten times?'"

"It wasn't a doctor's..." *Dammit.* Of course, it was a doctor's office, but I didn't need him to mention it like it was tattooed on his brain. "And why are you bringing up Del Taco?" I pointed my pen at him. "*You* insisted on buying me lunch. You *made* me eat."

"I didn't make you eat. No one can make *you* do anything."

"You...*encouraged* it."

He flinched. "And that's wrong?"

"Yes. No." I pinched the bridge of my nose and shook my head. "I don't know."

"I encouraged it because I was worried about you." He leaned forward. "I *am* worried about you."

"Well don't be, because I'm fine."

"And you're sure there's not anything you...need? Anything I can do?"

I dismissed him with a curt laugh. "I assure you, there is nothing—like, *literally* nothing—you can do." I paused before adding, "Because I'm fine."

"Okay." He blinked, like he was trying to convince himself of that.

"Okay," I said, clasping my hands in front of me, as if to say *case closed.*

But he hadn't convinced himself at all because he pushed a hand through his hair and continued. "But you've been—"

I groaned.

"Just let me fucking say this, Denise," he insisted, his voice loud and stern in a way I'd heard only once, when he'd had it with some asshole trying to talk over him during a meeting.

Oh. My eyes widened and dropped to the table. *Oh my.*

I crossed my arms over my chest, refusing to be turned on. *Fucking hormones.*

"Sorry, I didn't mean to..." He released a long exhale. "It's just that you've been practically falling asleep at your desk. You've looked like you're gonna puke during the Monday morning staff meetings, and then yesterday, I picked you up at a —sorry to bring it up again—*doctor's office*, and I'm fucking worried about you."

"Marcos," I said, adjusting my tone to try to sound like a less rattled, more rational human being. "People get tired. People" —*skip the puking part, skip the puking part*—"go to the doctor. It doesn't mean anything's wrong. So stop worrying, and let's finish the presentation, so I can go home, sleep, and hopefully look less *haggard* when we meet the investors."

"You don't look haggard."

"Whatever."

"And I can't stop worrying."

"Why not?"

"Because I care about you, Denise."

"Well, stop caring."

"*What?*"

"I said, *stop fucking caring*," I hissed.

Shit. I didn't mean that. I promise I didn't mean that. I'll take it back later, but I cannot do this right now.

He threw his hands up. "How do you expect me to stop—"

And I slammed mine on the table. "Jesus, Marcos! I'm not dying, I'm fucking pregnant, *okay*?"

He stared at me, wide-eyed, mouth slightly open, until my arms folded on the table, my head collapsed on top of them, and I started blubbering.

"Oh my God," I cried, my body heaving.

"Shit," he said, and the next thing I knew, he was sitting beside me, his hand on my back. "Denise, I—"

"Oh my fucking God, I cannot believe I said that out loud."

"I'm so sorry, Denise. I was just...I was freaking out because I had it in my head that you were sick, like, *really* sick, and I was being selfish, I guess, because all I wanted to do was take care of you and let you know that I..."

I lifted my head toward him. I normally wouldn't have let the tears fall so freely, but it was too late, I was too knocked up, and the truth was too exposed to pretend. "You what? Feel *sorry* for me?" I wiped my nose with the back of my hand because there were no tissues, and my pride had gone out the window anyhow. "Well don't, because like I said—"

"I am so fucking in love with you."

"Wha—" My voice was sticky with phlegm. I noticed the thin trail of snot on my skin and shoved my hand under my thigh. "What?"

"I love you. I'm *in* love with you." He sat back in his chair and massaged his forehead. "But you have to know that by now, right?"

He sounded defeated, but not like all the times we'd joked about why I wouldn't go out with him. This was different. His words weren't peppered with playfulness, and there was no laughter.

"I..." My eyes flicked around the room. I supposed I knew he *liked* me, or at least *thought* he liked me, but *love*?

"Clearly, this isn't a good time to tell you since you're with someone else." He raked his hands over his face and sighed. "Fuck."

I searched for the right words, astonishment fading to melancholy as I realized it couldn't possibly be true. "You're not in love with me."

"Uh..." He blew out a breath and let his hands fall against the armrests. "I mean, I'm pretty sure I am."

"But you can't be in love with me." I shifted my gaze to him. "You don't...know me. Not really."

You don't know that I'm not enough for you.

"We've worked together for nearly five years, Denise. More than that if you count your summers during college. We've had too many lunches and dinners and late nights to count."

"That's just work, Marcos."

There are other parts of me. Hidden parts that I'm afraid you'll eventually find, no matter how hard I try to keep them from you.

He tilted his head, hesitating like he was waiting for me to acknowledge an obvious truth. "You really think that all this time I haven't seen you for everything you are?"

You haven't. Because if you did, this wouldn't be happening. You wouldn't be telling me you love me.

"You think I haven't seen how you take Kathy a cup of coffee every morning when you make yours?" He gestured toward the hall that led to her reception desk. "How you hold doors for people, and you smile at waiters and say thank you every time they fill up your water glass? How you always get me to laugh when I've had a shitty day?"

Most people do those things. That's just being considerate. Nothing special.

"Or how at the Oscars party last year, you wore that gold strapless dress with your hair pulled back in that diamond clip, and you traced the tip of your finger right below the corner of your mouth to check your lipstick every time you took a sip of champagne."

You saw that? You remember that?

He gave me a wistful smile. "I totally missed my shot with Cindy Crawford that night but couldn't have cared less because I was already talking to the most beautiful woman in the room."

I sniffed and pinched my brows together. "You had a shot with Cindy Crawford?"

He shook his head. "Not at all."

A tiny laugh worked its way out of my throat.

"Anyway, uh...congratulations"—he nodded his head, then pressed his hands against the arms of the chair, poised to stand —"and let's, um...let's finish this presentation, so I can start looking for a new job because this has officially crossed over into the awkward as fuck territory."

"I'm not..." *Don't tell him anything. Just let it go.* "I'm not with anyone."

Or sure...tell him that.

Goddammit.

He relaxed back into the chair. "What? What do you mean?"

"The person who..." I took a breath and glanced down. "I'm not with him. We're not together."

Marcos took in a gasp of air. "Is he still...I mean, is he gonna be... around or..."

I held my fingers below my eyes, catching the tears before they could fall.

"Sorry," he said quickly. "That's none of my business."

"It's okay. It's not a secret." I shrugged. "I guess it *was*, but it shouldn't be. I decided to do...this. And he decided not to."

"Were you *ever* together or..." His hands tightened into fists. "No. You don't have to tell me. The only thing I want to know is where to find this dumb fucker so I can—"

"Save the alpha male shit for flexing and sweating while you're changing tires." I rolled my eyes and managed another small chuckle.

"The last person I punched was a pitcher who threw at me during a high school baseball tournament, so I'm not really gonna—" He blinked. "Wait, what?"

Baseball? Fuck, that's hot.

"Did you mean flexing and sweating...in a good way?"

What the hell. Why not let all of the cats out of all the bags?

My shoulders lifted. "Let's just say, I may have let you take me to dinner if I wasn't knocked up."

He swallowed. "I still wanna take you to dinner."

I snorted, dismissed him with a sarcastic "Please," and shifted to face the table. "Anyway, you don't need to find a new job. We can just forget about this and finish the presentation because I actually *am* tired and—"

"Marry me."

"—I want to go home."

Our words blended together, and I twisted my head, locking eyes with him. "What did you just say?"

"Marry me," he repeated.

"Marcos, stop, you don't have to..." I blew out a breath and swiped my palms across my cheeks. "Look, I'm fine. I don't need sympathy, okay? I can take care of myself."

I've been doing it for a long time now, and yes, I'm fucking exhausted. But if I've learned anything about life, it's how to live it on my own.

He leaned forward and reached for my arm. "I know you can, but I want this. I want *you*, and I have since that very first summer you gave me those go-fuck-yourself looks from the file room."

Oh God. The file room. The same one filled with all those metal cabinets I imagined him pushing me up against while he hiked up my skirt and—

"Denise," he said, his voice quiet and sincere. "Let me do this. Let me take care of you."

The fog clouding my thoughts cleared. *He's serious. He's actually serious.*

"I, um..." I rubbed my lips together as I attempted to gather my thoughts. "Marcos, you deserve someone..." *Better than me.* "You don't need me and this baby changing your life."

"I told you the other day, fun's only fun for so long," he countered. "And I don't want to get so tired of searching for someone like you that I settle for someone who isn't. Especially when you're *right fucking here*."

"But you deserve—"

"I know what I deserve *and* what I want," he insisted. "I also know that *you* deserve someone who wants to be there for you, for the baby...for everything that happens for the rest of your life."

I tried to look away. To turn back to my files and papers and pretend the last ten minutes had never happened. But I was captivated by the hope in his eyes.

"I know this sounds crazy. I do. And I'm not asking you to pretend you're madly in love with me, and this is what you've always imagined. But I think you know there's something beyond what we have here at work, and if there's a chance you might feel the same as I do one day, it's a chance I wanna take."

He took a deep breath, his gaze fixed on me like I was the only star he'd ever wish upon. And maybe I would be, as long as I could keep my light shining bright enough to hide the dark parts inside.

"So, I hope you can ignore the fact that I'm asking this in a conference room in Century City and not on a balcony in Italy with champagne and caviar and the biggest fucking ring I could find." He paused and clasped my hand. "But will you do this, Denise? Will you marry me?"

33

NOVEMBER 2009

I pulled my SUV into the small dirt lot, where Christian sat on one of the boulders lining the ridge above the water. He turned, offering a small wave and a cautious smile. I cut the engine and lifted my to-go coffee cup from the holder.

The sun had been up for only an hour, but it wasn't unusual for me to hit the gym early on a Saturday. There was always something going on—Marisol's soccer games, Lola's mall drop-offs, errands I couldn't get to during the week——that would prevent me from doing it later in the day. So, like any regular start to the weekend, I pulled on a pair of leggings and a tank top, gathered my hair into a ponytail, and grabbed my warm-up jacket on the way out the door while Marcos and the kids slept. I did my regular routine, cardio before weights, but when I was done, instead of steering my car left toward my house, I turned right toward the PCH.

"Hi," I said, my tennis shoes kicking up dust as I approached him.

He pointed to my cup. "I brought you coffee, but I guess you, uh..."

"Oh." My eyes fell to the cardboard holder on the ground next to his foot. "Yeah, I stopped after the gym. But thanks."

"You already went to the gym? That's impressive."

No, it's not, I wanted to say. *I'm a normal adult, and I do normal adult things like waking up and exercising and being responsible. Something which I'm still not sure you're familiar with.*

But I ignored his comment and sat on the flat top of the boulder next to him, my stoic expression hiding a mind weighed down by thoughts as heavy as the rock beneath me. Those thoughts, like stones, would have to come loose at some point, but I would be prepared. No unexpected avalanches, no people hurt beyond repair.

I took a deep breath. "So tell me about—"

"How are you?"

My muscles tensed.

"Sorry," he said. "You go."

"I think we should keep this..." *Formal? Professional?* Emotions were unnecessary. This was a fact-finding mission, plain and simple, and I'd promised myself I'd treat it as such. "I just have a lot of questions."

"Right." He took a sip of coffee before the twitch of disappointment on his face settled into a resigned sadness, and my chest instantly ached.

If I pull my heart out, how long can I stay alive till I have to put it back in? Can I hold it in my hand, find out what I need to know, then reattach the cords and drive away?

"So tell me about after..." I cleared my throat, swallowing my feelings along with the word *us*. "The album came out. What happened on tour, why the band broke up, how you got sober. Because if Lucas wants...this, he's going to want to know all these things." I gave him a pointed look, a reminder of what we'd agreed upon at the diner in Monrovia a little over a week before. "But I want to know them first."

"I'll tell you whatever you want to know, Denise." He tucked his empty hand in the pocket of his corduroy jacket, and there was a beat of silence before I gave him a curt nod to begin.

"The band broke up for exactly the reason you think it did. The reason the rest of them gave in every interview afterward. I'm a…I'm a heroin addict. Recovering now, but I'll always be an addict," he admitted. "Mike and Kurt have never really forgiven me for what happened. But Jordan…We've been in a good place since I got sober seven years ago."

Jordan. Hearing his name was like someone hitting rewind, sending me back to the bathroom at their house and the club in Reseda.

I took a breath. *Don't think about it. You're not there. You're here, doing what you need to do to protect your son.*

"Everything got worse on tour," he continued. "It wasn't terrible at first. I could function as long as I made sure I never went without and did just enough to maintain. I tried to be careful not to leave track marks, or I'd cover them up if anything showed. Just like I always did. But I'm sure the guys knew, and they let it go because the shows were good." He tipped his head back, watching an imaginary concert in the sky. "The shows were great, actually."

I looked past the shallow drop-off, images of him from before things had gone so wrong flickering along with the sun on the Pacific. Scenes that had flashed behind my eyes over the years, reminding me how scary and beautiful it was to show someone the pieces of me I'd hidden for so long. Someone who had those same tarnished and broken parts, who made me feel seen and understood, as though finally, *for the first time in my life*, I wasn't alone. Each time the memories came, I told myself I shouldn't be thinking about him. That I had a loving husband who'd do anything in the world for me, for our family. A husband who was perfect in every way imaginable and somehow believed I was, too.

"While we were finishing the second album, it got bad—

really bad—and then we were scheduled to go back on the road," Christian said. "Venues were booked, tickets sold, so much time and money invested. Jordan told me, looking back, he wishes we'd canceled anyway. That he'd handcuffed me, driven me to rehab, and told the label and the promoters and everyone else to fuck off."

"You looked sick." I cursed myself for externalizing the thought, but since the words were already out, I finished it. "Back then."

His laugh was hollow. "I looked a hell of a lot worse after you saw me, I guaran—"

"On TV," I added.

"Oh." He wrinkled his brow. "Did you—"

"I saw an interview." I set my coffee down, zipped my jacket, and crossed my arms over my chest. "I was up late one night with Lucas. I guess he was two, two and a half, and he was sick, and..." My eyes drifted back to the ocean. "It doesn't matter. Keep going."

He hesitated, and I glanced at him.

"I want to know everything," I said.

"Things went downhill on that tour. I was so out of it, I could barely make it through the shows. Crowds started to notice, and then one night, I just...blanked. Couldn't remember songs, couldn't remember words. Our tour manager got me offstage, and Jordan sang so they could finish out the show. That was it. The guys had had enough and gave me a choice. I could go to rehab, or I could be done."

He took a shaky breath as the water lapped at the rocks below us. "The band didn't last long once I was gone, but that didn't make me happy. I didn't feel like I'd *won* or anything. It just really fucking hurt to think what we could've been if I hadn't fucked it all up." His voice cracked. "If I hadn't fucked up every good thing in my life."

His gaze burned the skin on the side of my face, and I

wanted to turn to him—to ask him if he was talking about us, too—but I kept my focus straight ahead. "And then you went back home? To Seattle?"

"Yeah. Most of my old drug buddies had either cleaned up or they weren't..." He sighed. "Around anymore."

My heart plummeted to my stomach. *That could've been him. He could've died, too.*

"But a few were, and I had enough money to spend all my time getting myself and them high. Then, one night, a guy I'd known since high school, he OD'd at my house. I somehow had the sense to dial 911, then hid all the shit in my closet and sat in there crying and praying he was still alive. He was, thank God, but it scared the shit out of me, and I checked myself into rehab the next day." He cleared his throat and sniffed. "It was just an endless cycle after that. Something would scare me straight, I'd get clean, then start using again. Sometimes within weeks. I was sober for about six months when I was married, but... neither of those things lasted."

What did she look like? What was her name? Did you accidentally call her by mine sometimes? Did you love her, and do you still?

I wanted to know more but knew I shouldn't ask. I was there to find out facts, but those particular facts didn't matter.

"I don't think either of us were in love," he answered as though he'd read my mind. "But I guess she thought life with a famous—formerly famous—drug addict would be exciting. That faded pretty quickly, though, and she tried to help, but... there's just no saving anyone, you know?"

The truth was, I didn't know. Because there was still a part of me that believed if I'd been everything he needed, it could've been me. I could've been the one to save him.

"So, why'd you do it? Get married, I mean. If you weren't in love."

Why am I so fucking concerned about—

"Honestly?" His voice dropped lower, and I finally twisted my head to him. His lids were heavy, his eyes strained.

Is he trying not to cry?

"Sorry," I said quickly. "That was way out of line, you don't need to—"

"I wanted somebody to believe in me again. Somebody who understood how it feels to not have that. Someone I could believe in, too." He held my gaze until my eyes fell to the dimple in his right cheek. "You know how that is...right?"

I was staring at it so intently that it took a moment for his words to register. "Oh. I, um..." My chest instantly flushed, and I flinched. "So, how did you finally get where you are now? Sober, I mean. Hopefully sober."

"I'm sober, Denise," he said. "Really. I am."

The warmth on my chest spread to my cheeks. After all I'd been through with Christian, I had every right to question his sobriety, yet, somehow, I still felt bad for doing it.

"My brother came over to my house one day," he continued. "He was worried because I...I didn't show up for my dad's funeral. My dad had been sick, but I was too messed up to deal with any of it. When Carter found me, it was bad. I'd barely eaten. I could hardly walk. I was too weak to fight him, so he carried me to his car and took me to the hospital."

A new image formed in my brain alongside the ones of him on tour. It was even more terrifying, and I dropped my eyes.

"I know Carter wasn't always in my corner, but my mom had passed away several years before, we'd just lost my dad, and even though they were who they were, when Carter looked at me like I was the last piece of our family, he just...cracked. He fucking lost it, and I knew I couldn't leave him the way I'd left other people."

I lifted my chin to turn back to the ocean, but his pull was stronger than the tide.

"The way I left *you*," he said.

My arm quivered as I pressed my hand against the top of the chilly stone to steady myself from the flutter in my veins. *No. No emotions. Change the subject. Change it now.* "So you're, uh...you're close with your brother now?"

"Yeah. His kids, too. My nephew is just out of college, and my niece is actually not much older than Lucas." He chuckled. "Of course, they think I should cut my hair because they're mini-Carters, but I still love 'em."

Don't cut your hair. I love your hair. I've always loved your hair. I pushed my tongue to the roof of my mouth until the thought passed.

"I'm glad. For you and Carter. But I'm sorry about your parents," I said.

"Thanks. That's, um...complicated. But thanks." He tilted his head. "Can I ask about yours?"

"Oh. I, uh," I stammered, caught off guard by his question. "I don't...I mean, I..."

"It's all right," he said. "You don't have to—"

I started answering before I could give it any more thought. "My mom is...Well, she's a lost cause. But with my dad, it's better. He'll never admit the error of his ways, and hell, maybe there were no errors. I did what he wanted me to do, and my life is good."

Yes. Yes, it is. My life is good. My life is great.

His mouth turned down slightly as he pushed his hand through his hair. "So, you took over the business, huh?"

"Almost ten years ago."

"And your, uh...your husband. He seems like a good guy. I mean, the way Lucas talks about him, it's obvious he is."

My body shifted, and I gave him an uneasy smile. *This is wrong. Lucas talking about Marcos in front of Christian, having no idea. I have to tell them. I have to tell them soon.*

"Marcos is amazing. He loves Lucas. And our girls. More than anything."

"And you," he said.

"Hmm?"

"He loves *you*," Christian repeated.

"Oh. Yeah. Of course," I said, dismissing him with a wave of my hand.

His brows pinched together. "Why do you sound—"

"He does." *Love the idea of me. Who he thinks I am.*

His brows raised at my sharp tone, but he nodded. "You deserve that."

No, I don't.

"We got married when I was pregnant with Lucas, but we'd known each other a long time before that," I added, my voice still sharp with guilt for thinking about Christian in the past, for thinking about him now, for loving his fucking hair. But especially for keeping a secret like this from the one person I should've been sharing it with. "Marcos has always been there for me. And Lucas. Always."

"I know. I just...I can't lie, Denise. I wish it had been me."

I bit the inside of my cheek. *Sometimes I do, too.*

"Do you ever...think about that?" He studied my face as I tried my best to keep so much as a flutter of emotion from showing. "Like, what if we were..."

I wanted to say no, but the word was stuck in the part of my brain where good decisions were made. "It's better not to think about those things, Christian."

"Yeah." He looked off in the distance, then back to me. "But I do anyway."

Fuck.

All the emotions I'd tried to keep myself from feeling flooded my body at once, humming and buzzing and begging me to get up and either run away or run straight into his arms. But the conflicting impulses paralyzed me, and I could only stare into his eyes, trying to decide whether they looked like silver bullets or silver linings.

A seagull squawked, and I pulled in a tiny gasp of air, finally able to flick my gaze away. "So I, um…I don't want to move too fast with this. We should wait until after Christmas." There was a slight tremble in my voice as I picked up my coffee and stood. "Lucas said you guys are taking a break starting the middle of December, then getting back to work after the new year."

"Uh, yeah." Christian looked down at his cup, as though he'd forgotten it was in his hand. "I'm going home for Christmas, but I'll be back in January." His lips twitched before settling into a smile. "Thank you, Denise. This means…Just thank you."

"I need to know more, though," I said, nervously tapping the plastic lid on my coffee. "About your sobriety. I need to know you're committed. I need to know for sure this time."

"Yeah. Yeah, of course."

I nodded and started for my SUV. "I'll email you after Thanksgiving."

"Denise," he called after me.

I turned around as he stood up, hand on top of his head to keep the wind from whipping his hair across his face.

"Was it around Thanksgiving?" he asked, his voice softening. "When we…When you got pregnant with him?"

I froze, and my fingers curled around my car keys. "What?"

"I was just thinking the other day—wondering about it, I guess—and I started looking at these stupid calculators on the internet."

Saturday. It was the Saturday after.

"I don't remember," I lied, then pivoted on my heels, hurried to my car, and drove away.

34

JUNE 1991

"We can call someone to do that, you know." I stood in the doorway of the nursery and rolled my lips inward, trying to hide my smile.

"Call who?" Marcos asked from the floor where polished pieces of dark wood lay scattered around him on the carpet.

I chuckled. "A handyman. A crib putter-togetherer. A professional."

He scoffed, looking up from the paper booklet of instructions. "Absolutely not."

"I'm just saying, if you're trying to impress me, you already did that a few months ago when you changed my tire."

"You have no idea how glad I am you got stranded that day." He grinned, then nodded toward the bump under the thin white cotton of my nightgown. "How'd you sleep?"

I shrugged. "Eh. I'd say I'll sleep when he gets here, but I don't think that's happening, either."

Marcos stood, then stretched his arms overhead, offering me a peek at the toned area between his T-shirt and the waistband of his sweatpants. My limbs turned warm and fluid as the blood rushed from my head to other regions of my body, and I leaned against the frame of the door, reminded that the pregnancy libido was almost too much for even me to handle.

But I'd deal with that later. By myself.

Not that sex with Marcos wasn't good. It was fucking *great* when I could forget that I'd gotten pregnant by someone who wasn't him, but that was extra hard to do once I crossed over into my third trimester. The idea of sex with him happening at *all* was awkward at first. However, in a pledge to return to even just a slice of my former self, I decided to rip the awkwardness off like a Band-Aid. After everyone but us had left the office the evening after our presentation, I'd asked for his help with something in the file room, telling myself if he was as good as I imagined back when I was alphabetizing folders during summer break, I'd marry him.

He was. And I did.

But I would've married him regardless.

After Marcos had asked me that night in the conference room, I told him I'd think about it. We had a deadline to meet, we could discuss it later, and really, it was all so sudden, would he even feel the same way next week, month, or year? But the Monday meeting had gone off without a hitch, even as visions of gold rings and white dresses (*hilarious, by the way*) danced in my head along with the facts and figures we were presenting. And when he winked at me as we shook hands with the investors to seal the deal, I knew.

We were a fantastic team at work. And we could be a fantastic team in life.

"I can do this later. You want breakfast?" Marcos asked, stopping to give me a kiss as he headed toward the stairs.

My stomach fluttered, and I placed my hand over it, smiling as the baby repositioned himself. "Well, I guess we know the ears work. And *yes*. Tommy's is open twenty-four hours. Should I get dressed, or can I go like this?"

"Oh my God, Denise. You're going to turn into a fucking

cheeseburger." He laughed as he jogged down the steps to the first floor of the house, and I followed behind him. "How about bacon? Eggs? Pancakes?"

"Yes, yes, and yes." I weaved around several unpacked moving boxes as the cold kitchen tile sent a welcomed chill up through my bare feet. "Wait, do we even have all that?"

"I went to the store before I started trying to figure out that damn crib." He opened the refrigerator and began pulling out packages and cartons. "We've been eating takeout since we moved in here last month."

"You're too good to me," I said.

"You deserve it."

I cast my eyes downward.

"Hey," he said. "What's wrong?"

"Huh?" I glanced up to see his forehead creased with worry. "Oh. Nothing." *Just thinking about how one day you might realize I actually* don't. "I spaced out for a sec. You know, the shitty sleep and all," I added.

"Well, sit down, 'cause I got this," he assured me as he unstacked two mixing bowls and set a frying pan on the stove.

I eased into a chair at the kitchen table and twirled a finger in his direction. "Uh, did I own those?"

He gave me a proud grin. "I did."

"Wow," I said, shaking my head. "The things you don't know about a person when you marry him two weeks after he asks you."

He raised his eyebrows. "It's hot, right?"

"Totally," I said, dramatically fanning myself with my hand.

"My mom bought them for me when I got my first apartment."

I gritted my teeth. "Okay, it actually *was* hot until you mentioned that part."

"What's wrong with her wanting me to cook? Aren't you glad she didn't raise me to be a man who expects his wife in the kitchen, barefoot and pregnant?" Marcos clicked his tongue against the roof of his mouth and pointed to me. "Oh. Wait."

I rolled my eyes. "Ha ha. And yes, I'm glad, but I'd be glad... *er* if I thought she liked me."

"She likes you."

I narrowed my eyes at him. "Marcos."

"She just needs time to let it all sink in," he said as he set about making breakfast. "And she'll be so happy when she gets to show off pictures of her *nieto* to all her friends, it won't matter if said *nieto* isn't genetically a Navarro."

I sighed. "I hope so."

"Trust me. This woman has been wanting a grandchild since 1980. She's gonna fall completely in love with him, we'll make up for the courthouse wedding with whatever Catholic thing we need to do in Miami, and everything will be fine." He chuckled as he opened a box of pancake mix. "Meanwhile, all your father does when we tell *him* is look at me and say, 'It's still her company when I'm gone.'"

I snickered. "I might let you have some of it."

"No," he said, shaking his head. "As soon as we get settled, I'm finding another job. I don't need Tom Abbott sizing me up for the next however many years."

I smiled and winked. "We'll see. But, uh, speaking of parents...I called my mom."

"Oh." He turned around, spatula in hand. "What did she say?"

"She made a huge fuss, was all 'Oh, isn't this exciting,' then told me she had to go or she'd be late for her massage, but she'd send a gift soon." I shrugged. "Nothing about visiting, but what did I expect?"

His face fell. "I'm sorry."

I waved my hand in the air, pretending her disinterest didn't hurt. "That's just how she is."

"But, hey, Eva's gonna come out, right?" He cracked an egg

and immediately began digging for shells. *Must've skipped that day in Señora Navarro's cooking class.* "She didn't kill you earlier this month when you showed up for *her* wedding with your own ring on, so that was good. She actually seemed excited."

I nodded. "I think she wanted to kill me, but after meeting you for ten seconds three years ago, she told me I should sleep with you. So she felt..." I paused and yawned. "Vindicated."

"I knew I liked her." He bobbed his head toward the living room. "Why don't you go lie down? Take a quick nap?"

"Yeah. Maybe I should." I rose from the chair and waddled to the sectional couch. It was big and fluffy and not a hundred percent my style, but when I'd tested it out at the store, it was so comfortable that I'd handed the salesperson my credit card while still lying down.

Even with another human inside me, the sofa enveloped my small frame, and I sighed as I sank into the cushions, the smell of bacon making my mouth water. I closed my eyes and felt like I was floating, already lost in a dream. It was quite possible that I was. I still had trouble believing I owned a house with four bedrooms and two stories and apparently mixing bowls and a husband who knew how to use them. Sure, I'd slept with plenty of men, but when I thought about it, there wasn't ever much sleeping involved, and I'd certainly never lived with any of them. The change was scary, but I was adjusting more easily than I'd imagined. The nesting instinct that all the books talked about had kicked in, and the nice house on the quiet street with the devoted suit-and-tie husband overshadowed thoughts of the life I'd once imagined with Christian.

When I'd said yes to Marcos, I wasn't in love with him. But I believed that I could be, and every day after, I believed it a little more. Then, one early morning, two months after that night in the office conference room, I came back from my fifth trip to the bathroom to see him sitting up in bed. He asked me if I was all right, then settled back into sleep once I assured him I was.

He looked so peaceful, his eyelashes fluttering just slightly, chest rising up, then falling down, and I whispered, "I love you" to see if it sounded as right on the outside as it felt within. He smiled and said, "I love you, too," his eyes still closed as he pulled me into him, and I didn't just believe it anymore...I *knew*. I drifted off in his arms, determined that I would never let him see the parts of me that weren't worthy of all that he was and everything he had to give.

It wasn't so different from how I'd lived my life before. Feelings were messy, and they made *people* messy, which was fine for others, but something was already wrong with me. I didn't need to add messy to it. So, I vowed that I would pretend to be okay, to have my shit together, to have everything under control, inside and out. I'd show Marcos just enough to let him know I was human but never enough to make him want to leave. He'd fallen in love with who he thought I was, and I wasn't going to disappoint him. If not for my sake, for my son's. For *our* son's.

35

APRIL 1994

"Here, baby," I said, handing Lucas a plastic sippy cup. "Drink some of this."

He looked up at me from the sofa with his glassy gray eyes and sniffled. "Juice?"

"Yes. Juice." I sat down beside him and brushed the dark curls off his forehead, warm with fever.

"I watch Barney," he said, pointing to the television where the purple dinosaur clomped around his playground.

"You can watch him till you go night night, then I'll take you to your bed, okay?"

He coughed, and a thousand germs were released into the atmosphere as phlegm curdled in his throat. Two and a half years before, the thought of inhaling a plague like this would've sent me running from the room, but all I wanted to do was kiss him and hug him and squeeze him up. Motherhood was weird like that.

"We'll get you some yummy medicine that tastes like candy, and you'll be all better tomorrow."

He shook his head, sending the unruly curls bouncing. "No more med-cine."

"We'll see. You just need to get some sleepies, okay?" I tucked a soft throw blanket under his chin.

"Mama stay?"

"For a little while, then Daddy will stay in your room because Mama can't sleep on the floor." I patted my pregnant belly. "Your sister wouldn't like that."

He chewed on the spout of the cup. "Lucas has sissy."

I smiled and curled into the corner of the sectional, Lucas's head on the pillow against my thigh. "Are you excited to be a big brother?"

"Brudder," he repeated as his gaze settled back on the TV.

I chuckled and my head dropped against the back of the sofa while I fingered his silky locks. Even with a nose full of snot, he was the cutest fucking thing on earth. So cute that it hadn't taken much for me to say yes when Marcos asked if I maybe wanted another one. It was something we'd skipped over in the ok-sure-let's-get-married conversation, but I wanted to do it, not only for him, but because I'd always wondered if my childhood might've been less lonely with a sibling.

Not that being pregnant and giving birth were two of my favorite things. But being able to give the love I'd never gotten from my own mother to the tiny human I grew made it all worth it. And it made the wound she'd left me with hurt a little less, even though she'd only visited us once when on her way to some state-of-the-art seaweed treatment in Corona del Mar.

"You look tired. You should hire a nanny," she'd said as she passed baby Lucas back to me after *oohing* and *aahing* over him for approximately fifteen seconds.

"We have a nanny. During the day, while we're at work."

She furrowed her brow. "Then you should stop working. You look like you've aged at least ten years since I last saw you."

Maybe I should go wrap some seaweed around my fucking face, I wanted to say. But I kept my mouth shut, left the room, and put Lucas down for a nap, telling him a fairy tale about an evil queen who drove off a cliff on her way to the spa while he and Mommy and Daddy lived happily ever after.

The sound of the sippy cup rolling out of Lucas's hands onto the floor startled me. I glanced down, the light from the TV flickering across the long dark lashes skimming the top of his cheeks and the pouty pink lips shaped like a little O. His forehead was cooler, meaning the Tylenol I'd given him earlier had kicked in, so I lowered the volume on the television, deciding to wait just a little longer before moving him. I switched over from his Barney tape to scroll through the cable channels, hoping to find a late-night sitcom rerun. Infomercial...*Star Trek*...infomercial...*M*A*S*H*...infomercial...Christian.

I gasped, then cupped my hand over my mouth as Lucas sighed and snuggled into his blanket.

Press the button, change the channel, I told myself, but my finger wouldn't budge.

My blood froze, a thousand tiny sharp icicles pricking me from the inside. I'd seen pictures of him since the band had taken off—a quick glimpse of a magazine cover, a flash of a video—but this was the first time I'd allowed myself to really look at him. His collar bones cut through the top of his T-shirt, and his arms dangled like toothpicks from the sleeves as he scratched the crook of his elbow. A woman sat across from him, MTV-logoed microphone in her hand, nodding intently like Christian was saying something profound. Like she wasn't concerned in the least that he looked like he should be in the hospital instead of backstage at a festival in—I squinted to read the banner at the bottom of the screen—Brazil. He smiled at the interviewer, but his eyes were too sunken in for it to seem anything but sad, and for a moment, I wished the television worked both ways so he could see a picture of a life that might've been. Of possibilities he wished he hadn't abandoned *so fucking easily*, as if they had never meant that much to him at all.

He probably didn't care. He probably didn't even know where he was. He looked like a stranger, pale skin stretched over bones, a shell of the person I'd known and who'd known me. Who'd *really* known me. So, I continued to watch, the comfort in seeing him alive greater than the pain of seeing what he'd become.

A tear spilled onto my cheek, and I brushed it away at the sound of footsteps on the stairs, then cut the power on the television.

"How's the little guy doing?" Marcos whispered as he quietly made his way over to the couch.

"Better, I think." I smiled up at him. "Do you mind sleeping in his room?"

He lifted Lucas into his arms, and Lucas nuzzled into Marcos's shoulder, his tiny fingers grasping his dad's T-shirt. "I got you, buddy."

"Thank you," I said, softly clearing my throat. "I'm right behind you. Gonna take me a second to get up."

Marcos chuckled. "I can help you once I get him into bed."

"I'm good, you go ahead."

He nodded, told me he loved me, and carried Lucas from the room.

"I love you, too," I said. And I meant it, even though, as soon as I heard him start up the stairs, I picked up the remote and turned the television back on.

36

NOVEMBER 2009

"Well, I suppose that wasn't the worst Thanksgiving ever." I sat on the couch with a glass of red wine. "Lola only complained nine times about us not letting her go to Cabo with Jasmine, and I was really thinking it was going to be ten."

Marcos eased into the chair across from me. "Did you count when she tacked things she was *not* thankful for onto the end of things she *was*?"

I clicked my tongue against the roof of my mouth. "Dammit. Totally forgot that one. I guess it *was* ten, then."

"Whatever she did, your father is now considering taking all of us *plus* Jasmine to Cabo next year for Thanksgiving, so I suppose we should thank her for that."

I tucked one leg under me. "If I had complained like that when *I* was fifteen, he would've gotten up from the table, dropped an Alka-Seltzer in his whiskey, and never come back. Now he's offering up free trips to Mexico to right the terrible wrong I inflicted on his granddaughter."

"Yeah, well, there's no denying he's softened over the years." Marcos propped his feet on the ottoman in front of him.

"*Softened?* It's like he's a whole other person with them. He doesn't even hound Lucas about taking over the business one day. Which is good, I'm glad, but...Hell, I sound jealous of my kids." I took a sip of wine. "I'm going to shut up now."

"I think he's got his eye on Marisol for that anyway," he said, winking. "She's smart, quiet, calculating...a mini Tom Abbott, if you will."

I groaned. "*Please* tell me I'm not raising my father."

"Dee." He chuckled. "You're not. You're definitely not. But it would be kinda cool, don't you think? I mean, for Mari to one day be the boss of the whole place?"

"Oh." My skin tingled. "I don't know. I hadn't really thought about it."

"I mean, Lucas has his music, Lola will probably move to Miami and design a line of clothing that I don't ever want to see her wear." He shrugged. "Mari seems more finance-minded."

I dropped my eyes to the floor. Why was it all of a sudden hard to breathe?

"It's kinda fun to think about showing her the ropes one day," he added.

The pins and needles dug deeper into my veins. "I guess?"

What is he saying? Where is this coming from?

"We should give her space, though," I insisted. "To figure out what she likes, what she *wants* to do."

"I'm not disagreeing with you, but maybe she'll *want* to do this."

"And maybe she won't," I snapped, lifting my gaze and pinning Marcos with it.

He held his hands up. "I'm just—"

"You're just what?" I cocked my head, warmth spreading across my chest and creeping up my neck. "Deciding our kid's future before she graduates from middle school?"

"What the hell, Denise? Why are you so pissed off? You

followed in *your* dad's footsteps. Was that the worst thing in the world?"

I don't know, I wanted to scream. *I don't know if it was because I never had a choice. I didn't want to disappoint him. He was the only parent I had, and I couldn't lose him like I'd lost my mom—even though I always acted like I didn't care what he or she or anybody else thought about me.*

I took a sip of wine, hoping it would steady my nerves. "I just think we should let her choose her own path, without steering her in any certain direction."

He scoffed. "So then, I'm not even allowed to talk about it?"

"Not when she's fucking twelve, you're not," I said through gritted teeth.

"I didn't say I was going to call her down here right now and offer her equity in the goddamn company, Denise," he retorted. "I'm talking about later. *If* she wants it. *If* any of the kids want it. Lucas and Lola just haven't expressed an interest."

"And Marisol *has*?"

Marcos sighed and massaged his forehead. "Look, let's drop this. It's not that big of a deal. Seriously, forget I said anything. I was just making conversation."

Rein it in, Denise. Rein it in.

"I'm sorry." I inhaled through my nose, trying to calm my racing pulse. "I didn't mean to be an asshole. I just want the kids to be happy. That's all."

And I don't ever want them to feel like I'm not going to love them if they don't make the decisions that I'd make for them.

He nodded. "I know. I do, too."

"Yeah," I said softly. And even though I knew that was true, something inside me was holding onto what he'd said. Marcos wasn't my father, but the thought of any of our kids feeling like they had to fit into any type of mold scared the hell out of me. I'd lived that life. I was *still* living it. And I knew how painful it could be.

"Okay. So. On to something only slightly less controversial..." He smiled, clearly not having the same trouble I was forgetting our discussion. "Who's this guy Lola mentioned? The one she wants to hang out with this weekend."

"Right," I said, rolling my shoulders back. "His name is Elias. No, Elijah. I think. He's seventeen."

"Automatically no."

"Marcos."

"Okay, keep going."

"He's a senior at one of the arts high schools. I can't remember which."

He looked at me, brow wrinkled and nose scrunched. "He's an *artist*?"

"A painter. And what's with the face?" I twisted my lips. "Need I remind you that your son, the musician, is an artist, as well. And that we work in the film industry, which pretty much consists of"—I brought my hands to my face in mock horror and winked—"artists?"

"Yeah, but Lucas is the exception. And those people aren't dating our daughter," he reasoned. "All the others are tortured and eccentric and spend their time wooing women only to take them to Europe and—"

"Oh, dear God." I pinched the bridge of my nose. "She met him at the *mall*, Marcos. He wants to go to CalArts next year."

"Is that in Europe?"

"Santa Clarita."

He laughed, in spite of himself. "Oh."

"Anyway, I'm surprised she told me as much as she did about him, and I think as long as we meet the guy, it's fine, right? Like, if he comes to the house and we know where they're going, it should be okay. Obviously, she'll have her cell with her because she's fucking glued to it."

Marcos squinted and rubbed the back of his neck. "An *artist*, though?"

I raised my brows. "Would you like him to pull up to the house in a suit and tie, ready for a board meeting?"

"*No*, I just..." He threw his hands up in defeat. "All right. I guess it's fine. I mean, I like art. I buy art from artists. Well, you do that, of course, but I appreciate it." He grinned. "The art *and* you."

I smiled, swallowing the last of my wine. Even after I was a complete jerk about Marisol and the business, he appreciated me. I had to be more careful, though. Even-tempered. Not so emotional.

"But do you think we should maybe, like, check this Elijah guy out online?" Marcos asked, watching the TV as the crowd booed a flag on the football field. "What if he's a felon? Or a drug addict?" He paused and looked over at me. "She's too smart to get mixed up with a guy like that, though, right?"

My empty wine glass toppled out of my hand to the floor, landing with a soft thud on the rug, and the room began to spin.

I can't...What did he...Air...There's no air...I don't...I can't...

Marcos's mouth moved, but his voice was garbled, his face blurred. I rubbed my ears and blinked, shook my head, then blinked again.

"Denise. Babe. Are you okay?"

I sucked in a gulp of air and everything came back into focus. "What?"

"You dropped the..." My eyes followed his finger as he pointed to the floor. "Do you want some water or something? You look—"

"No." I shook my head. "I mean, yes. But I'll, um...I'll get it."

"You sure you don't want me to—"

"I'm fine, I'll be right back," I blurted out, nearly tripping over the glass before scooping it up. I hurried to the kitchen and leaned against the counter, pressing my damp palms onto the cool marble.

"She's too smart to get mixed up with a guy like that, though, right?"

A drug addict? Who would date a drug addict? Only stupid girls, obviously. Only stupid girls who were stupid, stupid, STUPID.

The echoes fell in time with my breath, fast and heavy, repeating the word over and over and over again. I stared at the countertop, as if I might find some wisdom in the twisty veins running through the stone surface.

I'd planned to tell Marcos about Christian on Saturday, while the kids were out of the house, fully prepared for the shock and confusion and anger that would come before I explained why I'd waited, how I'd wanted to make sure Lucas would be safe. Then, once Marcos understood, once he remembered how much I loved him and our family, he'd squeeze my hand and assure me that we'd figure out a way forward, together.

But now...now there was no plan. Not one that involved Marcos anyway. I'd promised myself long ago that I'd never disappoint him, that he would never see the real me, the fucked up me, the stupid and broken and unlovable me. And I wasn't going to break that promise.

I grabbed my purse from the kitchen table, fished out my cell phone, and opened my inbox, searching for Christian's very first message to me where he'd included his phone number. I didn't want him to have mine, so I'd never called, never texted, but this was urgent.

Me: *It's Denise. Are you in town?*

"Everything all right in there?" Marcos asked from the family room.

"Yep," I began, clearing the panic from my voice. "Just needed that water. All good."

My cell pinged, and I clicked on the notification.

Christian: *Yeah. You okay? Lucas okay?*

My hand trembled as I tapped out a response.

Me: *Yes but we need to talk. Can I come over tomorrow at*

I paused, a shaky finger hovering over the keyboard as I tried to think about calendars and schedules.

Me: *2pm?*

I chewed on my thumbnail, waiting for the reply to come in.

Christian: *Of course.*

Another ping.

Christian: *Been thinking about you. Hope you had a good Thanksgiving.*

My chest ached as I stared at the message until the type turned into a watery blur, then I deleted the texts and stuffed the phone back in my purse.

"I think I'm actually going to lie down, sweetie," I called as I started toward the stairs in the foyer. "The wine made me sleepy. You gonna come up soon?"

"Yeah, I'll be there in a bit," he said. "I wanna watch some of the game. You sure you're fine?"

I wasn't fine. I wasn't fine at all. But I told him I was anyway.

Just like I always had.

Just like I always would.

37

NOVEMBER 2009

You just have to tell him. Tell him Lucas can't know. No one can know. And he'll beg, he'll want reasons, he'll say his son has a right to know the truth, but don't let him change your mind. You don't owe him anything. Not one single thing.

I clutched and released the steering wheel of my SUV several times, hoping the tension would flow from my body with each stretch of my fingers. But it had buried itself deep inside the day Christian approached me at the coffee shop, and there were no pep talks or relaxation techniques strong enough to free it. The only cure was Christian promising to go back to Seattle and never contact me or Lucas again.

With one final deep breath, I got out of the car and walked to the guest house. Christian opened the door, wearing a slightly wrinkled T-shirt and faded blue jeans.

He smells like soap. Laundry detergent. Like he did on our first date in the dingy bar all those years ago.

Stop.

"Hey," he said, stepping aside to let me enter. "What's going on? You sure everything's okay?"

"Can we sit...and talk?" I asked.

"Uh, yeah." His eyes narrowed with concern as he swiped his hand over his goatee, then gestured down the hallway. "Yeah, come on in."

I took a seat in one of the chairs in the living room, avoiding the couch, so he couldn't sit next to me with his fresh shower or fresh laundry or whatever-the-hell-it-was scent.

"So, um," he began, perching on the edge of the sofa across from me, resting his elbows on his knees. "Is this about Lucas or..."

"Of course, it's about Lucas," I snapped.

He shrank back to dodge the poison I'd spit at him.

"What else," I began, clearing my throat and softening my tone, "would it be about?"

"Right." He rubbed his lips together as his gaze drifted to the floor. "It wouldn't be about...anything else."

I nodded.

Christian looked back up. "So, is he—"

"I can't tell him."

"What?"

"About you." I swallowed. "I can't tell him."

Christian sucked in a breath and laced his fingers together. "What do you mean, you can't tell him? You said if—"

"I mean, I'm his mother, and I'm not telling him." I tightened my jaw, determined not to give up the real reason I'd come to my decision. "And neither are you."

"Denise." He sighed. "If this is you worrying about whether or not I'm sober, *I am*. You've seen me over a couple months now, and I haven't been high once. I haven't been high in *seven years*, so I don't understand why you're changing your mind about this."

"I'm not changing my mind," I insisted. "All I ever said was that I was thinking about it, and I've realized that I can't do it. I

don't want to create chaos in his life, and if you care about him"
—*if you care about* me—"then you won't want to, either."

"But did I do something?" He held his hands out, palms up. "Did you read something or see something or...did something happen with him or your husband?"

"*No,*" I answered quickly. "No."

Shit. Am I that obvious? Does he know this is about Marcos?

"Well," he said, blinking. "Something had to have fucking happened because last time we met, you wanted to talk more about my sobriety, and now you don't. You've just all of a sudden decided that Lucas can't know."

"I don't have to explain my decision," I said, my eyes examining the paintings on the walls, the sculptures on the bookshelves—anything that wasn't Christian. "I'm just telling you right now that I don't want him to know."

He scoffed. "And you don't think he should be able to make that choice for himself?"

"No, I don't."

He slapped his hands on his knees and stood, pacing the floor. "But why? I've told you how sorry I am. I told you that I fucked up, and if I could go back and change everything, I would. But I can't, and I've worked so fucking hard to get where I am now." He stopped and turned to me, but I focused on the spots in the ivory leopard print throw draped over the sofa. "I deserve this chance, Denise. And Lucas deserves it, too."

I laughed sharply. "Are you fucking kidding me, Christian? He deserves better than you, and he *always* has."

Even if I don't. Even if I never *have.*

"You can say that about the person I was then, but not the one I am now," he bit back. "I've owned my mistakes, I've worked to be better, and I'm going to keep doing those things."

My eyes darted to his before I could stop them. "And how am I ever supposed to believe anything you say, Christian?

After you made me love you by pretending to be someone else. After you lied and lied and lied *again. After you said you didn't care about me or Lucas.*"

His shoulders fell as he shook his head. "I'm not...I didn't pretend to be someone else. I *am* that person you believed in, that you trusted, that you...loved."

"And if you had really loved *me*," I said, standing and jabbing my finger at him, "you wouldn't have let anything stand in the way of that."

"I'm a fucking addict, Denise!" He grasped the top of his head, the muscles in his arms straining. "And I could say I was young and stupid and make a ton of other excuses, but I was just...I was fucking powerless because the drugs were stronger than me."

I crossed my arms over my chest. "How do I know they won't always be?"

"That's the thing. They *will* be. I have to work every day to make sure I stay sober, and I'm not going to lie to you about that," he said, calm returning to his voice. "I'm not going to say it's easy, and I never think about getting high. Because I do. I fucking do, and that's the truth. But it's also true that I haven't gotten high today or for the last seven years."

I raked my hands over my face. "No. I can't, Christian. I'm not telling Lucas, and you're not telling him, either."

"I need to tell him, Denise."

My eyes went wide as adrenaline flooded my body. "*No.* Don't you fucking dare. Because I'll deny it. Or I'll call the cops. Or I'll...I'll do both. And he'll believe me. He has no reason to believe you. *None.*"

"Then tell me what the fuck is going on," he demanded. "Why did you change your mind? Why did you come over here panicking?"

"I'm not panicking," I insisted, chin raised in defiance. "I'm just a mother keeping her son away from a guy who passes out in fucking bathrooms with fucking needles in his fucking arms!"

"No, I know you, Denise." His nostrils flared as he shook his head. "And I know you'll do or say anything to protect yourself when you feel cornered. Which is why I know there's something going on. Something you don't want to tell me."

"You don't *know* me, Christian."

You do know me, and I fucking hate it and I love it, all at the same fucking time.

"I do, Denise. And I know you want people to think you're someone different from who you are. Someone who wouldn't be in this situation."

I narrowed my eyes at him. "You have no idea what the hell you're talk—"

"Are you afraid of Lucas and I having a relationship? Or are you afraid of him finding out about *us*?"

"*What?*"

He stepped closer to me. "Or is it your husband? Are you afraid of *him* finding out?"

I took a step back. "*No.* You do not get to talk about him. You do not get to—"

"Does he even know who you are?" He cocked his head.

"Stop, Christian."

"Does he know how fucking amazing you are? And how much *more* amazing your feelings and fears and all the things you think are flaws make you?"

He's too good to know those things. He won't love me if he does.

My hands began to tremble. "I—"

"*Does he?*" There were only inches between us as his fingertips skimmed my arm, sending a shock of electricity straight through me. "Because *I* know, Denise. And I love you. I always have. *I never stopped.*"

"No, Christian, I can't do this."

But I want to. Because this feels the way it did before everything went wrong. The way I imagined it would every time I dreamed of a life where it all went right instead.

"I don't think you ever understood what you meant to me. What you still mean to me," he said, the heat from his body flushing my skin.

"What do I…" I lifted my gaze and swallowed the lump my words were fighting their way around. "What do I mean to you?"

"Fucking everything."

His eyes bore into me until my heart ached, my core ached, my fucking *soul* ached. I grasped his neck, pulling him toward me, and as soon as our lips met, the pain melted. Its liquid warmth soothed my insides *and* set them on fire, a strange kind of magic only Christian could invoke.

Because he is who he is.

Because I am who I am.

Because we are the same.

I pressed against him, my fingers threading through his hair, my tongue tangling with his. My hands slid down, then up under the hem of his shirt, his skin burning me like a hot stove I wasn't supposed to touch, and he gripped the fabric, sweeping it over his head. I placed my palms on his chest and his stomach, then closed my eyes and let them glide up to his shoulders.

I should stop. I should leave. I should stop.

He cupped my cheek and gently tilted my head upward. "I know you," he said, tracing his thumb over my bottom lip. "The real you."

I raised my lids slowly and shivered before leaning into the familiar touch of his fingers spreading across my ribs and brushing over my nipples, hard against the lace of my bra.

"And I've missed every fucking thing about you." His hand traveled up my chest and settled on my other cheek as he held me with the same feathery gray eyes that had once seemed like the safest place in the world to land.

What if they still are? What if this is what I lost and have been trying to find all these years?

His lips met mine again, teasing them with soft kisses that became harder as I returned them. My shirt floated to the floor, and I unfastened my pants, pushing them down and kicking off my shoes. I fumbled with the button of his jeans, then slid my hands inside, working them down his hips until he was free. He cradled my ass, lifting me, and I wrapped my legs around his waist as he carried me to the wall and pressed my back against it. I wedged my hand between us, tugging my underwear to the side and guiding him into me.

I moaned, my head rolling as he pushed deep inside, the hair on his face scratching my neck, my cheeks, my lips. Our chests rose together with each frantic breath, and I lost all sense of space and time, forgetting that *befores* and *afters* and consequences in between them existed. There was only me and the person who'd once found my heart and made me feel free.

"I can't lose you again," he panted between kisses.

"Yes," I managed, my breath shallow. "Yes."

You can't lose me.

You can't...What?

No. What does that...what does that mean?

"Fuck," he groaned, thrusting deeper. "We're the same, baby. We belong together."

What is he saying?

What am I doing?

The couches, the chairs, and the windows around me came into focus. *This isn't my house. This isn't where I live. With my husband. And my kids.*

Old photos flickered in my mind. Our wedding ceremony in Miami. Lucas wrapped in a newborn blanket. Lola running to me after her first day of kindergarten. Marisol scoring her first soccer goal. Favorite stuffed animals, Christmas trees, birthday cakes, family dinners and—

Everything went black, and I gasped. *What am I doing? I belong there. I belong with them.*

"No." I pressed my hands against Christian's shoulders. "No, I can't...I can't do this, I need to—"

"I'm not gonna fuck things up this time," he began, his hips moving faster. "This is a whole new chance for us."

"Christian, please," I said, trying to free myself from his grasp.

He stopped and pulled back slightly, studying my expression as his chest heaved. "What's wrong? Are you all right?"

"No." I shook my head. "Let me go. Now."

His hands slid to my thighs, and as soon as my bare feet hit the floor, I began gathering my clothes.

"What did I..." He pulled his pants to his waist. "Did I do something wrong?"

"This was a mistake, okay? A horrible fucking mistake. And I'm a horrible fucking person." I stepped into my jeans, then pulled my shirt on. I reached down, hooking my fingers onto my shoes, yanking them off the floor, and took off for the door.

"Denise," he called, following behind me. "It's not a mistake. Just...just talk to me."

"I love my husband, I love my kids, and I shouldn't have done this. That's all there is to say." My voice shook with shame as I opened the front door and stepped onto the pathway to my car.

"No, we can figure this out." His feet tapped against the stones behind me, and I turned around. "It's you and me, remember? You and me, like we always said."

"Don't. *Please don't.* Just let me go home, and you go back to Seattle or anywhere but here." I wiped the back of my hand along my damp cheeks. "Please."

"Denise!"

I hurried down the rest of the pathway, flung myself into my SUV, and peeled out of the driveway, catching a glimpse of my red eyes and tangled hair in the rearview mirror as I checked to make sure he wasn't following me. Once on the main road, I searched for a place to pull over and try to collect myself before I went home, confessed my sins, and did whatever I could to hold onto the one thing I couldn't bear to lose.

38

NOVEMBER 2009

I parked my car in the garage, tore through the kitchen, then ran up the stairs to our bedroom. I closed my eyes and pressed my back against the bathroom door, barricading it like the person I was trying to outrun wasn't inside me. Like it wasn't already too late, and the damage wasn't already done. A flurry of thoughts blew through my brain, and my lungs struggled for air, my heart beating too fast for my body to expend energy on anything else.

I have to calm down.

My eyes darted to the amber prescription bottle on the counter.

No. Not when I have so much to tell him. But a shower...I should shower.

I dashed to the glass enclosure and turned the lever, then stripped off my clothes. Pellets of icy water rained down on me as my feet flattened against the pebble tile, and I grabbed the loofah, saturating it with soap, and scrubbing my skin. I wanted it all gone—his smell, his touch. But no matter how hard I tried, I couldn't wash away what I'd done. I couldn't erase the fact that he'd been inside me.

That I'd done something I hadn't ever imagined I was capable of.

When my skin was too pink and tender to scrub anymore, I finally managed a deep breath, releasing along with it sobs so jagged and raw they were painful for even me to hear. I covered my mouth as my body shook, spasming until my muscles were sore and strained, until my head ached and there were no more hot tears, just chilly droplets falling from above and trickling down my face.

After I stepped out of the shower and wrapped myself in a towel, I immediately grabbed the clothes I'd discarded on the bathroom floor and tossed them in the back of my closet to be thrown away later.

They could be washed a hundred times and never be clean, I thought as the small suitcase in the corner caught my eye.

I hadn't considered the possibility that he'd tell me to leave tonight.

What if he does? Will he ever want me to come back?

I can't think about that now. I just have to think about telling him—everything.

I hurried over to the dresser, pulling on a pair of running shorts and a sweatshirt. The sound of cabinets opening and closing echoed from downstairs as I walked from the bedroom down the hallway.

Marcos was home.

He'd texted while I was on my way back from Christian's, letting me know he was at the gym and he hoped I was having fun with the other soccer moms.

Just one of the many lies I would come clean about.

My handle trembled as it slid down the railing, one bare foot after the other tapping against the hard wood of the steps. I approached the kitchen, stomach churning as I cleared my throat and stood at the entrance.

"Hey," Marcos said, turning around, butter knife in hand as

he popped the top back on a container of mustard. "I know, I know. I should eat an apple or a carrot or something else I hate. But this is kinda healthy, right?"

My eyes brimmed with tears as I surveyed the lunch meat, bread, and condiments on the counter in front of him. *He's making a sandwich*, was all I could think. *He's making a fucking sandwich, and I'm going to tell him that I've ruined our lives.*

"What's wrong?" He slid the knife onto the counter, walked over to me, and brushed the damp hair from my face. "Did you shower again? Do you feel okay?"

"I, um...I need to tell you something." I dabbed at my wet lashes and folded my arms across my chest. "Some things. About Lucas's...biological father."

"Oh. Shit." He sighed and rubbed my shoulder. "Did he contact you or—"

The doorbell rang. I startled and twisted my head.

"Hey," Marcos said softly. "It's okay. That's probably the laptop we ordered for Lola. Lemme just go sign for it, and then we'll talk. Whatever it is, it'll be all right." He kissed my forehead. "Promise."

I closed my eyes as a tear traced its way down my cheek. *Please let him forgive me. I'll do anything. Anything except lie again. No more lying. No more fucking lying.*

"Oh. Hey...Christian. No, I'm fine, I was just expecting someone else. Lucas is at work, but do you, uh...do you want to come in or..."

Marcos's voice was replaced by a high-pitched hum that sent me sideways. My hand landed against the wall before I could crash to the floor.

No. No, no, no.

I pushed myself off the wall and rushed to the foyer. Part of a leather jacket and locks of dark hair were visible around Marcos's shoulder. The same fucking hair I used to lose myself in. The place I would go to forget that anyone else existed, that anyone else mattered in the world but us. Staring at it now, all I saw was guilt and regret, and I wanted to cut it, pull it, rip it out.

"Uh, yeah." Marcos turned from the door, raising his eyebrows when he saw me. "Oh, there she is. Is everything... okay?"

How could this...What is he...How does he know where we live?

I shook my head, trying to calm my thoughts. "What's, um... what's going on?" I asked.

Christian stared at me, lips pressed together as he tapped his fist against the side of his leg. "Did you tell him?"

My heart hammered in my ears. "We, um...we were just about to talk."

Marcos's eyes swung back and forth between us. "Tell me what? What's going on? Is Lucas okay?"

"Lucas is fine. You need to leave, Christian," I demanded, glaring at him.

"I'm sorry." His voice shook as he turned to Marcos. "Because you seem like a good guy. Like a really good guy, but—"

"Shut up, Christian," I warned him.

Marcos looked back at me. "What the fuck is going on?"

No more lies. I promised myself no more lies.

"Christian is..." My blood flashed hot and cold as sweat beaded on my upper lip and my voice grew quiet. "Lucas's father. Biological father."

Marcos blinked and grasped the handle of the door. "What did you say?"

"I'm his—"

"I asked her, not you." Marcos didn't take his eyes off me as he interrupted Christian. "What did you say, Denise?"

This is not how it's supposed to go. This is not how he's supposed to find out. What I did was bad enough, and this is making it worse.

"I...I was going to tell you in the kitchen ju-just now," I

stammered, wringing my hands. "I didn't know he would come over here. I...I didn't know, I swear."

Marcos clenched his jaw and dropped his gaze to the ground. "Leave, Christian."

"I didn't want to do this," Christian continued. "But you needed to know. And you need to know that I love her. That I'm in love with her."

Marcos raised his head, shaking it and letting out an incredulous laugh. "You came to *my* house to tell me you're in love with *my* wife? Are you...Is this serious?" He turned to me. "Is he fucking serious?"

"No. No, he's not in love with me," I insisted. "Stop saying crazy shit and leave, Christian."

Christian's nostrils flared, and his brows turned in as he looked to me. "I *am* in love with you, Denise. You know I am. And you love me, too. You just—"

"Get the fuck out of here," Marcos barked. "*Now.*"

"But I..." Christian's eyes pleaded with me.

Marcos stepped in front of him, blocking his view of me. "I said, get the fuck out of here right *fucking* now," he hissed. "And stay the *fuck* away from my wife, *and* my son."

A car accelerated, then squealed to a stop. My insides froze as a door shut and feet shuffled against concrete.

No. Oh my God, no.

"Hey, man." Lucas chuckled, surprised. "What are you doing here?"

I quickly wiped at my cheeks. Marcos looked back at me, and I bobbed my head, asking him to stand down. He stepped away from Christian, who slowly shifted his eyes to me.

No, I tried to tell him. *He can't find out like this. Please don't do this to him. Please.*

Christian's face fell, and he took a deep breath before turning his attention back to Lucas. "I just stopped by because I...I'm actually leaving. I've got to head back to Seattle and take care of some stuff, and I'll be up there till after Christmas, so I just wanted to let you know."

I looked at Marcos, hoping we could share a brief moment of relief, but he was so focused on Lucas that he didn't notice.

Of course. Because that's the type of father he is.

Lucas nodded, a hint of concern on his face. "Yeah. Yeah, I understand. But you should come in for a bit. I got off work early so—"

I gasped, immediately coughing to cover my fear.

"I actually have to get packed, so I need to head out," Christian said, thumbing toward his car. "But I'll, uh...I'll see you soon."

"All right, man. I'll see ya." Lucas gave him a small wave, then walked inside as Christian jogged down the steps, glancing at me once more before Marcos shut the door. "You okay, Mom?"

"I'm fine," I said, sniffing. "Just allergies or something. I'm good."

Lucas started upstairs. "Okay. I'm gonna change and head to Mia's."

"All right, sweetie."

Marcos turned to me as soon as Lucas disappeared from our sight, and the brief wave of relief I'd felt receded. "What's going on, Denise?" he asked, his voice quavering. "What the *fuck* is going on?"

His sad eyes glistened, slicing my heart in two.

"I'll tell you everything," I said, pressing my hand against my chest until it ached, hoping I was strong enough to keep the two halves beating until they became whole again. Although I wasn't sure they ever would.

———

"I still don't understand, Denise." Marcos finally stood and paced the sitting area in our bedroom. He'd been slouched in the chair across from me since we'd heard Lucas leave the house fifteen minutes before, and I'd begun telling the story of how Christian had ended up in LA again. Of how he'd come back into my world. *Our* world.

"Why didn't you tell me when you saw him at the coffee shop? Or at least that night after the show when we"—his jaw tightened—"when *I* first met him."

Tears wet my palms as I dropped my head into my hands. "I know. I should've told you. But I..." There was so much. So much I couldn't explain to him because even I didn't understand. "Maybe I...maybe I was hung up on the fact that you'd always said you didn't want to know anything about him. About Lucas's father. Or maybe I—"

"No," he snapped so loud that I jerked up. "You're not going to put this on me."

My fingers slid down my face. "You're right," I said. Because he was. That wasn't a reason. It was an excuse, and a shitty one, at that. "I just...I thought he'd go away. That I could *get* him to go away. But I...couldn't."

"And it didn't occur to you to tell me after you realized he wasn't going anywhere?"

"Yes, but I got worried about him being around Lucas." I wiped my nose on the back of my hand. "And I thought if I could make sure he was sober and then tell you, you'd feel better about it. Or even if he wasn't sober, we could figure it out from there."

"That doesn't make any sense, Denise." He stopped pacing and looked at me, his expression more disappointed than angry. "That doesn't make any fucking sense."

"I know it sounds ridiculous now, but it made sense at the time, and I just..."

He frowned, brows pinched, waiting for me to continue.

"I was so fucking *embarrassed*, Marcos. Embarrassed that I was with a heroin addict. That I stayed with him. That I let myself get pregnant by him."

"And you thought I'd judge you for that?" he asked, a hint of sadness in his voice.

"No. I don't know." I shrugged. "Maybe I did."

"So you lied because you didn't think I'd understand why you did the thing you did a million years ago? The thing that ultimately gave me a life with you and Lucas?" He blew out a breath. "How can you think so little of me, Denise? *How?*"

"I don't," I said, my voice cracking. "I don't think so little of you..." *I just think so little of me.* "Being with him wasn't something I was proud of, and I wanted to make sure he was sober before I let him into Lucas's life. And if I found out he wasn't, I was going to—"

"You were going to what? Tell him to go away and assume he'd listen because he'd be totally reasonable about it if he was still on drugs?" He inhaled sharply. "I mean, *what the hell?* You're so smart. You're the smartest person I know, but this was..."

Stupid. Fucking stupid. I held my breath, waiting for him to say it.

"We're supposed to be a team," he said instead. "We're supposed to figure shit out together. But you lied to me. For *months.*" He rubbed the back of his neck. "Was there something...*more* between you and him?"

"I..." *Don't lie. Don't lie.*

"Shit, Denise." He collapsed back onto the chair and let out a humorless laugh. "You can't answer that without having to stop and think about the goddamn question?"

His voice rose, and I pressed my palms together.

"Marcos, please. I'm trying to tell you. To be honest."

He rubbed his hand over his mouth as he dropped his eyes

to the floor. "Then tell me this." His eyes shifted back up. "Was what he said true? Are you in love with him?"

"No," I insisted, shaking my head. "I'm not. I swear, I'm not."

If someone had asked me that morning, during the time now distinctly marked as *before*, I wouldn't have known what to say. But looking at Marcos, I knew that while I may have thought I *deserved* Christian, I *loved* my husband.

"I guess part of it was because I wanted...closure." I swallowed. "I wanted to know why things worked out the way they—"

"So, did you think about him all these years?" He snorted. "Fuck, of course you did. He's Lucas's father, which, you know, *wow*, still trying to process that one." He ran his hand through his hair, stood up, and resumed his pacing. "But did you think about him other than that?"

"I..." I *had* thought about him, there was no denying that, but I didn't know how to explain the *why* to Marcos because I couldn't fully grasp it myself. "I don't know. I just...Don't people think about their exes? That's...people do that, don't they?"

"I don't," he said, pursing his lips. "I honestly don't. Not beyond a memory or two here or there. And I guess..." He exhaled. "I guess I can understand that maybe sometimes people wonder how their lives would've been different, but you were...*seeing him. Behind my fucking back.*"

"No, I wasn't. I mean, I was, but you make it sound like we had a relationship or something. And we didn't. It wasn't like that. I was just trying to find out more about his life before I told you, and we told Lucas."

He crossed his arms over his chest. "And how far did you go with that? How far did you go to 'find out more about his life'?"

My body tensed. *How do I do this? How do I tell him what I've done and that I'll do anything to make it right?*

His eyes narrowed at me in slow motion. "Did you sleep with him, Denise?"

I blinked, my breath heavy in my head and my ears as I stared at the floor.

"Did you sleep with him?" he asked again.

I nodded my head forward, then back, and tears streamed down my face as I looked up. "Once."

Crimson anger crept up Marcos's neck and spread across his face as he gripped his head. "God*dammit*, Denise. What the *fuck*?"

I opened my mouth and meaningless words began to tumble out. "It didn't...It barely happened because I knew it was wrong, it was *so* wrong, and I left, and I came back here, and I was going to tell you everything and then—"

"And then he showed up at *our fucking house*?" His voice boomed at the end, and I winced. "Jesus *fucking* Christ." My reaction, my silence told him all he needed to know. "You slept with him—no, I'm sorry, you *fucked* him *today*. You weren't having coffee with the soccer moms, you were having sex with your ex-*fucking*-boyfriend."

"Marcos, I'm sorry. I'm so sorry. I didn't mean to, I didn't. I don't know why I did it, it was...it was just for a minute, and like I said, I stopped it. I stopped it and I—"

"Oh. Well. That's okay, then," he said, his voice slathered in sarcasm. "He *did* put his dick in you, but neither of you came, so it's fine. That's not *really* sex." He brought his fists to his forehead. "Fuck!"

"Marcos, I—"

"This is messed up. This is so messed up." He began to pace faster. "What the hell is wrong with you? What the fuck kind of person are you? I don't...I don't understand this at all." He raked his hands down his face. "*What the fuck, what the fuck, what the fuck.*"

My entire body trembled. "I...don't know what else to say. Just please know that I am *so* sorry, and I don't want to be with him, and I don't love him. I love you and the kids and our life, and I...I know it's probably impossible for you to understand because I don't understand it, either, but I'll do anything to make it up to you. Anything for you to forgive me."

"I can't..." He shook his head. "I can't do this right now, Denise. I don't care if you fucked him for one minute or one hour. We've been married eighteen fucking years, and you just threw us in the *goddamn trash*."

"No," I cried as invisible fists squeezed the two halves of my heart, draining them, bleeding them dry. "Don't say that. Please don't say that. I love you. I love you so—"

"How am I supposed to be here? How am I supposed to even look at you?" The crimson had drained from his face, which was now pale. "I don't...I can't do this."

"Marcos, please."

"I, um..." He looked around the room. "I need to leave."

"Oh my God. No. No, please don't leave." I stood and stumbled toward him, reaching for his hand, which he snatched away.

"I'm going to a hotel," he began, walking to the closet. "I need to figure this out."

"No, Marcos, can you just...Can we talk more, can I—"

"I'll stay for a couple days," he said, pulling the carry-on out into the room. "You can tell the kids I had to go out of town at the last minute for work or something."

"I can't...I can't tell them that. They won't believe it, not on Thanksgiving weekend."

"Shit." He tossed the suitcase on the bed and unzipped it. "I don't know, then. Tell them—"

"I'll go," I blurted out. "I'll go to the Ojai house."

"How is that any different?"

"I'll tell them it's for, uh...a spa weekend. That I got a...last-minute invitation. You stay here. It's more believable, and I don't want them thinking anything." I moved toward him, cautiously. "I'll come back early next week. And I'll make sure

Lola and Marisol are taken care of, rides to and from school, all that stuff while I'm gone."

I didn't want to go, but it was comforting to know that he'd be home with the kids and wouldn't leave for good. At least not until I got back.

"I'll go," I repeated. "This is all my fault, so I'll go."

"You're right. It is your fault," he said. "And fine, go to Ojai. But we need to figure out a way to tell Lucas about..." He choked, then cleared his throat and wiped at his eyes. "If Lucas wants him in his life, I don't...*Fuck*, I don't know how to *fucking* do this."

"We have time. He's leaving. Christian told Lucas he's leaving." Acid burned the back of my throat as I said his name.

Marcos scoffed. "And you believe him? You really think he gives a shit how this is handled? He fucking showed up at our house and told me he was in love with you. *Lucas could've been here for that.* Any of the kids could have been here."

"I know." I nodded. "But I...I think he'll really go back, so we have time to tell Lucas."

"But what if he calls Lucas, what if—"

"I don't know. But I don't think he will." I didn't want to explain to him that the look on Christian's face when he told Lucas he was leaving was enough to convince me that we were safe for now. He knew he'd done enough harm. He didn't want to add hurting Lucas to his list of wrongs. "We'll tell Lucas. Together. Soon. This is just...This is all too much, and I—"

"Well, you should've thought about that, Denise, before you dug this fucking hole we're sitting in right now."

"I'm sorry. I'm so sorry." My voice was thick with tears.

I could say it a thousand times, but it would never be enough to undo what I had done, to fix the hurt I'd caused, to make Marcos see me as anything but the fucking liar and cheater I was.

He slid the suitcase toward me, then walked to the door, his hand on the knob as he turned around. "It's like I don't even know you," he said, shaking his head and leaving the room.

You didn't *know me*, I thought. *But now you do.*

I dropped to the bed, curling my legs tight against my aching body. Tears rolled onto the pillow as I tried to summon the strength to pack my clothes and get ready for a stay at the house in Ojai. The house my father had given to me when my mother left. The one I'd never sold, which mostly remained vacant except for a few random weekends each year with Marcos (and the kids before they lost interest).

The kids.

I'd tell them that I needed the time away at the spa with a few friends so I could unwind from work and life and get ready for the busy holiday season. Even though there was no spa, and there would be no unwinding. I'd be all alone in a quiet house where I would spend every waking hour imagining what my life would be like without them and without Marcos.

I don't want to be alone. I can't *be alone.*

I reached over to the nightstand and picked up the cordless phone, dialing one of the few numbers I had memorized. I placed it against my ear, pressing my fingers to my lips and closing my eyes as it rang. And when the call connected, I could only manage a few words before I broke down.

"I fucked up, Eva. I fucked up really bad."

39

NOVEMBER 2009

"Here," Eva said, handing me a mug of hot tea. "Let's hold off on the wine. Have you eaten?"

"I'm not hungry." I reached for her arm as she turned to head back to the kitchen. "And you should sit down. You've done enough."

"Are you sure? I got cheese and crackers and...more cheese." She gritted her teeth. "Mostly, I got cheese. I figured I could pick up something for dinner in a couple of hours, but I can go now if—"

"Sit," I insisted, pointing to the opposite end of the couch. "You flew all the way out here, stopped at the grocery store on your way to the house, then let me *literally* cry on your shoulder for an hour. We'll eat later."

"Well, it's not like Ojai exactly sucks." She winked, flopped down, and propped her back against the arm of the sofa. "And I always want to see you. I just feel like I should be doing something."

Eva had gotten in around 3 p.m., several hours after I arrived at the house. The kids hadn't batted an eye at my last-minute spa invitation story, and Marcos barely said a word as

I'd walked by him, hiding in my baggy sweat suit with my roller bag trailing behind me. The sky had turned a beautiful shade of blue as I drove into the valley, and I knew it would do me good to sit outside, letting the sun seep into my skin while taking in the view of the mountains from the patio. Instead, I'd landed on the sofa under a chenille throw, hoping my life would somehow magically put itself back together.

"Seriously, I feel like I should be helping," she added, gathering her blond hair into a ponytail. "What can I do?"

I swiped my fingers under my eyes, my husband's silence when I left the house still haunting me. "You not hating me is plenty."

She tilted her head, and her eyes softened. "Babe. I could never hate you."

"I just, um...I don't want you to think I'm Aaron. Because I feel like Aaron right now." I took a sip of my tea. "And I feel like I not only let Marcos and the kids down, but I...I let you down, too."

"Hey," she said, stretching her legs parallel to mine along the leather cushions. "Unless you've knocked up the girl you've been seeing behind my back for a year and plan on asking me for a divorce, *you're not him.*"

"But did you think about that, though? When I told you on the phone that I'd...you know." I dropped my eyes to my lap, and Eva sighed.

"You can tell me," I said, looking back up.

"I guess when you first told me, I did, but it's..." She took a deep breath. "It's not the same."

"But I did to my husband what your husband did to you, and I..." I tipped my head back to keep the tears from falling. "I don't know how to forgive myself for that."

"Denise. Aaron had a full-blown affair, which involved *so* much sex that he got the chick pregnant, for fuck's sake. *Then* he decided he wanted a whole new life and packed his bags before I even knew what the hell was going on. No *sorry*, no nothing. So, trust me. It's not the same."

"But—"

She held up her finger. "And even if it *was* the same, it's not, and I don't care if that doesn't make sense. You're my best friend, and I'm on your side, and I'm here for you. I'm *always* here for you."

"But it would make sense if you don't want to be around me. If you just came out of obligation because you're a good person. And friend. The *best* friend."

"What do you mean?" She leaned forward. "I'm here because I love you."

"I didn't want to tell you. About...*that* part. I didn't want you to think I'm like him, but also I...I didn't want to lie about it."

"You can tell me anything," she assured me. "And I want you to hear me say that and know, I mean *anything*. Because sometimes I think maybe you *want* to tell me things, but you don't. Like you don't think I'll understand or—"

"Oh my God, Eva. No." I held out my free hand to stop her thoughts. "That's not it at all. It's just, you're busy, you know? You've got two kids, you're starting back to work after Christmas, you've got this whole new relationship, which is amazing, and I'm so happy for you. You don't need me to burden you with my shit."

Her brows pinched together. "Burden me?"

Burden you and make you leave me, too, I wanted to say but nodded instead.

"Denise. You're never a burden to me. And I *want* you to come to me with your shit. I want to be there for you like you've been there for me. I couldn't get on that fucking plane fast enough when you called."

"I know. And I know it's not easy to leave on a moment's notice, so thank you. Truly."

"Please," she said, waving me off. "Aaron has the boys this

weekend anyway. They'll go over Eric's tomorrow night and stay with him till I get back. They're fine. They're more than fine. They're going to eat a bunch of crap and do whatever they want."

I managed a sad laugh as I placed my mug on the end table and curled my knees to my chest.

"So, um...did you talk to Marcos?" she asked, her voice faltering. "Let him know you got here this morning?"

"I texted him. He just said *Okay* and that's it, really. We agreed to talk about things when I get back, but..." Tears welled behind my eyes. "What if he doesn't stay, Eva?"

She reached forward and gave my foot a squeeze. "Right now, you just need to give him space to process things."

"But I...I slept with another man. And not just any other man, with Lucas's *father,* for Christ's sake. And for months, I hid everything about him from Marcos, and I...I just don't understand how I could've done this. I don't know how he isn't going to hate me forever." My body shook as I rested my forehead on my knees.

"I know, babe. It was a mistake. A big mistake, yes, but you got caught up in the moment, and you immediately realized it was wrong."

"I should've told Marcos about Christian as soon as I knew he was in town, though," I continued, lifting my head and smoothing my hair from my face. "That's what a fucking normal person would have done. And then none of this would've happened. But I'm not normal, and I fucked everything up."

"Have you thought about why you didn't tell him?" she asked, her voice quieting.

"I mean, it's, um..." I shrugged. "It's what I told you on the phone, I guess. I didn't want Marcos to get hurt, or Lucas to get hurt, so I thought maybe I could somehow deal with it myself. And then when it was clear Christian wasn't going away, I...I don't know. I told myself I was doing the right thing, making sure he was sober. I was just so embarrassed about the past."

There were other reasons, I was sure of it. But those reasons were butterflies, diving up and down and right and left, too quick to catch. And even if they made it into my net, they would slip away within seconds.

Maybe I was letting them go on purpose. Maybe I was afraid of what I might find if I actually captured them and peeled back their skeletons to see what was beneath.

"I know," she said. "I know those things are true, but have you *really* thought about why you didn't tell him?"

"What do you..." I wiped my nose on the cuff of my sweatshirt. "What do you mean?"

"Look, I don't know everything about Marcos, but I do know he loves you. And I don't think you ever need to be embarrassed to tell him anything, just like you don't have to worry about that with me." She pushed up, crossing her legs, one over the other. "It's like I said before about how I think you sometimes hold me at a little bit of a...distance. And I just wonder if..."

My shoulders fell. "I don't mean to, Eva. Really, I don't."

Except I do. I know I do so you won't see that I don't deserve someone as good as you in my life. So that you won't leave me, too.

"Babe, this is not me being angry." She scooted close to me, placing her hand on my knee. "When we were younger, sometimes I thought I'd done something wrong, but then I realized it wasn't that. It's not that you don't love me as much as I love you. It's just...maybe you're afraid? Like you don't want me to see any side of you that's vulnerable. And I don't know, but maybe you do that with Marcos, too? Does that...make sense?"

I opened my mouth to protest. To say, *No, I don't do that!* then try to change the subject. But the way she held me with her eyes made the truth feel safe.

"Yeah," I whispered. "It makes sense."

"Just please know I've never expected you to be anything but human. I want to know everything you want to tell me, the good *and* the bad, and I won't judge you, and I won't leave you. *Ever.*"

Does she mean that? It's so easy for people to say these things and then...

I bit my bottom lip. "But what if...what if it's too late with Marcos?"

"I don't know what's going on in his head right now, but I do know there are ways to get through this," she said. "Have you talked to your therapist? You still see her, right?"

I sniffed. "I don't...I mean, I don't really...*do that* with her. I just thought every female executive was supposed to have one, so I used to go when work was super stressful, and we'd talk about that stuff. I haven't actually seen her in months."

"Did she ever dig deeper than work issues?"

My body tensed at the idea of anyone knowing what lived inside me—the thoughts, the reasons, the *butterflies* that hid something sad and shameful beneath their hard shells flanked with pretty, patterned wings.

"She tried, and that's when I kinda...stopped going."

Eva raised her brows. "Could you think about opening up to her a little? I mean, therapy helped me so much in working through all the stuff I'd been dealing with for...well, for forever. I started to see why I did the things I did, why I put up with the bullshit, why I lost myself for so many years. And I know it doesn't automatically solve all the problems, but being able to understand the reasons was so...I don't know. It was almost like I could forgive myself and start to move forward."

Forgive myself. Ha. As if I ever could. As if I ever should.

"Yeah, maybe I can call her. I'll...I'll think about it."

Will I? Or am I lying again?

"Good," she said, smiling.

I nodded and took a deep breath. "So. Let's get my mind off

this for a bit," I began, stretching my hands over my head as though everything would flow up and out and be forgotten. "Tell me what's going on with you. Are you and Eric still gonna look for a house after the holidays?"

She eyed me cautiously. "Denise, we don't have to talk about this."

We do. Because I can't talk about me anymore and why no thera-pist is going to be able to fix me. I'm fucking broken, and all I can do to keep my family together is beg for forgiveness, then put the mask back on and never let it slip again.

"No, it's fine. I want to," I insisted, leaning in and clasping her hands.

"Are you sure?" she asked.

I smiled. "I'm sure."

"Well, then, yeah. We are." She squealed. "And sometimes I think it's kinda quick, and then other times, I think we can't do it fast enough. I mean, he's been in Nashville since July, and with how well he and the boys took to each other, it just seems silly that we're in the house, and he's in that condo."

I squeezed her fingers. "I'm so happy this is all working out for you, babe."

Eva sighed, the light that had once disappeared from her eyes back and brighter than ever. "Thanks. I feel like a fucking teenager again, before all the terrible shit happened. I'm excited and giddy and ridiculous and..." She paused and laughed. "Not in love with an asshole this time around."

"Aw, that's so sweet." My voice turned from sugar to spice as I pursed my lips. "Now, tell me about the dirty, dirty sex."

"Ah, right. Just when I think I've escaped." She uncrossed her legs and stood. "Fine. I'll give you all the juicy details, but let me open that wine first."

"Good idea," I said. "And hey."

She stopped and turned to me.

"I love you. Even if it's hard for me to say certain things." I brushed a tear from my cheek and smiled. "I don't know what I'd do without you."

"I love you, too," she said, returning my smile. "And don't worry. This is for life. I'm talking, going out in a South Florida retirement community eating cheesecake in our nightgowns, *Golden Girls* style."

"Deal. As long as it's not Miami." I grimaced. "My mother-in-law is there, and I'm fairly certain there'll be wanted posters of me on every street corner."

"Eh." Eva waved her hand in the air. "She won't be around by the time we're eighty, right?"

"You obviously don't know Marta Navarro," I said. "That woman is gonna live forever, just to spite me."

40

JANUARY 2010

Marcos walked into our bedroom—or was it *my* bedroom now?—and crossed his arms over his chest. "They're all here, so we need to do this. We need to tell them."

How is it time? How is it time to take down the Christmas tree, put away the decorations, and tell the kids that their happy family isn't happy anymore?

It seemed like just yesterday I'd left Ojai, holding onto a tiny bit of hope that I could fix what I had broken.

After I'd gotten home, Marcos and I spent our days trying to act like nothing had happened and our nights trying to sort through the mess I'd made of our lives. For a two weeks, I begged him to stay, swore I would do anything to keep our family together, and asked him what I could do to make him believe I loved him. But there was nothing. It would take time for him to believe that again, he'd said, adding, "And I'm not sure I ever will." We decided to talk to the kids after Christmas, after his mother went back to Miami, then figure out what to do about work and running the business together. And, of course, we'd tell Lucas about Christian.

"Can you let him know we're handling this?" Marcos had

asked me one night before heading to bed in the guest room (any questions from the kids about sleeping arrangements covered up with an excuse about snoring). "Text him or call him or fly up to Seattle and fuck him again. I don't really care what you do, he just needs to know we're telling Lucas after the holidays, and it would be great if he could keep his fucking mouth shut till then."

And now, Marcos was standing in the doorway of the bedroom once again, this time maybe the last he would ever do so. I used every bit of strength I had to force the tears back behind my eyes, down whatever tubes and trails would carry them to a burial place deep inside. He'd seen enough of them, and I was sure they only made him hate me more.

"Right. We have to tell them," I said. "Are they downstairs?"

"Lucas and Marisol are watching TV. Lola is in her room, so I'll..." His voice cracked. "I'll get her."

"Okay." My eyes met his, and I told myself that if he didn't look away, he didn't really want this, he hadn't really rented a condo in Century City, and his clothes weren't really packed in suitcases. All he wanted was to hear me say *I'm sorry* one more time, and he would stay. But he slid his hands in his pockets, and his gaze fell to the floor.

"I'll meet you downstairs," he said before he turned and left the room.

If I don't go, what will happen? Will he bring them to the bedroom? Will he make me tell them anyway? Will he call a lawyer, even though he said he wasn't going to do that right now? Even though he told me he just wanted space to figure out what he needed.

I already knew all *I* needed was for him to stay, and not because he was required in order to perpetuate the myth of my perfect life. As much as I'd hidden from people over the years, he and the kids were never part of the charade. They were unexpected gifts I'd somehow received along the way, and my love for them was never a lie, never for show.

A minute passed, and when I realized Marcos wasn't coming back, I pushed myself off the bed, trudged through the hallway, and started down the stairs. Each step felt heavy, like the truth was weighing me down rather than setting me free. I leaned against the wall at the bottom of the staircase until the sound of Lola's voice from above sent me through the foyer to the family room, which was lit by the colored bulbs on the Christmas tree, the television, and a dimmed lamp.

The tree. How can we do this when the Christmas tree is up?

"Hi," I said, my throat thick and dry.

Lucas looked up from the couch, where he was sprawled out with his phone. "Hey."

Marisol waved from one of the chairs without taking her eyes off the television. Her legs were tucked underneath her, and she was watching *Twilight*. I remembered she'd been watching it that day in October when she stayed home from school, and I'd gone to the store to get ginger ale. The same day Christian stopped me outside the coffee shop.

How did I manage to destroy my life in three short months?

I looked around the room, wondering where one sat to tell their children that their lives were being upended. Or was standing best? As I debated about the most appropriate location, Marcos and Lola appeared.

"So what's going on?" Lola asked. "What's *so* important that we have to 'talk as a family'?" She curled her fingers, quoting what I assumed Marcos had told her.

I looked at Marcos out of the corner of my eye, hoping he would understand what I was silently saying. *This is an ambush. We can't do this to them. We can't do this to our babies.*

He met my gaze with daggers and messaged back. *There is no we. You did this. This is happening because of you.*

"Your mom and I need to tell you something." His eyes flicked away from me. "Something that isn't easy, but we're going to deal with it as a family."

Lucas set his phone down and raised his head. "Huh?"

I wanted to speak but was afraid I might unravel into a string of *I'm sorrys*. Marcos and I had agreed we'd remain calm. Sometimes people needed time apart. It had nothing to do with them. It was nobody's fault.

Even though it was mine.

Lola's lips formed a thin line as she looked at me, then Marcos. "What's going on?"

"Mari, turn off the TV," Lucas said, sitting up and planting his feet on the floor.

Marisol swiveled her head and blinked. "What?"

"The TV," Lucas repeated firmly. "Turn it off."

She fumbled for the remote beside her and cut the power. "What's wrong?"

We can't do this, how can we do this, please don't make me do this.

"Your mom and I are going to…"

Please don't say it.

"Take some time apart."

All the air left the room, and I reached for the back of the chair beside me.

"What? What do you mean?" Lucas asked, turning to me before Marcos could answer. "Mom, what does he mean?" His expression flashed between confusion and sadness.

Don't cry, don't cry, don't cry.

"We, uh…" I looked in Marcos's direction.

"We need some time apart because we believe that's better for us right now while we work on our problems," he said, sticking to the script.

Lola narrowed her eyes at me. "What problems?"

Oh God. She knows. Somehow, she knows that I did this, that I'm the problem.

I opened my mouth, seconds passing as I tried to remember

the words I was supposed to say. "I didn't...I mean, we just need to..." My gaze shifted back to Marcos, who tightened his jaw.

I'm sorry, I wanted to say. *I'm sorry I'm fucking this up. I'm sorry I fuck everything up.*

"We just have some...differences," he explained. "And we need some space right now."

"So..." Marisol's voice quavered as she looked up at Marcos. "You don't want to live here anymore?"

Something shattered inside me, and I dropped my head, watching as a tear rolled off my nose. It exploded into a thousand tiny Christmas-colored droplets as it hit the floor, and a cacophony of voices sounded, stabbing my ears, one knife after another.

"Of course, I do, but sometimes it's better to live apart."

"I don't understand."

"It's okay to be confused. Just know we still love you."

"This doesn't make sense."

"Why is this happening?"

"Why are you doing this?"

"Why?"

"Why?"

"*Why?*"

The noise faded into a low hum, then stopped.

"Mom," Lucas said.

I gasped and looked up.

"Why aren't you saying anything?" he asked.

"Sorry, I..." I tried to focus through the ocean in my eyes.

Lola slumped on the couch. Lucas standing beside her, fingers threaded through his hair. Marisol sobbing from across the room, her face buried in Marcos's side, his arm wrapped around her.

"Mari," I said, hurrying toward her. "No, baby. It's going to be okay."

She let go of Marcos and landed against me. I stroked her hair and held her close. "I promise it'll be all right."

"So," Lola began, her voice sharp as she wiped at her face. "Who's moving out?"

"I'm..." Marcos's voice caught in this throat. "I have a condo close by. But we've worked out a schedule so I'll see you all the time, and neither of us will miss games or shows or birthdays or—"

"*Birthdays?*" Lucas snorted. "How long are you planning on doing this?"

"We'll figure that out," Marcos said. "Nothing is set in stone."

Lucas raked his hands down his face and blew out a breath. "But where is this coming from? You didn't seem...Everything seemed fine."

"These things can happen in marriages. But this family will always be our priority. *Always.*" Marcos's voice was steady and calm, making the guilt gnaw harder at my insides.

I almost wished he would tell them what I'd done, that I was the one to blame, that they should all move out so I would be alone because that's what I deserved.

"Let's sit down and—"

"I don't want this." Marisol said, cutting Marcos off as her body trembled against mine. "I don't want you guys to get divorced."

I looked up at Marcos. *What do I say? What do I fucking say?* "Sweetie, we're not getting divorced right now, we're just going to live apart for a while and see if that's better for us."

"That's divorce," Marisol cried.

"No, baby girl, it's not divorce," I assured her.

Not yet.

Lola stood and raised her chin, an attempted act of defiance that reflected more hurt than rebelliousness. "Whatever. I hate this family anyway. I don't care what you guys do."

"Lola," Marcos called after her as she marched from the room.

But there was only the sound of bare feet slapping against the tile in the foyer and the wood on the stairs, culminating with the distant slam of a door.

I pulled back from Marisol and held her face in my hands, brushing away her tears with the pads of my thumbs. "Can we sit down? Can Daddy and I explain this to you?" I looked at Lucas. "And your brother?"

Lucas sighed and walked around the arm of the couch, then flopped onto the cushions with his head down. I sat beside him with Mari snuggled against me, while Marcos settled into the chair across from us.

He leaned forward, elbows on his knees. "I know this isn't easy," he said, his hands clasped together. "But your mom and I both love you all more than anything in the world. And we *will* get through this."

I closed my eyes, pulled Marisol closer, and pretended he was talking to me, even though I knew he wasn't.

I was on my own.

Just like I'd always imagined I would be.

———

"Denise. Hey."

I opened my eyes to see Marcos leaning over me, gently shaking my arm. "Hmm?"

"You fell asleep," he said, standing upright.

"What?" I surveyed the room. "What time is it?"

"A little after eight. So we, um...we should talk to Lucas."

Lucas? Why should we talk to Lucas? Is he okay, is he—

"We need to tell him," he clarified.

My stomach twisted. *Right.* Marcos and I had agreed to do this after we talked to all the kids about the separation.

I pushed myself up to sit. "Where's Marisol? We were watching TV."

"She's in Lola's room."

"Oh." I looked up at him. "Are they okay?"

"I don't know. I mean, they will be. It'll just...take time." He massaged his forehead and gestured behind him with his thumb. "Lucas is out back in the music room."

The music room was a small space off the pool house, which Lucas had taken over several years before. Of course, he'd gone there. He probably wanted to forget that anything existed in the world but his guitars. And once he found out about his real father, he'd probably want to use all of those guitars to write a song about how much he hated me.

"Do you, um..." I cleared my throat. "Do you think we should wait? It's just so much on him in one day."

Marcos glared at me. "How long should we wait, Denise? You think doing it tomorrow will make it easier? Or should we wait a week, maybe two or three, and let him find out from your fucking boyfriend?"

"Marcos, he's not—"

"Oh, I'm sorry," he said, his tone telling me he was anything but. "I meant, should we let him find out from the guy you fucked nineteen years ago, and then fucked again after Thanksgiving."

I pressed my hand against my chest and winced.

"I'm..." He covered his mouth with his hand, rubbing his finger along his upper lip. "Look, this is the last fucking thing on earth I want to do right now. I don't know if..." The muscles in his face strained. "I don't know if I'm going to lose my son."

I scrambled up from the couch and reached for his arm. "No, Marcos. No, you won't lose him."

He stepped back, not allowing me to touch him, then took a breath and ran a hand through his tousled hair. His eyes were tired and rimmed in red, and I knew it would take so much more than a good night's sleep to make their browns and greens and golds shine again.

"I just need to get this over with," he said, then turned and strode out of the room.

I followed behind him, propelled by the tiny bit of strength I had left.

The night was chilly, and I hadn't bothered to ask Marcos for time to grab a sweater or shoes because I knew I didn't deserve that courtesy. My bare feet sank into the cold, damp grass, and I wiggled my toes to make sure I was still in control of my mind and my body. That I hadn't floated away, helpless to do anything but watch what was happening to me. A dog barked in the distance, and I had a thought that I should get the kids a pet. We'd once had a hamster and a fish, but never a dog or a cat. Never something they could cuddle with. *Maybe that's what they need. Maybe* that *will make them happy again.*

"Denise." Marcos's voice shook me from my thoughts. "We need to do this."

I blinked and all of a sudden, he was halfway through the backyard. A breeze blew through my veins, and I shivered. How long had I been standing there? Maybe I *had* floated outside myself.

"Oh, sorry," I said quietly. I folded my arms across my chest and rubbed my pebbled skin, forcing my legs to move forward.

The shed glowed ahead of me, the light from the window yellow and hazy. Marcos waited for me, then knocked and cracked the door.

Lucas looked up from the futon where he sat in a hoodie and jeans, plucking the strings on his acoustic. "Hey."

"Hey, kiddo," Marcos said, stepping to the side so I could slip by him. "You got a minute to talk?"

"Yeah." Lucas nodded and placed the guitar in its stand. "Are you guys...okay?"

"There's, um, one more thing we need to tell you." Marcos

sat on one of the amps along the wall and leaned forward, forearms resting on his thighs. "Something we didn't want to talk about in front of your sisters because...well, this is for you to share with them only if you want to."

Lucas's brows angled in. "Uh, all right. Is this something bad or..."

"It's...I'll let your mom tell you." Marcos's foot tapped against the floor as he nodded to me. "We agreed she needs to tell you."

Lucas twisted his head. "What's going on?"

I have to do this. This is my fucking mess, and I have to clean it up.

"I need to..." I pointed to the futon as I walked across the room and sat down, facing him.

Lucas took a shaky breath. "Seriously, you guys have to tell me before I freak out. Is someone dying?"

"No. But your...biological dad. He asked me if you wanted to maybe...get to know him."

"*What?*" Lucas's gray eyes went wide, but his voice was quiet.

My lungs seized, trapping my breath. It wasn't like I hadn't expected the surprise and the confusion, but seeing it in real time was something I couldn't have prepared myself for, no matter how many times I'd imagined his reaction in my head.

"I know it's a lot. And you don't have to do anything you don't want to do." I placed my hand on his shoulder. "I never expected him to come back into our lives, but it just... happened."

"Wha-what do you mean, it 'just happened'?"

I don't know. I don't know how it happened. Everything was fine, and then he showed up, and all of a sudden, it wasn't.

"It's, uh...He's someone you know, but I didn't know you knew him...until I did, I guess, and—"

"What the hell, Mom? Who is he?"

"He's, um..." *Say it. Say it because it's the right thing to do, because he needs to know, because you can't keep it from him any longer.* "It's Christian."

The name echoed off the walls of the room like we were standing in the middle of a canyon.

"Christian?" Lucas blinked. "Christian...O'Connor?"

"Yes," I said, searching his face for some sign of whether that was good or bad or if he hated me, regardless, for keeping something of this magnitude from him.

He looked at Marcos. "You knew this? You knew this, too?"

Marcos nodded. "Your mom told me."

"I mean, are you sure?" Lucas pushed his curls back, flattening them against his head. "Are you sure that he's—"

"Yes," I repeated, this time in a whisper as I let my hand fall from his shoulder to my side. "But you know your dad is always going to be your dad, he's always wanted to be your dad, and this has never mattered to him."

"But I don't...I don't understand." Lucas shook his head. "Did Christian...know about me?"

I took a deep breath. "He knew I was pregnant, but he...he said he didn't want to be a father, and he ended our relationship. He was using heroin, a lot of heroin, and he wasn't...safe. So, I didn't tell him when you were born because I wanted to protect you. I *still* want to protect you."

Lucas looked out the window before speaking. "And now does he expect me to—"

"He doesn't expect anything. After we broke up, he never reached out, he never asked about...it. I don't think he even knew I had you." My stomach tightened at the thought of Lucas not existing in this world, not existing in my life. "But when he saw you, and he saw me, it was...obvious. And he wanted you to know, and your dad and I thought since you all were working together, you *should* know. It wasn't fair to not tell you."

"But did he help with the album because of me? Was that on purpose?" Lucas asked, turning his head to me.

"I don't know," I said honestly. I could only go on what Christian had told me. "But he said it wasn't."

"So then, when he...At that show, when I introduced you, you already knew him. And you guys just let me be around him all that time without telling me?" Lucas's eyes darted back and forth between Marcos and me.

Marcos's chin quivered, and I knew I couldn't let Lucas believe that any of this was his fault.

"Your dad didn't know that night. It was...a while before I told him, so he didn't keep anything from you. This was all me. I was scared, and I didn't want you to get hurt."

"She needed time, Lucas," Marcos added, and my heart broke. He had no reason to defend me. None. But he was doing it anyway. "She just wanted to protect you. You mean the world to her. And me."

"And Christian knows everything we're telling you," I added, a tear trickling down my cheek. "I emailed him and told him to give you space, and he said he'd understand if you don't want him to come back to work on the album. He agreed to respect that, and no one would know it had anything to do with...this."

"I just...I don't know what to..." Lucas scrubbed his hands over his face. "Is this...Does this have anything to do with why you and Dad are splitting up? Is Christian the reason?" His hands fell to his lap, and he tilted his head at me. "Are you gonna...*be* with him?"

"No, Lucas," I insisted, shaking my head. "No. That's not happening. That will never happen."

"Yeah, but did you..." He stared at the floor as though he was imagining scenarios that a son would never want to think about his mother being involved in.

I need to come clean. He's old enough. He should know the truth.

"I, um...I made some mistakes," I admitted. "Your dad and I are working through that."

Lucas narrowed his eyes at me, the pieces of the puzzle locking into place. "So *you* did this? You guys splitting up...This is because of *you*?"

"Your mom loves you, Lucas," Marcos said. "She didn't set out to hurt anyone."

I was sure Marcos was biting his tongue, but I was grateful he didn't seem to want to rake me over the coals in front of our child.

"Yeah, but she did," he said, looking at Marcos before turning his eyes back to me. "You did."

"Sweetie, please. I'm so sorry for the mistakes I made. I'm beyond sorry, and I know that doesn't make it better, but I want you to understand that I love you and your sisters." I glanced at Marcos, but he shifted his gaze in the opposite direction. "And I love your dad. More than I could ever love anyone else."

"Then why'd you fucking cheat on him?"

I fell back against the futon, reeling from the gut punch Lucas had delivered.

I can't breathe.

I can't fucking breathe.

"Look, I know you're upset. I get it," Marcos said to Lucas, his tone sympathetic, yet stern. "But you can't talk to your mother like that."

"I can talk to her however I want after what she did."

He won't forgive me. He'll never forgive me. Marcos was worried about losing his son, but it's me who's going to lose him.

"Lucas, she's still your mother, and I'm not going to let you—"

"Fuck this shit." Lucas sprang up from his seat. My hand brushed along his arm, and he jerked it away. "I'm going to Mia's."

Marcos stood, reaching for him as he stomped toward the door. "Lucas, please, come back so we can—"

He turned to Marcos. "I love you. I do. You're my dad, you'll always be my dad, and Christian can go fuck himself. But I just...I need to go right now, okay? I need to go."

Marcos swallowed and nodded as Lucas left. I brought my hand to my mouth, the trickling tears turning to muted sobs.

Marcos squeezed his fists against his sides, nostrils flaring as he narrowed his eyes at the wall across from him. "Goddammit," he hissed, then stormed out of the room and slammed the door behind him.

41

—————

MARCH 2010

I peered around one of the drapery panels flanking the large window in our living room, watching as Marcos pulled his Audi into the driveway. I'd only seen him a few times since the end of February when I'd left the company for what we'd decided to call a sabbatical. Officially, I was stepping back for a while and taking some time to rest, be with my family, and pursue interests outside of work which had been on my to-do list for "much too long." Unofficially, I was waking up, going to the gym so I wouldn't completely lose my mind, then watching TV or staring at the ceiling until it was time to pick Lola and Marisol up from school. Marcos had offered to step back from the business, but that felt wrong. I had been the one to turn our world upside down, and he'd sacrificed enough already by moving out of the home we'd settled into a couple years after Lola was born. Why should he have to leave his job, too?

After the girls and I got home, our routine was to order dinner. We'd sit at the kitchen table while Mari, who'd been surprisingly resilient after the initial shock of the separation, told me about her day. Lola, on the other hand, would pick at the food she'd said she wanted, only to eventually push it away, insist she wasn't hungry, and go to her room.

I was fairly certain Lucas hadn't told them about Christian. Even though her resting bitch face had been on full display since January, Lola hadn't mentioned anything about it, and she was never one to shy away from calling me out. I wasn't even sure of the last time they'd seen Lucas. Maybe when they were at their dad's. Maybe they all went to lunch every Sunday, then got ice cream on the Venice boardwalk afterward and thought about how much better it was without me there as they licked their chocolate and strawberry and butter pecan cones, laughing and gazing out at the ocean.

Lucas had moved in with Mia a week after our conversation with him. I'd known he would be upset but hadn't seen that punch coming. Of course, I'd considered that he'd want to stay with Marcos for a while, but he had never lived away from us, and for him to leave because of this, to leave because of *me* was confirmation that I'd destroyed our family.

I'd texted him more than a few times—*Are you sure you have enough money for rent? Do you need me to get your groceries?*—before realizing I wasn't going to get a response. I only knew he was okay because he hadn't cut off the lines of communication with his dad.

"He needs space," Marcos had said. "But I'll try to talk to him."

Besides discussing how we planned to deal with our business until further decisions were made, and trying to ensure we were always on the same page with Marisol and Lola (school, soccer games, curfews), Marcos and I didn't talk much. Our conversations were cordial enough, but the formality of them was painful, each one reminding me of what I'd lost.

No. Not lost.

What I'd thrown away.

Nineteen years of marriage—to the day.

Which is why I stood in the living room, hidden by the fabric of the curtains, waiting to see if Marcos would follow behind Lola and Marisol as they got out of the car. I wanted him to come inside. I wanted him to tell me happy anniversary, and I didn't care if his voice had hints of contempt when he did. I just wanted him to acknowledge it because that would mean in some way he still cared.

The Audi pulled away, and though the waiting was over, I felt no relief. The kernel of hope I'd been holding on to dissolved, leaving me empty as the door opened, and I hurried into the foyer. I slowed down as I entered, pretending I was just passing through on my way to the kitchen.

"Oh, hey, girls," I said, my tone a little too surprised, too cheerful. "Did you have a good weekend? What'd you do?"

Marisol nodded, removing her duffel bag from her shoulder and dropping it on the floor. "It was good. We got pizza and watched movies on Friday night, then made empanadas on Saturday. Lola went out with her *boyfriend*." She giggled as her sister rolled her eyes.

Empanadas?

"Oh. Wow." I blinked, my mouth twitching. I wanted to smile because knowing that my daughter had spent quality time with her father genuinely *did* bring me happiness, but I couldn't deny I felt an unhealthy side of jealousy along with it. "Did you make the dough and everything? From scratch?"

"Yeah." She nodded. "They turned out really good."

I could never get that fucking dough right. I'd tried a dozen times over the years and ended up throwing it in the trash each time because I was embarrassed at how terrible it turned out.

I looked at Lola. "And you had a good time with Elias? Elijah?"

Fuck. I could never get his name right, either.

Lola huffed. "*Jah*, Mom. For the hundredth time, his name is Eli*jah*."

"Sorry, sweetie. I'm, you know, old. Can't remember things." I managed an awkward laugh as she stared at me.

"Anyway," Lola said, finally. "His mom invited me over for dinner tonight, so he's going to pick me up in, like, forty-five minutes." She tugged at the bag on her shoulder as she stepped past me toward the stairs. "That's okay, right?"

"Uh..." I placed one hand on my hip and the other on my forehead. "Yeah, I...Where do they live?"

"Silver Lake. She's, like, this really amazing sculptor, and her boyfriend is an independent airbrush artist."

"A *what?*"

Shit. Did I say that out loud?

"He just"—Lola flipped her long dark hair—"airbrushes things. It's super cool."

Oh my God, these are the people who make hash brownies and let kids drink at their house because "they're gonna do it anyway."

"Uh, okay. I just...Have you been there before or..."

"Yeah." Lola let out an exaggerated sigh. "And seriously, Mom. Not everyone wears a suit to work. It doesn't mean they're bad people. They're just creative. They...*express themselves.*"

Like, sexually? And do they hand out condoms to their son and tell him to express himself, too? Elias—fuck—Elijah seems like a good kid, but she's too young. She's too young for this.

I need to talk to Marcos. If he was here, we'd discuss it, we'd figure it out together. He'd probably be more worried than me. After all, I was the one who defended artists when he was wary about Lola going out with one. Maybe I shouldn't have. Maybe his concern was warranted.

"So, can I go?" Lola asked.

"Did you mention it to your dad?"

"No. Elijah's picking me up *here*, not *there*, so why would I?"

Because your dad and I make decisions like this together. Or at least we used to. When he was here...not there.

"Uh. Yeah. You can go. But we should have him over for dinner sometime, too."

"Sure. Fine. Whatever." Lola rolled her eyes, then headed up the stairs.

I turned to Marisol, took a deep breath, and smiled. "Okay, so it's you and me, kid. What are we eating tonight?" I started down the hall. "How about Indian? Extra naan, of course."

She followed me into the kitchen, and I began rifling through drawers for a take-out menu.

"Um," she said. "We had a big lunch with Dad, so I'm kinda full."

My stomach knotted. "Oh," I said, staring into the open drawer.

Does everything have to hurt so badly? Does everything have to remind me that Marcos doesn't live here anymore?

"Is that...okay?" she asked, her voice hesitant and small.

I swallowed and forced a smile before shutting the drawer. "Of course, sweetie. That's totally fine. You can have a snack later if you get hungry."

Her shoulders relaxed, and my chest squeezed.

She didn't want to upset me. My twelve-year-old didn't want to upset me by telling me that she was too full to eat with me because she'd eaten with her dad.

It felt wrong. It felt like I was *doing* something wrong. That I was inadvertently making them feel like there was a competition between Marcos and me.

"You know, I'm actually not super hungry, either," I lied. "I think I'm going to just get some cheese and crackers and watch TV."

"I have to work on my book report for Language Arts." She scrunched her nose. "I don't know why they make us read stuff that's not real. I like math better."

I remembered how worked up I'd gotten when Marcos had suggested that Marisol was more finance-minded and might take over the family business one day. Funny how I'd been so rattled back then, when hearing Marisol actually confirm his suspicions only made me chuckle now.

I shouldn't have freaked out on him.

"Reading is good for you," I told her, winking. "Now go upstairs and do it."

"I just don't think anyone is ever going to ask me about elves and wizards and rings and crap. Why does that matter when it comes to, like, *business*?"

Wow, maybe he really was onto something.

"You know, they actually make movies about those books now," I reminded her. "So it could totally come in handy."

She squinted at the ceiling, the wheels turning in her mind. Her braces gleamed as she grinned, nodded, and headed out of the kitchen.

If he was here, I thought, *we could laugh about this together.*

———

I shoved the last cracker from the sleeve of saltines into my mouth and pressed the down arrow on the remote.

16 and Pregnant? Absolutely fucking not.

Desperate Housewives? Oh God, that's me.

Dateline? People who are dead or in prison. So, worse off than I am—maybe.

As I clicked the button to watch the program, my cell phone pinged with a text notification. I reached for it on the sofa cushion beside me, and my body tensed when I saw the name on the screen.

Christian.

He hadn't contacted me since returning my last email, thanking me for letting him know that Marcos and I had told Lucas about him. I'd insisted he give Lucas time and space, and he agreed he wouldn't come back to LA unless Lucas wanted to see him.

Is he going to break that promise? Is he going to tell me he can't wait to hear from Lucas any longer? Or shit...Did Lucas ask him to come back, and he's already in town?

My thumb tapped the screen to open the message.

Christian: *Can you talk?*

I rolled my eyes and shook my head, typing out *If it's about how much I never want to hear your name or see your face ever again then yes* before erasing it.

Christian: *It's about Lucas.*

He answered the phone on the first ring. "Hey."

"Hi." My voice was purposely void of emotion. It wasn't his business what I was thinking or how I was feeling. I just needed to know whatever it was he wanted to tell me about my son.

He took a breath, as though he was deciding what to say next, and I silently dared him to ask me how I was doing.

"I, um...I wanted you to know that Lucas texted me. I wasn't sure if he told you he was going to do that."

I pressed the heel of my palm into my chest, trying to keep what was left of my heart from disintegrating.

Stay calm. Stay calm.

"Oh." He didn't need to know that Lucas hadn't mentioned it to me. He didn't need to know Lucas hadn't said a *word* to me for the past two and a half months. "What did he, uh...what did he say?"

"He asked me if you and I were together."

I moved my hand to my mouth and squeezed my eyes shut. How many times could I tell myself not to cry? As much as it hurt me to know my son believed I could love someone other than the man who'd raised him, I knew it hurt Lucas ten thousand times more. Even though I couldn't imagine a pain greater than realizing your child was devastated because of something you'd done.

"I said no," Christian offered before I could ask. "That we're not together."

"And did you add that we haven't been in nineteen years? And never will be again?" My tone turned sharp.

The line went silent until he cleared his throat. "So, does he know about what happened? I mean, when you came to the house that day?"

I shivered, remembering the ridges of the stucco wall against my back, Christian's calloused fingers on my skin, and the coarse hair on his chin scratching my face. The moment I understood that the safe space I'd longed for over the years wasn't really safe at all.

Bile rose to the back of my throat. If I hadn't slept with Christian and shattered my husband's trust...if it had just been a matter of not telling Marcos about my past...would he still be here?

"He's a smart kid, Christian. He figured out there was more to the story than just his long-lost father showing up."

"Yeah, I...I'm sorry about that. About what happened."

"No, you're not," I stated, even though I recalled the hint of remorse on Christian's face as he told Lucas he was going back to Seattle.

He sighed. "Anyway, he, um...he said he wanted to know a lot of things, but he didn't know how to ask them right now. I think he's angry. And he's afraid. He doesn't want me to fuck things up any more than I already have."

"Yeah, well, that's kind of impossible."

Christian continued as though my comment hadn't registered. Or maybe he just knew it was true, and there was no point in arguing. "And I think he's afraid *he'll* fuck things up if he tries to have a relationship with me."

I blinked, the realization that I had no idea what a relationship between Lucas and Christian would truly mean for any of us smacking me in the face. It was something that had gotten lost in the shuffle, buried under the logistics of the separation.

I had no answers, so I asked a question. "And what do you want me to do about that, Christian?"

"I...I'm just not sure how to handle this."

"Yeah, well, I didn't know how to handle you showing up at my house, telling my husband that I'm in love with you *when I'm fucking not*, but I'm figuring that out. I'm taking responsibility for my mistakes, and I'm dealing with them."

Barely dealing. Almost not at all. But he didn't need to know that.

"Look, I..." He paused and took another breath. "I know that was messed up, okay? I shouldn't have come there. But I don't want to screw things up with Lucas."

"You asked for this, Christian," I reminded him. "You *begged* for this. And now you want me to give you fucking step-by-step directions on what to do next?"

"I know I did, I just...I don't know what the hell to do, Denise."

"I don't either." I had expected the words to come out sharp and biting. But there was a genuine sense of confusion, a true lack of understanding of how even I was supposed to navigate these waters.

"So, should I—"

"I said, *I don't know*." My voice pulsed with shame and frustration.

"I'll just..." He sucked in a tiny bit of air. "I'll leave it alone until he tells me he's ready to talk."

"Good," I said, clenching my jaw. "You do that."

"I really am sorry. I'm sorry about all of this."

"I have to go." My thumb hovered above the button to end the call, but rather than hanging up, I brought the phone back to my ear. "But you need to know that even if Lucas wants a relationship with you, you and I will never have one, Christian. That time is done."

I disconnected the call and tightened my grip on the phone, my muscles contracting, shaking. The confidence in my voice shocked me, but I knew it was genuine. I loved Marcos and our children more than anything in the world—certainly more than anything I thought I'd felt when I was with Christian—and I couldn't hurt them more than I already had. Those feelings were just memories anyway. They weren't real. But my family and the love I had for them was.

I had to understand why I'd done something so terrible, something I hadn't thought even a person as fucked up as me was capable of. I had to understand, so I could fix it. And I had to figure out how to regain Marcos's trust, as well as Lucas's.

I opened my contacts, scrolled to the name I was looking for, and hit the Call button. The after-hours message played, and I took a deep breath.

I can do this.

"Hi. This is Denise Abbott. I haven't seen Dr. Shirazi in a while, but I need to make an appointment. As soon as possible, please."

42

APRIL 2010

"Denise." Dr. Shirazi smiled as she stepped inside her office, folding her hands in front of her. "So good to see you."

"Good to..." I paused, managing to swallow the spit pooling in my mouth, rather than throwing it up. "Good to see you, too."

She sat in one of the velvety barrel chairs across from me. "I looked back at my records, and I think the last time I saw you was about a year ago. How have you been?"

"I'm okay."

I am?

I'd given her a preprogrammed response to what I always assumed was a preprogrammed question.

But I'm paying her to care. Or at least paying her to fix this.

"Actually, things have been...difficult lately." My fingers rubbed the soft camel leather covering the arm of the couch. "But, you know, I'm...I'm all right."

"Your voice is leaving a whole lot of room for me to question that." She cocked her head, shiny black hair falling over her shoulder as she held me with her soft gaze and gave me the space to answer.

I'm here for my family. I want us to be together again. To be happy again.

Say that. Say something.

"Why don't you tell me what's been going on since we last spoke?" she asked when I didn't respond.

"This is, um...I mean, I don't really like to talk about my personal life, so this is..." I took a shaky breath. "Hard."

She offered me another warm smile. "I remember that's not on your list of favorite things to do."

"It's just that..." I flicked my eyes down to my lap. "My husband and I have separated."

"Oh," she said, crossing her legs. "I'm sorry to hear that."

"It's...it's all my fault, really." I slumped against the back of the sofa and picked at my cuticle. "And I hope you can help me make it right."

She inhaled and leaned forward, chin on her elbow. "I'd like to first help take some judgment out of the statement you just made about it being all your fault."

"There's no...That's not possible." I shook my head. "I'm the one to blame. I lied. And I cheated. I broke up my family, and I want to fix us. Those are just...facts."

"Well, some of those things may be true," she said. "But in my experience with separations, there's always more to the story. So maybe you can tell me in more detail what happened, and then I can ask some questions if you feel"—she tilted her head down slightly in what I assumed was an attempt to coax me out of myself—"comfortable with that?"

I raised my eyes, then nodded. "I can try. I want to try." There was a beat of silence, and I let out a sound that fell somewhere between a snort and a chuckle. "I mean, that's why I'm here, right? Didn't get on the 405 at 3 p.m. for nothing."

She gave me a polite but knowing look. "Start wherever you want to."

I began in October when Christian first reappeared and ended in January when we told Lucas about Christian. I recounted the times and places we met behind Marcos's back, how we had sex the day I'd gone to tell him Lucas couldn't know the truth. I talked quickly, wanting to get it out and over with, and Dr. Shirazi took notes. And then, when I was done, I sucked in a breath and sat wide-eyed, waiting for her to tell me either how I could make it all better or that it was hopeless and there was no use in trying.

"Thank you," she said, gliding her pen across the notepad on her lap before looking up. "I know that was hard to share, so thanks for trusting me with it."

I nodded and rubbed my lips together.

"And I think if we really want to figure out where you *go* from here, we need to figure out how you *got* here."

"Oh," I said, my knee bouncing. "Well, I got here because I'm not—"

No. I can't say this. I can't say this out loud. I've never said it to anyone except Christian, and look how that turned out.

Dr. Shirazi narrowed her eyes. "What were you going to say?"

I shifted my gaze to the abstract piece on her wall. *Is that a Richter? Jesus, how much did that cost? What am I paying this woman again?*

"Denise? I feel like you want to say something. That those things happened because you're not..."

I can't say it. I can't.

"I don't want you to feel pressured, but this is a safe space. I can guarantee that."

Safe space, safe space. Is anyone really safe? I thought Christian was, but I was wrong. People tell you they won't judge you, they won't leave you, and maybe they think those things are true, but they're not. I'm surprised Eva's stuck around after all the shitty things I've confessed to her. Maybe she'll be the next to go.

Dr. Shirazi cleared her throat. "It's okay, we can move on from that if you're not ready to—"

"I'm not a good person," I blurted out, twisting my head to her.

I expected her to agree. To say she'd always suspected that about me and since I'd confirmed those suspicions, there was no point in continuing our session. But she took a breath and sat back in her seat, concern settling on her face.

"Why do you say that?"

"Because it's true. I'm not." I crossed my arms and pressed a fist to my mouth.

Her lips turned down, then up ever so slightly. "I think we just confirmed that there's definitely more to the story."

"What do you mean?"

"You took me from point A to point B. And that's important. I needed to know everything you told me, so please don't think otherwise. But it was almost like you were reading me a news report. I don't know how you were *feeling* while those things were happening, and if we talk about that, we can also explore *why* they happened. That's the *more* I'm talking about."

"But it's like I said. There's something wrong with me." I shrugged. "It's just another...fact."

"Look, Denise." She shifted in her seat. "If you want to continue seeing me, and I discover during our time together that you're a psychopath or sociopath or anything along those lines, then maybe we can discuss whether or not something is truly wrong with you. But until then, I'm going to wager this is a *belief* you have, and that belief was put there by something...or some*one*."

I shook my head. "No, it's just...it's always been that way."

"So, you think you were born broken, for lack of a better word?"

"I..." My eyes brimmed with tears. "I guess so."

"And you think you need to be fixed?"

"Yes. Be fixed, be better, whatever I need to do to get my family back. To make my husband believe nothing like this will ever happen again. To help my kids deal with everything that's been thrown at them. Especially Lucas." My throat tightened. "Sorry. I'm so sorry I'm crying."

"You don't have to apologize for expressing emotion, Denise."

I coughed and nodded, even though I didn't believe that was true.

"Back to what you said you wanted to accomplish. I understand you want your family back together. But that goal is very outward focused. And I know it's hard to hear this and even harder to accept it, but it's not really within your control."

My body deflated.

"There are things we can work on that may help, though. Things that will make a difference in *your* life, regardless of the outcome with your family."

"But what does that matter? I mean, I was happy with *them*. And my life without them is...I just can't imagine it."

"Is there a possibility you weren't as happy as you thought you were?" She raised her hands slightly. "And there's no judgment in that question. I'd just like for us to consider if maybe there was a bit of *un*happiness that guided your decisions."

"I don't...I mean, no. I was happy. I had every reason to be happy." The muscles in my forehead strained as I questioned what I'd just said.

And then she answered me out loud. "Whose reasons were those, Denise?"

I pinched my brows tighter. "I don't know."

"So, would you be open to figuring that out? Maybe starting with a different goal in mind?" she asked softly.

"What goal?"

"How about we place our focus on simply starting to heal?"

I sniffed and wiped at my nose. "Starting to heal what?"

She placed her notepad on the chair beside her, then laced her fingers together. "The parts of you that were hurt long before any of what you just told me happened."

43

MAY 2010

Dear...*Me?* I wrote, then rolled my eyes and tapped the tip of the pen against the blank page of my journal.

"It doesn't have to be perfect. Just give yourself what you needed back then."

Dr. Shirazi's voice rang like a delicate bell in my head, making the exercise seem less intimidating. But it still wasn't something I wanted to do. Contemplating my childhood had never been an activity I'd seen as productive, and the idea of writing a letter to my younger self was damn near beyond comprehension. I'd been able to journal some of my thoughts, but the letter felt weird, and there were a million other things that seemed more appealing at the moment.

My eyes wandered around the kitchen. *Unloading the dishwasher. Sorting through the mail. Rearranging the cabinets. Everything should be lower. I can't reach things, and he isn't here to help me.*

I didn't normally need to access a whole lot in the kitchen, but I'd started to cook more, promising myself we'd have at least three meals a week that didn't involve restaurants. Things that were simple enough. Breakfast for dinner. Tacos. Chicken parmesan. And since Lola had recently ventured into vegetarianism in solidarity with El*ijah* by the time I'd gotten to that dish, I'd even had to learn how to deal with an eggplant.

Cooking was something I'd never done a lot of because I'd been so busy with work, and the last thing I wanted to do was run around the kitchen after a long day. But with the job on hold, I had more time. At first, I thought the idea was born out of guilt (I *should* be doing this), but then I realized it was something I really wanted to do for the girls. Even if they eventually decided they hated the whole idea of it, I wanted them to have at least *some* memories of sitting down with their mom and eating a home-cooked meal—the kind of memories I wished for but didn't have. Plus, it occupied my time while Marcos and I avoided discussing the topics of our marriage and our business. He was running the day-to-day operations, while I was still on my *sabbatical.* It wasn't like I longed for the nonstop meetings or constant stress, but it was really the only thing I'd ever known. My return to work was so intertwined with the status of our marriage, though, that broaching the subject scared the hell out of me. Marcos didn't bring it up, either. Maybe he still didn't know what he wanted. Or maybe he was in the process of hiring a lawyer.

"I mean, there should be *some* discussion of what we're doing, right?" I'd asked Dr. Shirazi during our last weekly session. "Some discussion of the future? It's been four months since he left, and I'm just out here in limbo. I want to talk to him. I want to know what he's feeling, and I want to tell him what *I'm* feeling. But he never brings it up, so I guess he still needs time."

"Which is understandable. But you're allowed to tell him what you need."

"No." I shook my head. "I'm actually not allowed to do that. I'm the one who fucked up. I'm the one who lied and cheated."

"You're beating yourself up," she said. "And you're still

hiding yourself from him, even though he's seen what you would consider the absolute worst of you. There *should* be open and honest communication during a separation, Denise. What you want, what you *need*, is actually healthy."

I pursed my lips and shrugged.

"Just remember, you're human," she continued. "And by virtue of that alone, you deserve the right to communicate your needs in a healthy way. I'd like for you to try to do that the next time you see him. Don't let it all out while you're at a soccer game or anything, but do tell him you'd like to schedule time to talk."

"But what if I do that and it, I don't know...triggers something inside of him, and he tells me he wants a..." I swallowed, afraid to say the word, as though I might speak it into existence. "Divorce?"

Dr. Shirazi took a deep breath. "I assume if that's what he's thinking he wants, you simply asking him for time to talk wouldn't be the deciding factor. But of course, I don't know that for a fact, and I think that's a chance you're eventually going to have to take."

"It's just that I don't know what would happen if..." I trailed off, refusing to let my mind go to a place where our family didn't exist as it had in the past.

"This is a chance for you to put some of what we've talked about into action. You being able to express yourself is so important, Denise."

"Maybe what I need is something to *do*," I suggested, circumventing a commitment to her request. "Like, a distraction."

"I'd say you actually need the opposite."

I cocked my head. "What do you mean?"

"You've distracted yourself for a long time. From a lot of traumatic things that happened in your life."

"Traumatic things?" My face twisted in confusion. "That...

that doesn't make sense. Nothing *traumatic* happened to me. I haven't witnessed a murder. Or fought in a war. Or survived a plane crash."

"Those are what we call *Big T* traumas," she explained. "And though we might discover you experienced one or more significant events on that level, the *Little T's* are smaller occurrences that added up over the years. All the times your mother emotionally neglected you. All the times your father told you to hide your feelings and dismissed any ideas of yours he didn't agree with. These are things that made you believe you aren't good enough. Why it's difficult for you to trust people. Why you're afraid to let them see anything you think might make you vulnerable or 'needy.'" She curled her fingers into quotation marks. "You have to allow yourself time to heal because even if you and Marcos decide to work on your marriage, you don't want to fall back on those old patterns."

"But those things are just part of life." I waved my hand in the air. "There are so many heavier things that happen to people."

Dr. Shirazi raised her chin. "Think of 'those things' as rocks in a backpack you're carrying, then. The backpack was empty until your mother or father did something that hurt you, and one rock went inside. You probably didn't even notice it was there. Then they did it again...and again...and again, and each time, a rock was added."

My chest tightened as I sat at the island in the middle of the kitchen, hunched over the journal in front of me, remembering what she'd said next.

"You're carrying around hundreds of rocks, Denise."

I sat up straight, rolled my shoulders back, and imagined the backpack sliding off me. I closed my eyes and breathed a sigh of relief.

My lids flipped open as my cell phone rattled against the marble counter in front of me.

Tom Abbott.

Fuck.

He rarely called these days—only to give me advice I hadn't asked for—so he'd clearly gotten wind of what was going on with the business. He and Gina had been in Costa Rica for the past few months, so we hadn't told them about the separation. Now that he was back home, he was going to ask me what the hell was going on and scold me for not calling him with the news. My thumbs hooked around the straps of the imaginary backpack, and I started to slump forward, ready to carry the load once again.

I pushed the button to answer. "Hello?"

"Denise. What the hell is going on?" My father's voice was still commanding but had developed a perceptible weakness to it that signaled he'd gotten older. "Did you sell the business to Marcos? Why didn't you tell me?"

"I didn't sell the business to him." I sighed. "I'm just...taking a break."

He scoffed. "And may I ask why?"

"Because I..." I swallowed, choking down the instinct to justify every single thing I did to him. "Because I needed to, Dad. Because Marcos and I are also on a break."

"What the..." I heard a thud, like he'd dropped the phone. "I told you when you got married that he should find another job, and this is why. This is exactly why. Although, I don't even know why I'm calling right now because you didn't take my advice then, and you clearly don't want it now, since you didn't even bother to tell me this was happening."

My throat tightened even more as I fought the urge to capitulate to him. *He doesn't know everything. Even if he acts like he does. Even if he's always told you he does.*

"You're right, Dad. I don't."

"You don't what?"

"Want your advice."

"Denise." In my mind, I could see his nostrils flaring. "I've been in this world for much longer than you have, and I know how these things work. This is not good. This is not good at all. Have you talked to the attorneys?"

"No, we're not there yet."

"Well, you could be any second, and you need to be prepared in case—"

"Dad. Stop. Just stop." I took a deep breath. "It's my company now. It's my fucking company, and I'm handling it."

Inside me, a surge of fear clashed with a surge of pride. *Did I say that? Did I really just say that?*

Hems and haws sounded through the speaker. "I don't even know what the hell to say to that. Maybe I'll call you tomorrow and see if you've come to your senses. Or maybe *I'll* call an attorney."

"I don't care what you do," I whispered.

"What?"

My chest puffed out. "I said, I don't care what you—"

"No, I'm talking to Gina. What? What do you need?" he asked in response to a muffled voice in the background. "I... Hold on a second. Denise, are you there?"

He's flustered. Ha! I made him flustered. I rolled my lips inward at the realization, trying not to smile in case he could somehow see me through the phone. "I'm here."

"Gina needs to talk to you about Lola's birthday present. But you and I are going to discuss this later."

I gave myself permission to smile. "We're not, Dad."

"Goddammit." There was rustling in the background, and I covered my mouth to stifle the laughter that flowed from inside as his power over me waned. "Here, Gina. Take the damn phone."

"Good Lord, I don't know what's got his feathers so ruffled, but just ignore him," Gina said as she came on the line.

I will, I thought. *For the first time in my life, I will.*

44

JUNE 2010

"Hi, Mom."

"Hi, sweetie. How was—"

Before I could finish my question, Marisol breezed by Marcos, who stood on the front porch just outside the door.

"Hey," he said.

"Uh...hi." My mouth twitched into a hopeful smile.

I hadn't seen him other than at Marisol's club soccer games and a few events at the girls' schools before summer break began. We'd made small talk about the business, the weather, and the kids, then gotten into our separate cars and drove to our separate homes. I worried that each time would be *the* time he'd tell me it was over, that he officially wanted a divorce, so I hadn't worked up the courage to ask him if we could meet to discuss things.

"Do you have a second to sign these?" he asked.

I blinked, then dropped my eyes to the folder in his right hand. My heart hammered against my ribs, and my brain buzzed.

What? Are those divorce...Oh my God. Oh my God. This is it. This is the time.

"I didn't know if you'd have time to stop by Jean's office next week, so I figured I could bring them here."

Jean...Jean...

"I need to get them to her by the fifteenth."

Oh Jesus. Jean the accountant. Jean the CPA. Jean the fucking CPA.

A cool river of relief rushed through me, and I was finally able to look up at him. "Oh. Quarterly taxes. Yeah. Yeah, come in."

Come in? To your own house?

He hesitated, then nodded and stepped inside.

"How was Mari's practice?" I asked over my shoulder as I headed through the foyer, and he followed behind.

"Good. I was going to take her to grab some food afterward, but she said you were making dinner."

"Oh." I dismissed him with a wave as we entered the kitchen. "It's nothing big, just cheeseburgers. Well, veggie burgers for Lola and Elijah."

He pointed to the long spatula and tray of patties on the counter. "You're grilling them?"

I turned and nodded. "I finally had time to figure out how the grill works."

"I could've...I mean, I would've shown you. If you wanted."

My heart squeezed. *You could've? You would've?*

"Nah, it's all right," I said, sounding much more casual than I felt. "No one was harmed. The house is still standing."

He nodded, tapping the folder against his leg.

"I can..." I extended my hand to him.

"Oh." He looked down before passing the folder to me. "Right."

I placed the papers on the island, then scanned the room for a pen, freezing as I caught sight of my open journal with a ballpoint lying in the crease.

Shit. Shit, shit, shit. I want him to know how I'm feeling, but not all the gibberish I've been vomiting onto those pages.

Marcos and I both started around the island, our hands touching for a second as we reached for it.

"I got it," I said, picking up the pen.

His gaze shot away from the open notebook, and he shoved his hands in the pockets of his gym shorts.

I closed the journal and gave him an awkward smile. "Just some stuff I'm working on."

"Did you...Are you doing another job right now or..."

My pulse picked up. *It's okay,* I told myself, attempting a few discreet calming breaths. *This could be good. Maybe this is how I let him know I want to talk.*

"No, it's just some stuff I'm doing for...me. For therapy," I said, cautiously lifting my eyes to gauge his reaction.

"Oh."

Blank face. Nothing that says Good for you, *nothing that says* You're wasting your time. *No emotion. But this is a chance, and I should take it. Dr. Shirazi is right. We need to communicate, and I can at least try to open the door.*

"Yeah," I said, my insides swirling. "It's actually going really well. I've, um...There are a lot of things that I'm starting to understand better now, a lot of things I'm working on."

"That's great," he said, his tone flat. "Where's, uh...where's Lola?"

He looked around the room, and my heart dropped into my stomach at the sound of an invisible door slamming shut.

Does he not care? Does he truly not care?

"She's out back in the pool with Elias. Elijah. Let me, uh...let me sign these real quick." My hand trembled as I scribbled my signature in a couple boxes, then slid the folder across the counter.

"Thanks," he said, placing his left hand on top of it.

The light from the pendants hanging above the counter

reflected off the gold band on his finger, and I took a deep breath. It was usually the first thing I checked for when I saw him, but I'd been so caught off guard when he appeared at the front door, I'd forgotten.

"No problem," I said, twisting my own rings. "I actually need to get the burgers on the grill. Do you want to"—*stay for dinner?*—"say hi to Lola?" I picked up the spatula and pointed it toward the back of the house, my grip tightening as I thought of all the things I wanted to say to him.

I miss you. And I want to tell you that. I want to ask you to stay, and I want to eat dinner together as a family, and then I want us to talk about how we can figure out a way forward. But I'm afraid of what you'll say. I'm afraid I'll make you upset or piss you off, and you'll never want to come back.

"Uh..." He rubbed the back of his neck. "Sure. And let me get that."

He carried the tray of patties through the house, and I opened the door to the patio to see Lola and Elijah standing on the stone pool surround, her arms around his neck, his hands on her hips.

"Oh shit," Marcos muttered under his breath as he diverted his eyes.

I gritted my teeth. *Fuck.* Was he going to think I'd turned the house into the damn Playboy Mansion? That I was a terrible mother who let teenagers run wet and wild all over my backyard?

Lola and Elijah separated at the sound of the door shutting.

"Oh. Dad. Hey," she said, folding one arm over her stomach.

He gave her a tense smile and wave, then set the tray by the grill. "She's so grown up. I'm freaking out right now. *Should* I be freaking out?" His hazel eyes darkened with concern.

"No," I whispered back.

"Give me a reason to not freak out." His voice was quiet, and he briefly twisted his head over his shoulder as they jumped in the pool.

"They're not having sex," I said.

He raised his eyebrows. "How do you know?"

"I talked to her about it."

"You did?"

I nodded, and he released his breath.

"But you know she probably *will* do that one day," I said.

He massaged his jaw. "I know. It's just hard having been the teenage boy, and now I'm the dad." He shook his head. "Anyway, thank you. For talking to her. I wanted to ask you about it, I just..."

"No problem." I gave him a tiny smile. "It was a good talk."

It hadn't been as easy as I made it sound but diving into the details when he'd stopped in to have me sign tax forms didn't seem ideal. As I'd watched Lola and Elijah get closer, I thought more and more about myself at fifteen. Needing someone to love me so badly but confusing love with desire. It hadn't taken seeing Dr. Shirazi for me to understand that, but she *had* helped me see that as I'd gotten older, I wasn't so much confusing that need as I was replacing it. I didn't necessarily feel shame about the casual hookups, but losing my virginity in the way I had was fucked up, to say the least. And I didn't want my daughter to feel an ounce of what I'd felt that night.

It had been hard to admit to Lola that I was her age the first time I had sex. But I was so grateful she didn't scream and run away when I'd told her I wanted to talk about her and Elijah's relationship that I was honest when she asked. It wasn't a good experience, I said, but that didn't mean her experience would be the same. She needed to decide for herself when she was ready. I loved her, nothing would ever change that, and she could always tell me anything.

"Oh, don't worry," she'd said. "You'll know because you're totally taking me to get on the pill before it happens."

"I am?" I coughed and cleared my throat. "I mean, yes. Of course. I absolutely am."

"Babies are *so* not my thing." She flipped her hair over her shoulder and picked up her phone. "Anyway, can you drive me and Katie to The Grove? Jasmine is grounded."

I smiled, thinking about how she'd so confidently told me she was already planning to let me know when she decided to take that step. I could've never opened up to my mother like that. She never would have given me the opportunity to do it, and quite honestly, she wouldn't have cared.

"Good. I'm glad it was good." Marcos's voice shook me from my thoughts. "Well, I guess I should get—"

"Hey," I said, reaching for his arm. I held my breath, waiting for him to pull away, but he didn't. "Can I ask if...Have you talked to Lucas?"

He sighed.

"It's okay. You don't have to...I mean, he's obviously still not ready to talk to me, so..."

"I just..." His expression was pained. "I can't make him, Denise. And it's not that I don't want to, but I—"

"Yeah, no, it's fine." My arm fell to my side. "I get it. He actually texted me back *Okay* when I asked him how he was doing the other day, so, hey...that's progress."

"Look, I'm sure I said some things back when everything...happened." He raised his shoulders and cleared his throat, as if trying to maintain his composure. "But you're a good mother, Denise. And he'll come around eventually. He will."

You're a good mother. But a shitty wife.

And even though there were times when I thought I *was* a good mother to Lola and Marisol, I couldn't get past the feeling that I'd ruined Lucas. *Eventually* seemed like a code word for never, like something Marcos was saying just so I wouldn't have a breakdown on the patio before I could feed my kids dinner.

I bit my lip. "Are you and he in a good place, at least?"

Marcos nodded. "Yeah. We are. Truly."

The ache in my chest eased slightly, and I nodded as I walked over to the grill and turned one of the dials. The ignition clicked against the silence until the flames burst through the rack, and a surprising sense of courage sparked inside me as well. "Do you want to stay for dinner?"

"Oh." He took his USC ball cap off and ran his hand through his hair. His eyes met mine, and for a moment I thought I saw them soften into a yes. "I, uh...I've actually got plans." He worked his hat back on his head. "But I'm sure Mari will tell me how good the burgers were when I see her this weekend."

I tried to smile but couldn't manage it. The tax forms were just tax forms. Him coming over wasn't anything more than a kindness so I didn't have to drive to the accountant's office next week. He probably had a date he had to go home and get ready for. Maybe tonight was the night the wedding ring finally came off. Or maybe it had been off, and he just put it on around the kids.

"Don't forget the, um...the folder." Tears welled behind my eyes as I gestured toward the house.

He nodded, pausing briefly as he allowed his gaze to meet mine once more. Then he told Lola goodbye, opened the door, and stepped inside.

45

JULY 2010

"So, how have things been? I know we didn't get to see each other last week. Catch me up." Dr. Shirazi's tan skin popped against her sleeveless ivory blouse, and her eyes sparkled in the morning sun streaming through the floor-to-ceiling windows of her downtown office. Maybe all *I* needed was a week's stay in Punta Mita to make things right again.

"Uh, let's see..." I drummed my fingers on the arm of the leather couch. "Marcos came over. It wasn't anything planned. He just came inside when he was dropping Marisol off after soccer practice."

She raised her eyebrows. "Really? Did you talk?"

"He just needed me to sign some tax stuff."

"Were you able to tell him you wanted to discuss things?" She tapped the end of her pen against her chin. "Plan a time to do it?"

"No." I shook my head. "I tried. Sort of. My journal was open on the kitchen counter, and he saw it. I told him it was for therapy...stuff."

"And what did he say?"

"He said 'That's great,' like I'd just told him we were going to start saving money on our car insurance or something."

Dr. Shirazi gritted her teeth. "So, not the level of enthusiasm you were hoping for?"

"No," I said, sighing. "And obviously, I was hoping he'd ask me more about it so I could bring up needing to discuss things with him, but he didn't."

"I think you're going to have to ask him point-blank. Which is good." She bobbed her head. "I know it's disappointing that he didn't pick up on your signals, but I want you to feel comfortable being straightforward with him."

"Did he not pick up on them, or did he ignore them?" I asked, even though I knew she couldn't provide an answer.

"Hard to say. Which is why you need to be straightforward." She winked.

"Well, I did very straightforwardly ask him to stay for dinner, but he said he had *plans*. So, I'm not sure it matters now."

"What do you mean?" she asked.

"I mean, he obviously had a date."

She arched a brow. "Why do you say that?"

"Because how could he not?" I tossed my hands in the air.

"That's just a big assumption."

I looked at her like the degrees on her wall meant nothing if she couldn't use common sense. "Marcos is a catch. He's gorgeous, successful, an amazing father..." I counted off his attributes on my fingers. "He's the guy every woman wants, and trust me, they can spot the gorgeous and successful parts from a mile away. I'm sure they're lined up outside his condo right now, probably taking numbers from one of those things they have at the fucking deli counter."

I groaned and slouched against the back of the couch before popping back up. "And also, if it wasn't a date, why wouldn't he tell me what his plans were? Why wouldn't he tell me he was, I don't know, getting a beer with his buddies, or going to the grocery store, or joining a fucking bowling league or something?"

"So it rattled you." Dr. Shirazi tilted her head. "What other feelings did it bring up?"

"I was..." I looked down at the red heat spreading across my chest above the V-neck of my tee. "I was *pissed*."

"Why were you pissed?"

"Because he was so vague," I explained. "And I kept thinking, *Is he doing this on purpose? Does he want me to sweat this?* Because if he did, he succeeded. I can't even fucking sleep now, thinking about him kissing another woman, having sex with her, making fucking breakfast with her." I stared at Dr. Shirazi, my chest pumping frantically, sure she was going to tell me to calm the hell down.

"That reaction makes total sense."

I blinked. "What?"

"I mean, I don't *want* you to panic, and we'll work on ways to deal with that. But I also don't want you to think it's not normal to spiral."

I let out a long exhale, soothed by her validation.

"But I'm curious," she began. "Did you talk about seeing other people when you separated?"

"We didn't." I chewed on my bottom lip. "He probably just thought I would since it was apparently so easy for me to screw someone behind his back even when we were together."

"Denise. You're beating yourself up again."

"Well, it's true."

She sighed. "I think you have a right to ask him about it, just like you have a right to tell him what you need. And I know that's uncomfortable for you. You don't want him to know you're carrying anything inside that could ever be seen as burdensome. You don't want him to think he has to *deal* with you, for lack of a better word."

"Right. I'm afraid it'll send him over the edge. One wrong move on my part, and it's done." My shoulders fell, and I dropped my head into my hands. "*Fuuuck.* Why is it so hard for me to do this? I just want it to be easy."

"Which is why you were drawn to Christian."

I nodded—reluctantly.

"It was easier for you to express your feelings to him," she added. "And that made you feel…"

I took a deep breath as my fingers slid over my face, and I looked up. "Free."

"And you like feeling free."

"Who doesn't like feeling free?"

"I just mean, especially after all the years of believing you had to act a certain way, that you had to hide who you are, it must've felt especially good."

"Yeah," I said. "It did."

"And when you opened up to Christian, did he judge you? Did he think you were a bad person?"

"No. Not until he decided drugs were better than me. But he was messed up, too, so of course, he wanted me to be myself. He…*insisted* I be myself."

"And Marcos doesn't do that?"

I narrowed my eyes and frowned. "You're making it sound like Marcos is the bad guy here."

"No, not at all," she stressed. "I don't think he had intentions of doing anything bad or wrong. I'm just wondering if it was easier for him that way. Maybe he thought, *If my wife is telling me she's happy and things seem good, why rock the boat?*"

"But I *was* happy."

She pursed her lips. "Even with everything you were keeping inside?"

"Yes," I maintained. "And I love him. I do. I love the person he is, the husband he is, the father he is. We had fun, we laughed, we loved being together, and we were happy...until I fucked it all up."

"But there was something else you needed. And that's what took you down that path with Christian."

I swallowed and dropped my gaze to my foot as I slipped it in and out of my sandal.

"Again, that doesn't make you bad," she said. "And I don't believe you were in love with Christian. Not this time around. I think you remembered who you were with him all those years ago, and you loved *that* girl."

My body tensed, and I curled my toes.

"And since you lost her," Dr. Shirazi continued, "there's been a certain amount of *un*happiness in your life. Nothing you couldn't fake your way through, but you wanted that girl back. That led to a lot of confusing emotions and reinforced your feelings about not being good enough for Marcos."

"But I..." My mouth went dry, and it was hard to speak. "I didn't have to fucking *sleep* with Christian. I don't know what I was thinking. I don't know why I did that."

She leaned forward. "Sometimes we do things to prove to ourselves we're the person we *think* we are. It's tied up with low self-worth, especially from having experienced trauma. I believe what happened with Christian was not only about you wanting to feel free again, but also about you engaging in self-sabotaging behavior."

"So, I..." I slowly raised my head to look at her. "I put myself in the situation I thought I deserved?"

She nodded. "Exactly."

I stared at the ground, the tiny blue threads running through the gray carpet pulsing along with the blood in my veins.

"Are you okay?" Her voice echoed in my head. "Denise?"

"It's just that...it's still hard for me to believe the whole thing with my parents. The *trauma*." The word made me uncomfortable and sent an inexplicable blush of shame sweeping across my cheeks. *Look at her, there she goes down the street, a victim of trauma!* "I feel like it's an...*excuse.*"

"Excuses are used to justify behavior, and you're not trying to justify anything. You're trying to understand the reasons. The *whys.*" She sat back in her chair. "But let's not pick apart words right now. I'd like to know, if one of your daughters experienced what you did growing up and acted in a way that was hurtful to someone else, would you tell her that was no excuse for her behavior?"

"No." I lifted my eyes and shook my head. "Oh my God, no."

"You would try to understand."

I nodded. "Of course."

"Then give yourself that grace. And maybe let Marcos have the opportunity to give you that grace as well. Even if this separation is permanent, you're still going to have a relationship with him as the father of your children. It's important to be honest with him. You can't automatically assume he doesn't want you to be."

She scanned my face, which I was sure looked like it had just been hit with the backpack full of rocks she'd talked about during one of our early sessions. "That was a lot. Let me get you some water," she said, retrieving a bottle from the mini fridge in the corner of the room. "How are you feeling?"

"I'm..." I took a long swallow of the cold liquid, then set it on the table like it weighed a thousand pounds. "I'm fucking tired."

"Pretending is exhausting. And you've been doing it for years." Dr. Shirazi paused and placed her notepad down on the chair beside her. "Have you been able to work on the letter to your younger self at all? It's okay if not, but if there's anything you want to share, I'm listening."

"I've written some of it. I...I'm trying."

"Trying is good. I know this is something completely new to you."

"I, uh..." I reached for another sip of water. "I did tell my dad to fuck off, though."

Her lips mirrored mine as I smiled.

"Wow. That's...amazing. And I honestly don't even care why you did it," she said, laughing.

"He was giving me a hard time about the business, Marcos running it for now, me not telling him. And I don't know. I'd just had enough."

"Well, whether you know it or not, you told your dad what you needed in that moment."

"Yeah, I guess I did." I managed a small chuckle. "But it made me wonder...Do you think I should try to talk to my dad about things? Like about how I felt when I was growing up? My mom, I just...I can't with her, but it's a little different with him."

"I understand about your mother, and we can talk about that in another session. But your father..." She bobbed her head side to side, considering. "I don't think it's a terrible idea. You probably don't want to do all of this at once, though. It might be good to spend some more time on the letter, thinking about what you needed then and what you need now. Then see if you're ready to talk to him."

"Okay. And I'll...I'll work on talking to Marcos." *Even though the second I find out he's seeing someone, my heart will stop, and none of this will matter anyway.* "But then there's Lucas." I cleared my throat. "He's still not really speaking to me."

"That's tough, I know."

"I've felt so much more connected to Lola and Marisol lately. I was able to talk to Lola about her boyfriend, and I've been cooking, and Mari's started helping me. It feels really good. But I don't know what to do about Lucas." I slipped my sandal back on my foot. "Should I keep trying? What if I'm making things worse?"

"Unless he's told you to stop reaching out to him, I don't see any harm in letting him know you're there when he's ready to talk. In fact, if you want my off-the-cuff, non-psychobabble opinion, I think it's what a mother *should* do." She gave me a reassuring smile. "It's what *I* would do."

I sniffed and pressed my fingers beneath my eyelids. I could only hope she was right. My mother had walked out on me, but there were other ways to abandon people. And if I lost Lucas forever, if I'd hurt him like my mother had hurt me, I would never be able to forgive myself.

46

JULY 2010

I sat on the couch and opened the journal to where I'd begun to jot down my thoughts after my early sessions with Dr. Shirazi. I was starting to get answers to the questions I'd scribbled on the pages, and things were starting to make sense, but I knew there was more work ahead of me.

Dr. Shirazi was right. I didn't love Christian. Not anymore. I loved who I was with him twenty years before. He gave me something I didn't get from Marcos, but not necessarily because Marcos couldn't give it. I'd just never offered Marcos the chance. Maybe he'd never really asked or pushed or *insisted* on knowing if I was truly happy, if there was something missing, or if I needed something more. But I was a master of disguise, honing my craft over many years, and ultimately, it was my responsibility to tell him.

I flipped through the notebook, past other thoughts I'd jotted down each day as I was walking out the door to the gym, after I hopped out of the shower, or as I was marinating chicken for some recipe that had popped up as an internet ad. There were at least ten pages with *Dear Me* and *Dear Younger Self*

written at the top, some with more words written underneath.
Proof that I'd tried to start the letter but never gotten very far.

I turned to a blank page and wrote it again.

Dear Me —

Then crossed it out.

Dear Younger Me —

That felt wrong, too.

HEY! DENISE!

Jesus. Am I trying to re-traumatize myself?

Maybe without the *HEY!*

Denise —

I took a deep breath. Okay. What now?

I'm sorry if this seems strange.

Keep going. Don't stop. Just write.

But it's important that you know what I'm about to tell you because even if you don't exist physically anymore, you're still inside me. That sounds weird, but I guess this whole thing is.

The biggest thing I want you to know is that your mother never should've treated you the way she did. Like you were an inconvenience. Always an afterthought. Like you didn't matter in her life or at all, really. You were a kid, and you needed her. You needed her love and her attention, and she gave you neither.

I wish I could go back and tell you how amazing your science project was and clap for you when she didn't. I wish I could go back and hug you when she told you she was leaving, when she said you should be able to take care of yourself at fifteen. She should've never put that on you. So please, whenever you feel like you aren't good enough, remember that she didn't abandon you because there was something wrong with you. She abandoned you because there was something wrong with her.

And because your father stayed, you thought you should be grateful, even though there wasn't a moment when his love didn't feel conditional. If you didn't do what he thought was right, what he wanted, what he thought was best for you, then you were a failure. A disappointment. Stupid. I'm sorry the only pride he ever showed in you was pride in your accomplishments—the ones he believes he contributed to. You were always so much more than those things.

I wish I could go back and erase what you learned from him. When he told you not to feel, it was cruel. It made you scared. It made you not trust people. It made you cry alone, then pretend you hadn't.

Your parents made you believe you were unlovable, and you did what you thought you had to do to survive. You pretended you didn't care. But there was still a piece of you that wanted to love and be loved, so on the outside, you became the person you thought everyone wanted you to be. You were never needy. You were never vulnerable. You always had your shit together.

These aren't excuses, and it doesn't matter if someone tells you (or if you tell yourself) that there are worse things that could have happened. The older you—the one writing this letter—still has a lot of work to do. But the most important thing she can do right now is tell you that you were not bad. There was nothing wrong with you. You did the best you could. And one day, you'll have a son and two daughters of your own, and you'll know that no child should ever have to go through what you did.

My phone pinged, and I shook my head

I looked down at the journal and blinked—Where was I? Had I written all those words?—then snapped it shut, as though the person texting me might see it. It was hard enough to say these things to myself, much less to...

Lucas?

I gasped, then picked up my cell from the cushion next to me and opened the message. It took a moment to slow my pulse so I could focus on the text.

Lucas: *I'm sorry I haven't really responded to your messages. I'm still fucked up about things. Sorry for writing fucked up.*

My eyes stung as I smiled and placed my hand over my mouth and continued to read.

Lucas: *I've only talked to Christian a couple times, but it doesn't feel right to be speaking to him and not you. I don't know if he loves me, but I know you do. I'm going to Colorado with Mia for a couple weeks at the beginning of next month. Can I come over when I get back?*

Hot tears streamed down my cheeks, each one formed from the words I'd written in the letter to myself and the words my son had written to me. My hands trembled as I typed my reply.

Me: *Yes. I would love that. And I love you. Always.*

I hit Send and put the phone down before snatching it back up.

Me: *Be safe on your trip. Sorry I'm such a mom.*

A colon followed by a parenthesis appeared on the screen, and I returned his smile.

I pressed my cell against my chest. Lucas wanted to talk to me. He knew I loved him, and for the first time since he'd walked out of the house that night, I believed that maybe there was a chance I hadn't ruined him. Not only that, but after nearly four months in therapy, I'd finally written the letter I didn't think I could write. There was probably more to say, I probably hadn't said everything exactly right, but what was *right* anyway? Getting all of that out on paper felt good, and that's what I was going to hold onto in the moment. Because if I could tell that girl she wasn't a bad person *then*, maybe I could start to believe she wasn't a bad person *now*.

Yes, she'd made mistakes. But she deserved to be heard.

With that thought, I lifted the phone and brought up Marcos's number. My thumb hovered over the screen until I forced it down.

He answered on the second ring. "Hey. Is everything okay with the kids?"

"Yeah, they're fine."

"Oh. Good," he said, breathing a sigh of relief.

Of course, this was his first thought, and I loved how much he cared about them. I was sure I would've been concerned, too, had he been the one to call, but I couldn't help but wish he'd sounded more excited to hear from me once I assured him they were fine.

"I didn't mean to worry you. I just, um...Well, Lucas texted, and he wants to talk." I took a deep breath. "And I wanted to let you know, I guess."

"Great." He paused. "That's great."

"That's great." Again with "That's great."

My cheeks warmed, as though I should be embarrassed for calling him with this information. "I don't know if you talked to him, if maybe you encouraged him to do that, but if so, thank you."

"Yeah, he, uh...he wanted to reach out to you. I just gave him a little nudge, I guess."

"I appreciate it. Really."

Now's the time. Now's the time to ask. You don't have to discuss it all this minute. Just ask for the opportunity. Tell him what you need.

"And also, I was..." I closed my eyes and swallowed. "I was wondering if maybe you and I could talk, too?"

"About Lucas?"

My eyes snapped open. "Uh, no. I meant about...us?" I cleared my throat. *Don't make it a question.* "About us."

He was quiet for a beat, and my heart sank before he even spoke.

"I'm not there yet," he said, his tone void of emotion.

"Oh." My eyes brimmed with tears. "Well, I'm not asking for a resolution right now. I just want to, you know, tell you how I'm feeling. And maybe you could tell me how you're feeling, too." I waited for a response, but none came. "I've realized I haven't done that very much—or maybe at all, really—in the past."

More silence, making me feel like I was in a field, thick with mud, barely able to put one foot in front of the other but still trudging ahead.

"Anyway, I've been doing a lot of work in therapy, revisiting things that happened with my parents," I said. "There's just a lot I want to share with you."

He snorted. "So, your mother and father are the reason you lied to me? The reason you cheated on me?"

One tear dropped onto my cheek, followed by another. I didn't know exactly what I'd expected—maybe I was flying too high from writing the letter and talking to Lucas—but his words felt like daggers.

"No," I choked out. "No, that's not it at all. I'm just asking for a chance to explain some things to you."

"You had eighteen years to do that, Denise."

"But I didn't because I was afraid that you would—"

"That I would what?" he asked, and I couldn't decide whether he was genuinely curious or mocking me.

"That you would find out I wasn't perfect," I confessed. "That I had feelings that weren't always nice and neat and that maybe I didn't really have my shit together after all."

"I never expected you to be perfect."

My voice rolled over the lump in my throat. "I know, and I'm starting to understand that now, but for a long time, I didn't. I'm realizing I never gave you the opportunity to tell me you didn't expect that of me. I never really allowed myself to be vulnerable or let you see when I was hurting and—"

"I can't." He sighed. "I really can't do this."

A desperate pain ached deep within me, penetrating my bones. *There has to be something I can say. Something I can do.*

"But it's been six months. It's been six months since you moved out, and we haven't talked about this at all. And I know I fucked up, Marcos. Trust me, I know this. But I need to talk to you. We need to talk to each other. I want us to be honest about what we're thinking and feeling, and I'm not asking to do it right now, but if we could plan for next week or—"

"Denise, I..." He pulled in a breath, then blew it out. "Look, I've got to go, but I'll...I'll talk to you later, okay?"

"I...Okay," I said, waiting for him to tell me goodbye. But when I looked at the screen, he was already gone.

47

———

JULY 2010

"I, um..." I pressed the Kleenex against one eyelid, then the other. "I think it's over."

"What do you mean?" The faint lines in Dr. Shirazi's forehead creased. "You think your marriage is over?"

I sniffed and nodded.

"Tell me why you think that."

"I talked to..." I paused and cleared my throat, trying to find my voice. "I asked Marcos if we could find time to talk, and he, um...he said no, he didn't think he could do that. He didn't *want* to do that."

I recounted the details of our conversation to her, and she set her notepad aside, listening as sympathy spread across her face. When I was done, I shrugged and shook my head. "I was hopeful, you know? I was starting to believe I was getting better, and I could make *us* better, but I guess that's not true."

"No, Denise," she said as I looked up from the tissue I was rubbing between my thumbs. "You've come so far, and I can't let you say that you haven't."

"But...he doesn't see any difference in me."

"Do *you* see any difference in you?"

"I...I thought I did."

She tapped her finger against her lips. "That letter you sent me. The one you wrote to your—"

"Yeah, I'm sorry I bothered you with that." I waved my hand, dismissing my email to her. "It was silly to send it to you, I just...I wanted to share it with someone who understood. Or maybe I wanted you to tell me I did my assignment correctly. I don't know."

She smiled. "I thought it was beautiful. And I thought it was beautiful that you wanted to share it with me."

I gave her a quick bob of my head, then flicked my eyes down.

"Do you think you could've written that before you came in here four months ago?" she asked.

I inhaled, my breath shaky. "I guess not."

"Well, I don't have to guess," she said, leaning forward. "I *know* you couldn't have. And not because you didn't have those feelings, but because you didn't know what to do with them."

"Yeah," I whispered.

She sighed. "You know how in the letter you told your younger self that she did the best she could?"

I nodded, still focused on the shredded tissue.

"I think it's time you tell forty-six-year-old Denise that," she said firmly. "Tell her that no one ever gave her the tools to cope with the things she encountered in life. That while she made mistakes and thought she should've known better as an adult, she was emotionally still that fifteen-year-old girl whose mother walked out on her and whose father belittled her. But now she's learning. She's taking steps to change things. And she needs to acknowledge how amazing that is."

I raised my eyes to her, swallowing as I struggled to find my words.

Dr. Shirazi leaned forward. "Can you do that, Denise?"

"I, um..." I dropped the tissue in my lap, then wiped my

fingers beneath my eyes. "Yes. I'm making changes. I've *made* changes. Important ones, and I've worked hard to do it."

She smiled. "You deserved to hear that from yourself."

"I just wish Marcos wanted to hear it, too," I said.

"And I want that for you because I really do believe you want to make your marriage work. And maybe he does need more time to sort things out for himself. But I think..." She twisted her lips as if considering whether or not to let the thoughts behind them come out. "I think at some point, you might start to ask yourself how long you can wait before it becomes too much. And I'm not talking about the separation. How long that lasts is something you all will have to figure out, but in order to do that, you have to communicate. He has to be willing to listen and hear you. And if he can't do that...is that really a marriage you want to be in? After all you're doing to get to a point where you feel comfortable expressing your feelings, do you want to be shut down?"

Her words froze my insides. They felt cold and harsh, like she was blaming Marcos, when I was the one who ruined us. I stared at her, wanting something to make sense, hoping that the last four months hadn't been time wasted paying someone solely to make me forget that *I* had been the one who'd broken my marriage vows.

"I just know how much it hurts to keep things buried inside," she continued. "And now that you're letting them out, I don't want that hurt to be replaced by the pain of not being heard. Because sometimes that's the worst pain of all."

"But..." My eyes searched her face for some sign that she understood the facts of the matter. "*He's* the one who has to forgive *me*. I don't get to make these decisions."

She laced her fingers together and pointed at me. "But you *do*, Denise. You *do* get to decide what you need. And you *do* get to decide to forgive *yourself*."

"I..." My eyes drifted to my lap, tears falling too quickly for my shredded tissue to absorb them, their warmth slowly thawing the icy chill that had consumed me.

She was right. I'd made progress, but I hadn't been able to shake the belief that my bad decisions made me a bad person who deserved to be punished for the rest of her life. I was waiting for someone else to forgive me, but that might not ever happen. I would have to try to set myself free.

"How do I...how do I do that?" I asked.

"You've already started the process," she said, offering me an encouraging smile. "We just need to keep moving forward."

48

AUGUST 2010

"So we're supposed to sift the flour." Marisol's face twisted. "Is sifting like when you put it in that...thing?"

"Oh. Shit. I mean, crap." I scrunched my nose at her. "Yes, that's what it is, but I don't know if that matters?"

Although, maybe my failure to sift is why I've never been able to get this fucking dough right.

I scanned the kitchen, then headed for the bottom cabinets where we kept the pots and pans. "I'm sure we have one. Your *abuela* used it when she made them last Christmas."

I stood, opening some of the overhead cabinets, but it was nowhere to be found. "Ugh." I slumped forward. "I guess we can use a colander?"

"What's that?" she asked.

"The thing you use to drain spaghetti." I pointed to the left side of the stove. "Can you grab it from there? The holes are probably too big, but if it doesn't work, we'll find a sifter for next time."

I shrugged, examining the metal contraption as she held it up. *It doesn't have to be perfect. My daughter wanted to spend time doing this with me. And having fun with her, making one of her favorite foods, is all that matters.*

I took a calming breath and opened the bag of flour. "So, remember. Even if they turn out weird, we're gonna eat them." I turned to her. "Do not let your mother throw them away."

"Okay. But you can't ground me when I talk back to you," she warned.

My brows angled in. "You're going to talk back to me? You never talk back to me. You just..." I twirled my hand in the air. "Negotiate."

"I think I'm gonna start, now that I'm a teenager," she said, grinning.

No, you've still got purple braces, and you're still my baby.

"You know," I began, motioning for her to hold the colander over the mixing bowl while I poured the flour into it. "I was excited about you and Lola hanging out when she got her license, her giving you rides everywhere, but she might actually be a bad influence on you."

She giggled and set the colander on the counter. "So what's next?"

"You can put the salt in. Use that little measuring spoon. Yep." I nodded. "And I think this next ingredient is the key. The *secret.*"

Marisol side-eyed me.

I chuckled. "I have, in the past, refused to use lard, insisting that butter would work just as well."

"What's lard?"

"Uh..." *Pig fat? No big deal?* "It's like butter, just...different. I'll add it."

Once I had the dry ingredients in the bowl, I retrieved the cooled brown sugar cinnamon syrup we'd made earlier. "Actually, *this* is what *Abuela* says makes it so good."

"*Perfecto.* And now, we mix," she said, acting as master of the empanada ceremony.

I picked up an extra-large spoon and grinned.

She shook her head, a wry smile on her lips. "Hands, *Mami*."

"Okay. You're right. I want to do this the *correct* way." I sighed and twisted my rings, knowing I should take them off rather than getting them dirty, but not wanting to imagine a world in which they were permanently gone.

"What's wrong?" she asked.

"Huh? Oh. Nothing." I managed a faint smile. "Just thinking about putting my hands in there."

"I'll start," she offered. "But you have to help knead—"

The doorbell sounded, and she jumped.

"You expecting someone?" I winked as I brushed my palms along my thighs, leaving a trail of white on my black leggings.

"Nope," she answered, gathering the ingredients into her hands and forming the dough.

"Maybe it's *Elijah*," I said, padding through the kitchen to the foyer, laughing to myself.

I swung open the door, ready to sign for a package or tell Lola's boyfriend she was out back with her friends in the pool. "Oh." My eyes went wide. "Hi."

Marcos gave me a cautious smile. "Hey. I'm sorry to show up without calling, but I was in the neighborhood and wanted to drop off Mari's cleats. She left them in my car."

"Yeah, sure, I can..." I reached for the shoes.

"They're muddy," he said. "You want me to put them..." He gestured to the tile floor just inside the door.

"That's fine." I stepped back to let him pass. "Thanks."

My eyes traveled down his gray T-shirt and faded jeans, then over to his left hand. I breathed a sigh of relief even though I didn't know if the ring meant anything. He'd been with Marisol that morning, and he'd probably put it on just for her.

Over the past several weeks, nothing had changed with

Marcos. He hadn't mentioned my calling and asking him if we could talk, and with Dr. Shirazi's encouragement, I was trying to keep the focus on my own progress in therapy. I couldn't make him give me what I needed, but I could decide how I would handle that. I just hadn't reached that point yet because I knew I'd first have to forgive myself for what I'd done.

"What's, uh…" He pointed to my legs. "What's all that?"

Oh my God. The empanadas. The fucking empanadas.

Did I tell him I was making one of his mother's signature dishes? All of a sudden, it felt sort of…sad. Pathetic.

"Oh. Mari and I are just making…"

Empanadas, I tried to say. *Em-pa-na-das.*

For fuck's sake, spit it out.

"We're making empanadas." I managed an awkward laugh. "Is that…weird?"

His eyes grew wide. "*You are?*"

I gritted my teeth. "You didn't answer my question."

"Oh. Shit. No." He shook his head. "No, that's not weird. I just know you get so frustrated with those." A smile spread across his face as he pointed at the white dust on my leggings again. "*Are* you frustrated?"

My body tensed. *Was that a joke?*

He cleared his throat. "That was a joke. Sorry, now *I* feel weird."

"No, I'm just…" *Sensitive. Confused. Worried. Missing you.* I inhaled, and a tiny laugh escaped from within as I noticed a subtle pink coloring the olive skin on his cheeks. "This whole thing is weird."

I flinched, afraid of his reaction to how freely I'd let the thought come out of my mouth. But the fear quickly turned to surprise, and a cautious sense of pride flowed through me. *You're being yourself,* I thought as my shoulders relaxed.

"Yeah. Yeah, it is." His voice was quiet, and his mouth turned down before flicking up into a sad half smile.

My heart squeezed.

"Anyway," he continued. "Is Mari here? They're changing up some of the practice schedule, so I just wanted to fill her in."

I nodded. "She's in the kitchen."

He followed behind me, and I turned to see him beaming as she kneaded the dough on the counter.

"*Ah, mi niña,*" he said. "*La masa se ve perfecta.*"

She laughed. "*Gracias, Papi.* But Mom has to take over now."

I winced. "I do?"

Marisol wiped her hands on a towel. "Violet just texted and asked if I could sleep over there instead of her coming here. They have a theater room, and we decided we wanna watch horror movies. Her mom can come get me."

"Uh…" I looked at the bowl on the counter. "Yeah, that's fine. The dough will keep in the fridge, and we can have these tomorrow night."

"Thanks," she said, grabbing her cell, fingers flying furiously over the keyboard as she headed toward the stairs. "I'll get my stuff together."

"We never should've gotten her a phone for her birthday. She's like Lola *número dos* these days." Marcos winked as I looked up at him.

"So true," I said, my lips easing into a smile.

Our eyes locked in a few moments of silence before I spoke.

"I should, um, finish kneading this so it can rest." I walked over to where Marisol had been doing her handiwork.

"Right. Important business." He inhaled and motioned behind him. "I guess I'll head out then."

My stomach twisted, part of me wanting to ask him to stay, part of me thinking it would be easier to not deal with the disappointment of him saying no. But when he didn't turn toward the door, my *want* took the wheel. "You don't have to go."

One corner of his mouth turned up. "Are you trying to get me to knead?"

I chuckled. "No. Maybe. Probably."

"I, uh...I think you should do it," he said, sweeping a hand over his mouth, then rubbing his chin. "You never believed you could get that dough right, but I know you can."

I braced myself against the counter, dropping my eyes and letting the sadness flow through me before looking back up. "Thanks for vote of confidence," I said, my voice cracking slightly.

It's okay to show him you're disappointed that he doesn't want to stay. It's okay to let him know you really wanted him to. And when he goes, you'll be okay, too.

"But I, uh..." He slid his hands into his pockets. "I did want to tell you that I'm sorry about what I said on the phone. A few weeks ago...when you asked if we could talk."

My insides hummed, and my mind wrestled with what to say, torn between the familiarity of dismissing my feelings, and the freedom that I knew would come from expressing them.

"That wasn't the right thing to do." His throat tightened as he swallowed, and he took a step toward me. "Because I agree that we should be open. And honest."

I gripped the marble lip of the counter, my spiraling thoughts nearly pulling my body into the tornado with them. *Is that an invitation to talk? Or is that a heads-up that the twenty-five-year-old girlfriend who lives in my head is actually real and moving into his condo? Either way, I want to know...don't I?*

"Yes," I said, letting out a slow exhale. "We should."

"I've just...I've struggled with this because I'm still angry, you know? And hurt." The overhead light caught the glossy sheen in his eyes.

My chest tightened as emotion rose behind my own. "I'm sorry, Marcos. I am *so* sorry."

"I know," he said. "I know you are."

I placed my hand over my mouth and nodded.

"But I realized the only way I'm going to work through that anger and hurt is to talk to you. To listen to you." He took a deep breath. "Fuck, this is hard."

I closed my eyes, a tear spilling onto my cheek before I opened them again.

"I think maybe I knew there were things you wanted to tell me over the years. Things about your life, about your parents..." He sniffed and shook his head. "Anyway, it doesn't make everything that happened okay. It doesn't mean I shouldn't be completely fucked up over it, and hurt and angry just like I said, but...I want to understand." He raked his teeth over his bottom lip. "Because I think if I can understand, I can..."

My breath became shallow as I desperately searched his face, trying to anticipate what he was going to say next. *You can work on our marriage? You can leave me for good?*

He sighed. "I just want to understand, Denise."

My shoulders fell. I wanted answers so badly, but I couldn't make him tell me what he wasn't ready to say, just like no matter how much I talked or how much he listened, I couldn't make him understand. All I could do was tell him the truth, tell him what I was feeling, and tell him what I needed—then hope he would.

I nodded, cautiously at first, then more confidently. "There are a lot of things I want you to know."

"So, can I listen while you knead that dough?" A gentle smile broke through the pain. "Or would you rather me take you out for a cheeseburger and talk there?"

Laughter coated the sound of my tears, turning sadness into hope. "I know I may be pressing my luck here, but can we do both?"

"Yeah," he said, chuckling. "We can do both."

He settled onto a barstool at the island, his smile growing wider as he winked, then pointed toward the dough.

And in that moment, it was all I needed.

ACKNOWLEDGMENTS

There are so many people to thank for so many reasons.

My critique partner, Melissa, for making my stories better and always offering me the support she knows I need. She's the Mick to my Keith, the Plant to my Page, the Morrissey to my Marr.

My incredible alpha reader, Kate, who insists on the best and never lets me get away with "just okay."

My other early readers—Reah, Ali, Jackie, Jennalee, Kayla, Elise, and Leila—for the catches, feedback, support, and love.

My editor, Chris, for knowing all the grammar rules and making me look like I know what I'm doing.

My dear friend, Ali, for her unwavering support and helping me promote both this book and *For Eva* with her incredible graphics and ideas.

My old pal, David (aka Ding), for the badass band name (and always getting me into the coolest RVA clubs back in the day).

My sweetest Gaby and my new friend, Al, for making sure my Spanish was on point. Also, huge shoutout to Al for guiding me on all things Cuban.

My parents for their love and support in helping me get across the finish line.

My daughter, who constantly amazes me with everything she does.

My husband, whom I'd normally say I don't deserve...but we've learned lessons from this book, haven't we?

And last, but certainly not least, all the readers who took a chance on *For Eva* and gave me the confidence and courage to do this all over again. Words cannot explain how much you all mean to me.